Praise for Jane Bites Back

"Michael Thomas Ford has struck gold.... The plot is inventive and funny, and the story progresses with the kind of light touch that compares favorably to the ... Stephenie Meyer Twilight series. Ford manages to strike just the right tone ... and consistently delights."

—*Bay Area Reporter*

"Hilarious ... I thoroughly enjoyed reading this book and know you will too!" —The Vampire Librarian

"A rollicking good read ... Ford is wickedly funny: I cackled my way through half the book, especially the vampire stuff.... I eagerly await *Jane Goes Batty.*" —Dirty Laundry

"Ford approvingly cites Seth Grahame-Smith's *Pride and Prejudice and Zombies,* but his own mashup is better integrated, more knowledgeable about Austen and considerably funnier." —*Kirkus Reviews*

"Readers who fall under Jane's spell will be eagerly awaiting her next adventure." —*Library Journal*

"Ford's Jane is a very fun and funny heroine to root for as she endures the indignities of publishing and bookselling, fends off danger and (perhaps) finds love. Her hilarious smack downs with Violet hint of more madness to come in this first of a series." —*Publishers Weekly*

"FIVE STARS! This is one of the most thoroughly entertaining stories I have read in the past few years! I feel that the author succeeded in capturing Jane Austen's proper personality, as well as how the legendary author would have reacted had she found herself an immortal vampire. Michael Thomas Ford has crafted a vivid, charming and witty tale to delight readers of any age. Absolutely fantastic!" —Huntress Reviews

"A witty and entertaining read with just the right amount of bite . . . This book will appeal to Austen fans and vampire fans alike."

—Night Owl Romance

"Jane Austen's novels brim with irony, witticism, and in the end, a gentle reproof or two. It is why I love her writing. Few authors can deliver this dry, deft and wickedly funny style. Michael Thomas Ford is one of them. . . . Light, campy and a bit Buffyish . . . Read with tongue-in-cheek and a full glass of suspended disbelief, you will chortle and guffaw until the last bite. This Janeite was truly 'glamored.' 5 out of 5 Regency Stars."

—Austenprose

"A well cultivated tale with great character development that holds its own against the real-life history of its main character, Jane Austen."

—Best Fantasy Stories

"A confection of a novel."

—*The Advocate*

"Such a fun read. I especially love to imagine Austen duking it out with fellow literary blood-suckers, both literal and figurative." —BookBitch

"In the past year, I have read quite a few Jane Austen spin-offs, but none quite as original as *Jane Bites Back* by Michael Thomas Ford. What a fantastic premise for a book . . . I am so excited to say that I really, really enjoyed this book."

—Booking Mama

"Vampire Jane is much more human and enjoyable than the chocolate-box saint that many Janeites have created in her image. She's a lady—but with a bite. . . . We really liked the book, and look forward to the sequel(s). . . . In the meantime, Jane, we'll keep swinging the Cluebat of Janeite Righteousness on your behalf."

—AustenBlog

Jane
Goes
BATTY

A Novel

Michael Thomas Ford

BALLANTINE BOOKS TRADE PAPERBACKS NEW YORK

A Ballantine Books Trade Paperback Original

Copyright © 2011 by Michael Thomas Ford

Published in the United States by Ballantine Books,
an imprint of The Random House Publishing Group,
a division of Random House, Inc., New York.

BALLANTINE and colophon are registered
trademarks of Random House, Inc.

Library of Congress Cataloging-in-Publication Data
Ford, Michael Thomas.
Jane goes batty: a novel / Michael Thomas Ford.
p. cm.
Sequel to: Jane bites back.
ISBN 978-0-345-51366-3 (trade pbk.)—ISBN 978-0-345-52434-8 (ebk.)
1. Austen, Jane, 1775–1817—Fiction. 2. Women novelists—Fiction. 3. Women
booksellers—Fiction. 4. City and town life—New York (State)—Fiction.
5. Motion picture locations—Fiction. I. Title.
PS3606.O7424J37 2011
813'.6—dc21   2010041173

Printed in the United States of America

www.ballantinebooks.com

2 4 6 8 9 7 5 3 1

Book design by Elizabeth A. D. Eno

For Nancy,
who will always be older than I am

Chapter 1

"NOT AGAIN."

Jane Fairfax gripped the steering wheel so tightly her hands hurt. Two dozen women stood on the sidewalk. Three of them were peering in Jane's living room windows. All of them were dressed in imitation Regency period dresses. The thought occurred to Jane that instead of adopting the clothing of her time, they might have chosen to copy the tradition of waiting for an invitation before dropping in unannounced.

A tall, thin woman in a ghastly pink pantsuit emerged from a parked tour bus and called out loudly, "Miss Fairfax doesn't appear to be at home today, but we can still get a lovely photo!"

"It's Beverly!" said a deep male voice beside Jane with lascivious glee. "We should say hello."

"We should *not*," said Jane, giving Byron a withering look.

Jane had seen the woman—and her pantsuit—before. Her name was Beverly Shrop. A retired kindergarten teacher, Beverly had devoted the past five years to becoming the number-one-ranked reviewer of romance novels on a very popular bookselling site. That her "reviews" consisted largely of regurgitating a book's cover copy mattered little to her readers. Nor did it apparently occur to them that in order for Beverly to have amassed

12,729 reviews she would have had to have read an average of 6.9 books a day.

Beverly had subsequently started a website of her own—ShropTalk.com—on which she not only posted her reviews but also featured interviews with romance writers and kept her readers abreast of what was happening in the world of romantic fiction. This, naturally, had increased her profile even more, to the point where publishers started not just paying attention to her but actively courting her.

When *Constance* was published, Jane had done the requisite interview with Beverly. She'd found the woman dull and her questions insipid (Do you wear any particular perfume when you write? If you were a flower, what would you be?) and had been relieved when it was over. She'd hoped never to encounter Beverly Shrop again.

Beverly, however, was determined to make the most of her talents. This took the form of offering romance-themed tours to readers who wanted to visit the hometowns of their favorite authors or to visit the locations that had inspired their favorite books. She had several itineraries, among them The World of Edith Wharton, Love and Lust in Santa Fe (a surprising number of romance writers lived there), and Jackie Oh!: The People and Places of Jackie Collins.

Most recently Beverly had designed a field trip around writers of New York and New England. Brakeston was included on the itinerary primarily because of Byron, who the previous year had revealed himself to be the real author behind the very popular novelist Penelope Wentz. Complicating matters, he had chosen to use yet another pseudonym in making his announcement, and so the world at large knew him as Tavish Osborn, a name he now adopted for everyday use.

"You just don't like her because she wasn't going to include you on the tour until I suggested it," Byron said.

Jane snorted. "I hardly think so. I don't like her because she turns literature into a spectacle."

Byron laughed, earning him another fierce look from Jane. "Literature has *always* been spectacle," he said. "Do you really think we held all of those literary salons so that we could exchange ideas? Of course not. It was so we could gossip about everyone who wasn't there. And don't you remember how James Joyce used to wander through Paris mumbling nonsense words until people recognized him?"

He cleared his throat and in a perfect imitation of Joyce's impish Irish brogue said, "Spifflepond puppetdingle griffintide! Woozlewoozle crumpetpeal dirf! Why yes, I *am* James Joyce. You enjoyed *Ulysses*? Bless you, madam. Bless you."

Jane stifled a laugh. It was true. Joyce had often wandered back and forth between La Closerie des Lilas and the Dingo Bar, hoping to be noticed. He denied it, of course, but they all knew.

"It's hardly the same thing," she told Byron, still not giving in.

Byron made a vague noise. Much to Jane's irritation, he reveled in the attention that Beverly Shrop's tours brought him. He frequently welcomed Beverly and her clients into his home, even offering them tea. Jane, on the other hand, avoided them as much as possible, finding the whole business unseemly. Although even her book publicist had encouraged her to cooperate at least a *little*.

And now Beverly and her minions were preventing Jane from getting into her own house. She seethed. Beverly never stayed less than half an hour, and from the look of things they'd only recently arrived.

"We'll just have to leave until they're gone," Jane said as she began to turn the car around.

"Wait," Byron said. "I have a better idea."

Jane paused. "I doubt it," she said. "But go on."

"This is a perfect opportunity for you to practice making yourself invisible," said Byron.

For the past few months—following an attack on Jane by an undead and very angry Charlotte Brontë—Byron had been teaching Jane more about her vampire powers. Despite living for more than two centuries, Jane had studiously avoided delving into the mysteries of being immortal. She had been convinced, however, that it was in her best interests to learn what she was capable of, particularly in the event of another attack.

Unfortunately, in nine months she had succeeded only in improving the quality of her glamoring. She had long been proficient in the basics—at least enough to seduce those she used to quench her occasional thirst—but now she was able to implant thoughts into the heads of others, as long as her subjects weren't overly bright to begin with.

Invisibility, however, was proving more troublesome. Despite practicing every day, she had so far managed only brief periods of dimness. Her meager results were irritating both to her and to Byron, who just that afternoon had accused her of not trying hard enough.

"I don't know," Jane said.

"Why not?" asked Byron. "Avoiding Beverly is the perfect incentive for vanishing. In fact, I can't think of a better opportunity for you to prove yourself."

"I'm really not in the mood," Jane said. "I have a headache, and—"

"It's time to sink or swim," Byron interrupted as he opened his door. He gave Jane a wink as he sauntered toward the crowd of women. "Beverly!" he called cheerfully. "How lovely to see you."

Jane ducked down. "Horrid man," she hissed. "How I loathe you."

She could just turn the car around and leave. That would be the easiest way out of the situation. But now Byron had made it a matter of pride. If she fled, he would never let her forget it.

Which is just what he wants, she thought. *He doesn't think I can do it.*

"We'll just see about that," she said firmly.

She closed her eyes and took several deep breaths. *Imagine you're made of glass,* she told herself.

She tried to hold that picture in her mind. Other thoughts intruded, but she brushed them aside. When she could envision her body as completely transparent, she opened her eyes and held up one hand. Behind it she could see the steering wheel.

"I did it!" she cried, and immediately her hand became solid again.

"Damn!" she muttered.

She closed her eyes and once more let the image of her invisible self fill her mind. Again she opened her eyes, and again she could see through her hand. But this time the illusion held. She sat for several minutes to make sure she wasn't going to pop back into view, then opened the door and got out. She hoped no one would notice the door opening and closing seemingly by itself.

Slowly she approached Beverly and her group, all the while trying to keep her thoughts calm. Several of the women were circled around Byron, but still Jane's path to the front door was blocked. She would have to go around to the back and get in through the kitchen.

You don't have the key to that door, she reminded herself. *You never go in that way.* Still, she had no choice. Her lawn and stoop were littered with gawkers.

"No," she heard Byron say. "I haven't seen Miss Fairfax. Perhaps you should try knocking again."

Shut up, Jane thought, knowing full well that Byron could tell she was nearby. Something in her vision changed for a second. She looked down and saw that she was becoming visible. She was very faint, but nonetheless there. Panic gripped her, and she grew more solid. She had to get into the house.

She ran, slipping past a woman who was examining her rose-bushes. The woman looked up, a puzzled expression on her face. Jane ignored her, reaching the corner just as she winked back into sight.

She tried the door and found it locked, as she'd known it would be. The only way in was through the kitchen window. She went to it and pushed up on the frame, praying that she hadn't locked it. It slid up with only slight hesitation.

Gripping the sill, she jumped as hard as she could. Her head passed through the window, and for a moment she felt the relief of having succeeded. This, however, was a momentary joy, as she now found herself stuck. Below her Tom stared up at her with a mixture of bemusement and disgust.

"Don't look at me like that," Jane told him. "I will not be ridiculed by a cat."

She was hanging over the windowsill, her front half in the kitchen and her back half kicking uselessly at the air. Finally, with enormous effort, she managed to propel herself forward and onto the linoleum, almost landing on Tom. The black-and-white cat stepped neatly to one side, avoiding her. Moments later Jasper, the springer spaniel Jane had adopted after he'd helped her escape from Charlotte Brontë's house, trotted in. Looking at her, he gave a soft woof.

"What a wonderful guard dog you are," Jane told him as she got up and dusted herself off. She turned and shut the window.

And now you're a prisoner in your own house, she told herself. *If you'd just step out and say hello, they'd go away.*

But she knew they wouldn't. A simple greeting would turn into requests for autographs and pictures. Then someone would ask—ever so sweetly—if they could have just a *peek* at the room in which she wrote her books. And of course she couldn't say no without seeming churlish, and then it would descend into madness. She imagined hysterical women rifling through her drawers and peering into her bathroom cabinet, and it made her head ache.

The phone rang, startling her. Noting the number on the caller ID display, she picked up.

"Well, you're not going to believe this," a voice said.

Jane was slowly getting used to Satvari Thangavadivelu's manner of launching into a conversation with no preliminaries. At the insistence of her editor, Kelly Littlejohn, Jane had signed with the Waters-Harding Agency to represent her in her business dealings. Satvari was the head of the firm's film department and had shepherded *Constance* through the Hollywood minefield.

"What won't I believe?" Jane asked.

"They want to film there," Satvari said.

"There where?"

"*There* there," said Satvari. "Brakeston. They want to film *Constance* in Brakeston. Well, the exterior shots, anyway. Apparently they've decided it will be more authentic than shooting on a soundstage."

"They're bringing everything here?" Jane said, not quite understanding. "The cameras and . . . and lights and . . . actors?"

"All of it. And they'll be there in a week."

"A *week*?" Jane exclaimed. "How am I supposed to get ready in a week?"

"Relax," said Satvari. "You don't have to have anything to do with it, remember?"

Jane breathed more easily. "That's right," she said. "I forgot."

"Unless," Satvari said.

Jane heard an unsettling tone in the agent's voice. "Unless what?"

"Unless you *want* to be involved," said Satvari. "It seems they'd like you to maybe help out a little bit with the script."

"You told me that was a bad idea," Jane reminded her. "You told me not to even see the film."

"I told you not to try to *write* the script," said Satvari. "But this isn't writing it. It's more like rewriting it. Just a little. You know, some dialogue here and there."

Jane sighed. "Can I think about it?" she asked.

"Of course," Satvari answered. "But don't think too long. If you say no, they're going to ask Penelope Wentz to do it."

"Penelope!" Jane exclaimed.

"Sorry, Tavish Osborn," said Satvari. "And yes, they're going to ask her. I mean him. She's a him, right? I can't keep it all straight."

"I'll do it," Jane said.

"Really?" asked Satvari. "You're sure?"

"Absolutely sure," Jane assured her.

"Great," said Satvari. "I'll work out the details and call you tomorrow." She hung up without a goodbye.

"Penelope Wentz," Jane remarked to Tom, who was sitting in a spot of sun, washing his face. "Honestly. As if Byron could ever do justice to my novel."

"What about me?" Byron materialized in the room, startling Jane.

"Nothing," said Jane. "It's not important."

The doorbell rang, and for a moment Jane almost picked up the phone, thinking someone was calling. Realizing what it was, she was overcome by a desire to go hide in the closet. She had visions of Beverly Shrop standing on her front steps, grinning like the Cheshire cat while her minions crowded behind her.

"I heard you say my name," said Byron. "You might as well tell me."

Again the air was filled with an electric trill. Jane, still ignoring Byron, was beginning to retreat to the bedroom when she saw that the little light on her phone was blinking. *Now someone is calling,* she realized.

Grateful for the distraction, she picked up without looking at the caller ID. "Hello?"

"It's me." Walter's voice had a strange tone to it.

"Are you all right?" Jane asked. "You sound peculiar."

"I'm hiding behind a hedge," said Walter. "There's a gaggle of Shropheads outside your house."

"I was hoping they'd be gone by now," Jane said. "Best to keep yourself hidden. Beverly knows who you are. If she sees you, you're done for."

"Is that Walter?" Byron called out. "Tell him I say hello."

"Is that Brian?" asked Walter. "What's he doing there?"

Jane heard a slight edge in Walter's voice. Although he and Byron were cordial to each other, Jane knew Walter was still a little suspicious of the man he knew Jane had once been involved with.

"He just stopped over to borrow a book," Jane said.

"Oh," said Walter. "Well, I wanted to do this in person, but I guess this will have to do," he continued.

"Do what in person?"

"I have something to tell you," said Walter. He took a deep breath. "My mother is coming."

"Your mother?" Jane said, feeling immensely better. "Is that all?"

"You don't understand," said Walter.

Jane interrupted him. "Walter, from everything you've told me, your mother sounds like a lovely woman. She even sent me that thank-you note after she read my book."

"Yes," Walter said. "I know. But there's something I sort of haven't told you about her. About me too, I suppose."

Well, that makes us even, Jane thought. She had yet to tell Walter that she was a vampire, a situation that was becoming more and more difficult to excuse as they grew closer.

"I'm sure whatever it is—" she began.

"I'm Jewish," said Walter. "Well, *technically* I am."

Jane paused. "Fletcher isn't a very Jewish name," she commented. "Not that it matters to me."

"My mother's maiden name is Ellenberg," said Walter. "Miriam Ellenberg. She's Jewish, so by default so am I. Not that I practice or even really think about it much. But she does."

Suddenly there was a lot of static coming through the phone.

Jane pressed the receiver to her ear, trying to hear. A moment later Walter's voice returned.

"Sorry. I had to get between the bushes," he whispered. "They're on the move. I think they're heading to Brian's house. I mean Tavish's house. What are we supposed to call him again?"

"Tavish is fine," said Jane. Another secret she was keeping from Walter was Byron's true identity. As far as Walter knew, his real name was Brian George.

"Did you tell him I say hello?" Byron asked. He was crouched on the floor, tossing a ball for Jasper. Jane ignored him.

"Anyway, I think that's where they're going," said Walter. "As soon as they're gone I'll run to your back door."

"I'll unlock it," Jane told him, and hung up.

A brief glance out the front window confirmed that Beverly had moved the tour away from Jane's house. Jane saw the back of the bus as it turned the corner. A moment later she heard knocking on the kitchen door and hurried to open it.

"She's relentless," Walter said as he stumbled into the house, collapsing into one of the chairs around the table. "I swear she has spies all over town."

"I wouldn't doubt it," said Jane.

"She's really not that bad," Byron remarked, entering the room. "And it would do wonders for your career if—"

"Shouldn't you be getting home?" said Jane.

Byron sighed. "I suppose so," he said. "Oh, but I still need to borrow that book."

"What boo—" Jane began to say before a look from Byron reminded her of her earlier lie to Walter. "Yes, of course. Just a moment."

She went into the living room and pulled a book at random from the bookcase. Back in the kitchen she handed it to Byron.

"*Frankenstein,*" Byron said. "How delightful." He turned to Walter. "Have you read it? It's one of my favorites. And there's a perfectly *delightful* story behind its authorship. You see—"

"There's no need to return it," Jane said as she pushed Byron toward the door. "I've never much cared for it."

Byron paused at the door. "You did very well," he whispered. "Congratulations."

"Thank you," said Jane. "Now get out."

She shut the door behind Byron, went to the refrigerator, removed a pitcher of iced tea, and poured a glass for Walter. "Now let's get back to the drama over your Jewishness," she said as she handed him the drink.

Walter took a long drink, then set the glass down. "It's not me," he reminded her. "It's my mother."

"You said that," said Jane. "But I still don't understand the issue."

Walter drummed his fingers on the tabletop. "I'll put it as simply as I can," he said. "My mother wants me to marry a nice Jewish girl."

"Oh," Jane said. "Now I see. May I ask, was Evelyn Jewish?" They seldom spoke about Walter's deceased wife, but Jane thought the question pertinent to the discussion.

Walter nodded. "She was," he said. "Again, like me she didn't really *do* anything about it. But the fact that she was Jewish was enough for my mother."

"Let me make sure I understand completely," said Jane. "Your mother is coming to visit and you're concerned that she will be upset because I'm not Jewish."

"Yes," said Walter. "That's it."

"Hasn't the question come up before now?"

"It might have," Walter said vaguely.

"And what *might* you have told her?" Jane asked.

Walter, looking uncomfortable, drained his glass before answering. "I *might* have told her that you were thinking of converting."

"Converting!" Jane said. "Becoming Jewish? Me?" She paused for a moment. "Can you *do* that?" she asked.

"You can," said Walter. "You have to take a class or something."

"A class," Jane said. "On being Jewish. How novel."

"I'm sorry I didn't say anything before now," said Walter. "Honestly, I thought I would tell her you were converting and then it wouldn't come up again until we got mar—" He stopped and looked away. "Until later," he concluded.

Jane too looked away. The subject of marriage was another one they didn't discuss. *We really should make a list of forbidden topics,* she mused.

"All right," she said. "Your mother thinks I'm converting to Judaism. We'll just let her think that I am. I don't see why that should be a problem."

Walter leaned back in his chair. "She's a Jewish mother," he said miserably. "They can tell when you're lying."

"Nonsense," Jane said.

Walter looked at her. "You don't know," he said. "I'm telling you, they're mind readers. When I was a boy, my mother *always* knew when I wasn't telling her the truth. Always."

"Then shouldn't she have figured out by now that you're fibbing?"

Walter shook his head. "That's over the phone," he said. "But once she sees me in person, it's all over."

Jane stifled a laugh. Part of her thought Walter was joking, but the expression on his face, and his continued nervousness, said otherwise.

"So as far as she knows, I'm considering converting, correct?" she said.

Walter nodded.

"Then we'll just keep pretending that I'm considering it. That won't be a lie."

"I told her you've already begun studying with a rabbi," Walter said.

"A rabbi?" Jane felt a flush of anger, which she forced down.

"All right," she said when she'd calmed down. "I'm studying with a rabbi. How long have I been doing this?"

"Just a couple of months."

Jane nodded. "And what would I have learned in that time?"

"I don't know," Walter answered.

"You don't know?" said Jane. "How can you not know?"

"I didn't have to convert!" Walter said. "It came built in."

"Then we'll just have to find out what it entails," said Jane. "I'm sure I can catch up enough to be able to answer any questions your mother might have. When is she coming?"

"In two weeks," Walter said.

"Two weeks!" Jane slumped in her chair. There was no way she would be able to learn what she had to learn before then, especially if the film company was coming as well. She looked at Walter, shaking her head. *"Oy vey!"* she said.

Chapter 2

"HERE ARE THE SALES TOTALS FOR LAST WEEK."

Jane looked up at the young man standing in front of the desk. Small of stature, he had fair skin, blond hair, and eyes the pale blue color of Arctic ice. When he smiled a dimple appeared in his chin, rendering him even more striking.

"Thank you . . ." She glanced at Lucy Sebring, who was standing behind the young man, looking over his shoulder.

Ned, Lucy mouthed.

"Ned," Jane said. "Thank you, Ned."

"You're very welcome," said Ned. "If there's anything else you need, just ask me or Ted." He smiled, revealing perfect teeth, and left the office.

"I don't know how you tell them apart," Jane remarked as Lucy took a seat in the chair beside the desk.

After her novel topped the bestseller lists and Jane had become busy promoting it and working on her follow-up, running Flyleaf Books had become impossible. She had made Lucy manager and hired Ned and Ted Hawthorne as clerks. Twins, the boys were completely indistinguishable.

There were only two differences between them: one was gay and the other was not, and one was a vampire and the other was not. Jane could never remember which was which, and even when she successfully attached the correct name to the correct young man, she could not then recall which one was—as Lucy so cleverly put it—playing on her team.

It was due to Byron that Jane had come to employ the twins. They were former students of his from a short stint teaching English literature at a small college in the Midwest. Byron had become infatuated with the young men and cultivated an intimate friendship with them. Eventually he came to favor one over the other and one night, fueled by too much wine, made the decision to turn him so that they could be forever together.

Unfortunately, he had as much trouble telling the twins apart as everyone else did and turned the wrong one. Curiously, the other twin had so far refused to be similarly transformed. With the passage of time one of the Hawthorne boys would continue to age while the other remained forever twenty-one. At the moment the difference was not noticeable, but inevitably it would be, and time was running out for the nonvampire twin to make a decision.

"I have no trouble telling who's who," said Lucy. "You just need to spend more time around them."

"Which is the gay one?" asked Jane.

"Ted," Lucy answered. "The one who *wasn't* just in here."

"And he's the vampire one as well?"

Lucy shook her head. "Ned—the straight one—is the vampire. Hence the problem. And by the way, shouldn't you be able to tell the undead from the not undead?"

Jane sighed. "One of my many failings as a creature of the night," she answered. "Remember, I didn't even realize Our Gloomy Friend was a vampire."

Our Gloomy Friend was a joke, but also something of a precaution. Jane half feared that if they spoke Charlotte Brontë's name aloud it would somehow cause her to appear. Lucy and Byron humored her in this, although Jane suspected they agreed with her more than they cared to admit.

"Speaking of Our Gloomy Friend," said Lucy, "her books have

been selling like crazy lately. We moved twenty-three copies of *Jane Eyre* last week. Apparently the high school assigned it as summer reading."

"How nice for her," Jane remarked. "Pity she won't see any of the royalties."

"Says the woman who should be collecting half a million a year from the sales of her own books," Lucy teased.

"At least *I* have a recent bestseller to my credit," Jane countered.

"There's that," said Lucy. She hesitated. "Do you think she's really gone for good?"

Jane, who had been wondering the same thing, heard herself say, "I do. If she was going to try anything, she would have done it by now."

"I hope so," Lucy said. "I still check under my bed every night."

"Monsters only hide under the bed in horror films," Jane said. "Where you really need to check is the closets."

Lucy laughed. "I'll keep that in mind," she said. "And since we're on the subject, what's happening with the *Constance* film?"

Jane groaned. She told Lucy the news about the production crew's imminent arrival in Brakeston.

"That's so exciting!" Lucy said.

"It's horrifying," said Jane. "You have no idea what Hollywood people are like. They talk far too quickly, are forever fidgeting with their phones, and don't eat anything yet manage to end up with two-hundred-dollar tabs. For *lunch.*" She shuddered, remembering her three days meeting with producers in Los Angeles following the purchase of the film rights to *Constance.* "They're terrifying," she whispered.

"I still think it's exciting," Lucy told her. "And Portia Kensington as Constance! She's the hottest thing around right now."

"So I understand," said Jane. "To be honest, I was hoping they'd get a more *serious* actress. Like Maude Firk."

Lucy made a face. "Don't you want people to actually *see* the film?"

"Maude Firk is an excellent actress," Jane argued. "She's won two Oscars."

"And both of them before 1924," said Lucy. "Anyway, at least you got the director you wanted. If anyone can make a good film out of your book, it's Julia Baxter."

"There is that," Jane admitted. "I suppose it will be nice to spend some time with her."

"That's the spirit," said Lucy, standing up. "I should get back to work."

"Oh," Jane said as Lucy walked out. "Do you know if we have any books on becoming Jewish?"

Lucy popped her head back in the office. "On *becoming* Jewish?" she asked.

"Yes," said Jane. "You know, converting."

"We have *Judaism for Dummies*," Lucy said.

"I suppose that's as good a place to start as any," Jane said. "Could you set a copy aside for me?"

"Sure," said Lucy. "May I ask why?"

"It's a long story," Jane replied. "Actually, it's not so much *long* as it is *complicated*. I'll tell you later, though. I promise."

"Okay," said Lucy. "I'll go find the book." She gave Jane a peculiar look before leaving without another word.

I might as well get used to that look, Jane thought. *I have a feeling I'm going to see quite a lot of it.*

She returned to looking through the store receipts, but it took her all of five minutes to see that Lucy, Ned, and Ted were doing just fine without her. She felt a pang of jealousy. Although she didn't want anything bad to happen in her absence, she liked to think that she was crucial to the store's continued well-being.

"Here's the book you asked for," said a male voice.

"Thank you," Jane said. She glanced up and saw Byron standing beside her.

He held out the book. "Interesting reading," he remarked.

"Yes," said Jane, taking the book from him. "I'm doing some research for my novel. One of my characters is Jewish."

"And how *is* the new book coming along?" Byron inquired.

"Brilliantly," said Jane.

"That well?" Byron remarked.

Jane picked at a loose thread on her blouse. "It's very difficult producing art under pressure," she said. "I'm not a machine."

Byron nodded. "I imagine it must be very trying."

"Stop gloating," said Jane irritably.

"Me?" Byron objected. "I'm not gloating."

"You are," Jane insisted. "I can tell by your tone."

"You wound me," Byron said. "You know I wish you nothing but success. Why, I bought six copies of *Constance* to give as gifts."

"Be that as it may, you're still gloating. Might I ask how *your* writing is going?"

"Splendidly," Byron answered. "I just finished the latest Penelope Wentz novel. It's called *The Scent of Love.*"

Jane stifled a snort. Her opinion of Byron's recent literary efforts was not high. But she envied his sales. Although *Constance* had sold extraordinarily well, Byron's Penelope Wentz novels did even better.

"It's about a *parfumeur* who has had her heart broken one too many times," Byron continued, ignoring her. "Yet she manages to create scents that make people fall wildly in love. Then one day a man comes into her shop and asks her to make a perfume that will remind him of his beloved wife, who died tragically a year before. Our heroine does, of course, but in the process she falls in love with the grieving widower and finds herself altering the formula to make him fall in love with *her.*"

"Scandalous," Jane remarked.

"Isn't it?" said Byron. "Of course the gentleman does fall in love with her, and then she doesn't know if he really loves her or if it's merely the scent. She hates herself for tricking him. Yet she really does love him. What can she do?"

Jane shook her head. "That *is* a puzzle," she said.

"Naturally the only solution is for her to stop wearing the perfume and see if he remains in love with her," Byron concluded. "Et cetera, et cetera, et cetera, and they live happily ever after."

"I believe I smell another bestseller," said Jane dryly.

"Very amusing," Byron replied. "I have to write *something* to keep myself living in the style to which I've become accustomed. Heaven knows we don't see any royalties from our real books."

"I consider *Constance* a real book," Jane told him.

"You know very well what I mean," said Byron. "How many copies of *Pride and Prejudice* did you sell last year?"

"I don't want to talk about it," Jane said. "Anyway, why are you here?"

"He came to moon over the twins," said Lucy, brushing past Byron. She stood by the desk as she sorted through the day's mail.

"Have you been able to talk any sense into Ned?" Byron asked.

"You mean Ted," Lucy answered as she handed a postcard to Jane. "Ned's the one you turned."

Byron made a face. "I can never remember," he said.

"And no, I haven't," said Lucy. "Frankly, I'm sort of surprised. I would have thought the gay one would be all excited about staying young forever. It seems more their thing somehow."

"This is all I get?" Jane asked Lucy. "A postcard announcing a half-price sale at Bed Bath and Beyond?"

"I could try getting them drunk again," Byron said thoughtfully.

"You keep out of it," said Jane as she dropped the postcard into the trash. "It's bad enough you turned . . . Ted?" she asked, looking at Lucy.

"*Ned,*" Lucy said. "Honestly, is it really so hard?"

"Ned," Jane continued, ignoring her and speaking to Byron. "You just can't help yourself, can you?"

"It was a momentary lapse in judgment," Byron argued. "He read my work so *beautifully.*"

"Oh, well then," said Jane. "That's perfectly understandable."

"Would you two please shut up," Lucy hissed. "They're right outside."

Byron and Jane looked at her with wounded expressions. Lucy, unmoved, held up a finger. "Not another word about turning anyone," she said to Byron. She looked at Jane. "And yes, that's all the mail for you today. I'll handle the rest. And anyone else would be ecstatic about getting half off a duvet or waffle iron or whatever, so don't give me that look."

Byron watched her leave. "She's quite a girl, isn't she?" he remarked.

"Yes, she is," said Jane.

"Pity she doesn't have a boyfriend," Byron said.

"We've been through this before," said Jane. "Don't even think about it."

"I'm not talking about *myself,*" Byron said. "I'm just thinking out loud."

"Did you really come here just to see that boy?" asked Jane.

Byron shook his head as he shut the door. "Well, that was an incentive," he admitted. "But I really came to congratulate you on your vanishing yesterday."

"Well, thank you," Jane said. "I did a rather neat job of it, I think."

Byron shook his head. "I've seen year-old vampires who could dematerialize more successfully," he said. "But it's a start."

"Beast!" Jane exclaimed. "You can't expect me to do it instantly. I'm not a trained dog, for heaven's sake."

"You won't always have time, Jane," Byron said. "What would you do if you were confronted by a vampire killer?"

Jane sighed. "I would glamor him—or her—as much as possible and then summon you to deal with the problem."

"You can't," said Byron. "I've been staked. You're on your own."

"Oh, bother. Well, I suppose I could drain him—or her—myself, but you know I draw the line at murder."

"You did kill Our Gloomy Friend," Byron reminded her.

"She was already dead," said Jane.

"You didn't know that at the time," Byron countered. "You thought she was a psychotic blogger who was trying to blackmail you."

Jane huffed. "Anyway, I didn't push her into that fire. She *fell*. And she came back and tried to kill *us*, in case you've forgotten." She paused, remembering Lucy's earlier question. "Speaking of Our Gloomy Friend, I wonder where she is. Do you think she'll try again? It's been nine months."

"That's barely a second in vampire time," Byron answered. "I wouldn't be surprised if she was planning something. But that's even more reason for you to perfect your vanishing. When you are faced with someone wishing to do you harm, the best course of action is to simply disappear." He looked thoughtful. "Of course, you could always transform yourself into a bat, but—"

"A bat?" Jane exclaimed. "I thought that was a myth."

Byron shook his head. "No, it's quite true. But it's a very advanced technique. You're not nearly ready for it."

"What else can I turn into?" asked Jane.

"That's it," said Byron. "Just a bat. And no, I don't know why. That's just how it is."

"But if one can turn into a bat, then doesn't that suggest that the power of transformation might be more widely—"

"A *bat*," Byron repeated sternly. "Not a cat, not a wolf, not a giant sloth. A bat. And *you* can't even do that. Not until you master disappearing."

"I wasn't aware there was a larger goal," said Jane. "Perhaps

I just needed some incentive. I mean, a bat . . . well, that's something." A thought occurred to her. "What *kind* of bat?" she asked.

Byron sighed. "I don't know," he said. "A vampire bat, I suppose."

"But there are lots of kinds of bats," Jane countered. "Fruit bats. Spotted bats. Little brown bats. And of course the flying foxes, which aren't foxes at all but—"

"Tell you what," Byron interrupted. "One night I'll turn into a bat and you can look me up in a field guide."

"Don't think I won't," said Jane. "Now let me try disappearing again."

"No," Byron said. "I don't want *trying;* I want *doing.* Go home and practice, and don't call me until you're absolutely sure you can vanish and stay vanished for at least five minutes."

"That could take centuries," said Jane moodily.

Byron smiled. "Then it's a good thing we're vampires." He opened the door. "Now I'm going to see if Ned would like to get some lunch."

"Ted," Jane said without thinking. "You mean Ted."

"Whichever," said Byron. "They're both delicious."

When Byron was gone Jane picked up *Judaism for Dummies* and opened it. She sighed. *I hope being Jewish is easier than being a vampire,* she thought. *There has to be something I'm good at.*

Chapter 3

Ha, noch einen ganzen Tag,
Überlang ist diese Zeit.
Zwei Opfer sind mit schon geweiht
Und das dritte ist leicht gefunden.
Ha, welche Lust aus schonen Augen
An bluhender Brust neues Leben
In wonnigem Beben
Mit einem Kusse in sich zu saugen.

"FLOWERING BOSOM, INDEED," JANE SIGHED AS SHE TOOK A SIP OF wine from the glass next to her keyboard. The glass was almost empty. *Should I have some more?* she asked herself, knowing full well that she should not. She'd already refilled the glass twice. Although her altered constitution allowed her to tolerate more than a normal human body could, she was nonetheless feeling the effects of the merlot.

"I believe I'm tipsy, Jasper," she announced. The dog, splayed on the rug beside her chair, thumped his stub of a tail.

"I must be if I thought listening to Marschner was a wise idea." She picked up the CD case and looked at it. The cover depicted a naked woman seated on a bed, her back to the viewer. In front of her stood a dark-haired man wearing a tuxedo. Only if one looked very closely would one see the drops of blood on the man's shirt and the two tiny punctures on the woman's neck. *"Der Vampyr,"* Jane said in a deep voice, then giggled. "Honestly."

Marschner's opera was not really to her liking. For one thing, she found the German language completely without appeal. As a friend had once said, "It always sounds as if they're on the verge of coughing something up." For another, the libretto was ridiculous. "Not that most of them aren't," Jane remarked to Jasper. "But this one is particularly melodramatic. You see, Lord Ruthven is a vampire. One night—I don't know why—the Vampire Master comes to him and informs him that unless he is able to kill three virgins before the clock strikes one the next morning, he'll die. If he *can* kill three of them, he gets to live another year."

Jane took another drink of wine. "Of course there is no such thing as a Vampire Master," she continued. "And the rest is equally silly. Something about a cave and moonlight and Ruthven pretending to be his own brother. It all ends badly for him and he goes to hell."

Jasper yawned.

"My sentiments exactly," Jane agreed. "Still, I can't help feeling a bit sentimental toward it."

In the spring of 1828 she had been dead for nearly eleven years and the novelty had not yet worn off. For reasons she could not now recall she was in Leipzig. Hearing that a new opera about a vampire had recently premiered, she was curious to see it. When she found out that the opera was based on Dr. John Polidori's novel *The Vampyre,* she was even more intrigued. It was Polidori, after all, who had vacationed with Byron at the villa on Lake Geneva the summer Jane was turned.

"I suppose I thought I might understand him better or some such foolish notion," Jane informed Jasper. "Byron, that is. I hadn't quite given up hope that he might yet love me."

The opera had devastated her. Sitting in the darkness of the balcony she had watched with mounting terror as the young woman, Janthe, fell under the spell of the handsome vampire and became his first victim. Several times she had to stop herself from crying out to the girl to run. But just as Jane had been entranced by Byron's beauty, Janthe fell prey to Ruthven's charms. During the soprano's final lines Jane had wept uncontrollably, and at the intermission she had fled into the night.

She had returned to the opera a week later, determined to see it through to the end. This time as she watched Lord Ruthven seduce and destroy first Janthe and then Emily, her sorrow was replaced with anger. At the finale, when Ruthven's evil plan to marry the chaste and virtuous Malwina and thus secure his immortality was thwarted by Malwina's true love, Edgar, Jane applauded fiercely, not only for the fine performances but for the triumph of good over evil.

For years she had hated Byron and often thought about what she would say or do should she see him again. Then, when he'd first appeared in her bookshop, she had immediately felt the draw of him as if no time at all had passed. He was still dashing, and his wit had grown even sharper over the centuries. She had even succumbed to his charms once again and spent a night with him.

They had since come to terms with each other, and although Jane knew they could never again be lovers, there were still moments when she thought she was meant to be with him. She wouldn't have to explain anything to him, or worry about him growing old.

"And I wouldn't have to become Jewish," she told Jasper.

But she wasn't in love with Byron. Now she was in love with Walter, and she and Byron were merely friends. Besides, Byron was always falling in love with other men, which made it considerably more difficult to imagine spending an eternity with him.

Jane pushed thoughts of Byron and vampires and Leipzig from her mind and turned back to the computer screen. She had decided to play *Der Vampyr* out of some hope that it might inspire her. She had a vague idea that she wanted to write about longing and loss, and she thought perhaps listening to Marschner's opera would put her in the mood.

It had not. At the top of the page of the open word-processing document was "Chapter 3." Beneath that was precisely one sentence. *And it's not even a good one,* Jane thought miserably.

Her new book had been due on her editor's desk at the first of the year. Six months later—despite assuring Kelly that she was almost finished—she had barely begun it. Every day she sat down at the computer determined to write a chapter, and every day the hours passed with excruciating slowness as she did everything but write. After several months of this she had reduced her daily goal from a chapter to a page, and a few months after that from a page to a paragraph. Now she would be content with a sentence or two.

She should, she knew, be ecstatically enthusiastic about writing this novel. *Constance* was a huge success. Her bank account was full. The letters and emails from fans were gratifying. There was the movie to look forward to. And the reviews had been wonderful.

Well, most of them had been wonderful. There was one that continued to gnaw at Jane's confidence. And like most stinging reviews, this one irked her because it mirrored her own fears about her novel's flaws.

Instinctively she directed the mouse's cursor to her Favorites folder and clicked on the link to Failures of Mimicry. The blog's front page filled her browser window. Its tagline, "In which we prosecute crimes of literary identity theft," leered at her in mocking accusation. She blushed.

She glanced at the latest entry. "Faux Faulkner: Peter Nesbitt's Yucknapatawpha County," she read. Much to her annoyance she found herself laughing at the play on Faulkner's celebrated fictional setting. She did not, however, read the accompanying text. Instead, she went to the blog's listing of earlier entries. For a moment she considered looking at "The Last Brontësaurus: Is Mary McTennant's Ice Age upon Her?" Then she selected "Austenish: Jane Fairfax's *Constance* Has an Identity Crisis."

She had read the review so many times that she had memorized it. Still, there was something about seeing it in its original form that made revisiting it even more painful. As she read the words Jane mouthed them silently. She flew through the opening paragraphs quickly, slowing when she reached the heart of the post.

> Jane Fairfax's *Constance* is not the worst of the recent novels to unabashedly borrow from Austen, but it is arguably the most disappointing, for it contains a hint of its inspiration's charm and wit but smothers it in a heavy sauce that leaves a bitter taste in the reader's mouth. Where Austen is light and gay, Fairfax is dark and broody. Her characters are interesting, to be sure, but they seem intent on unhappiness. Constance is predisposed to sulkiness, and even when she finds love with Charles she seems restless and unfulfilled. One can almost imagine her happier with the brutish Jonathan, who at least exhibits some amount of passion, however twisted it might be. Ultimately one is left with the impression this is the novel Austen might have written following a blow to the heart. Or possibly the head.

Jane shut the window and leaned back in her chair. Not for the first time since stumbling across the site (damn Google and its ability to ferret out every last mention of her and her book) she considered writing the author a note. But she knew that would end poorly. Kelly had told her—and she'd soon found that he was quite right—not to read everything written about her. Unlike the past, when critics were allowed to criticize because they knew something about books and writing, the invention of the Internet made it possible for anyone with an opinion to share it. This was not, as far as Jane was concerned, a good thing.

She had to admit, however, that despite her relentlessly snarky tone the blog's author was not stupid. Her name was Wen Bao, and if her biography was to be believed, she was thirty-three and lived in Fargo, North Dakota. What she did there was unclear, but Jane liked to imagine that she worked some dreary minimum-wage job simply in order to afford the books about which she wrote. As an ear piercer in a mall, perhaps, or a gift shop clerk at the Roger Maris Museum.

This was unkind of her, Jane knew, but it allowed her to not dislike Wen Bao as much as she might otherwise. She *had* disliked her upon first encountering the blog. That was only natural given her maternal feelings toward *Constance*. But after a few days (or perhaps it was weeks, or months) she had been able to read the post with a little more objectivity, and when she did so she was able to see that what Wen Bao had so succinctly stated were the very fears she herself had about her novel.

No, not fears. Truths. For she knew—had always known—that this novel was different from her others. But that was because she herself was changed. She had written *Constance* in a fever brought on by her infatuation with Byron. Their correspondence had awakened things in her, and these feelings found their way into her pen. *Constance* was, after all, her love letter to him. It was only natural that some of his infamous melancholy should color it.

And then there was what happened at Lake Geneva.

"They can hardly expect me to remain myself," Jane told Jasper. "Not after that. And yet they don't want me to change.

They like me the way I am. Was. Not that they even know that I'm me. Still, it hardly seems fair to expect a woman to stand absolutely still for two hundred years. I'm *not* Jane Austen any longer, at least not *their* Jane Austen."

She'd seen this before. She remembered when Amy Heckerling had borrowed liberally from *Emma* in creating her movie *Clueless.* A certain segment of Jane's readership had cried foul, going so far as to say that Jane would be scandalized by what had been done to her novel.

"But I rather liked it," said Jane as Jasper got up and padded out of the room. "How are they to know what I would and would not like, anyway? It's not as if they *know* me. Really, knowing a writer through that writer's books is about as likely as understanding the inner workings of a clock by listening to its chime."

Still, she had fooled a great number of people. More than one critic had compared *Constance* favorably to her previous books. *But not Wen Bao,* Jane thought. *She saw through me.*

It occurred to her now—and she was positively astonished that it hadn't already—that perhaps the change in tone of *Constance* was what had caused the novel to be rejected so many times. Her earlier novels had brought into popularity a certain kind of story, one that *Constance* was not. Well, not completely, but enough that it was troubling to editors. *At least for the first twenty or so years,* Jane thought. *I can only assume that later editors simply hated it. Until Kelly.*

The phone rang. Jane, glancing at the clock, saw that it was after eleven. *Who's calling at this hour?* she wondered as she picked up.

"I hope it's not too late." Kelly said.

"No," said Jane, suddenly seized with a panic that he was calling to ask about the undelivered manuscript. She tapped her fingers on the keyboard loudly. "I'm just writing."

"Good," Kelly replied. "Because that's why I'm calling."

Jane's anxiety doubled. "It's coming along *very* well now," she said. "I've had a breakthrough. I think I can have it to you before Labor—"

"I'm not checking up on you," interrupted Kelly.

Jane hesitated. "You're not?" she asked.

"Do you really think I'd call you this late to see how the book is coming along?" Kelly said.

"Well . . ." Jane said slowly. "You *did* say you were calling about the book."

"I did," Kelly agreed. "But it's not about when it will be finished. That will be up to your new editor to worry about."

Jane breathed a sigh of relief. Then Kelly's words sank in. "My new editor?" she said.

"That's the big news," said Kelly. "I've got a new position. I'm going to be an agent at Waters-Harding. Actually, I'm going to be *your* new agent. I made that part of the deal."

Jane was at a loss for words. "Congratulations," she managed.

"You don't sound very excited," said Kelly.

"Oh, I am," Jane said. "Very excited. It's just that I didn't know you were looking to leave editing."

"I wasn't, really," said Kelly. "But last week I had a meeting with Knut Amundsen about another author they represent and out of the blue he asked if I'd ever considered being an agent. I guess he was impressed with my negotiating skills. I said I hadn't given it much thought, and he said I should. Then he offered me a job."

"That really is wonderful," Jane told him, her composure regained. "I know you'll be a wonderful agent." She paused a moment so as not to appear anxious. "So who will my new editor be?"

"A wonderful young woman," Kelly said. "Jessica Abernathy. She comes from Fourth Street Books. She adores *Constance*. Didn't stop raving about it the whole interview."

"Jessica Abernathy," Jane said. The name was familiar, but she couldn't place it.

"She's young," Kelly continued. "But she's edited some really good books. I really think you'll—"

"Jessica Abernathy!" Jane exclaimed. "Of Fourth Street Books?"

"Yes," said Kelly. "Do you know her?"

Indeed I do, Jane thought. *She's number 116.*

"No," she said, trying to calm herself. "I must have seen her name somewhere." *As in on her rejection letter,* she fumed. *Adores* Constance *my foot. I'm sure she said it just to get the job.*

But she couldn't tell Kelly that. It would seem petty of her. Besides, it was possible Jessica Abernathy had never even read Jane's manuscript. She could have just rejected it out of hand, then not recognized it when she read the finished product.

It will be all right, she told herself. *You can handle this.*

"When do you start?" she asked Kelly.

"Two weeks," Kelly replied. "Then I'll be your agent. We'll get you a much better deal than the one you got last time." He laughed at his little joke.

Jane tried to laugh, but ended up coughing.

"Are you okay?" Kelly asked.

"I just swallowed a little wine," said Jane. "I'll be fine."

I'll be fine, she repeated to herself as Kelly continued talking excitedly about his new job. *I'll be fine.*

Twenty minutes later she hung up, having listened to only about half of what Kelly had said. His excitement had only deepened her sadness, and now she felt as she had that first night sitting in the balcony at the opera. She didn't want to lose Kelly as her editor. She particularly didn't want to have to work with Jessica Abernathy.

She turned the music back on and sat back in her chair, her eyes closed. Whatever incentive she'd had to work on her novel was now gone. What was the point? Jessica Abernathy was going to hate it anyway.

Jane listened as Lord Ruthven wove his spell on the doomed

Janthe. Despite knowing it would always end the same way, Jane couldn't help but hope for the girl's salvation. As Ruthven sang Jane translated his words in her head.

> *Yes, beloved, I belong to you forever,*
> *And forever, beloved, you are mine!*
> *Ah, only love, love makes me happy,*
> *I devote my life to you alone!*

Jane opened her eyes. "Don't believe him, Janthe," she said. "He's going to break your heart. They always do."

Chapter 4

"I'M SORRY, WHAT WAS YOUR NAME AGAIN?"

"Anthony," the man answered as he rummaged around in one of the many bags he had with him. "But you can call me Ant. Everyone does."

"Ant," Jane repeated. "Of course. And you say you're with the film people."

Ant nodded. "They were supposed to tell you we were coming," he said as he fiddled with the controls on the video camera in his hands.

"Yes, well, I'm afraid they didn't," said Jane, squinting as a bright light blinded her.

"Sorry," said the girl who was positioning the lights behind Ant.

They were in Jane's living room. Jane was seated on the couch, anxiously watching Ant come perilously close to knocking over a ceramic figure of a badger that had been given to Jane in 1908 by Kenneth Grahame as a thank-you for convincing him to change his lead character from Miss Slug to Mr. Toad. When Ant turned his back Jane retrieved the badger from the side table and placed it safely under the couch.

"Like I told you," Ant said. "We're shooting scenes for the DVD extras."

"The DVD?" Jane said. "But they haven't even made the film yet."

Ant snorted. "Tell me about it," he said. "But they want this stuff done earlier and earlier." He pulled a roll of duct tape from one of the bags and unrolled about six inches of it. "If you ask me," he mumbled, tearing the tape with his teeth, "it's because they want to get the interviews when everyone's still excited about the project and doesn't hate each other."

He applied the tape to the side of the video camera while he continued to talk. "We used to do the DVD stuff six months, sometimes a year after the movie wrapped. But then you run the risk of losing people for one reason or another."

"Losing them how?" Jane asked, shifting uncomfortably in her chair.

Ant shrugged. "Costars who fell in love on the set break up," he explained. "The director has a falling-out with the studio. Someone is in rehab and can't film." He laughed. "Well, *that* always happens. Anyway, if you get this stuff done before shooting even begins, you've got it in the can and ready to go."

"That seems prudent," Jane remarked.

"One film I worked on a couple of years ago, the leading lady got divorced after the film wrapped," said Ant. "She dealt with it by eating everything in sight and blew up like a Macy's Thanksgiving Day Parade balloon. When I went to shoot her interview for the DVD we could only shoot her from the chest up. Even then her face was so fat she looked like one of those bodies that wash up on the beach a week after a plane crash. Every time she talked I kept waiting for a crab to come out of her mouth."

Jane put a hand to her cheek. *Do I look puffy?* she wondered. The girl working on the lights was also the makeup person, and she had put powder on Jane's face fifteen minutes earlier. But suddenly Jane felt sweaty. She started to ask if the girl could refresh her makeup, then stopped herself. *You don't want to seem demanding,* she reminded herself.

"You ready to go?" Ant asked the girl, who was still fussing with the lights.

"Almost," she said just as one of the bulbs in a light popped. The girl swore loudly.

Ant rolled his eyes and sighed wearily. "Let me guess," he said. "You don't have a spare."

"I think there's one in the van," the girl told him. "I'll be right back."

With the girl gone Jane took the opportunity to ask Ant a question that had been on her mind. "I understand why they might want interviews with the stars of the film," she said cautiously. "Or with the director. But why me?"

Ant nodded. "It's weird, right? I mean, you're just a writer. You didn't even write the script." He shook his head. "That's Julia Baxter for you."

Jane's interest grew with the mention of the film's director, whom she had yet to meet or even speak to. "Julia Baxter asked for me to be included?" she said.

"No offense, but she thinks people actually give a crap about who wrote the book a film is based on," said Ant. "Like anybody reads *books* anymore."

"Imagine," Jane said. "The idea."

She eyed Ant with growing dislike. She was already annoyed with him, ever since he'd arrived at her bookstore that afternoon and immediately started bossing her around. As she hadn't been expecting him, his behavior was even more upsetting, and until he'd explained his presence she had considered biting his neck.

He reminds me of George Wickham, she realized. *He's all bluster and no substance.*

"I don't think I've read a book since high school," Ant said, oblivious to the fact that he was making himself even more unappealing to Jane. "I just wait for the movie." He laughed.

"No books?" Jane said. "Not a single one?"

"Not a whole one," Ant admitted. "Sometimes I'll grab one at the airport when I fly to L.A. You know, in case the in-flight movie sucks. But I've never finished one."

"I imagine you *could* finish one on the way back," Jane suggested, wondering just how long it took Mr. Anthony Doolan to read a book designed to appeal to air travelers.

"Nah," Ant said. "I forget the story as soon as I get off the plane. I'd have to start all over again, and what would be the point?"

Before Jane could suggest what the point might be, the girl returned with a new bulb for the light. Jane caught her eye, and the girl smiled. *She seems nice,* Jane thought. Ant had not introduced them.

She started to ask the girl's name, but once again the light came on, making her blink. When finally her vision cleared she saw Ant pointing the video camera at her. Staring into its large black eye, she found herself feeling very self-conscious.

"Don't look at the camera," Ant instructed her. "Look at Shelby."

Shelby, Jane noted. She smiled at the girl.

"All right," said Ant. "I'm going to ask you some questions. Just answer them naturally. But try to be interesting. If you can."

Jane took a deep breath. *You're lucky I fed last week,* she thought as she focused on Shelby's face. *Otherwise I'd give you more interesting than you could handle.*

"How did it feel when you heard your book was going to be made into a movie?" Ant asked.

"Of course it was very exciting," Jane said. "It's always a pleasure when your work is exposed to a wider audi—"

"Cut," Ant said, putting the camera down.

"What's wrong?" asked Jane.

"It's boring," Ant said. "I told you, be interesting."

Jane nodded. "Interesting," she repeated. "I see." She paused for a moment. "How would I do that?" she asked.

Ant sighed. "This is exactly why writers should never be

interviewed," he said, looking at Shelby. He turned back to Jane. "Let's try something else," he said, lifting the camera and pointing it at Jane. "Did you ever think a book you wrote would be made into a movie?"

Jane resisted the almost overwhelming urge to tell him that her books had been made into *dozens* of movies. "No," she said instead. "Frankly, it never occurred to me that fans of modern cinema would be drawn to something with actual content. Nothing at all blows up in my novel, you know."

She noticed Shelby suppressing a smile, but Ant seemed pleased with the answer. "Tell me something about your writing process," he said. "Do you have any interesting ways to inspire yourself?"

"I drink quite heavily," Jane said pleasantly. "I find that my best ideas come when I have to focus on the computer screen to keep the room from spinning. Also, I write in the nude. Oh, except for the earrings. I wear a pair given to me by the king of Norway."

Shelby let out a short laugh, which she cut off when Ant glared at her. "Do you mind?" he said.

"Sorry," said Shelby. She looked at Jane and bit her lip. "Sorry," she said again, her eyes twinkling.

"It might also interest people to know that I write precisely seven hundred and thirteen words every day," Jane said.

"Hold on," Ant said. "I'm not shooting." He hit the record button on the camera. "Say that again."

"I write precisely seven hundred and thirteen words a day," Jane repeated.

"So how long does it take you to write a whole book, then?"

"Oh, at least a month or two," said Jane, maintaining a serious tone. "Longer if there are more than two characters. It gets a bit confusing once there are three. But I use dolls to act out the scenes. That helps."

"Kind of like a movie," said Ant. "Have you ever wanted to write a screenplay?"

"Heavens, no," Jane answered. "I'm not nearly clever enough for that. I can only manage novels."

Ant set the camera down. "That's better," he told Jane.

"Do you think so?" Jane asked. "I tried my best."

"It's your first time," said Ant. "You'll get the hang of it. Now I want to get some footage of you writing."

"But I'm not drunk," Jane protested.

"Or nude," Shelby added.

"Precisely," said Jane. "Perhaps if you give me half an hour?"

"We'll do it later," said Ant. "Maybe we can shoot some scenes at the bookstore. You know, with customers and whatever."

"Whatever indeed," Jane said.

Ant set the video camera down. "Shelby, pack this stuff up," he said. "I'm going to have a smoke."

When Ant was safely out of the room Shelby looked at Jane and the two of them burst into laughter. "Is he really that stupid?" Jane asked the young woman.

"Hard to believe, isn't it?" Shelby answered. "Do you know what the duct tape is for?"

"I was wondering about that," said Jane.

"It's so he knows which buttons to push on the camera," Shelby explained. "He draws little arrows pointing to the ones he needs to use."

Jane laughed.

"Sometimes I'm amazed he can put his pants on without killing himself," Shelby said. "You handled him really well."

"I suppose," said Jane. "But I'm afraid my answers are completely inappropriate."

Shelby folded up one of the light stands. "Don't worry about it," she told Jane. "You and I can reshoot it all later."

"Really?" Jane said. "You can do that?"

"I always do," the girl told her. "Ant hasn't shot a usable interview yet."

"Then why go through all this?" Jane asked.

"There's one thing Ant *is* good at," said Shelby as she rolled up an electrical cord and tucked it into a bag. "He speaks bullshit fluently. And in Hollywood that's a major skill. Sort of like speaking Russian if you work for the CIA."

Jane laughed. "I see. So why do you work for him?"

"He's my brother," Shelby said.

"Oh," Jane said. "I'm sorry."

Shelby laughed, and Jane realized what she had said. She also recalled calling Ant stupid. "I didn't mean—"

"It's all right," Shelby assured her. "I know what you meant. And he is stupid. But I've been covering up his messes since we were kids. I guess I'm just used to it."

"But don't you want to get credit for the work you do?" She thought about the centuries she'd spent not being able to take credit for her novels, and felt herself becoming angry for the young woman.

Shelby shrugged. "I like doing it," she said. "But I don't speak bullshit. Having Ant do that part kind of makes up for everything else."

No, Jane thought. *It doesn't.* But she kept her opinion to herself. Later, she told herself, she might have a talk with Shelby. But not now.

Ant poked his head through the door. "What's taking so long?" he snapped.

Shelby ignored him and looked around the room. "I think that's everything," she said. "I'll just take this stuff to the van and we can go." She picked up one of the heavy bags and walked to the door. Her brother barely stepped aside as she left the house.

"Let me help you with this," Jane said, reaching for a bag and following after the girl. As she passed Ant she shot him a withering look, which he didn't notice because he was busy looking at something on his iPhone.

"Shel!" he yelled, his brow knitting up in confusion. "How do I make a call on this thing?"

I believe I will *have a talk with your sister,* Jane thought as she walked to the van. She felt her fangs slip into place, and ran the tip of her tongue over their needle-sharp points before drawing them back up again. *And then I may just have a few words with you as well.*

Chapter 5

"AUSTEN A GO-GO?"

Jane looked at the pink flyer that one of the twins had just handed her.

"What is it?" Ant asked, pointing the video camera in Jane's face before she could answer. "Is it something bad?"

Jane, who was reading the rest of the flyer, ignored him. A sick feeling was blooming in her stomach, followed closely by a rush of rage.

"How dare she?" she said furiously, balling the flyer up and flinging it into the trash can beneath the front desk. Several people browsing Flyleaf's shelves turned to look for the source of the noise.

"She dropped them off while I was at lunch," said Lucy. "If I'd been here, I would have told her where to go with her stupid—"

"It's all right," Jane assured her. "I just can't believe the gall of that woman."

"What woman?" Ant asked, still following Jane and filming her.

"Nobody," said Jane. "And turn that thing off!"

"Sorry," Ant replied. "I've got to get everything. Besides, this looks like it might be good."

"It's many things," said Jane. "And *none* of them is good."

"I apologize for upsetting you," said the twin who had given Jane the flyer. "I didn't know who she was, and she seemed pleasant enough."

"It's all right. . . ." Jane hesitated.

"Ted," the young man said.

"It's all right, Ted," said Jane.

"Who *is* she?" asked Ned, appearing beside his brother.

"Beverly Shrop," Jane answered, her teeth grinding on the name.

"The ShropTalk woman?" said Ted, or possibly Ned.

"Yes," Jane said. "That's the one."

"She's a moron." Shelby's voice emerged from the uncomfortable silence that had descended.

"Quiet," Ant hissed at his sister.

"I'm sorry," said Shelby. "But she is. Have you seen her site? It's crap."

Jane suppressed a smile. "Not the word I might have chosen, perhaps," she said. "But vividly accurate nonetheless."

"So what's this Austen A Go-Go?" Ant pressed.

Jane sighed. "Apparently Beverly Shrop has organized a festival of sorts for fans of romantic novels, of which she considers Austen's prime examples."

"And that's bad?" asked Ant.

"In theory, no," Jane answered. "But Beverly has an uncanny ability to make things . . . inconvenient."

"She's a horror show," Lucy clarified. "She's turned writers and books into a cottage industry, when really she knows nothing at all about them. Austen A Go-Go. Honestly."

"There's going to be a Darcy look-alike contest," Shelby said, reading one of the flyers. "And a Team Austen versus Team Brontë softball tournament."

Jane groaned. "Fabulous," she said.

"Someone named Tavish Osborn is a guest speaker," Shelby continued.

"What?" Lucy and Jane exclaimed in unison.

"Tavish Osborn," Shelby repeated. "Do you know him?"

"Vaguely," Jane muttered, thinking, *How could he?*

"He's going to be giving a lecture called 'The Real Jane Austen,'" said Shelby.

Lucy and Jane exchanged looks. *That's it,* Jane thought. Why hadn't Byron said anything to her about Beverly's ridiculous event? And what exactly did he mean by the *real* Jane Austen?

"Oh, good. You've seen the flyer."

Jane turned to see Beverly Shrop approaching at a brisk clip. As usual, she was dressed in pink, and her face wore a cheerful smile that appeared to be painted on with copious amounts of red lipstick, much like a clown's ghastly perpetually grinning mouth.

"Beverly," Jane said without enthusiasm.

"Doesn't it sound *delicious*?" Beverly asked. "I'm especially looking forward to Tavish's talk."

"Aren't we all?" asked Jane.

"I would have asked *you* to speak," Beverly said. "But I know how very busy you are trying to get your next book written."

And how would you know that? Jane wondered. Just what had Beverly and Byron talked about? She would most certainly have to have a word with him.

"It's true," Jane said. "I *am* quite busy at the moment."

"Well, I hope you'll at least grace us with your presence," said Beverly. "Oh, and if you'd like to sell your book at the event, feel free to bring a few copies. Blockstone's will be selling copies of Tavish's Penelope Wentz novels."

"Blockstone's?" said Jane, the name of the rival bookstore bitter on her tongue. "Why not have *us* sell his—"

"I have to run," Beverly said. "Lovely seeing you."

Fuming, Jane watched Beverly leave the store.

"Wow," said Shelby. "She really is something."

"You're breaking the wall!" Ant shouted at her. "Rule one. Don't get involved with the subject!"

Shelby ignored him. "You should have a big sale on this Tavish guy's books right before the event," she suggested to Jane. "That would really piss her off."

Jane nodded. "Yes," she said, smiling at Shelby. "It certainly would." She was liking the young woman more and more.

"Jane, you have a phone call." One of the twins leaned over the counter, covering the receiver with his hand. "It's a Jessica Abernathy."

For a moment Jane couldn't remember why the name was familiar to her. Then it hit her. "Oh!" she said. "Of course. I'll take it in the office." She turned to Ant, who was beginning to follow her. "This is private," she informed him. Without waiting for him to object, she went into the office and closed the door behind her, relieved to finally be alone.

She took a moment to calm herself before picking up the phone.

"Hello, Jessica," she said. "Sorry to keep you waiting."

"Don't worry about it," said a husky voice. "I hear we're used to waiting for you around here." Jessica laughed. It sounded like sandpaper rubbing against an obstinate board.

"I'm sorry?" said Jane. "Waiting for me?"

"It's a joke," Jessica said. "You know, waiting for your manuscript. Wasn't it due six months ago?"

"Something like that," said Jane. "I'm working on it."

"You might want to think about working faster. We're already going to miss the holiday shopping season. Now you're into spring at the earliest and more likely summer. You don't want to come out in summer. You'll get buried. Nicholas Sparks has a new one out in June. So does Jodi Picoult. And I heard King has *three* hitting the stores in time for vacation season. You'll be lost in that bunch."

"My last book did very well," Jane reminded her. "It was number one for—"

"Three weeks," Jessica said. "I know. But the remainder bins are filled with second books that flopped. You can't assume anything. Especially if you wait too long between books. People will forget you."

Jane wondered if Jessica remembered rejecting *Constance*. It certainly sounded as if she wasn't entirely thrilled about working with Jane on the new book. At the very least she was hardly being encouraging.

"Anyway, I'd like to have it by the end of the month," Jessica continued.

"I don't know if—"

"Great," said Jessica. "We'll talk then."

The line went dead. Jane stared at the phone for a moment. She felt shaky and disoriented, as she had as a girl when her brothers would hold her by the wrists and swing her around and around. Then she had enjoyed the giddiness that resulted. Now she merely felt sick. *That didn't go at all well,* she thought.

The phone rang again. She picked it up with some hesitation, wary that it might be Jessica calling back to tell her that her book had been canceled altogether. But it was Kelly.

"I'm calling from my new office," he told Jane. "Wait till you see my view."

"I just spoke with Jessica Abernathy," said Jane, skipping the pleasantries.

"How did it go?" Kelly asked.

"I'm not sure I know," Jane said. "She's rather difficult to read."

Kelly laughed. "Don't worry," he said. "She loves your work."

"Really?" Jane said. "I'm not so sure I got that from our little talk."

"When I interviewed her she just *raved* about *Constance*," Kelly said. "She said she couldn't wait to get her hands on your new manuscript."

Yes, Jane thought. *So that she can toss it in the shredder.*

"You're just anxious about working with someone new," Kelly

continued. "But you've still got me. I'll read whatever you have before you give it to Jessica. In fact, why don't you email me what you've got and I'll take a look."

"Maybe," Jane said. She couldn't bring herself to tell him that there was nothing more for him to read than there'd been the last time he asked.

"I saw Satvari at a publishing party last night," said Kelly. "She tells me a film crew is invading Brakeston."

"Yes," Jane said. "Some of them are already here. Did she tell you they were following me around documenting my thrilling existence?"

"No," Kelly replied. "Are they really? Are they there now?"

"Lurking just outside the door, I expect," said Jane.

"It sounds like things are crazy there," Kelly remarked.

"You have no idea," said Jane. "Did I tell you Walter's mother is coming to visit?"

"I sympathize," Kelly said. "Bryce's mother was just here for a week. I thought I was going to kill her. She's pressuring us to get a baby so she can have a grandchild. She says she wants a black one because they're more exotic than white babies and everyone else has Asian ones. If you'd heard her, you'd swear she was talking about a cat."

"She sounds intriguing," Jane said. "And perhaps the tiniest bit racist."

"She's a loon," said Kelly. "Oh, and she wants us to name it after her grandmother. Her name was Parsimony."

"Do you and Bryce even *want* a baby?" Jane asked.

"Not really," said Kelly. "But it might be fun. We could dress it up and buy it toys."

"Now who sounds as if he's talking about a cat?" Jane teased.

"I know," said Kelly. "It's ridiculous. But just think of it. Parsimony Littlejohn-Manx. It's kind of cute."

"It's horrid," Jane told him.

Kelly sighed. "It really is," he admitted. "What do you think of Aida Littlejohn-Manx?"

"Only slightly less horrid," said Jane.

"Does Walter want children?" Kelly asked.

The question took Jane by surprise. "I don't know," she said. "We've never discussed it. But it really doesn't matter. I'm far too old for that sort of thing."

"You aren't," Kelly said. "They can do wonderful things with in vitro these days. A friend of ours is pregnant for the first time at forty-seven. With twins. Can you imagine?"

Jane did imagine it. And she was horrified. It had never occurred to her that Walter might want children. She wasn't even sure she *could* have children. *Of course, the girl in the Twilight books did,* she mused.

"You know I'm joking," Kelly said after Jane had been silent for some time.

"Of course," said Jane. "I was just trying to imagine going to my child's graduation at the age of two hundred and fifty-three."

Kelly laughed, not knowing that she was serious. "You don't look a day over a hundred and sixty-two," he told her.

"Moisturizer," Jane joked. "And you're too kind. Anyway, I don't think children are in our future."

"His mother may have different ideas," said Kelly. "Do you have any idea what she's like?"

"None whatsoever," Jane said. "I'm sure she's lovely. After all, look at her son."

"That's what I thought about Bryce's mother," said Kelly. "Look how well that turned out." He paused for a moment. "But I'm sure you're right."

Jane heard another voice, muffled, on the end of the line. Then Kelly said, "I have a client here, so I have to go. But don't worry about Jessica. Or the film crew. Or Walter's mother. It will all be fine."

Jane hung up. Not wanting to face Ant and his camera quite yet, she remained seated at the desk. She hoped Kelly was right. She had enough to worry about without adding stress about her new editor hating her work to the list. *And I haven't even told him about Austen A Go-Go,* she reminded herself.

A crash coming from the other room made her jump. She instinctively started to get up to investigate; then she sat down again.

"Let someone else deal with it," she said. "I quit."

Chapter 6

RABBI BEN COHEN WAS NOT AT ALL WHAT JANE HAD EXPECTED. As he rose to shake her hand she found herself taken aback by both his age and his appearance. Much younger than she would have thought possible for a religious leader, he was also much more handsome. She had envisioned someone well into his later years, perhaps with a bushy beard and glasses through which he peered out at the world with sad eyes. But Ben Cohen appeared no more than thirty, had no beard or glasses, and looked as if he'd just walked off a rugby pitch.

"Welcome," he said. "Please. Have a seat."

There was a desk in Rabbi Cohen's office, but he did not sit at it. Instead he settled himself onto one end of a stylish black leather couch while Jane took one of two sleek armchairs opposite it. Looking at the rabbi, she couldn't help but notice the large painting on the wall behind him.

"Is that a Pollock?" she asked.

The rabbi nodded. "It is," he said. "A gift from him to my grandmother in 1948. She was quite a beauty," he added without further explanation.

What with the painting and the furniture, Jane felt as if she were in the living room of a New York socialite instead of the office of a rabbi of a small upstate synagogue. But Ben Cohen's easy demeanor was anything but snobbish, and Jane suspected he'd grown up in far different circumstances.

"I prefer outsider art myself," Ben said. "That painting behind you, for instance."

Jane turned to look at the canvas hung on the wall opposite the couch. The same size as the Pollock, it was entirely different in mood and appearance. A figure composed of rectangles and circles stood surrounded by odd birdlike creatures breathing fire. The figure was of indeterminate gender and appeared to have several faces, each in its own circle and looking out in all directions. Above the figure what was unmistakably an angel reached down with open arms.

"It was done by a patient of mine," Ben said. "A woman who suffered from multiple personality disorder. This personality— William—was an artist."

"Patient?" said Jane.

"I'm a psychologist," Ben explained. "I interned at Bellevue as part of my postgraduate work."

"When did you become a rabbi?" Jane asked.

Ben smiled, and his eyes momentarily took on an air of sadness. "Six years ago," he said. "I decided I wanted to know more about God."

Jane turned back to him. "And do you?" she asked.

"No," Ben said, shaking his head. "Not so much."

Jane couldn't help smiling. The rabbi's honesty was charming.

"Do you believe in God, Jane?" he asked.

Jane's smile faded. "Not so much," she admitted.

It was Ben's turn to smile. "May I ask why?"

Jane sighed. "My father was a reverend," she told him. "An Anglican. Naturally, so was I. It wasn't until . . . later that I began to question things."

"Later," the rabbi said. "Was there a specific incident?"

When I became one of the living dead, Jane thought. She wondered what Ben Cohen would say if she told him she was a vampire. Would he treat her as if she had multiple personalities? Would he recommend hospitalization in a psychiatric facility?

"Not really," she told him. "More like an accumulation of them."

"And yet now you want to convert to Judaism," said Ben. "That's an interesting decision for someone who isn't sure she believes in God."

I might as well tell him the truth, Jane thought. "My boyfriend's mother wants me to be Jewish," she said, her cheeks reddening at the word *boyfriend.* It sounded so juvenile.

"I see," said Ben. "Well, you wouldn't be the first person to convert for that reason."

"It's all rather silly," Jane said. "Walter wasn't even really raised Jewish. His father and stepmother were Episcopalian. But his mother is Jewish, and that makes *him* Jewish."

"I've heard that," said Ben.

Jane put her hand to her forehead. "Of course you have," she said. "I'm sorry. It's just that it's all a bit much to handle right now on top of everything else."

"Everything else?" said Ben.

"The new book, my new editor, the film, Beverly Shrop." Jane looked up. "You don't need to hear all this."

"It *is* what I do," said Ben.

"Yes, but it's not why I'm here," Jane replied, composing herself. "Although I imagine you're going to tell me that I'm a poor candidate for conversion, so I might as well go."

"Why would I say that?" Ben asked.

Jane wrinkled her brow. "Well, I can't say with any amount of honesty that I'm terribly sincere about it," she said.

"Not now," Ben said. "But maybe we should talk some more. It doesn't even have to be about conversion."

Jane, taking his meaning, asked, "You mean like therapy?"

"Yes," Ben said. "Like therapy."

Jane found herself laughing. "I don't think that will be necessary," she said.

"It's up to you, of course," said the rabbi. "But if you ask me—which you didn't, but I'm going to pretend you did—you're dealing with a lot of issues. It might help to talk about them."

Jane considered this for a moment. Ben was watching her. *But he's not judging,* she thought, looking into his eyes. "Perhaps you're right," she heard herself say.

"You have my number," said Ben, standing up. "I hope you'll use it."

Jane stood too, gathering up her purse and preparing to leave.

"Have you met the mother?" Ben inquired.

"This afternoon," said Jane. "Walter is picking her up as we speak."

"May I give you some advice?"

Jane nodded. "By all means."

"There's one key thing for you to remember when dealing with a Jewish mother."

"Which is?" asked Jane.

"They're always right," said Ben. "Always."

"But that hardly seems—"

"*Always,*" Ben repeated. "Trust me. I've had one for thirty-four years."

"I'll keep it in mind," Jane assured him.

Twenty minutes later she pulled up outside Walter's house. His car was in the driveway. *So you've arrived,* Jane thought as she checked her hair in the rearview mirror. She applied some lipstick, sighed deeply, and got out of the car.

Walter answered the door even before she'd rung the bell. "You're here!" he said, a little too loudly. He leaned in and gave Jane a peck on the cheek. "She's already making me crazy," he whispered.

"Is that the girl?"

Walter stepped aside, revealing a small, thin woman perched on the couch. Her hair, which was black with only hints of gray, lay flat against her head like a swim cap. Her blue eyes focused in on Jane like a bird of prey sizing up a rodent far below, and the look on her face told Jane that she had yet to make up her mind about her son's choice of girlfriend.

She was dressed in white slacks and a billowy black blouse patterned with yellow and red flowers. Numerous rings covered her fingers, and beside her on the couch sat a small brown Chihuahua with enormous ears that stuck up like a bat's. Something about the dog didn't seem quite right, and then Jane realized that it was missing its right front leg and was leaning against Miriam for balance.

"Jane, this is my mother," Walter said. "Mother, this is Jane."

"I can see that," Miriam said. She extended her hand. "Who else would she be?" she asked.

"It's a pleasure to meet you, Mrs. Fletcher," Jane said as she shook Miriam's hand.

Miriam drew back her hand. "Ellenberg," she said. "*Ms.* Ellenberg." She looked at her son. "You didn't tell her? You should have told her."

Jane, realizing her mistake, instinctively moved to protect Walter. "Oh, he did tell me," she said. "I'm so sorry. It's not Walter's fault. I've been so looking forward to meeting you that it completely slipped my mind that you and Walter's father—"

Miriam shook her head. "All the trouble I went through to divorce that man, the least I could get was my name back. How is that little *shiksa* he married?" she asked Walter. She glanced at Jane as she said it, and Jane couldn't help but see that the barb was aimed partially at her.

"Bethany is fine, Mom," said Walter.

"That's too bad," Miriam remarked.

Jane decided to change the subject. "What a handsome little dog," she said. "What's his name?"

"*Her* name is Lilith," said Miriam.

Hearing her name, Lilith perked up her ears and looked up at Miriam. "I found her in Jerusalem," Miriam continued. "She was wandering around the streets."

"What were you doing in Jerusalem?" Jane asked.

"Hunting," Miriam replied. "For antiques," she added.

"Mother has traveled all over the world," Walter told Jane.

"I still do," Miriam said. "I'm not quite dead."

"Of course not," said Walter. "Mother travels all over the world," he said to Jane.

"Walter's father hated traveling," Miriam said. "It's one of the reasons I divorced him. That and the fact that he was a lazy, no-good son of a bitch."

"I'll just go get us some drinks," said Walter.

"I'll help," Jane told him.

"No," Miriam said. "You sit. We'll talk."

Jane looked at Walter, who nodded. Jane sat down in an armchair beside the couch and smiled at Miriam. "I'm so pleased you're here," she said.

"Bullshit," Miriam said. "You're terrified of me. You're afraid I won't think you're good enough for my son. And I don't. But nobody is, so don't worry too much. Walter tells me you're converting."

Jane cleared her throat. "Well, I have been talking to a rabbi," she said.

Miriam snorted. "Talking to a rabbi," she said. "It takes more than that to be a Jew. Being a Jew comes from here." She tapped her chest over her heart.

"Ms. Ellenberg," Jane said, "I care very much for your son, as I see you do as well. I would like us to be friends. However—"

"Don't however me," Miriam said. "And let me make one thing perfectly clear. You will never marry my son."

Jane stiffened. "And why is that?" she asked, trying to keep her tone civil.

Miriam leaned closer, until Jane thought she might jump off the couch and leap into her lap. "Because," said Walter's mother, "I know what you are."

Chapter 7

"I don't know *what* she meant," Jane told Lucy.

They were in the living room of Lucy's apartment. Jane had gone there after excusing herself from the evening with Walter's mother as early as she could without appearing rude. It had been a tense couple of hours, although Walter hadn't seemed to notice that anything was wrong. Even Miriam had behaved perfectly normally, complimenting Walter on the roast chicken and asking Jane the usual sorts of questions two people ask upon meeting for the first time.

"Maybe I imagined it," Jane suggested.

"Why didn't you just ask her?" said Lucy, handing Jane a glass of merlot.

"I was startled," said Jane. "And Walter came in just at that moment. I could hardly say anything with him there."

Lucy sat down on the couch. "It's the sort of thing you say to someone you think is a gold digger," she said.

"Precisely," said Jane. "But Walter hasn't any money to speak of, and at any rate I have more than enough of my own. I certainly don't need his."

"My guess is that she's just trying to put a scare into you," said Lucy, sipping her wine. "You know what you should do?"

Jane shook her head.

"Bite her," Lucy said.

"I'm tempted," Jane said. "What a horrible woman."

"I'm serious," said Lucy. "Didn't you tell me that feeding on people can make them more susceptible to your charms?"

"Well, yes," Jane replied. "In a manner of speaking. But I wouldn't feel right feeding on Walter's mother. I think that crosses some sort of line."

"What about glamoring her?" Lucy asked.

Jane shook her head. "Glamors are temporary. I'd have to keep doing it, and that would be exhausting. Besides, truth be told, I'm not terribly good at it. I mean, I can get by, but something like that would take more power than I've developed."

"Maybe you should sic Byron on her," Lucy suggested. "I imagine he could glamor anyone."

"I'm not so sure of that," said Jane. "He's not done very well with Ned."

"Ted," said Lucy.

"That's what I meant," Jane said. "With Ted."

"No, he hasn't," said Lucy.

Something in Lucy's voice caught Jane's attention. "You know why, don't you?" she said.

Lucy shifted uncomfortably. "No," she said defensively. "Why would I know anything?"

"You *do*!" Jane insisted. "Out with it."

Lucy sighed. "All right," she said. "But you can't say *anything* to Byron. It will hurt his feelings."

"You're assuming he has any," Jane said.

"Be nice," Lucy told her. "I think he's behaved rather well, all things considered. He hasn't hit on me once since our battle with Our Gloomy Friend."

"Anyway," said Jane, waving her hand dismissively. "What do you know?"

"Well," Lucy said. "Apparently Ted isn't at all attracted to Byron. He thinks he's too old."

"He *is* old," said Jane. "He's two hundred and twenty-three."

"I mean too old for Ted," Lucy said. "How old was he when he died? I mean when he turned?"

"Thirty-six, I think," said Jane.

"Is that all?" Lucy said. "I would have guessed early forties."

"Eternal life isn't as easy as it might seem," Jane remarked.

"Ted is only twenty-two," said Lucy. "Those fourteen years make a big difference."

"Not after a century or so," Jane replied. "He'd catch up." She drank some more wine. "Besides, the way he acts most of the time, Byron might as well be twenty-two."

"You sound as if you *want* Ted to be turned," said Lucy.

"I suppose I do," Jane admitted. "Not for Byron's sake. He'd tire of the boy within a month after he got what he wanted. I'm thinking about the other one. Ned."

"What about him?" asked Lucy, tucking her feet under her and leaning against the back of the couch.

"I hate to see him lose his brother," Jane explained. "I know what that's like."

"But didn't you once tell me that you wouldn't have turned Cassie even if she'd asked you to?" said Lucy.

Jane nodded. "I did feel that way," she said. She hesitated. "I don't know that I do now."

"What if *I* wanted you to turn me?" Lucy asked.

Jane looked at her friend. "I've never turned anyone," she said.

"That's not what I asked you," said Lucy.

"I know what you asked," Jane snapped.

Lucy looked stung. Jane got up, went to the couch, and sat beside her. She took Lucy's hand. "I'm sorry," she said. "I didn't mean to sound so angry."

"It's all right," Lucy told her. "I shouldn't have asked."

"No," Jane said. "You have every right to ask. You're my best friend. I suppose that's why I reacted as I did."

"I don't understand," said Lucy.

Jane continued to hold Lucy's hand as she spoke. "I've had many friends over the past two centuries," she said. "Many of them I liked very much, and I was sad to lose them. But the only person I've missed every single day is Cassie. She's the only one I've ever even thought about wishing I'd turned."

Jane stopped speaking and looked down at the floor. She felt she was going to cry, and she didn't want to. Only when she thought she could continue without weeping did she speak again.

"Then you came into my life," she told Lucy. "And you've given me back a part of my sister. When I think that someday I might lose you too . . ."

Her voice trailed off as the tears began to flow. Lucy sat up and hugged her, holding Jane tight. "It's all right," she said softly.

"I don't know what I would do if you asked me," Jane whispered. "I don't know that I would be able to refuse. And that frightens me."

They held each other for a long moment and then let go. Lucy too was now crying. She got up and went into the kitchen, returning with a box of tissues. She held the box out to Jane, who took two tissues and blotted her eyes.

"I won't say I haven't thought about it," Lucy said as she sat down. "But I promise not to put you in that position. Besides, I'm sure Byron would do it if I asked."

Jane looked at her, horrified. Then Lucy smiled. "Joking," she said.

Jane pointed a finger at her. "Don't even think about it," she said. "This isn't like when you were seven and if your mother said no to something you went and asked your father."

Lucy shook her head. "You're absolutely right," she said. "It's more like if I asked my great-great-great-great-great-grandmother for something and she said no."

Jane couldn't help but laugh. She wiped her eyes again and

picked up her glass of wine, taking a sip. She felt a little bit better, but the feeling that had started her down this path lingered. Lucy really was going to age while Jane remained the same. Someday they *would* have to say goodbye. *Just as you would have to say goodbye to Walter,* a voice in her head whispered.

She brushed it away, or at least tried to. But it buzzed around her head like a bee at a picnic, the ever-present threat of a sting making Jane anxious.

"I should go," she said, standing up.

Lucy looked at her, a puzzled expression on her face. "Is everything all right?" she asked. "I didn't mean to—"

"You didn't do anything," Jane assured her. "I just had an idea for my new book, and I want to get home and work on it for a bit before my confidence in it wears off."

Lucy stood up. "Okay," she said. "But promise me you won't say a word to Byron about what Ted told me."

"As much as it would bring me joy to see the expression on his face when he discovered that there's someone immune to his charms, I promise," Jane said.

She gave Lucy a long hug, then left the apartment and went to her car. She had no intention of going home and writing anything. Her new book was the last thing she wanted to think about. Well, the second-to-last thing. Lucy dying was the first. Lucy or *anyone* she loved. Although that list was fairly short, containing only Lucy and Walter. Byron was already undead. *Not that I love him,* she told herself. But of course she did. Despite everything, she did love him. *Just not in the same way I love Walter,* she concluded.

Now that she was thinking about what she didn't want to think about, it was all she *could* think about. She found herself tearing up again as she imagined attending Lucy's funeral. The logical thing—the thing almost every vampire she'd ever encountered did—was to move on and leave old friendships behind before the inevitable separation by death. It was only slightly less painful than watching a friend die, but at least you didn't have to witness the end grow nearer and nearer.

This was something that nonvampires could perhaps never understand, the inherent horror of knowing that you would continue on even as everyone and everything around you turned to dust. Yes, you could turn anyone you loved. There was nothing preventing you from doing that. But there were impracticalities with that as well. For one, where did you stop? Having turned, say, your favorite sister, were you then obliged to turn her husband, or lover, or children if she had them? If you turned your mother, were you then required to turn your aunts and uncles (all of whom she would likely miss when they passed on) as well as *their* children?

"There really would be no end of it." That's what the vampire with whom Jane had first discussed this matter had said. Her name was Olivia Rhodes. When Jane first met her she had been alive for almost five hundred years, having been turned toward the end of the Black Death. Since then she had watched scores of husbands and lovers die. Each time, she told Jane, she'd had to force herself not to turn the man. When Jane asked her why she didn't turn just one, to spare herself the endless cycle of grief, Olivia had smiled and said, "Eventually we would resent each other for not dying."

At the time Jane had not understood. Now, two hundred years later, she did. Still, she couldn't help thinking that there must be exceptions. Surely there were people with whom one could comfortably share eternity. People like Lucy. *Or Walter,* she thought. Wasn't it possible that they could continue to find each other interesting throughout centuries? Or would they get tired of telling the same stories again and again, until hearing a phrase such as "Remember that time in Pompeii" made them want to hurl themselves off cliffs?

She started the car. Sitting there in Lucy's driveway being

gloomy wasn't achieving anything. She could just as easily be miserable at home, where at least Jasper would sit beside her and she could stroke his ears. (Tom, being a cat, was useless as a source of comfort.) But thinking about *that* brought on another round of tears, as she imagined having to say goodbye to her pets. Animals could not be turned, so there was no question of creating a lifelong companion out of one of them. Jane had always thought this a great pity.

She pulled out of the driveway and headed for home. A few minutes later she found herself approaching Walter's house. Although she'd intended to pass right by, she felt herself step lightly on the brake to slow the car. Then she was coming to a stop at the curb.

She turned the engine off and sat in the dark, looking at the windows of the house. The lights in the living room were still on, and behind the curtains Jane saw shadows moving. She imagined Walter and his mother sitting, having coffee, talking. Were they discussing her? Was Miriam telling Walter that she didn't think Jane was suitable for him? Was Walter telling his mother that it was really none of her business?

She thought about trying to go invisible and sneaking up to the windows for a look. But that seemed slightly desperate. Yes, Miriam's remark earlier in the evening had bothered Jane. But had she really meant something sinister by it? Or was she just being an overly protective mother?

You're being silly, Jane told herself. *You just need to give her a chance.*

Suddenly the light in the living room went out. Jane waited, and a moment later a light on the second floor came on. Jane pictured the layout of the house in her head and realized that she was looking at the window to the guest room. *Miriam's room,* she thought.

She imagined Miriam getting ready for bed. Washing her face. Brushing her teeth. Putting on her favorite nightgown. Now she would go to bed in her son's house, a reversal of the years when she had tucked him into his bed in her house.

Jane thought of her own mother, and suddenly she was overcome with stirrings of affection for Miriam. Yes, they had gotten off to a bad start. But they could start again. Jane would just have to be a little more patient and understanding. *I can do that,* she told herself.

As she gazed up at Miriam's window the curtains parted unexpectedly. Miriam stood there, holding Lilith in her arms as she looked out at the night. The moon, nearly full, cast its light over the lawn. Jane's car was sitting in a pool of light, right in Miriam's line of vision.

Jane ducked down, her heart pounding. Then she remembered: Miriam hadn't seen her car. She would have no idea that it was Jane sitting there. Slowly Jane raised her head and peered over the edge of the window.

Miriam was staring at her. For a moment their eyes seemed to lock. Then Miriam closed the curtains. Her shadow remained visible for another minute. Then the light went out and Jane was left looking at a black space.

She started the car and drove away, feeling Miriam's eyes on the back of her head. *Or maybe I'll just stay out of her way,* she thought. *Just until she warms up to me a little. Or until she dies.*

Chapter 8

"HERE YOU ARE."

Sherman Applebaum slid into the booth, sitting opposite Jane, who was holding a cup of coffee in her hands and staring at a half-eaten jelly donut sitting on a plate in front of her.

At seven o'clock in the morning the Rise-N-Shine coffee shop was not particularly crowded. The handful of customers were mostly delivery truck drivers, people getting off late shifts, and retired men who dreaded the long days of having nothing to do and came to spend an hour or two among people who would gladly trade places with them. Tired and preoccupied with their own lives, none of them paid any attention to Jane, which is precisely why she had chosen to come there.

Jane looked at Sherman, who even at this early hour was dressed in a gray flannel suit complete with waistcoat, pocket watch, and a perfectly knotted tie in a lovely lavender and black pattern that complemented his alert blue eyes. His gray hair was neatly combed, and the faint scent of bay rum surrounded him. He looked as if he was on his way to a garden party instead of sitting in a greasy spoon. And yet at the same time he seemed to fit in perfectly.

"What are you doing here?" Jane asked him.

"I might ask you the same question," said Sherman.

A waitress approached the table before Jane could answer. "Morning, Sherm," she said. "The usual?"

"Thank you, Rhonda," said Sherman. "That would be lovely. And how did little Britney's recital go last week?"

The waitress beamed. "Great," she said. "I've got some pictures if you want to see them."

"I would be delighted," Sherman assured her.

As Rhonda walked away Jane said, "Little Britney's recital?"

"Rhonda's daughter," Sherman explained. "She's five. Her ballet class had a recital. If I'm not mistaken, Britney played the role of a daffodil."

Jane took a sip of coffee. "How do you know all this?" she asked.

Sherman's eyes twinkled. "My dear, when you're the editor of the town's second-largest newspaper, it's your job to know *everything*. Why do you think I'm here?"

"I believe I already asked that question," Jane reminded him.

Sherman nodded. "So you did," he said. "I'll tell you why. The people in this room know more about what happens in this town than the mayor, the council, and the police department combined. If you want to know what a place is *really* like, talk to the people who keep it running."

Rhonda reappeared with a plate of scrambled eggs and two pieces of bacon, which she set in front of Sherman. "There you are, hon." She fished several photographs out of her apron pocket and handed them to him. "Isn't she a doll?" she said.

Sherman looked at the photos, murmuring his approval. "A doll she is," he told Rhonda. "Tell her I'm sorry I couldn't make it."

"Danny got it all on video," said Rhonda. "I can make you a copy if you want."

"Please do," Sherman said brightly. "That's very kind."

Rhonda left to attend to another customer, and Sherman turned his attention back to Jane. "I was wrong," he said as he sprinkled pepper on his eggs. "She was not a daffodil, she was a daisy."

Jane laughed. "They really like you, don't they?" she said.

Sherman set the pepper shaker down. "Who does?" he asked.

"Them," said Jane, nodding at the people around them. "Everybody, really."

Sherman picked up a piece of bacon, bit the end neatly off, and chewed. "I listen to them," he said once he'd swallowed. "It's amazing how much people like you when you listen. It's also amazing the things they'll *tell* you."

"Now we're getting to the reason you're here," said Jane.

Sherman took a bite of eggs, leaving Jane waiting until he'd eaten it. "I understand that Hollywood has invaded our little corner of the world."

Jane sighed. "It would appear so," she said.

"And am I right in guessing that the reason you're here instead of at home or at your wonderful bookshop is because you've already tired of fame?" Sherman asked.

"You have no idea," Jane told him. "I can't get away from these people. They film *everything*. Well, one of them does. The girl—his sister—I quite like."

"Shelby," said Sherman. "Yes."

"Is there anything you don't know?" Jane asked.

"Oh, all sorts of things," said Sherman, wiping his fingertips on a napkin. "Brian George's real identity, for instance."

Jane, who was about to take another sip of coffee, paused with the cup just short of her lips. "Real identity?" she said, trying to sound casual.

"Yes," Sherman replied. "It's the oddest thing. For some time now I've wanted to do a series of profiles on Brakeston personalities. Of course you are on my list, but I know how busy you are at the moment, so I thought I would begin with Mr. George."

"How thoughtful of you," said Jane.

"I know about his books, of course," Sherman said.

"Book," Jane said, correcting him. "There's just the one."

Sherman smiled. "Of course," he agreed. "Under *that* name. But then there are the Penelope Wentz novels, which I understand are quite successful."

"They are," said Jane.

"Yet supposedly the writer of those books is a man named Tavish Osborn," Sherman continued.

He opened a briefcase that had heretofore gone unnoticed by Jane and removed from it a magazine, which he opened and placed on the table. Looking at it, Jane saw a photograph taken at the previous year's Romance Writers' Guild conference. In it a beaming Byron stood between novelist Chiara Carrington and Rebecca Little, the editor of *Romance* magazine. A tiny bit of Jane's left arm was visible to Rebecca's right, but the rest of her had been cropped out.

"Brian George *is* Tavish Osborn," Jane explained. "Rather, Tavish Osborn is Brian George. Tavish—Mr. Osborn—adopted the name Brian George when he wrote *Winter Comes Slowly,* as he didn't think a work of serious poetry would be well received by someone known for writing romances."

"But he *wasn't* known," Sherman said. "That's the point. Nobody knew Penelope Wentz was a man, so Tavish Osborn could have gone right on hiding in plain sight. So why the nom de plume *de plume,* so to speak?"

"I don't know, really," said Jane. "Why don't you ask him?"

"I will," Sherman said, putting the magazine away. "Sometimes, however, it's better *not* to go to the source first."

"What made you think I might know anything?" Jane asked.

Sherman poked at the remaining eggs with his fork. "It's no secret that you're friends," he said. "I thought that perhaps you might be able to shed some light on the subject." He hesitated. "I just find it peculiar that trying to find out anything about either Brian George *or* Tavish Osborn leads to nothing but dead ends."

"Dead ends?" Jane repeated.

Sherman nodded. "It's as if neither of them existed prior to the publication of Mr. George's novel."

Jane felt that she might be sick. What was Sherman suggesting? She'd never known him to be anything but amiable. Now, though, she almost felt as if she—or at any rate Byron—were being threatened in some manner.

"Well, as I said, I know very little about his past," she said, trying to sound nonchalant. "But I hardly think there's anything sinister hidden there." She drank some coffee and laughed, managing to choke instead.

"Oh, I don't suspect there is," said Sherman, handing her a napkin. "The old newshound in me can't help but wonder, though. People keep the strangest secrets. You weren't living here then, so you wouldn't know, but in '83 a fellow by the name of Clyde Dibble dropped dead from a heart attack while shoveling his driveway. A real nice guy, Clyde was. Ran a little grocery store, coached Little League for a bunch of years, was a deacon at the Presbyterian church. When his kids came to clean out the house they found a locked trunk in the attic. When they got it open they found it was full of pictures of a whole lot of the lady neighbors in their underpants. Turns out Clyde liked to roam around at night looking in windows and taking snapshots of what he saw."

"Oh my," Jane said. "Not very neighborly of him, was it?"

"Not very, no," said Sherman. "Anyway, you can see what I mean about never knowing what people are really like. I guess it's become an occupational hazard with me."

"And just what secrets are in *your* attic?" Jane asked, leaning forward.

Sherman grinned. "Oh, terrible things," he said. "Just terrible."

They both laughed, although Jane couldn't help but sense a little uneasiness in both their voices. "Is that all you wanted to talk to me about?" she said. She had a feeling it wasn't.

"Well, I did want to ask a favor of you," Sherman said. "I was wondering if you might help me get an interview with Julia Baxter."

"The director?" said Jane. "Well, I don't know. I haven't met her myself. But I can certainly try."

"I would very much appreciate that," Sherman said. "I'm a big fan. Unfortunately, it won't be any mean feat. She abhors the press."

"All we can do is try," said Jane. "I have no idea when any of them are arriving."

"Oh, a number of them are already here," Sherman informed her. "They arrived last night."

"And Julia Baxter?" asked Jane.

"Tomorrow," Sherman said. He took a wallet from his pocket and removed several bills, laying them on the table beside his plate. "Now, alas, I have to go and pen a stimulating article about the garden club's zinnia festival. If the excitement doesn't kill me, I'll see you anon."

"I look forward to it," said Jane. "And I'll let you know if I can get a word with Julia Baxter."

"Thank you, my dear. I appreciate anything you can do on my behalf." Sherman walked a few steps, then turned back and approached the table. "By the way," he said in a low voice. "I meant to tell you. Do you remember our friend Miranda Fleck?"

"Of course," Jane said, grimacing. How could anyone forget the overbearing assistant professor of English at Meade College? Not only was Miranda rude, she was a Brontëite. She and Jane had butted heads at Walter's most recent New Year's Eve party, a confrontation that had ended with Jane giving Miranda the tiniest of bites and secreting her beneath a pile of coats. She hadn't seen her since.

"Well," said Sherman, his voice taking on an excited tone, "you may be interested to know that she won't be returning to the college in the fall. It seems she was giving certain students superior grades in exchange for, shall we say, extra-credit assignments. *And* she preserved it all on film. Well, digital video. Apparently the footage was discovered when she took her laptop to the college's IT department to have it upgraded."

"Really?" Jane said. "I would never have believed her capable."

"Yes," Sherman said. "I understand she's a very emotive actress. At any rate, she's been let go."

"I'm terribly sad to hear that," Jane said. "Miranda added so much to the department."

"Didn't she though," said Sherman. "I'm sure she'll be missed by . . . someone."

He turned and once more headed for the door, leaving Jane to finish her donut and coffee and marvel at the never-ending surprises of which human beings were capable. Imagine, Miranda Fleck a seductress.

"She certainly didn't learn *that* from any Brontë novel," Jane assured the donut as she popped the last bite in her mouth.

A sharp pain in her side caused her to flinch. For a moment she wondered if some foreign object in the donut had pricked her insides. Then the pain—now more of a cramp—came again, and she recognized it as a sign of hunger. Not for more food, but for blood.

Jane groaned. *Wonderful,* she thought with no small amount of irritation. *Now I'm going to have to bite somebody.*

She added some bills to the ones Sherman had left, made sure Rhonda saw them so that she could collect them, then hurriedly left the Rise-N-Shine. Her stomach had begun to make very unladylike sounds, and the cramps were growing stronger.

She got into her car and sat for a moment, thinking. She hated having to feed during the day. Not only did it involve greater risk, it interrupted her schedule. *Not that you have anywhere to be,* she reminded herself. *You're trying to avoid people, remember?*

A tap on the glass startled her, and she gave a little shriek.

Looking to her left, she saw Walter's smiling face peering in at her. Behind him stood his mother, holding Lilith. Jane rolled the window down.

"I didn't mean to scare you," Walter said, giving her a peck on the cheek.

"What are you doing here?" asked Jane.

"Mother wanted pancakes," Walter explained. "This is the best place for them."

Jane glanced at Miriam, who met her gaze and smiled grimly. "I adore pancakes," said Miriam.

"How nice," Jane replied. Then she realized she would shortly be expected to explain *her* presence at the Rise-N-Shine. "I came for donuts," she blurted, hoping he wouldn't notice that there were none in the car. "For the film crew. I thought it would be a nice gesture." She was speaking too quickly, but found she couldn't stop. "Well, I should be going."

"Hold on," said Walter. "We were hoping you would spend the day with us."

Jane hesitated. "The day?" she said. "As in all of it?"

Walter laughed. "That's the idea."

"Of course, if you have something *better* to do," Miriam said, "we don't want to *inconvenience* you."

Hearing the tone in the woman's voice, Jane knew she was being tested. She also sensed that Miriam wanted her to fail.

"Don't be silly," she said. "I'd love to spend the day with you." Her stomach knotted and she gasped slightly.

"Are you all right?" Walter asked her.

"Fine," Jane said as the hunger pains returned. "Just a little cramp."

"I always found that hot compresses helped with my monthly troubles," Miriam announced.

Jane began to inform Miriam that she had quite the wrong idea, but then thought better of it. "What a charming suggestion," she said instead. Then, to Walter, she said, "I'll just take the donuts over to the shop and meet up with you after you've had breakfast. Where shall we meet?"

"I want to show you both the Carlyle House," said Walter.

"A wonderful idea," Jane replied.

The Carlyle House was one of Walter's restoration projects. He'd purchased the property when the last of the seven Carlyle sisters—none of whom had married—died the previous year, just three days shy of the century mark. Had it not been for an ill-timed tumble down one of the house's several staircases (thought to have occurred when one of the eighteen cats that lived in the house tangled itself in its mistress's feet), Mehitabel Carlyle would have been the guest of honor at a surprise one hundredth birthday party thrown for her by her friends at St. Andrew's Episcopal Church. Instead, on the day of her birth she was lowered into the ground of Resurrection Cemetery.

Mehitabel's misfortune was Walter's gain. The house, long in disrepair, was sold for a pittance. He had spent the past year working on it, and now it was almost completed. Although anyone passing by could see the dramatic change in the house's exterior, Jane had been banned from setting foot inside until the project was done. She thought this very silly, but it had seemed an inconsequential matter over which to quarrel and so she had not objected. She was, however, enormously curious to see what the house looked like.

"All right, then," said Walter. "You know where it is. Meet us there at ten?"

"Perfect," Jane said. She looked past Walter to Miriam. "See you then!" she chirped.

Miriam smiled weakly and turned away, walking toward the restaurant. "She's really looking forward to getting to know you," Walter told Jane.

"I can tell," Jane said.

Walter followed his mother, and Jane pulled out of the parking lot. Her stomach was growling audibly, and the cramps were closer together. There was no way she could spend the morning—let alone the entire day—with Walter and his mother unless she fed first.

"If only there were a drive-through for this sort of thing," she mused, looking longingly at the line of cars queued alongside a fast-food restaurant's take-out window.

But there wasn't, so she was going to have to come up with another solution to her hunger. And she was going to have to do it soon.

Chapter 9

JANE WAITED IMPATIENTLY FOR THE GROUP OF TEENAGERS TO cross the street. Although it was true that pedestrians had the right of way despite the absence of a stop sign or light, this particular group seemed to be taking advantage of their position. They moved more slowly than Jane had thought possible, oblivious to everything but their own conversations and the screens of their cellphones. Worst of all, just as one group made it across the street and Jane started to inch forward, another gaggle would step directly in front of her without so much as looking—like wildebeest crossing a river.

Her stomach knotted up and she gripped the steering wheel tightly. As she did so she inadvertently took her foot off the brake and the car jumped forward. Startled, the group of teenagers jumped back, some of them shouting obscenities. One of them— a girl wearing a T-shirt that read NO HATE!—banged her fist on the hood of Jane's car and gave Jane the finger.

Jane hit the gas, roaring through the now enraged group and sending them scattering. Watching their indignant faces in the rearview mirror, she felt a not-insignificant measure of satisfaction. Her joy was short-lived, however, as a moment later she saw, too late, that she was traveling past a stop sign at which she ought to have paused and was about to be hit on the passenger side by a silver Ford Eclipse.

The impact was not as bad as she would have thought, most likely because neither she nor the other driver was going terribly fast. Still, the sound was unsettling and the resulting crash pushed Jane's car sideways and sent bits of window glass raining around her.

The driver of the Eclipse emerged from his car, paused for a moment to survey the damage, and then walked around to Jane's window. In his forties, he was short, stout, and balding. His face, which Jane imagined was usually a pinkish color, was now red. One eye twitched as he stood staring down at Jane.

"Nice stop," he said.

"I'm very sorry," Jane said. "I'm afraid I—"

"Save it," the man snapped. "I don't have time to hear about how you're late picking your kid up or how you have to get your husband's suit to the dry cleaners, or whatever bullshit excuse you're going to use." He turned to look at his car. "Jesus Christ," he said. "I hope you've got good insurance."

Jane, who was looking in the glove box for her insurance card, said, "If you'll just calm down, we—"

"Calm down?" the man said, his voice rising. "*You're* telling *me* to calm down? Lady, if anyone needs telling what to do around here, it's you."

"I really don't think—" Jane replied.

"No, you don't think," said the man, interrupting. "That's the problem. If you *thought*, you wouldn't do something as stupid as running a stop sign." He shook his head. "Forget your insurance," he said, taking a cellphone out of his pocket. "I'll just call the cops and let them figure it out."

"I understand that you're upset," Jane said. "But there's really no need—"

"Just shut up," the man snapped. "I'll deal with this."

Anger rose in Jane's chest, and she made a decision. "You will not call the police," she heard herself say in a commanding tone.

The man glared at her, started to speak, and then stopped. Something in his expression changed, becoming almost childlike. He closed his cellphone. "I guess we don't have to," he said.

"Now get back in your car," Jane said, focusing her glamoring abilities.

The man turned and walked back to his car, opening the door and sliding into the driver's seat. A moment later Jane opened the passenger-side door of the Eclipse and got in beside him. So far no other vehicles had come through the intersection, but she knew it was just a matter of time. She had to act quickly.

As she leaned toward the man her fangs clicked into place, piercing his skin and causing the blood to flow. Jane didn't take much, just enough to stave off the hunger pangs. It took only a minute. When she was done she turned the man's head so that she was looking directly into his eyes. "You're going to forget," she told him. "In thirty seconds you will wake up and not remember what happened."

The man's eyes clouded over and he seemed to fall asleep. Quickly Jane got out of the car and went back to hers, looking around first to make certain that there were no witnesses. She turned the key in the ignition and was relieved when the engine came to life. There was a scraping sound as she pulled away, and the Eclipse's bumper fell to the pavement with a clatter.

She wasn't out of the woods. She would still have to explain the state of her car. But she would worry about that later. The important thing was that the immediate problem was taken care of and she had been able to feed. All things considered, she was actually rather proud of herself for handling it with such aplomb.

Besides, he was quite rude, she thought. Speaking to a lady that way was most uncalled for.

She did need to get another car, though. She didn't want to

show up for the tour of the Carlyle House in her damaged vehicle. Not only would it cause Walter to worry, it would probably give Miriam the impression that Jane was unreliable.

She elected to go to the bookstore. When she arrived she parked in the back, out of sight, and entered through the rear door that led into the storage room. Peering out, she made sure there was no one in the store she wished to avoid.

"Don't worry," she heard Lucy say. "They're gone."

Jane looked into the office off the hallway and saw Lucy sitting at the computer. "Who's gone?" she asked.

"Ant and Shelby," said Lucy. "They were here looking for you about twenty minutes ago."

"How did you get rid of them?" Jane inquired.

Lucy's fingers tapped on the keyboard. "I told them you were meeting with your parole officer," she answered. "I thought it would add some color to their profile of you."

"How very kind of you," Jane said. "May I borrow your car?"

Lucy looked up. "My car? Why? What's wrong with yours?"

"I had a small—*very* minor, nothing to even speak of— encounter with another vehicle," Jane explained. "Also, *they* won't be on the lookout for yours."

Lucy opened the desk drawer and removed a set of keys. "I don't even want to know," she said. "Go. I haven't seen you all day. I don't know where you are or when you'll be back."

"Thank you," said Jane, taking the keys. "I promise to bring it back in one piece."

"Put gas in it," Lucy called after Jane as she left. "And not the cheap stuff!"

Lucy's car—actually a fire-engine-red 1963 Ford F-100 pickup truck—was parked near Jane's old Volvo. As she got in, Jane wondered if perhaps she should also disguise herself, perhaps with a wig. Then she spied a baseball cap lying on the seat next to her. It bore the logo of the Boston Red Sox, the team to which Lucy was devoted. Jane picked it up and placed it on her head.

Looking at herself in the truck's side mirror, she adjusted the brim, pulling it lower over her eyes.

Imagine if we'd had these for cricket teams, she thought. *I can just see Henry and the others wearing Steventon Sledgers hats.* The image was amusing, but thinking of her brothers made her a little sad. She wondered what they would make of the world in which she now lived. She wished they were there to tell her.

She started the car and left the parking lot, keeping her eyes peeled (a loathsome expression, she thought) for Ant. Perhaps one of these days she could get Shelby alone and have a nice chat with her. Until then, however, Jane wanted to avoid running into the pair.

She drove without incident to the Carlyle House and parked in front of it. Walter's car was already there, and before Jane was even halfway up the stairs to the front porch the door opened and Walter stepped outside.

"Right on time," he said. "Are you ready for the grand tour?"

"Absolutely," said Jane, taking his arm. "I've been dying of curiosity."

Walter escorted her into a foyer paneled in mahogany. A blown-glass chandelier in the shape of an open poppy hung from the ceiling. Seeing Jane looking at it, Walter said, "It's meant to be a lamp. I turned it upside down. What do you think?"

"I think it's beautiful," Jane told him.

"Do you?" Miriam emerged from another room. Lilith followed alongside, using her single front leg much as a human might use a crutch.

Sensing an opportunity to win points with Miriam, Jane ignored the question and bent down so that she was closer to the dog. "Hi, Lilith," she said, holding out her hand.

Lilith bared her teeth and lunged at Jane's hand. Jane retracted her hand and stared at the dog, shaking, as Lilith continued to bark at her.

"She doesn't care for strange people," Miriam said. "Walter, I'd like to see the rest of the house."

She turned and walked away, Lilith once again at her heels. Jane looked at Walter. "I seem to be a hit with both of them," she said.

"You're doing fine," said Walter. He took Jane's hand. "Come on. I think you'll like this."

For the next hour Jane admired the William Morris wallpapers and painstakingly restored wood floors. She appreciated the kitchen that was at once functional and of a period, and the bathroom with its claw-foot tub and black-and-white-tiled floor. When Walter brought them into one of the house's five bedrooms and showed them a series of framed prints that Miriam attributed to Albert Joseph Moore, she refrained from pointing out that they were actually by John William Godward. Nor did she point out that the woman in the painting bore a remarkable resemblance to herself, or that they were wearing the same necklace. (She did, however, wonder if Walter saw the similarities, and if he had chosen the print with her in mind.)

Miriam, Jane was pleased to see, appeared to be impressed by her son's handiwork. Despite the occasional comment about a color she did not care for or a piece of furniture she found not quite right, she was very complimentary. She particularly seemed to appreciate the sheer amount of work that had gone into the restoration, especially after Walter showed them a photo album containing before and after shots of each room.

"You've done a remarkable job," Jane told him. "The house is extraordinary."

"Do you really think so?" he asked.

"I do," said Jane. "I think anyone would be happy living in such a beautiful place."

"I'm pleased to hear you say that," Walter said. "Because I'm going to be moving in."

"Are you?" Jane exclaimed. "That's wonderful!"

Walter smiled. "I'm hoping you'll live here as well," he said. "You know, after we're mar—" He stopped and blushed.

Jane and Miriam both looked at Walter with surprised expressions.

Walter, clearing his throat, said, "Oh, dear. That just slipped out." He took Jane's hand. "I didn't plan on asking you this way," he said. "But now that it's out, I—"

"Walter," Miriam said sharply.

Jane's heart raced as she processed what was happening. Had Walter just asked her to marry him? That was impossible. *Not impossible,* she told herself. *Unexpected.*

"Walter," Jane heard Miriam say again. "Don't you think you're being a bit hasty?"

"I know you haven't known Jane very long," Walter said. "But I have, and I know that I love her." He squeezed Jane's hand. "And I believe she loves me."

Miriam turned her gaze to Jane. "Is that true?" she asked, her voice cold.

Jane looked into Miriam's dark eyes and was surprised by the hatred she saw there. Then she recalled Miriam's words of the other night. *I know what you are.* She still didn't know what Miriam had meant by that, but thinking about it angered her. *No,* she thought while staring back at Miriam. *You don't know what I am. You don't know anything about me.*

"Yes," Jane said. "It's true. I do love him."

She dreaded what she had to say next. Steeling herself, she looked at Walter's smiling face. "I do love you," she said. "But I can't marry you."

Chapter 10

"BUT I THOUGHT YOU *WANTED* TO MARRY HIM."

Jane wiped her eyes and looked at Ben Cohen, into whose office she had been surprised to find herself walking ten minutes earlier. After the awkward moment with Walter she had quickly excused herself and fled the Carlyle House, leaving a smirking Miriam Ellenberg and a shocked Walter to watch her retreat. She had first driven to her own home, only to find it overrun by yet another of Beverly Shrop's tour groups. Next she had gone to the bookstore, but the presence of Ant's van had forced her to turn around.

That's when she'd found herself driving in the direction of Sukkat Shalom. She hadn't even realized she was going there until she pulled into the parking lot. She'd almost turned right around again. After all, she had met Rabbi Ben Cohen only once. She really knew nothing about him, or he about her. And yet she'd gotten out of Lucy's truck and entered the synagogue as if some other force were controlling her actions.

Now she was seated once more in the chair across from the couch, staring at the Pollock hanging on the wall behind the rabbi. Ben Cohen, dressed in jeans and a shirt the color of cornflowers, waited patiently for her to speak.

"I do," she said, sniffling. "That's why I came here in the first place, right?"

"You tell me," Ben said.

"It is," said Jane. She hesitated. "Well, because of Miriam, anyway."

The rabbi nodded. "You wouldn't have come otherwise?"

"Why would I?" Jane replied.

Ben shrugged his wide shoulders. "I don't know," he told her. "Why would you?"

"Stop doing that!" said Jane.

"Doing what?"

"That!" Jane said. "Answering everything I say with another question."

"Is that what I'm doing?" said Ben, one side of his mouth lifting slightly, as if he were trying very hard to remain composed.

Jane snorted. "Very funny."

Ben laughed. "You obviously haven't met many Jews," he said. "Or therapists. But we're getting off track. Walter asked you to marry him. You said no."

"I said I *can't*," Jane clarified.

"Can't," said the rabbi. "However, you've known all along that it would come to this. Which, by the way, brings us back to why you came here in the first place."

"Oh, I *know*," Jane said, her frustration audible in her voice. "But that was before."

"Before?" Ben said. "Before what?"

"Miriam," Jane replied. "Before Miriam. When she was just his mother I could handle her. The *idea* of her. The reality, however, is not at all agreeable."

"A lot of women clash with their potential mothers-in-law at first," said Ben. "It seems to come with the territory."

Jane shot him a look. "Are you married?" she asked.

Ben surprised her by looking away. "I was," he said. "My wife died giving birth to our daughter."

Jane felt terrible for having asked the question. "I'm sorry," she said. "I didn't mean to pry."

Ben held up a hand. "It's all right," he said. "You're not prying. You thought I had no experience with mothers-in-law."

"No," Jane objected. "I just . . . well, yes, that's what I thought."

The rabbi laughed. "As it happens, my mother-in-law is a wonderful person," he said. "And my mother loved Naomi very much. But I've heard stories."

It was Jane's turn to laugh. "I imagine you have," she said. She paused before asking her next question, afraid she might cause Ben pain by voicing it. "Your daughter," she said. "Is she . . ." She fumbled for her next words.

"She's six," said Ben. "Her name is Sarah."

Jane was suddenly overcome by sadness. She felt a tear slip from her eye. She wiped it away, but another soon followed. She couldn't help but think about her own family, particularly Cassie. How she missed her sister. How she longed to have her there to confide in and to laugh with, to say "Do you remember when?" to, and to just be quiet with.

"Would you like a tissue?"

The rabbi's voice jarred Jane from her thoughts. She realized to her horror that she had been crying freely. Her cheeks were damp, and her nose was running. "Yes, please," she said, sniffing.

Ben located a box of tissues and handed it to her. "There's a Jewish proverb," he said. "'What soap is for the body, tears are for the soul.'"

Jane blew her nose. "In that case, I seem to be having quite a good scrubbing," she remarked.

"My people specialize in grief," Ben said. "If they awarded degrees in it, every Jew would hold a doctorate."

Jane laughed as she dried her face. "My people are just the opposite," she told Ben. "Our upper lips are so stiff they prevent us from smiling."

"How did we get here?" asked Ben. "Oh, yes. Your potential mother-in-law and how the reality of her is far worse than what you'd imagined."

Jane sighed deeply. "I expected her to be protective of Walter," she said. "But honestly, she's like something out of an old Norse legend—or Grendel's mother. Oh, and you should see her little dog, Lilith. She's adorable, what with having only three legs and all, but what a little monster."

"Lilith?" Ben said. "That's interesting."

"Why?" asked Jane.

"In Jewish folklore Lilith is the name of Adam's first wife," Ben explained. "Supposedly she left him because she found him weak and stupid. Some stories say she was a demon with the feet of an owl, and that she came at night to suck the blood of children. Essentially, she was the world's first vampire. If you believe in that kind of thing."

Jane considered this information for a moment. "And do you believe in that kind of thing?" she asked the rabbi.

Ben shrugged. "Who's to say what's real and what isn't?" he replied. "The world is a strange and wonderful place."

Jane nodded in agreement. "So Judaism allows for the existence of vampires?"

"Among other things," said Ben. "Some people say that Lilith was actually trying to suck the souls out of her victims, not just their blood."

Jane felt herself growing uncomfortable. More than once during the past two hundred years she had wondered about the state of her soul and what had happened to it when she died and was reborn. She'd never had anyone with whom she could talk about such things. Now she wondered if she dared.

"Assuming she really was a vampire—or whatever—do you think Lilith had a soul?" Jane asked.

Ben got up and went to a bookcase. He returned with a small book, its covers stained with age. As he flipped through the pages he said, "There is a Jewish poet—a philosopher, really, although those two often go hand in hand—named Solomon ibn Gabirol. Lived in the eleventh century. He wrote a number of poems about humankind's relationship with God. My favorite is called 'Kether Malkuth.' A large part of it is devoted to the nature of the soul."

He stopped at a page and ran his finger down it. "Here we are," he said. "Listen to this.

> *O Lord, who can reach Thy wisdom?*
> *For Thou gavest the soul the faculty of knowledge*
> *that is fixed therein,*
> *And knowledge is the fount of her glory.*
> *Therefore hath destruction no power over her,*
> *But she maintaineth herself by the stability of her*
> *foundation,*
> *For such is her nature and secret;*
> *The soul with her wisdom shall not see death.*
> *Nevertheless shall her punishment be visited*
> *upon her;*
> *A punishment bitterer than death,*
> *Though be she pure she shall obtain favor*
> *And shall laugh on the last day.*
> *But if she hath been defiled,*
> *She shall wander to and fro for a space in wrath*
> *and anger,*
> *And all the days of her uncleanness*
> *Shall she dwell vagabond and outcast;*
> *'She shall touch no hallowed thing,*
> *And to the sanctuary she shall not come*
> *Till the days of her purification be fulfilled.'"*

Ben shut the book. "I love that idea of the soul being indestructible," he said. "It endures despite everything."

"But it also has that bit about an unclean soul wandering in wrath and anger," Jane pointed out.

"Which brings us back to Lilith," said Ben. "Some scholars would argue that her soul, being unclean, is what caused her to turn into a demon. A vampire, if you will. Her bloodsucking is simply her attempt to steal a clean soul from someone else. But that in itself makes her own soul even more unclean, and so she can only be purified by being destroyed and allowing her soul to come back in the body of another, to have another chance at redemption, if you will.

"That's kind of a lot to put on a three-legged dog," Ben said as he stood and returned the book to its shelf.

Jane suddenly felt very cold. She had long ago decided that she no longer had a soul, that whatever had existed in her had departed at the moment of her transformation. Now Ben Cohen was suggesting that perhaps she was wrong about that. *Not that anybody really knows,* she reminded herself. *It's all a lot of guessing.*

Still, she was shaken.

"So now that we've determined that you're facing Grendel's mother and her vampire dog, what are you going to do about it?" Ben asked.

Jane shook her head. "I was hoping you would tell me," she said.

"I think you need to figure out what exactly it is that upsets you about her," Ben suggested. "I don't think it's just the fact that she's Walter's mother. There's something else going on."

"If there is, I don't know what it is," Jane told him.

"Keep looking," said Ben. "You'll figure it out."

"I suppose so," Jane said, standing up. "I should go speak to Walter first. He probably thinks I've gone mad."

"We're all mad here," Ben said. When Jane looked at him he

added, "Sorry. It's from *Alice in Wonderland*. Sarah's favorite book. I've read it so many times I've memorized most of it."

"She sounds like someone I should like to know," Jane said. Then a thought came to her. "If you don't think it's inappropriate, would the two of you like to come to dinner at my house?" she asked. "You could meet Grendel's mother for yourself."

Ben hesitated.

"I know," Jane said. "You don't normally socialize with people you counsel. I think, however, that we're becoming something of friends."

The rabbi smiled. "I believe you're right," he said. "And in that case, I accept."

"Excellent," said Jane. "How about tomorrow night?"

"As it happens, we're free," Ben replied.

"Good," Jane said. "I'll expect you at six."

She wrote down her address for Ben, inquired after Sarah's likes (hamburgers) and dislikes (anything involving celery), and returned to the truck. She got in and sat there for some time thinking about things. The whole question of her soul and its status was upsetting her more than she cared to recognize. But her more immediate problem was Walter and, to an only slightly lesser degree, Miriam.

She took out her cellphone and dialed Walter's number. Part of her hoped he wouldn't answer, but he picked up after only one ring.

"Where are you?" he asked, sounding anxious. "I've been trying to call you for the last two hours."

"I'm sorry," said Jane. "I must have turned the ringer off."

A silence stretched between them like a thin, tight wire. Jane knew that, having caused the problem, it was up to her to make the next move. "We should talk," she said. "I don't suppose you can get rid of your mother?"

"Not permanently," said Walter.

Despite the tension, Jane found herself laughing. "How about long enough for lunch?" she said.

"I think I can manage that," Walter said.

"Meet me at the bookstore in half an hour," said Jane. "We can go from there."

"All right," Walter said. "I love you."

Jane bit her lip as tears came to her eyes for the second time that day. "I love you too," she said.

As she drove to the bookstore she fought back feelings of panic. So much was going on in her life—and going poorly. She felt out of control, and that in turn made her want to retreat. Part of her longed for the quiet, secure life she'd had before *Constance* had come out and turned everything upside down.

But it was too late. Now she had no choice but to face her new life and all of the challenges it was presenting. *Your characters manage to do it,* she reminded herself. *If they can, you can. After all, you're the one who told them what to do.*

Chapter 11

"JANE!"

"Jane."

"Jane?"

"Oh, Ja-aaane."

The voices came from all around her. Jane turned, trying to locate the sources, and saw Ant Doolan coming at her with a video camera. Behind him was Byron, behind Byron was Walter, and behind Walter was Beverly Shrop. Seeing them all, Jane's heart began to pound.

"Jane," one of the twins called. "There's a phone call for you. A Jessica Aber—"

"Tell her I'll call her back," Jane told him as she walked toward Ant and the others, holding up her hand.

"Stop," she commanded.

Her four visitors formed a neat line in front of her, like soldiers falling in for inspection. Before any of them could speak, Jane did.

"I'm taking the day off," she told Ant. "Go find something else to do."

She next faced Byron, who looked at her with a puzzled yet amused expression. "Yes, of course we'd love to do a signing for your new novel," she said.

"That's not why I'm—" he began.

"Just speak to Lucy about it," said Jane, moving on to Walter. "You wait out front," she instructed her boyfriend. "I'll be just a minute."

Lastly she addressed Beverly. "And what do *you* want?" she asked.

Beverly beamed. "It's about the festival. As you may know, there's a rivalry between Janeites and Brontëites."

"Is there?" said Jane dryly.

Beverly nodded. "There is. So we—and by that I mean *I*—thought it might be fun to arrange some kind of game with teams composed of each group."

"What kind of game?" Jane asked.

"Softball," Beverly answered. "It seems easiest to manage. Of course, *I* would prefer croquet, but what with so many people—"

Jane sighed. "What has this got to do with me?"

"Oh," Beverly said. "Well, I was hoping you might captain one of the teams. Mr. Osborn has graciously agreed to captain the Brontëites, and—"

Jane once more interrupted Beverly. "Have you now?" she asked Byron, who was in the process of pretending to ignore the conversation.

"What? Oh. Yes, I believe I have. It should be great fun, don't you think?"

"I had no idea you were so fond of the Brontës," Jane remarked. "Or softball."

Byron feigned surprise. "Who *isn't* fond of them?" he said. He winked mischievously at Jane, who glowered back.

"Very well," Jane told a waiting Beverly. "I'll do it. We can talk about it later."

She turned and walked toward the front door. Walter was waiting outside, and she could see him pacing. But to her annoyance, Byron was following her.

"I suppose you think this is amusing," Jane said. "Honestly. Softball?"

"I knew you would be enthusiastic about it," said Byron. "But that isn't why I came." He gently took Jane's elbow, forcing her to stop.

"Unhand me," Jane objected, pulling away. But Byron's grip tightened.

"You're in danger," he said in a low voice. "We're *all* in danger."

"What are you talking about?" asked Jane. "All *who*?"

"All of *us*," Byron said. He smiled, and for a moment Jane saw his fangs. Then he retracted them. "Someone is here who means us harm," he said.

"And just who is it?" said Jane. "Don't tell me Our Gloomy Friend is back."

Byron shook his head. "I don't think it's she," he said. "Although I suppose it could be. For the past day or two I've just felt something wasn't right."

"Oh, well then," Jane said. "Now that's much clearer."

Byron leaned in even closer. "Listen to me. I don't know who it is. But I sense something. Maybe if you'd developed your powers instead of running from them, you would sense it too."

"I've *been* practicing," Jane said.

"Just be careful," said Byron. He stepped away. "We'll just see about that," he said loudly and cheerfully, confusing Jane. "I'll have you know I pitched a mean softball game when I was younger."

"Is that so?" Jane replied, playing along. "Well, we'll just see how many touchdowns you get!"

Byron shook his head.

"How many goals you get!" Jane said as several customers began to laugh.

Byron grimaced.

"Baskets?" Jane asked.

"Just go," said Byron, rolling his eyes. "Now."

Jane walked quickly to the door and went out into the warm afternoon sun. Walter immediately descended upon her, taking her hand. "I'm so sorry about this morning," he said. "I shouldn't have sprung it on you like that. I don't know what came over me. One minute we were talking about the house and then I was talking about getting married. And my *mother,* well—"

"It's all right," Jane said. "I'm the one who should be apologizing. The way I ran out of there, I can only imagine what your mother thinks."

"She seems fine with it, actually," Walter said.

"Well, that makes me feel better," said Jane.

Walter indicated the store with a nod. "Shouldn't you get back?" he asked. "It sounds as if everybody wants something from you."

"No," Jane said. "I asked you to lunch, and that's where we're going."

"Okay," Walter said. "What would you like?"

Jane thought for a moment. She didn't want to go anywhere near the store, as it would be too easy for people to find her there. Then she had an idea.

"Come on," she told Walter. "I know just the place. Oh, but you'll have to drive. My car is . . . indisposed."

With Jane directing him, Walter drove to the restaurant she'd chosen. When they pulled into the parking lot he looked at Jane quizzically. "Here?"

"Absolutely," Jane said, opening the car door. "You'll see why."

The broad front doors of Tiki-Tiki featured the giant, grinning face of some unnamed god carved into the wood. Walter grabbed the handle somewhere in the vicinity of the tiki's nose and pulled, the enormous face parting neatly down the center to allow him and Jane entry. Inside, the restaurant was a re-creation of someone's idea of a Polynesian village, complete with burning torches, booths seemingly made from bamboo lashed together with rope, and a smiling hostess wearing a grass skirt and a bikini top printed with garish pink hibiscus.

"Aloha," the girl said. "Welcome to Tiki-Tiki." She stepped forward and placed around each of their necks a garish lei made of gathered plastic strips intended to look like flowers.

"More like Tacky-Tacky," Walter whispered to Jane as the hostess led them to a booth.

"Which is exactly why no one will think to find us here," Jane said. She removed her lei and dropped it on the table. Walter left his on as he picked up the laminated menu and perused it.

"Aloha," said a cheerful voice. "Can I start you off with a drink?"

Jane regarded the young man standing next to the booth. He wore a shirt made of the same hideous print out of which the hostess's top was made, but instead of a grass skirt he wore surfer shorts and flip-flops. The effect was a grotesque parody of Polynesian culture as filtered through the mind of someone who had clearly never experienced the real thing. Jane found it fascinating.

"Something with rum," she told the waiter. "And an umbrella."

"I'll have the same," said Walter. He looked across the table at Jane. "I have a feeling I'm going to need it."

The waiter withdrew to get their drinks, and Jane leaned back against the cool vinyl of the booth's bench. "It's all too much," she said. "The movie. The DVD nonsense. The new book I can't seem to write. Beverly Shrop."

"My mother," Walter added. "Me."

Jane shook her head. "You're the one thing that isn't too much," she said.

Walter cleared his throat. "Except when I proposed," he said.

Jane fidgeted with her menu, pulling at the corner where the laminate had begun to peel.

"I know it was awkward," said Walter. "Like I said before, it just popped out. I'd actually planned this really romantic thing. It was a kind of treasure hunt where you followed clues that eventually led you to a box with a key in it and a map to the house. When you got there I was going to be waiting with dinner and champagne and . . . and . . . a ring."

He stopped speaking and scratched his nose—a gesture Jane knew meant he was embarrassed. She took his hand and held it while she spoke.

"That sounds wonderful," she told him.

"I know," Walter agreed. "But now it wouldn't be a surprise, and anyway you already said no, so—"

"I didn't exactly say no," said Jane.

"You said you can't," Walter reminded her. "That's more or less a no."

"I know it sounds that way," said Jane. "But you must understand—"

"Jane, stop," Walter said. He withdrew his hand from hers.

Jane looked into his face and saw something there that troubled her. It was a kind of weariness mixed with resignation. Suddenly she was very frightened.

Walter swallowed hard. "Since the first day I met you I knew I loved you," he said. "I know that sounds ridiculous, but it's true. And when I asked you out and you said no, I promised myself I would keep trying until you said yes. Then when you finally did say yes, I was terrified I would do something to drive you away."

"But you haven't," said Jane.

Walter shook his head. "No, I haven't," he said. "All I've done is tell you how I feel, and that's something I can't change. Maybe I didn't do it in exactly the right way, but I think your answer would have been the same no matter how I'd asked. It's always been 'I can't,' Jane, and I don't think it will ever be anything different. Am I wrong?"

Before Jane could answer the waiter returned and set two huge hollowed-out pineapples on the table. Tiny umbrellas were stuck into the rims, and straws made to resemble stalks of bamboo protruded from the dark liquid inside.

"Two Pele's Potions," the waiter said. "Have you decided on your food yet?"

"Another few minutes," Walter told him, and the young man went away again.

"These are rather imposing," Jane said, trying to lighten the mood. "I think Pele is trying to get us drunk."

"You haven't answered my question," Walter reminded her.

"No," Jane said. "I suppose I haven't."

"The answer will never be yes, will it?" asked Walter.

Jane took the umbrella from her drink and twirled it in her fingers. She wanted Walter to stop talking. She wanted him to look at the menu and laugh at the silly names of the dishes. She wanted him to take her hand again, and for everything to be all right. More than anything she wished she could tell him why she couldn't answer his question.

"I love you, Walter," she said finally. "It's just that I . . ." Her words trailed off. She was tired of making excuses for herself and hoping they would buy her more time. It wasn't fair to Walter. Yet she couldn't wait forever. *When* would *be a good time to tell him?* she asked herself. *After you're married? After he notices that you don't age? When he's on his deathbed?*

She knew that there would never be a good time. What she had to tell Walter would come as a horrible shock under the best of circumstances. There was no way to prepare him for learning that she was undead, no gradual working up to it so that the final revelation was not so bad. Her only options were to tell him and hope he would understand, or not tell him and deal with the guilt of deceiving him. Neither option appealed to her.

"I won't say I understand, because I don't," Walter said. "And I'm not even sure you know. But I know I can't keep doing this."

"What are you saying?" asked Jane.

Walter sighed. "I'm saying maybe we should go back to just being friends," he answered.

"Friends," Jane said, testing the shape of the word on her tongue and finding it uncomfortably sharp.

"I don't know what else to be to you," said Walter. "You won't be my wife, and frankly, both of us are too old to be anyone's boyfriend or girlfriend. That's for twenty-year-olds who want to keep their options open. I don't want options, Jane. I want you."

Walter's words made Jane want to tell him right then and there that she *would* marry him. She even opened her mouth to say as much. But she couldn't. The words stuck in her throat, choking her, and refused to come out. *You can't do that to him,* her own voice commanded her.

The waiter appeared again. "Have you decided?" he asked.

Jane shook her head as she began to cry.

"Yes," she heard Walter say. "I think she has."

Chapter 12

Jane's backyard was teeming with movie stars.

"They're like ants at a picnic," Jane remarked.

"Well, they *are* at a picnic," Lucy reminded her.

They were standing in Jane's kitchen, looking through the window at the group of people milling about on the lawn. Jane had counted them half a dozen times, and each time had come up with a different number. Finally she had decided that there were slightly fewer than two dozen of them and left it at that.

"Do you think we have enough tables?" Jane asked, looking at the four redwood tables Ned and Ted had recently purchased for her at the local home improvement center and set up in her yard. Now the twins were helping Byron figure out the propane grill.

"You'd think he'd want to stay away from fire," Lucy mused, watching as Byron tried—and failed—to get the grill lit. "And yes, I think there are enough tables."

The cookout had been a mistake. Well, not so much a mistake as a slip of the tongue. When earlier in the day a striking woman had entered Flyleaf Books and introduced herself to Jane as Julia Baxter, Jane had been so thrilled to meet the director that she'd invited her for dinner. A moment later, when she recalled that she'd also invited Rabbi Cohen and his daughter, she'd heard herself say aloud something she should have kept to herself: "There's room for everyone."

Julia Baxter, hearing this, had smiled warmly and replied, "That's so kind of you. I'll tell the others."

And so a cookout had been arranged. The "others" had turned out to be the principal cast and a handful of assistants, as well as Ant Doolan and Shelby, who were filming the whole thing. To balance the equation Jane had invited *her* staff, as well as Byron. She had found herself picking up the phone to invite Walter and his mother, but then she'd remembered that their situation could currently best be described as uncertain, and so had not made the call.

She didn't want to think about that. "Tell me again who they all are," she asked Lucy, focusing her attention on her guests.

"Okay," said Lucy. "That one over there—the girl with the long, dark hair—that's Portia Kensington."

"Yes, I recognize her," Jane said, trying to place the young woman's face. "She was in that movie about the girl who . . . did something."

"She's your Constance," Lucy said, ignoring her. "And don't start about her being too young or not looking the way you picture Constance in your head. She's big box office. Oh, and she used to date one of the guys in Endzone, but she broke up with him when she found out he cheated on her with her best friend, Tanner Bixby, while Portia was recovering from her nose job."

"Why do you know this?" Jane asked.

"I can't help it," said Lucy. "I'm a pop culture sponge." She next indicated a woman of about fifty with short, curly red hair and a face—Jane thought—that Cassandra would have described as "looking like a boiled pudding." "That's Anne Simon," said Lucy. "She's one of those people you know you've seen before but can never remember what you saw her in."

The actress was holding a glass of red wine in her hand and talking to a handsome man with dark hair and a solid build.

"Is that Tucker Mack or Riley Bannister she's talking to?" Jane asked, throwing out the names of the actors she recalled were playing the two male leads.

"Tucker Mack," said Lucy. "That's Riley over there." She pointed to a man who was in every visible way slightly less than Tucker Mack. He was slightly shorter, slightly thinner, slightly younger, and slightly less dark. However, he was arguably more handsome.

"He's playing Charles," Lucy said. She sighed. "He's my movie husband."

"Your what?" asked Jane.

"My movie husband," Lucy explained. "You know, when you pick one guy from the movies who you would want to marry? I also have a TV husband, a music husband, a sports husband, and a book husband." She looked at Jane. "You and your girlfriends never did that?"

Jane was about to say that no, they never had, but then she remembered something. "Well, I *did* have rather a crush on William Pitt the Younger when I was about fifteen or so."

Lucy looked at her. "You're joking. William Pitt the Younger?"

"He was prime minister," Jane said defensively. "He had lovely eyes. Also, he worked to abolish the slave trade. I imagine that's more than you can say for your imaginary husbands."

"You're probably right about that," said Lucy. "But Riley Bannister has a cuter butt."

Jane peered at the young man, whose backside was facing her. "I must agree with you on that point," she said. "So that means Mr. Mack is playing Jonathan. I believe he'll do admirably as a villain. He has the eyebrows for it."

"Then we have Cecilia Banks," Lucy continued. "She's Minerva." She indicated a thin girl with olive skin and short black hair that reminded Jane of the style popular with the flappers of the 1920s. *She resembles Josephine Baker,* Jane thought, her mind briefly flashing back to a raucous evening spent with Baker, F. Scott Fitzgerald, and a trio of French modernist painters. How that girl had loved to laugh.

Cecilia was talking to another young woman who was her opposite in coloring, having unnaturally blond hair and skin like milk. The blonde was smoking a cigarette, and Jane could smell its acrid fumes from across the yard. "And she is?" she asked.

"That would be Chloe," said Lucy.

"Chloe who?" Jane inquired.

"Just Chloe," Lucy answered. "Like Madonna. Or Cher. She's a pop star. *The* pop star at the moment."

"She can't be more than seventeen," said Jane. "Can she act?"

Lucy shrugged. "We'll find out," she said. "This is her first movie."

"Tell me she's playing a small part," said Jane, watching the singer toss her cigarette butt into the grass and regarding the girl with dislike. "A *very* small part."

"Barbara Wexley," Lucy informed her. "So not all that big. Besides, isn't Barbara supposed to be something of a troublemaker?"

"Well, yes," Jane admitted. "Still, a pop singer?"

"She'll put butts in seats," said a male voice.

Jane and Lucy turned to see Ant Doolan standing behind them. As always, he was holding his camera. "Chloe's a real piece of work," said Ant, taking a handful of potato chips from a bowl of them on the counter. "Just between us, I wouldn't be surprised if she pulled a Richie on us."

"A Richie?" Jane repeated. "Is that a film term?"

Ant laughed loudly, potato chip crumbs dropping from his mouth. "Leslie Richie," he said. "You know, she was the rising star of Hollywood a few years ago. Won an Emmy. Was on the cover of every magazine in town. Dated one of them Italian princes. Only she got a little taste for the nose candy and vodka. That's not a big deal—most of them do—but she got out of control. Six trips to rehab in two years, but it never stuck. One night she and her boyfriend got into a fight and he beat her head in with her Emmy."

"What a delightful story," Jane remarked. She glanced out the window at Chloe. "I hope she won't come to *quite* so unfortunate an end."

"Probably not," said Ant. "She doesn't have an Emmy. Anyway, Cecilia is the one with the talent. That girl is pure magic. Wait till you see her on set. Unbelievable."

Jane heard genuine admiration in Ant's voice and was surprised by it. He seemed all too typically jaded by his life in Hollywood. Yet Jane could tell that he really was moved by Cecilia Banks, and not from any lecherous motivations. It would be interesting to see what the girl could do with her character. *It's too bad she isn't playing Constance,* Jane thought. She was not at all confident that Portia Kensington could do the role justice.

"At any rate, Chloe will bring in the teenyboppers, and *they'll* come with their mothers," said Ant. "Besides, it doesn't really matter how bad she is. They can fix all of that in editing." He looked at Jane. "So where's the can?"

"Can?" Jane asked.

"Bathroom," Ant explained.

"Of course," said Jane. "It's down the hall, on the right."

Ant took another handful of chips and walked away. Jane looked at Lucy. "Remind me not to eat anything he's had his hands near," she said.

The *ding-dong* of the doorbell broke through the sounds of the party. Jane left Lucy in the kitchen and went to see who had arrived. She was pleased to discover that it was Ben Cohen and his daughter standing on her doorstep.

"I'm afraid it's all going to be a bit casual tonight," Jane said as she welcomed them inside. "I hope you don't mind."

"Not at all," said Ben. "The more the merrier."

"You must be Sarah," Jane said, extending her hand to the little girl.

"And you must be Jane," the girl replied, taking Jane's hand and shaking it firmly.

"You mean Ms. Fairfax," Ben said, correcting his daughter.

"Why?" asked Sarah. "She didn't call me Ms. Cohen."

Ben looked at Jane and shook his head, as if he couldn't believe his child's impertinence.

Jane laughed. "It's all right," she said. "As long as *you* don't mind me calling you Sarah."

Sarah grinned, revealing a neat row of teeth with a single gap where one of her incisors had fallen out. "I don't mind," she said.

"Wonderful," said Jane. "Now why don't we go into the kitchen and see about getting you something to eat. I hope you like hamburgers."

"I *love* them," Sarah told her. "Is there corn on the cob too?"

"There just might be," said Jane, winking. "And apple pie."

As Sarah darted ahead, Ben took Jane's arm and stopped her. "Are Walter and his mother here yet?" he asked. "I can't wait to see what Miriam is like."

"I'm afraid you won't get the chance," Jane told him. "They aren't able to make it." She felt a little guilty telling the rabbi an untruth, but she wasn't in the mood to discuss her and Walter's relationship. She would tell him later what was really going on. *Once I figure it out myself,* she thought glumly.

Ben smiled kindly. "Another time, then."

He knows something is up, Jane realized as Ben continued on into the kitchen. She was amazed at the man's ability to pick up on the feelings of others.

In the kitchen Sarah was talking to Lucy, with whom she had apparently already made friends.

"Daddy, there are *movie stars* out there," Sarah exclaimed, pointing out the window.

"Is that right?" said Ben. He looked at Lucy. "I'm afraid I'm not really up on my movie stars."

"You're not missing anything," said Lucy. "By the way, I'm Lucy Sebring."

"Ben Cohen," said Ben.

"Ben's the rabbi I've been meeting with," Jane reminded Lucy. To Ben she said, "Lucy is the manager of my bookstore. More important, she's my best friend."

"An enviable position to have, I'm sure," said Ben.

"It has its moments," Lucy joked. "Would you like something to drink? We have soda, wine, beer—pretty much everything."

"A beer would be great," said Ben. "Thanks."

"And how about you?" Lucy asked Sarah.

"Ginger ale," she answered immediately. "Please," she added when she noticed her father watching her.

"One beer and one ginger ale," said Lucy. She opened the refrigerator and handed a bottle to Ben and a can to Sarah.

"Wow. Great service you have around here," Ben said to Jane.

Lucy laughed and tucked a stray length of hair behind her ear. Ben leaned against the counter and popped the cap from his beer. "So, you manage a bookstore. Who are some of your favorite authors?"

Jane, who was opening another bag of chips, suddenly felt a tingling down her spine. She looked around, half expecting to see another vampire standing there. But only Lucy, Ben, and Sarah were in the room. Sarah was sitting on the floor playing with Jasper, who was busily snuffling about looking for any dropped food that might be lying around. Then Jane's gaze moved to Ben and Lucy.

Around both of them there was a slight rippling in the air, barely noticeable. Tiny sparks, infinitesimal and glittering like diamonds, swirled and spun. Jane's skin tingled with millions of electric pinpricks. For a moment she had no idea what was happening. Then it hit her.

They're attracted to each other, Jane realized. But how was that possible? They'd just met. Surely she was imagining things.

"No, you're not."

Byron's voice startled her. She looked at him. "I'm not what?" she asked.

"You're not wrong," Byron whispered. "They're falling in love. Well, they're interested, at any rate. But it's looking pretty sparkly."

"How do you know what I'm thinking?" asked Jane, annoyed.

"Relax," Byron said, smiling mischievously. "I'm not reading your mind. Although I *can* if I try very hard. I just saw the expression on your face, saw the energy field around those two, and made a good guess."

"Energy field," said Jane. "Is that what that is?"

Byron nodded. "Your powers must be getting stronger if you can see it. Congratulations."

He picked up a bottle of red wine, poured himself a glass, and started to leave. Jane grabbed his elbow.

"Wait a minute," she said, dragging him away from the kitchen. "You mean I can *see* when people are falling in love?"

"Falling in love, really angry, in despair," said Byron. "Overcome by lust," he added, taking a deep drink from his glass and winking at her.

"What a lot of bother," Jane remarked. "I'm not at all sure I want to be able to do that."

"Oh, you don't *have* to," said Byron. "You can learn to turn it off. But that will mean more practice. Until then, don't be surprised if you see this sort of thing now and again."

Jane sighed deeply. "Just when I think I have one thing mastered, another rears its ugly head."

"I would hardly call falling in love ugly," Byron remarked.

Jane glanced back into the kitchen, where Lucy and Ben were still surrounded by a cloud of sparks. "You're right," she told Byron. "It's beautiful." Suddenly she realized fully what was going on. "Lucy!" she exclaimed. "And Ben!" She grabbed Byron's hand. "It never occurred to me," she babbled. "I mean, I never thought . . ." She couldn't form a complete sentence. "*Lucy,*" she said. "And *Ben.* I don't know why I didn't think of it before."

"Don't get too excited," Byron warned her. "It could be temporary." He watched the electrical storm surrounding the two humans. "But that *is* a pretty spectacular display."

Before Jane could respond the doorbell rang.

"Who could that be?" Jane said. "Everyone who could possibly be here is already here."

She walked to the door. As she approached it her skin began to tingle again. She stopped, waiting to see if the sensation ceased. It didn't. She took a few more steps toward the door and the tingling increased. Whoever was waiting behind the door was feeling something incredibly strong. But what? She had no way of identifying the specific emotion.

For heaven's sake, I've only been able to do this for ten minutes, she thought.

The bell rang again. Jane reached for the doorknob but found herself afraid to turn it. Her fingertips rested against it, the electric sparks of emotion coursing through the metal and up her arm. The feeling was more intense than the one she'd gotten from Lucy and Ben, and somehow less pleasant.

There was a sharp, impatient rapping on the door. Jane hesitated a moment longer and then opened it, revealing a petite woman whose closed fist was coming toward Jane with great purpose. It stopped just short of hitting her in the face.

"Sorry," the woman said. "You weren't answering."

The woman was thin, with pale skin and black hair that was pulled into a tight chignon. She was wearing a smartly tailored skirt and jacket—also black—and a scarlet silk blouse open at the neck. Her shiny black leather pumps had heels that meant business and added another three inches to her height. Small, perfect pearls adorned her ears. Her eyes were impossibly blue.

"Hello," Jane said tentatively. She was distracted by the aura of particles emanating from the woman. They were moving rapidly, as if agitated, and they were as scarlet as her blouse.

"You wouldn't come to me, so I came to you," the woman said, her pert red lips forming what would only very generously be called a smile. Something about her voice was vaguely familiar, but Jane was unable to place it. She was feeling slightly sick. Then it came to her.

"Jessica," she said weakly.

Chapter 13

JANE WAS TRYING TO HAVE A CONVERSATION WITH JULIA BAXTER, but Jessica's presence beside her was distracting. The editor was holding a glass of white wine (*Of course she likes white wine,* Jane thought) and talking animatedly about one of Julia's previous films.

"And I thought what you did using the Laundromat as a symbol for Victoria's need to wash away her sins was *brilliant*," she said.

"How perceptive of you to notice that," Julia said.

"I noticed that as well," Jane said.

Julia and Jessica looked at Jane as if she were a child who had just interrupted the grown-ups.

"I'll be back in a moment," Jane said as she used the opportunity to escape. She went outside and took a seat on one of the chairs on the deck. A moment later Cecilia Banks sat in the chair beside her.

"I just wanted to tell you how much I like your novel," she said shyly.

"Thank you," said Jane. "An author can never hear that too often."

"I'm not saying that in the Hollywood way," Cecilia said, smiling. "I actually did read it."

Jane laughed. "I take it your co-stars haven't?"

Cecilia shrugged. "I've found that most people in L.A. think of books as scripts with too many words," she said.

Jane liked the young woman's sense of humor. "And I find that most editors feel the same way," she said.

"It must be wonderful being a writer," said Cecilia.

"Not always," Jane said. "But sometimes. When you're working on something you love. I imagine being an actress is the same."

"I thought so too," said Cecilia. "Now I'm not so sure. I can't say I love most of the things I've been in. But I think this will be different."

Raucous laughter caught their attention, and they both looked across the yard. Chloe was talking to Tucker Mack, who had his arm around her waist.

"I understand this is her first film," Jane remarked.

"Yes," said Cecilia.

Jane looked at her. "You sound doubtful," she said.

"Do I?" said Cecilia. She paused. "I suppose I am," she admitted. "This afternoon we were talking about our favorite films and she said hers was *Beverly Hills Chihuahua.*"

Jane grimaced. "Really?" she said.

Cecilia nodded. "And that's not the worst part," she continued. "She said she couldn't believe they'd taught the dogs to move their mouths like they were talking."

"She didn't," Jane said, laughing.

"I didn't have the heart to tell her it was all done with computers," said Cecilia.

"That was very kind of you," Jane told her.

"I suppose," said Cecilia. "I think underneath all that makeup there might be a nice girl." She glanced at Chloe, who was nibbling Tucker Mack's ear. "Maybe."

"There you are." Jessica's voice was like ice water on Jane's mood. "Let's talk about your book."

"We were," Cecilia said. "I was telling Jane how much I like it."

"Oh, *that* book," said Jessica, pulling up a chair. "I don't care about that one. I'm trying to pry a new one out of her. But she's determined not to give me what I want."

Cecilia raised an eyebrow, then looked at Jane. "I'm sure it will be wonderful," she said. "Now if you'll excuse me, I think I should go back to the hotel and study my lines for tomorrow."

"You're an actress?" Jessica said. "I never would have guessed."

Jane was unsure how to take this remark, but she could tell Jessica meant it to be an insult. Cecilia, however, reacted with grace. "Given the usual opinion people have of actresses, I'll take that as a compliment," she said. She smiled at Jane. "Good night."

"Good night," said Jane. "It was lovely meeting you."

"It was lovely meeting *you* too," Cecilia replied, pointedly not addressing Jessica.

As Cecilia walked away Jessica said, "Now we can have an actual conversation. So, what are we going to do about this book of yours?"

"I'm working on it," Jane lied.

"You've been 'working on it' for a long time," said Jessica, using her fingers to put quotes around her words.

"A book isn't a cake," Jane said. "You can't just throw a bunch of ingredients into a bowl, mix it up, and end up with something people want to eat."

"That's exactly what a book is," said Jessica. "And that's how you need to be thinking. It's a good thing I decided to come up here. Clearly someone needs to put you on the right track."

"Is that why you came?" Jane asked. "To put me on the right track?"

"Only partly," said Jessica. "I was also invited to this silly little conference that's going on. Austen A Go-Go, I think it's called. Have you heard about it?"

How clever she thinks she is, Jane thought. *Suggesting I'm not important enough to know.*

"Yes," she said. "I recall someone mentioning it."

"I normally don't attend things like this," Jessica informed her. "They're almost always useless. Just a lot of people who want to be writers trying to get you to listen to their ridiculous ideas. But I thought it would be a good opportunity to see you as well."

"How thoughtful," Jane said.

"Yes," Jessica agreed. "Did you know Jacqueline Susann's editor used to sit with her in a hotel room and go over each page as she typed it?"

"Is that what we're going to do?" asked Jane anxiously.

"If that's what it takes," said Jessica. She sighed. "If only you could write a book as good as *Valley of the Dolls,*" she said.

"I can only aspire to such heights," Jane said. She wished Jessica would stop tormenting her, and she resented Kelly for inflicting the woman on her. "You know they *are* making a film out of my novel," she added. "And it *was* a bestseller."

"Not a thirty-million-copy bestseller," Jessica countered. "That's how many copies of *Valley of the Dolls* have been sold."

"Over forty-five years," said Jane. "That's not even a million a year."

"Which is still seven hundred and fifty thousand more than *Constance* has sold," Jessica said. "You need to start thinking *big.*

"We'll start tomorrow. Let's have lunch and brainstorm."

Jane shuddered. She hated that word—*brainstorm.* It was one of those ghastly made-up words that tended to be used by people in unfortunate professions such as advertising. *Next she'll say she wants to throw ideas around.*

"We can throw ideas around," Jessica said on cue. "See what sticks."

"What a delightful image," said Jane. "I can't imagine anything more invigorating than throwing around sticky ideas."

"I knew we could work this out," Jessica said, standing up. "I'll see you tomorrow."

"You're leaving?" Jane said hopefully.

"No," said Jessica. "I'm going to talk to someone else. That handsome man over there. I'm sure *he'll* have something interesting to say."

Jane looked and saw that Jessica was talking about Byron, who was standing on the lawn chatting with Chloe. From the smile on his face, Jane could tell that he was flirting with the young woman. Jessica's arrival was sure to annoy him. As her editor slinked away, Jane thought, *I should tell him to seduce her and drain her. But she'd probably give him food poisoning.*

"She seems . . . intense," said Lucy. She started to sit in the chair Jessica had vacated, looked at it, then switched to the one Cecilia had formerly occupied.

"Let's talk about something pleasant," Jane said. "How do you like Ben Cohen? The two of you seemed to be hitting it off."

"He's very nice," said Lucy.

Jane couldn't help but notice the sparks still emanating from Lucy's body. They were less plentiful now, but glittered brightly around Lucy's head. Seeing them raised Jane's spirits and erased some of the darkness Jessica had brought with her.

"Maybe you should ask him out," Jane suggested.

"Really?" said Lucy. "Wouldn't that be a little weird? I mean, he's a rabbi."

"Rabbis don't date?" Jane asked.

Lucy raised her eyebrows. "I never really thought about it," she said. "Most of the rabbis I've met have been old and, well, not so attractive."

"He *is* handsome, isn't he?" Jane said.

Lucy giggled. "He really is," she said. "Have you seen his eyes?" She placed her hand over her heart. "They're gorgeous."

Jane laughed. *A yard full of movie stars and she goes for the rabbi,* she thought. It was typical of her friend. She was always looking for what was inside people, regardless of the package in which it came. It was one of Lucy's many admirable traits.

"Ask him," she said.

"Maybe I will," said Lucy. "But enough about me. What's up with you and Walter?"

Jane's mood darkened. She took a deep breath. "I don't know," she said. She hadn't told Lucy the details of her lunch the day before, and although she had tried to hide her feelings she was sure that Lucy had sensed something was wrong.

"He asked me to marry him," she said.

"Again?" Lucy said. "Let me guess—you said no again."

"Don't lecture me," said Jane.

"I'm not going to lecture you," Lucy said. "You're a big girl, and you can make your own decisions." She was quiet for a moment. "But I *will* say that you're an idiot."

"I said no lectures."

"It's not a lecture," Lucy argued. "It's a statement of fact. Walter is the best thing in your life. Besides me, of course."

"Of course," Jane agreed. "But there's the whole—"

"Vampire thing," said Lucy, groaning. "I know. That's always the excuse."

"I think it's a fairly sound one," Jane said.

"I handled the news, didn't I?" said Lucy.

Jane nodded. "Yes. But you're an unusually accepting person."

"And Walter isn't?" said Lucy. "How will you know unless you try?"

"What will I do if he isn't?" Jane asked. "Leave town? I can hardly stay here once I've told him I'm one of the undead. He'd think I was mad. And can you imagine what would happen if he told anyone else? There's simply too much to lose."

"Yes," Lucy said. "But there's even more to gain."

Jane said nothing. She knew Lucy was right. But that didn't make her any less afraid. The idea of having to start over somewhere new, become someone new, terrified her. After so many years she had finally found a place to call home. Was it worth risking all of that for something that *might* work out?

She just didn't know.

"I'm not going to say another word about it," Lucy told her. "Whatever you decide, I'll support you."

"No, you won't," said Jane, not unkindly. "You'll make me feel guilty about not doing what you want me to."

"Nobody can make you feel guilty except yourself," Lucy replied. "Remember that."

Jane did know it. She also knew that despite what she said, Lucy would indeed try to make her feel guilty. *She thinks she knows what's right for me. And maybe she does. Cassie always did.*

Would she too tell Jane to risk everything on a chance at love? *You know she would,* she told herself.

"I'm going to go see what Rabbi Ben Cohen thinks about the work of Bernard Malamud," Lucy said, getting up. "And maybe then I'll ask him what he thinks about the possibility of having dinner with me."

"That's an excellent idea," said Jane. "I'm just going to sit here and make myself feel guilty for a little longer."

"You do that," Lucy told her. "I'll send Byron out to keep you company."

"Oh, good," said Jane. "I can't imagine anything more cheering."

Lucy smiled. "I'm always happy to help," she said.

"Away with you," said Jane, flapping a hand at her. "Leave an old woman in peace."

Lucy walked off in search of Ben. Jane, left alone, leaned back in her chair. She shut her eyes and listened to the sounds of the party. The many different voices tumbled around in her head, forming a whirlwind of sound. She allowed herself to be surrounded by it so that it blocked out everything—her irritation at Jessica, her fears about Walter, her disappointment in herself. It was all swallowed up by the meaningless roar of idle chitchat.

Exhaustion overtook her, and, surrounded by her own party, she fell asleep.

Chapter 14

JULIA BAXTER REACHED INTO HER POCKET AND WITHDREW A small plastic container of the kind generally used to hold prescriptions. Twisting the top off, she tipped the bottle and several round tablets poured out onto her outstretched palm. They were pastel in color—yellow, pink, blue, and orange. Julia popped them all into her mouth at once. Her teeth made a grinding sound as she closed her eyes and chewed.

She held the bottle out to Jane. "Do you want some?"

Jane shook her head. "I don't think so. But thank you."

Julia opened her eyes. "Good call. They're terrible." She put the cap back on the bottle and stuffed it back into her pants pocket.

"What are they, exactly?" Jane asked. She assumed they were drugs of some kind—something exotic from the wonderland of Hollywood.

"Gerrit's Satellite Wafers," said Julia. "Candy from the fifties. When I was a kid we used to get them at the penny candy store by our school. We used to get them and bottles of Orange Nehi and put ourselves into sugar comas."

"If they're so terrible, why do you eat them?" asked Jane.

"Nostalgia," Julia answered. "They're hard to find now. I buy them from the same store I did back in 1957. Strothman's

Candies and Soda Fountain in Baltimore, Maryland. I guess having them around reminds me how I felt then, like nothing was wrong with the world."

She watched as two burly men walked by carrying coils of extension cords. "It also puts me in the right mood."

"Right mood for what?"

"Shooting these scenes," said Julia.

Jane looked confused.

"You know, the whole fifties vibe. I like to connect with the time period I'm working with."

Jane was now thoroughly puzzled. "But *Constance* takes place in the eighteenth century," she said.

Julia looked at her. "They didn't tell you?"

"Tell me what?" Jane asked.

"We've moved it to the nineteen fifties," said Julia. "Costume dramas aren't doing well. People are in love with the fifties now." As Jane stared at her, speechless, Julia continued. "It actually makes a lot of sense. The forties are a little *too* far back, and the sixties have that whole hippie thing going on." She paused. "Nobody likes hippies."

Jane found her voice. "You're setting my story in the nineteen fifties," she said, more to herself than to Julia.

"Uh-huh," said Julia. "In America. Foreign films are a hard sell."

"England is hardly foreign!" Jane objected. She felt her heart racing, and thought that she might faint. She was shaking.

Julia, completely oblivious to Jane's distress, called out instructions to some crew who were setting up lights. When they failed to do what she wanted, she left Jane and walked over to them, gesticulating wildly.

Jane willed herself to breathe. *This isn't happening*, she told herself. *You misheard. She can't really be setting your novel in 1950s America.*

Just then she saw Portia Kensington emerge from a trailer.

The actress was wearing a red pencil-skirt dress and red heels. Her hair—it must, Jane realized, be a wig—was now blondish, the bangs a row of pin curls and the back neatly rounded. Portia carried a pair of white gloves in one hand, and with the other she toyed with the string of pearls around her neck.

I'm going to be ill, Jane thought. This was not *at all* what Constance was supposed to look like. She had to get away before she saw any more. *If they put Charles in a sharkskin suit, I might do something I regret.*

She walked down the street, away from the commotion of the shoot. Taking her cellphone from her purse, she dialed Satvari Thangavadivelu. The agent picked up after only one ring. Jane explained, as quickly as she could, what was happening.

"I guess I forgot to tell you," Satvari said when Jane was finished. "Sorry."

"You mean you *knew*?" Jane said.

"Well, I knew it was a possibility," said Satvari. "When the producers bought the rights they bought the right to make minor changes."

"Minor changes?" Jane said. "Jumping ahead two hundred years is minor?"

Satvari sighed. "It's all in the contract," she said. "Didn't you read it?"

"Of course I didn't," said Jane. "That why I have an *agent.* Besides, I thought they were paying *me* to make changes."

"No, you're just there in case they need any last-minute rewrites."

"Then who did all of these other rewrites?" Jane asked.

Before Satvari could respond, a scream rent the air. Jane turned around to see a woman running out of one of the trailers. She screamed again and then darted over to Julia Baxter. Jane saw the woman point toward the trailer. The next moment Julia and some other people were running toward it.

"I'll have to call you back," Jane told Satvari, and hung up. A minute later she was standing outside the trailer out of which the hysterical woman had come. A dozen other people were gathered there as well. All of them were watching the closed door of the trailer.

"What happened?" Jane asked a man standing beside her.

"That's Chloe's trailer," he said. "I don't know what's going on, though."

"She probably passed out again," said a woman nearby. "I hear she's been hitting the bottle pretty hard."

"But she's practically a *child*," Jane said. She was surprised at the casualness with which the crew spoke about the young woman.

The man beside her chuckled. "They just tell everyone she's seventeen," he said. "She's really twenty-two."

"Well then," said Jane. "That makes it all better."

The door to the trailer opened and Julia Baxter looked out. Seeing Jane, she motioned for her to come inside. Jane pushed through the small crowd and climbed up the steps to the trailer. Julia shut the door behind her.

"I don't want any of them in here," Julia said. "Any one of them would take pictures and sell the story to the gossip rags."

A couch upholstered in hot pink velvet was positioned against one wall of the trailer. Chloe lay on it, her head lolling to the side and one arm hanging off, the fingertips touching the bright pink shag carpet that covered the floor.

"Is she . . ." Jane started to ask.

Julia shook her head. "No. At least I don't think so."

"You didn't check?"

"I make movies," said Julia. "I'm not a paramedic."

Jane rushed to the couch. "Call 911," she ordered Julia.

Julia fished a cellphone from her pocket.

Something caught Jane's eye. Just below Chloe's left ear were two small puncture wounds.

"Don't make that call!" Jane barked.

Julia, startled, paused with the phone in her hand. "Why not?"

Jane thought quickly. "Because," she said, "you don't want any publicity, remember? If you call an ambulance, this will be all over the papers."

"But she needs help," Julia said.

"She's okay," Jane lied. "Or she will be. She just needs some looking after. I have a doctor friend who can come. Nobody will know."

Julia nodded. "That's probably a good idea. Smart thinking."

"Go out there and tell everyone that Chloe is fine," Jane said. "Tell them she just fainted. I'll call my friend."

Julia opened the trailer door and slipped out. A moment later Jane heard her speaking to the onlookers. Quickly she dug her phone from her purse and called Byron.

"I can't believe you," she hissed as soon as Byron answered. "I thought we were trying to *avoid* drawing attention to ourselves."

"What are you talking about?" Byron asked.

"You know very well what I'm talking about," said Jane. "I'm in Chloe's trailer."

There was a long pause. "Is there more to this story?" Byron asked.

"She's been bitten," said Jane. "Don't tell me you didn't do it."

"I didn't do it," Byron said.

Jane hesitated. "Are you sure?" she asked.

"I think I would remember something like that," said Byron.

Jane glanced at Chloe's still form. "Then I think you'd better get over here."

Byron promised to be there as soon as possible. No sooner had Jane finished speaking with him than Julia came back into the trailer.

"Okay," she said. "They bought it. Now what?"

"Now you go back to work," said Jane. "My friend will be here in a few minutes. The more normal things look to everyone outside, the better."

"Right," Julia agreed. She glanced at Chloe. Jane had rearranged the girl on the couch so that she indeed looked as if she were sleeping peacefully. "Is she really all right?"

"Yes," Jane assured her, although she was not at all sure this was the case.

After Julia left for the second time, Jane tried to wake Chloe by gently tapping her cheeks. When that achieved nothing, she tapped harder. Still the girl didn't wake up. Jane felt for a pulse and was relieved to find one. However, it was very faint.

Hours seemed to pass, but finally the door opened and Byron slipped in.

"Did anyone see you?" Jane asked.

"Some of us know how to stay invisible," Byron said dismissively. "Now what's this about someone being bitten?"

Jane showed him the marks on Chloe's neck. They were almost completely healed, but there was no mistaking their purpose.

"You didn't do this?" Byron asked Jane.

"Of course not!" Jane said. "This is something I would expect of *you*. After all, you were flirting with her at the barbecue last night."

"Well, I didn't do it either," said Byron. "And I flirt with everyone. You know that."

There was a lengthy silence. "Do you think it was Our Gloomy Friend?" Jane asked, voicing what she knew they were both thinking.

"It's possible," Byron said.

"You did say you sensed danger," Jane reminded him.

Byron nodded. "But I was almost certain it had nothing to do with her," he said, sounding angry.

Jane looked at Chloe. "Is she going to be all right?"

"Unfortunately, no," Byron answered. "She's too far gone."

Jane, horrified, turned to him. "She's going to die?"

"Either that or end up insane," said Byron. "Whoever did this drained her too much. If she survives, her mind will be gone. She'll spend the rest of her life having horrific visions. Frankly, she's better off dead." He hesitated before continuing. "Of course, we could always turn her."

Jane was shocked. "Turn her?" she said. "Into a vampire?"

"Those are the options," said Byron. "She can die, she can go mad, or she can become a vampire. I'll let you choose."

"Why me?" Jane exclaimed.

Byron sighed. "Because—as loath as I am to admit it—you have the greater character. Were it up to me, I would finish her off. However, I realize that there may be reasons to choose otherwise."

Jane sat in one of the chairs near the couch. She didn't know what to think. If Chloe died, there would be an investigation. Also, she would be dead. If she lived, she would be insane. That was, frankly, a bigger problem. Being dead was unfortunate, but being insane created the possibility of further disaster.

Jane sighed. "We have to turn her," she said.

Byron raised an eyebrow. "You're certain?" he asked.

"No," Jane said. "I'm not at all certain. But do it anyway."

"You're going to do it," said Byron.

"Me?" said Jane. "Why me? I didn't do this to her."

"Neither did I," Byron reminded her. "And you're going to turn her because you need to learn how."

"No, I don't," Jane objected. "I'm never going to turn anyone, so I don't need to know how."

"Turning also increases your powers," Byron told her. "You need all the help you can get. Besides, this is a perfect opportunity. The girl is already nearly dead, so it's not as if you're killing her. Well, not exactly. At any rate, you're saving her."

Jane looked at Chloe's face. "Well, when you put it like that," she said.

"Now that that's settled," Byron said, "come here. I'll show you what to do."

Jane moved to the couch, kneeling on the floor beside Chloe.

"It's just like feeding," Byron said. "Only keep feeding until her heart stops."

"What then?" asked Jane.

"Then you have to feed her some of your blood," Byron answered. "Don't you remember what happened when I turned—"

"I've tried to forget," said Jane. "Apparently it worked."

Byron sighed. "Well, haven't you seen the movies?"

"I never know what's true and what isn't," said Jane. "There's no need to be mean about it."

"Just bite her," Byron ordered. "There's not much time."

Jane took Chloe's head in her hands and gently turned it away from her. Closing her eyes, she clicked her fangs into place. Then, before she could stop herself, she leaned down and bit into the soft flesh of the girl's neck.

She couldn't think about what she was doing. Instead, she shut her eyes and imagined herself in her childhood room, tucked into bed beside Cassie. It was dark, and outside the house a storm thundered. Jane was frightened, and Cassie was comforting her.

Sleep, my child, and peace attend thee, Jane sang silently as Chloe's blood slipped down her throat. *All through the night.*

She thought about Cassie holding her, and imagined her sister's warm breath against her face.

Guardian angels God will send thee,
All through the night
Soft the drowsy hours are creeping
Hill and vale in slumber steeping,

I my loving vigil keeping
All through the night.

Jane felt the life drain from Chloe's body. The girl's heartbeat thudded in Jane's ears like the slow steps of a giant.

While the moon her watch is keeping
All through the night
While the weary world is sleeping
All through the night.

The flow of blood slowed. Jane clutched Chloe to her, forcing herself to keep feeding as she rocked the girl to sleep.

O'er thy spirit gently stealing
Visions of delight revealing
Breathes a pure and holy feeling
All through the night.

The flow of blood slowed, then stopped altogether. Jane ceased sucking and sat back.

"Is she . . . ?" she asked.

"Yes," Byron said. "Now quickly, feed her. It's easiest if you use your wrist."

Jane hesitated only a moment before biting the underside of her wrist. As blood poured forth she pressed the wound to Chloe's lips.

"How long does it take?" she asked Byron.

"Not long," he said. "You'll know when it begins."

Jane waited. Her wrist ached. Then she felt a gentle sucking, and she realized Chloe's lips were moving against her flesh.

"There she goes," Byron said.

The sucking increased. It was accompanied by a strange

sensation—a kind of dizziness—that filled Jane's mind. It began as a faint feeling of confusion, but the more Chloe drank from Jane's wrist the stronger the emotion became. Suddenly Jane was frightened. She tried to pull her wrist away.

"No," Byron commanded, his fingers closing on her wrist and holding it against Chloe's mouth. "Remain still."

Jane fought him. The dizziness had become an overwhelming sense of falling, as if she had tumbled from a great height and was turning head over heels on the way to her death. Colors rushed by her, and her ears were filled with the sound of voices laughing maniacally. *I'm going insane,* she realized. *And I can't stop it.*

Around and around she spun, her body thrown like a rag doll in a tornado. She screamed, although no sound came from her throat. Then, just before her mind went completely blank, she felt Byron pull her arm away from Chloe's mouth. She collapsed on the floor, heaving.

Byron took her in his arms. "Just breathe," he told her. "It will pass."

Jane allowed herself to sink into his embrace. The spinning of her mind slowed, and piece by piece she felt herself come back together. The dizziness faded away until she felt almost herself again. She opened her eyes.

On the couch, Chloe had also opened hers. She turned her head and looked at Byron and Jane. "Where's Ned?" she asked.

"Ned?" Byron said. "Who's Ned?"

"Ned from the barbecue," said Chloe, trying to sit up. "He came over this morning and brought me those." She nodded at a vase of pink roses that sat on a table opposite the couch. "He's really sweet."

Byron looked at Jane. "Ned from the barbecue," he said, a hint of anger in his voice.

"Ned," Jane repeated. Her brow wrinkled. "Wait. I thought Ted was the vam—"

"Ned had to go," Byron said loudly, drowning her out. "But you'll see him later. Right now you need to rest."

"Why?" said Chloe. "I feel fine. Just a little hungry." She ran her tongue over her teeth, which were still stained with blood. "Actually, I'm starving."

Jane looked at Byron. "Now what?" she mouthed.

She saw a change come over Byron's face as he looked into Chloe's eyes. *He's going to glamor her,* she thought.

"Chloe, you need to rest now," Byron said in a soothing voice. "You're very tired."

Chloe yawned. "You know what? I am. Maybe I'll take a nap." She snuggled into the couch and closed her eyes. "Wake me for my scene," she said. A moment later she was asleep.

"I didn't think we could glamor other vampires," Jane said.

"She's new," said Byron. "There's still enough human in her to respond."

"I must say, this doesn't seem to be terribly traumatic for her," Jane remarked. "I remember my turning as being much more dramatic."

"It's different for everyone," said Byron. "Believe me, when she wakes up and realizes what she is, there will be drama. I can tell. In the meantime, we have to get her to my house so I can look after her. The first day or two will be the worst."

"But she's expected on the set," Jane reminded him. "What will I tell Julia?"

"Tell her Chloe needs rest, and to shoot around her."

Jane suddenly remembered something. "And what about Ted?" she asked.

"Ned," Byron corrected her. "I plan on having a chat with him as soon as I see to this young lady. But first we need to get her out of here. If I carry her, I can make us both invisible. See if the coast is clear."

Jane went to the door and peered outside. Nobody was out there, so she opened the door and stepped out. As she did she saw a flash of movement to her left. She turned her head just in time to see a tiny tail disappearing around the side of the trailer. *It's just a dog,* she thought with relief.

Then she looked down. In the dirt around the stairs were several sets of footprints, all of them different. But there was also a set of paw prints, and there was something peculiar about them. At first Jane couldn't make out what it was, but then it dawned on her.

There were only three of them.

Chapter 15

"This would be a lot easier if we could levitate," Jane said as she looked up at the parlor windows of Walter's house. The sills were just about at the height of her head, and even standing on her tiptoes she could not see into the parlor. Byron, taller than she, had a better view, but not by much. "Is she in there?" Jane asked.

"Yes," said Byron. "She's sitting on the sofa with the dog. She appears to be speaking to it."

"What is she saying?"

Byron sighed. "I don't *know*," he said testily. "In case you hadn't noticed, we're *outside*."

"I realize that," said Jane. "But aren't you—aren't *we*— supposed to have extraordinarily acute hearing?" She paused. "You know—if we *try*."

"It would be much easier if the window were open," Byron replied.

"Or if we could levitate," Jane repeated. "Can't we do that?"

"Do you know how?" asked Byron.

"No," said Jane. "That's why I asked you."

Byron frowned. "Then it doesn't really matter whether we can or not, does it?"

Jane, annoyed, sighed deeply. "I wonder where Walter is," she said. "That's a rhetorical question," she added as she saw Byron open his mouth to speak. "I know you don't know."

"Actually, I do," said Byron. "He's just come into the room."

Jane turned and again tried to see through the window. She jumped as high as she could, and for just a moment she caught a glimpse of the parlor. As Byron had reported, Miriam sat on the sofa opposite the window. Lilith sat beside her. Walter stood to one side, his back to Jane.

"Stop that," Byron ordered as Jane prepared to jump again. "You look ridiculous."

"This is maddening," said Jane, leaning against the side of the house. "We need to get inside." She looked at Byron, who caught her eye and immediately began shaking his head. "No," he said.

"I've gotten *much* better at it," Jane said. "Last time I stayed invisible for what, fifteen minutes?"

"More like six," said Byron.

"Fine. Six," Jane said. "That's long enough to get in, have a listen, and get out again."

"And what if you lose your concentration and appear?" said Byron. "How are you going to explain that?"

"We'll stay in the hall," Jane said. "We won't even go into the parlor. There's no way they'll see us."

"You mean you," said Byron. "I know they won't see me." He hesitated. "Fine. We'll go in. But if I see so much as a *flicker,* we're leaving."

"Absolutely," Jane agreed. "Now how do we get in?"

"Most people go through the front door," Byron said. "Let's start there."

"The front door?" said Jane. "Shouldn't we go through the cellar, or the back, or . . . I don't know, the chimney?"

Byron turned to her. "Do you *enjoy* making things as difficult as possible?"

"To the contrary," Jane replied. "But it just seems to me that if we're going to go sneaking around and using our powers, we might as well have some fun at it." She thought for a moment about what she'd just said. "Goodness. That's not like me at all."

"It's because you turned Chloe," said Byron, continuing around to the front of the house. "It makes you a bit giddy."

"Really?" said Jane. "Now that you mention it, I do feel slightly tipsy. Do you think Chloe will be all right?"

They had left Chloe sleeping in Byron's guest bedroom. Byron had assured Jane that the girl would sleep for several hours at least. What would happen after that was something they hadn't discussed.

"She'll be fine," Byron said, coming to a halt behind one of the large lilac bushes that screened the side of the house from the street. "Just concentrate on disappearing."

Jane nodded. She closed her eyes, cleared her throat, and filled her mind with the image of herself made out of glass.

"Excellent," she heard Byron say. "That was very quick."

"I told you I could do it," said Jane, feeling quite proud of herself.

A second later Byron blinked out. "All right," Jane heard him say. "Here we go."

"How will I know where you are?" asked Jane.

Byron reached out and took her hand. His fingers gripped hers firmly but pleasantly. "Don't let go," he said.

Jane allowed him to lead her around the corner of the house and up the front steps. When a boy went riding by on his bike, startling her with the sound of playing cards tucked into the spokes of his wheels, *whap-whap-whap*, she felt her invisibility waver. A ghostly image of her hand appeared for a second before she focused her mind and regained control.

"You're certain you can do this?" Byron whispered.

Jane nodded, forgetting that Byron couldn't see her. "Yes," she added quickly. "Just get inside."

She watched as the front door opened slowly. The foyer was empty, and the faint sound of voices came from the parlor. Jane felt Byron pull her inside. Then the door shut again. Jane breathed deeply, steadying her nerves.

Again she felt Byron tug at her hand, and she crept behind him down the hallway to the parlor. They stopped outside the door. Inside, Walter and his mother were talking.

"You did the right thing," Miriam said.

"I don't know about that," said Walter. He sounded weary, almost sad.

"Walter, she told you she wouldn't marry you," his mother said.

"No, she said she *couldn't* marry me," Walter countered.

His mother snorted. "It's the same thing," she said. "Anyway, she wasn't right for you."

"Why do you say that?" asked Walter. "Because she's not Jewish? Mother, I think you should know that apart from the few holidays I've spent with you, I haven't set foot in a synagogue in twenty years."

"It has nothing to do with her being a *shiksa*," Miriam said. "And shame on you for not going to temple. That's not how I raised you."

Walter groaned. "I don't want to talk about this," he said.

"Who said we had to talk about it?" said Miriam. "I'm just saying you can do better. You should come stay with me for a while. Ruth Solomon has a lovely daughter you should meet. She lost her spouse, like you."

"Mother, I don't need you to set me up with anyone," Walter barked. Suddenly he groaned loudly, as if he were in pain.

"What?" Miriam said. "What's wrong?"

"You're giving me a headache," Walter told her. "I need some aspirin."

He came toward the door. Jane flattened herself against the wall, in the process losing connection with Byron as he stepped in the opposite direction. She held her breath as Walter passed between them. A moment later a breath tickled her ear. "Stay here," Byron whispered. Then he was gone.

Jane looked into the parlor. Miriam still sat on the sofa. Lilith was on her lap, and Miriam stroked the little dog's ears.

"I'm tempted to tell him what she is," she heard Miriam say in a low voice. "Of course, he would never believe it. Not unless we provoked her into revealing her true form."

She's talking about me, Jane realized. *So she does know. But how?*

"And I would have to explain about myself as well," Miriam continued. "That would be inconvenient. Also, it would put everything in jeopardy, and she's hardly worth it."

There was a long pause during which Miriam continued to pet Lilith. Jane wondered what Miriam meant by telling Walter about herself. *Surely she isn't a vampire herself,* Jane thought. *But how else would she know about me?*

"Who would have thought he would take up with one of them?" said Miriam, a new edge in her voice. "They're everywhere these days, like cockroaches. It's a good thing we arrived when we did. This one isn't getting my son. I'm going to see to that."

Jane gasped. She saw Miriam's head turn. A moment later Lilith leapt off the couch and came trotting toward the door in her peculiar hop-step manner. Her ears were alert, and her eyes were fixed on Jane. A low growl rumbled in her throat.

Jane didn't know whether to run or stay put. Could Lilith see her? She didn't know if the invisibility trick worked on all living things or just humans. But the way Lilith was looking at her, she feared she was about to find out.

Suddenly she felt herself jerked backward. "Quickly," Byron hissed.

That answers that question, Jane thought as she hurried after Byron. Lilith had reached the doorway and was looking down the hall in their direction. She bared her teeth, barked once, and scampered toward Jane and Byron.

Byron reached for the door, but just as he did there came a knocking from the other side. Walter, responding to it, emerged into the hallway, and he and Lilith advanced toward the door—and Jane and Byron.

Jane once again felt herself jerked sideways, this time toward the staircase leading to the second floor. They reached it just as Lilith came sliding to a stop, her feet slipping on the bare wood of the floor. She collided with the bottom step and gave a bark of frustration, looking up at the retreating figures of Jane and Byron.

"What's gotten into you?" Walter asked the little dog, picking her up as he went to open the door.

Lilith whined and growled, but Walter held her tightly. Jane and Byron continued up the stairs, pausing on the second-floor landing and looking over the banister.

"You might have told me that dogs can see us," Jane said to Byron.

"It slipped my mind," Byron said.

"Lovely," said Jane. "And who—or what—else can see us?"

"Cats, of course," Byron answered. "Most birds. Mice. Actually, rodents of all kinds. Goats."

"Goats?" said Jane. "How odd."

"I didn't make the rules," Byron replied.

Their conversation ceased as Walter opened the door and they looked to see who had thwarted their escape. Jane was expecting to see a UPS delivery person, or perhaps a neighbor. She was unprepared for the sight of Beverly Shrop.

"Good morning!" Beverly said brightly. "Is Miriam in?"

Walter, also seemingly taken aback, replied, "Yes, she is. One moment please."

Walter returned to the parlor, and a moment later Miriam came out. Lilith was at her heels and immediately began sniffing the steps and growling.

"Quiet," Miriam said to the dog. "You know this one." She looked at Beverly. "Why are you standing out there?"

"He didn't invite me in," Beverly replied. "You know I can't enter unless—"

"Of course," said Miriam. "I'd forgotten that your abilities are diminished."

Beverly smiled nervously. "It's part of the arrangement," she said.

"I am aware of the arrangement," said Miriam. "Not that I approve of it."

Beverly glanced down at Lilith, who had not turned her attention away from the stairs. "She seems to have found something," she remarked.

Miriam looked back at the dog. "It's probably the stench of that woman," she said. "She did spend a great deal of time here. The scent lingers."

Beverly, ignoring the insult, said, "I just came by to ask what you would like done with Tavish Osborn."

"Nothing at present," said Miriam. "Are you still in his favor?"

Beverly nodded. "He suspects nothing," she said. "He's so vain, I don't think he notices anyone but himself anyway."

Jane felt Byron stiffen beside her. She felt for his hand and held it tightly, afraid he might bolt down the stairs and throttle the Shrop woman. *Not that it would be a bad thing,* she thought. Who *was* Beverly Shrop, and how had she come to be acquainted with Walter's mother? Equally important, who was Walter's mother? Nothing was making any sense.

"He may still be useful to us," Miriam said. "He can't be allowed to go on, of course, but none of their kind can."

Beverly looked as if she'd been struck, but said nothing.

"I'm sorry, my dear," Miriam said with a tone of false apology. "I wasn't referring to you."

Beverly nodded. "I should be going," she said. "Give my regards to your son."

Miriam said nothing, shutting the door and turning to go back to the parlor. She noticed Lilith still pawing at the steps, and picked the dog up. Lilith's ears perked up and she barked loudly, her nose sniffing the air.

"Calm down," Miriam said. "You're just excited from sniffing out the Fairfax woman this morning. I only wish I could have gone with you to see what exactly she was up to."

Miriam disappeared, still talking to Lilith. Byron tugged at Jane's hand and the two of them descended the stairs. This time no one interrupted their exit from the house, and minutes later they were sitting in Byron's car, which they had parked one street over to lessen the chance of Walter or someone else who might recognize it seeing it. Both Jane and Byron had rematerialized, and they looked at each other with a mixture of relief and puzzlement.

"Correct me if I'm wrong," Jane said carefully. "But from that conversation I gather that Walter's mother wants to do us harm."

Byron nodded. "It would appear so," he said.

"And Beverly Shrop is aiding her in some manner," Jane continued.

"Miriam Ellenberg is a hunter," said Byron. "And Beverly Shrop is her eyes and ears. She also happens to be a vampire."

"What?" Jane said, surprised.

"Weren't you listening?" asked Byron. "Didn't you see that she couldn't enter the house because Walter hadn't invited her in?"

"I thought she was just being unusually polite," Jane said.

"And didn't you hear her talk about her diminished powers and an arrangement?"

"I was preoccupied with trying to stay invisible," Jane admitted.

"Which you did rather well, by the way," said Byron. "Congratulations. Turning Chloe does seem to have upped your powers. At any rate, yes, Beverly Shrop is a vampire."

"Did you know this before?"

"No," Byron replied. "But if she's been diminished, then I wouldn't have sensed her, as her powers are likely very weak."

"I still don't understand," Jane told him.

"Miriam is a hunter," Byron said, his voice filled with barely concealed disgust. "Surely you know about the hunters."

"I've heard of them, of course," said Jane. "But I always assumed they were a legend, or that they'd died out long ago."

"They're not a legend, and they haven't died out," Byron told her. "Their ranks have thinned, but they still seek us out." He sighed deeply. "I haven't encountered one since I toured with ABBA in the seventies."

"ABBA?" said Jane. "What were you doing touring with ABBA?"

"I was their head of security," Byron answered. "They'd gotten some threats and needed someone they could trust."

"ABBA are vampires?" said Jane.

Byron nodded. "Why do you think they look so young? Anyway, a hunter posing as a journalist with *Rolling Stone* tried to get to them. In Copenhagen he got into Björn and Agnetha's room and would have staked them if I hadn't stopped him."

"I had no idea," Jane said.

"Oh, the hunters are crafty," Byron continued. "You know, of course, that Abraham Lincoln was a hunter."

"You mean the book is true?" said Jane. "Good heavens. Anyone else I would know?"

Byron nodded. "There are dozens throughout history," he said. "Cleopatra. Guy Fawkes. Brigham Young. Princess Diana."

"Not Diana!" Jane exclaimed. "Oh, and I did love her so."

"Of course, most of them are just ordinary people," said Byron. "Those are only some of the more high-profile ones."

"How in the world did Walter's mother become involved with them?" Jane wondered.

"New members are always recruited by current members," Byron said. "Someone had to invite her."

Jane doubted she would ever know the answer to that question. "You said that Beverly has made some kind of arrangement with Miriam," she said. "What did you mean exactly?"

"Occasionally a vampire who is captured will make a deal," Byron said. "Continued existence in exchange for helping the hunters find other vampires."

"That's a bit traitorous," Jane remarked.

"Generally their fangs are removed," said Byron. "Because they can't feed normally, their powers grow weak. They subsist on the bare minimum of blood required to keep them alive, and that blood has to be given to them by their human masters."

"It sounds like slavery," Jane said.

Byron shook his head. "The traitors have a choice," he said. "No one forces them to betray us."

"How long do you think Beverly has known about us?" Jane asked.

"It's difficult to say," said Byron. "My guess is not terribly long. Otherwise there would have been hunters before Miriam Ellenberg."

"I can't believe that Walter's mother is a vampire hunter!" Jane said. "It seems a bit too coincidental that when I finally decide to attempt a relationship with a man his mother turns out to be part of some secret society dedicated to eradicating my kind from the world. Don't you think?"

Byron looked at her and grinned. "Not really," he said. "After all, we're talking about *you*. You don't exactly have the best of luck when it comes to men."

"True," Jane agreed. "Still, this seems excessive, even for me."

"Forget about your failed love life for a moment," said Byron. "We have to decide what we're going to do."

"Do you have any ideas?" Jane asked.

"We have to fight back," said Byron.

"Fight back?" Jane said. "How? There are only two of us. Who knows whom else Miriam has on her side."

"There are not just two of us," said Byron. "Besides ourselves we have Ted and Ned. That makes four. Five if you include Chloe."

"Which I don't," Jane said. "She was just turned. How much use can she be? And only Ted is a vampire. Or Ned. Anyway, how exactly are we going to fight back? I'm not killing anyone. Especially Walter's mother. That would be beyond the pale."

"That woman would have no qualms about killing *you*," Byron reminded her. "She'd chop off your head as soon as look at you."

"Pleasant," Jane sniped. "Thank you."

"Well, it's true," said Byron. "She's your enemy now, Walter or no Walter, and enemies must be destroyed. Besides, you had no problem killing Our Gloomy Friend."

"Why does everyone keep bringing that up?" Jane said. "I didn't mean to *kill* her. I just sort of . . ."

"Pushed her into a fire," said Byron, helpfully completing the thought.

Jane huffed. "I'm *not* killing Miriam," she said firmly. "And neither are you."

Byron opened his mouth and started to speak.

"No, Ned isn't killing her. Or Ted. And before you even think it, Chloe isn't going anywhere near her."

Byron looked at his watch. "Speaking of Chloe, we should be getting back to her," he said. "We can worry about this little problem later."

They drove to Byron's house without speaking. Jane knew that the issue of what to do about Walter's mother and Beverly Shrop could not be ignored forever, or even for much longer. But she didn't want to think about it. There were no scenarios in which things ended well. *Especially for me*, she thought as they pulled into Byron's driveway.

The front door was open. Exchanging looks, Jane and Byron got out of the car and dashed across the lawn. Once inside, they went quickly up the stairs and down the hall to the guest bedroom.

It was empty.

Chapter 16

JANE FELT ONLY SLIGHTLY GUILTY ABOUT LEAVING BYRON TO DEAL with the Chloe situation. After all, it was he who had forced Jane to turn the girl. She never would have done it on her own.

But really, you ought to be angry with Ted . . . or Ned, she told herself. *It's his fault the girl needed to be turned at all.*

This was true, and Jane planned on giving the young man—whichever one it was—a stern talking-to. But first she had another odious task to perform. She had agreed to meet Jessica Abernathy for lunch to discuss the new book. Foolishly she'd thought she might be able to churn out twenty or thirty pages to give to her editor as proof that she was working on something, but she had written nothing. Nor did she have any idea what she might *want* to write.

I suppose I could just feed on her, Jane thought as she walked down the sidewalk toward the restaurant at which she'd told Jessica to meet her. It was not a place she liked, and she'd chosen it precisely for that reason. If the meeting with Jessica went poorly—as she fully expected it to—she would not feel any sense of loss that might later occur due to associating the restaurant with the experience. It was, Jane thought, rather clever of her.

She more than half hoped that Jessica would have forgotten or by some miracle (or unfortunate tragedy requiring her immediate attention) have returned to New York. But there she was, sitting at a table in the rear of the restaurant. Jane almost overlooked her, as Jessica was sitting with another woman. The woman was quite short and uncommonly wide, with hair dyed candy-apple red, and Jane had no idea who she was. The two women were talking animatedly as Jane approached the table.

"Hello," Jane said pleasantly. "I hope I'm not late."

"Just a few minutes," said Jessica, failing to stand or otherwise greet Jane.

Jane, who knew full well that she was exactly on time, bristled but said nothing. Instead she extended her hand to the strange woman. "I'm Jane Fairfax," she said.

The woman beamed. "I know," she replied. "I love your books."

"Book," Jessica said. She gave Jane a curt smile. "There's just the one."

The woman laughed. "I'm sure there are more on the way," she told Jane.

Jane pulled out a chair and sat down. "Thank you." She paused expectantly, hoping someone would tell her the woman's name. When no one did she added, "I don't believe we've been introduced."

"This is Posey Frost," Jessica said, her tone more than suggesting that Jane ought to already know this.

Jane regarded the woman beside her. "Really?" she said. "Posey Frost of the Vivienne Minx novels?"

The woman nodded and giggled again. "I know," she said. "I'm not what you expected."

This was an understatement. Jane had always imagined the author of the Vivienne Minx novels to be young and sultry, someone who would be comfortable wearing only stiletto heels and diamond earrings as she lounged on her black leather couch sipping champagne. Never had she imagined the very ordinary woman who was now picking pieces from her dinner roll and popping them into her mouth.

"No," Jane said. "It's just that—"

"It's all right," Posey interrupted, patting Jane's hand. "I *have* looked in a mirror before."

Jane was unsure how to respond. Posey Frost seemed quite comfortable with herself. Still, it seemed rude to agree with her. Jane decided to avoid the subject altogether. "Are you here for the festival, Posey?" she asked.

"Oh, no," said Posey. "I don't do any public appearances. My publisher doesn't want to spoil the fantasy for my readers. When the books first got popular they thought about hiring an actress to play me at readings and whatnot, but then they decided it would generate more interest if people didn't know anything about me. Also, they would have to get a new actress for every book, because who would want to make a career out of pretending to be Posey Frost? Oh, and you can call me Shirley. Posey isn't my real name."

"Does it bother you that your readers don't know who you really are?" Jane asked. She couldn't help but compare Shirley's situation to her own, and she was curious to hear how Shirley felt about her own anonymity.

"Not at all," Shirley said as she dabbed butter on a roll. "My own family doesn't know. Well, Harvey does. That's my husband. But no one else. Not even the kids. They think we got all our money from my Uncle Horace when he died." She laughed. "Horace was a drunk and had about three dollars in the bank, but we told the kids he'd put everything into bonds during World War I."

"What do they think you do all day when you're writing?"

"I don't write during the day," Shirley told her. "I do regular mom stuff—clean the house, bake cookies, chauffeur the kids to soccer and piano lessons. I get an hour or two here and there, but mostly I write at night."

Jane was shocked. "So they've never read one of your books?"

"Tara—my thirteen-year-old—thinks the Vivienne Minx novels are, and I quote, 'fast-food fiction.' She likes Jane Austen,

Virginia Woolf, and Banana Yoshimoto. Ryan is sixteen, and he's more interested in baseball than books. Harvey read the first book, but it wasn't his thing. He's a Tom Clancy kind of guy."

The conversation was interrupted by the arrival of a waiter, who took their drink orders and went away again. Jane wanted very much to question Shirley further, but she felt she'd already pried enough. "So you're not here for the festival," she said. "Just for fun, then?"

"I'm here for the movie," Shirley told her.

"The movie?" said Jane.

Shirley nodded. "They've asked me to do some rewrites on the script. Well, they asked Posey to do them. I guess they want to sex it up a little."

Jane, confused, didn't understand what Shirley was saying. Then it hit her. "You mean *my* movie?" she said. "*Constance?*"

"That's right," said Shirley. A worried look crossed her face, and her eyes darted to Jessica and then quickly back to Jane. "Didn't anyone tell you?"

Jane shook her head and looked meaningfully at Jessica, who was examining the menu in her hand. "No," Jane said. "No one did."

"I'm sorry," said Shirley. "I thought you knew. Jessica said you were too busy working on the new novel to do it, so she recommended me."

Jessica set the menu down. "I worked with Shirley on the first Vivienne Minx novel," she said quickly, as if that explained everything.

"Of course, I'm still not Posey Frost," Shirley said. "We're telling the director that I'm Posey's assistant, and that Posey can't come out of the hotel because she's afraid of paparazzi finding her."

"Hollywood people will believe anything as long as you throw paparazzi into the story," Jessica remarked. "They're *terrified* of them."

"And you say they want to *sex up* the script," said Jane, ignoring the editor and addressing Shirley.

"That's what I understand," Shirley replied. "I'm meeting with the director this afternoon to discuss it. It all happened very quickly."

"It must have," said Jane. She looked at Jessica and narrowed her eyes. "As I said, this is the first I've heard about it."

"It was all very sudden," Jessica said. "Kelly called me yesterday afternoon to see if I thought you had time to do both the script and the new novel, and I said I didn't think we should—"

"Kelly?" Jane interrupted. "Kelly Littlejohn?"

"Well, yes," said Jessica. "Is there another one?"

"I'm just surprised he didn't call *me,*" Jane said.

Jessica waved a hand dismissively. "Oh, I told him not to bother you. As I was saying, I didn't want to overburden you. I know you've been having trouble with the novel."

"I'm not having trouble!" Jane exclaimed. "It's just that there's a lot going on at the moment and—"

This time Jessica interrupted. "See? That's exactly what I'm saying. You have a lot going on." Her tone made her sound as if she were talking to a small child.

Shirley, who had been listening to the exchange and systematically reducing her roll to tiny balls of dough that she pinched between her thumb and forefinger, suddenly stood up. "Will you excuse me?" she said, taking up her purse. "I need to go to the ladies' room."

As soon as Shirley was out of earshot Jessica said, "Now look what you've done. You've upset her."

"Have I?" Jane countered. "Well, perhaps we should see what Kelly has to say about his." She fished in her purse for her cellphone and started to dial Kelly's number.

"I wouldn't do that," said Jessica.

Jane paused mid-dial. "And why not?"

Jessica cleared her throat. "I gave Kelly a choice," she said.

"You can either deliver the manuscript within thirty days or you can pay back your advance and take the project elsewhere."

"Thirty days!" said Jane. "No one can write a novel in thirty days!"

"Tell that to Anthony Trollope," Jessica said. "Anyway, it states quite clearly in your contract that if you fail to deliver on time—which you have—we can request that you submit the manuscript in thirty days, and if you fail to do that, it can result in cancellation of the contract and recovery of all monies paid out against it."

"I know what it says," said Jane, although this was only partly true. Kelly had mentioned something of the sort when she'd missed several deadline extensions, but he'd assured her that publishers never acted on the clause. Especially not when an author's book had done as well as Jane's had. She hesitated a moment, then clicked her phone shut and held it tightly in her hand, which was very sweaty.

"So you see, we're only doing what's best for you," Jessica said. "Now let's have lunch, and afterward you and I can discuss the novel." She paused for a long moment. "Of course, if you prefer to work on the film, I imagine Shirley might be persuaded to assist with the novel."

"Excuse me?" said Jane.

"Of course, it would still be your name on the book," Jessica said. "And she wouldn't be writing the *whole* book. She could just, you know, outline it and get it started for you."

Jane was stunned. She sat staring at Jessica, unable to move her mouth. When she finally regained her senses she said, "You don't think I can write it, do you?"

Jessica took a drink of water. "To be perfectly frank, no."

"And why not?" Jane asked.

Jessica glanced around, as if checking to make sure Shirley wasn't on her way back to the table. "Look, I don't want to embarrass you if I don't have to, but we both know you didn't write *Constance*."

"What are you talking about?" said Jane. "Of course I wrote it."

"Violet Grey has evidence to the contrary," Jessica said.

Jane gave a start, as if she'd been slapped. "Violet Grey!" she said. "She has no evidence of any kind!"

Jessica smiled thinly. "She said you'd say that."

"Let me guess," Jane said. "She told you that I found a long-lost Charlotte Brontë novel and passed it off as my own." She shuddered at hearing herself say Charlotte's name.

"Hardly," Jessica told her. "It's not good enough to be a Brontë novel, even a minor one. It's not even good enough to be an Austen novel. Why do you think I rejected it when you sent it to me?"

"You're a Brontëite," said Jane. "I should have known."

"Violet didn't say *whose* manuscript you stole, just that you found one and passed it off as your own. But she says the evidence is there, and I trust her."

Jane sniffed. "How can you trust that vile little liar?"

Jessica frowned. "Because that vile little liar happens to be my sorority sister."

Jane was about to ask Jessica if "sorority sister" was a euphemism for something more sinister, but Shirley's reappearance stopped her.

"What have I missed?" Shirley said as she pulled her chair out and sat down.

"Just girl talk," Jessica chirped. "Jane was saying how grateful she is that you're able to help us out. Right, Jane?"

Jane forced herself to smile. "Right," she said. "So very grateful."

"Then you don't mind?" asked Shirley. "I was a little worried when you said no one had spoken to you about it."

Jane laughed lightly as she imagined sinking her fangs into Jessica Abernathy's throat. "Not at all," she said. "It was just a little miscommunication."

Shirley smiled. "That's a relief," she said as she picked up a menu. "So, what's everyone having for lunch?"

"The Cobb salad looks wonderful," Jessica said, acting as if she hadn't moments ago told Jane that she was a plagiarist, a liar, and a lousy writer. "What about you, Jane?"

Jane was thinking dark thoughts about having Jessica for lunch when the waiter appeared.

"Oh, there you are," Jessica said. "I'll have the—"

"I'm sorry," the waiter said. "I'll take your order in just a moment. Is one of you Jane Fairfax?"

"I am," said Jane.

"There's a call for you at the host stand," the waiter informed her. "You can follow me."

Jane excused herself and trailed behind the young man. When they were out of sight of the table the waiter stopped. "There is no call," he said in a low voice. "But there's a gentleman outside who says it's very important that he speak with you."

Jane peered toward the front of the restaurant. All of a sudden Byron's face appeared. Seeing Jane, he motioned for her to come quickly.

"Thank you," Jane told the waiter. "Will you tell my friends that I had to leave to attend to an emergency at work?" She fished a ten-dollar bill from her purse and slipped it into the young man's hand. "Tell them I'm *very* sorry."

The waiter nodded. "Of course," he said. "And may I just say, I loved your novel."

Jane raised an eyebrow. "Did the man outside tell you to say that?" she asked.

"No," the waiter said. "I recognized your picture from the jacket. I just pretended not to know you in case you were trying to be anonymous."

"Which of the characters in the novel is your favorite?" Jane asked.

"I'm ashamed to say so, but Jonathan Brut," the man said.

Jane smiled. "He's terrible, isn't he?" she said. "But so handsome. Don't be ashamed. We've all fallen for him at some point."

She looked toward the window again, but Byron had disappeared. "Anyway, thank you for the kind words. They came at just the right time."

She hurried out the door and found Byron pacing on the sidewalk.

"It's about time," he said.

"Bite me," Jane snapped. "I didn't realize we had an appointment."

Byron looked wounded. "What's the matter with you?" he asked.

"Sorry," said Jane. "It's not important. I'll tell you later. What's the emergency? Did you find Chloe?"

Byron was walking quickly down the sidewalk. Jane hurried to keep up with him. "Oh, I found her all right," he said. "She'd made her way back to the film set. I caught her just as she was about to feed on the best boy."

"The what?" Jane asked.

"Best boy," said Byron. "A crew member. Works under the gaffer."

"The what?" said Jane.

"Never mind," Byron said. "She was about to feed. I had to glamor the boy to forget."

They'd reached Byron's car, and Jane waited for him to unlock the doors. "So where's Chloe?" she asked.

Byron patted the trunk. "In here," he said. "And she's none too happy about it."

As if in response, a loud thud came from inside the trunk. Byron opened the car doors and he and Jane got in.

"Where are we taking her?" Jane asked.

"Back to my house," answered Byron as he started the car. "But first we have a stop to make."

Chapter 17

JANE WALKED INTO THE BOOKSTORE AND GLANCED AROUND FOR any sign of the Hawthorne boys. Neither seemed to be there, but Lucy was behind the front counter.

"Have you seen Ned?" Jane asked. "Or Ted?"

"Does it matter which one?" asked Lucy.

"A bit, yes," said Jane.

"Gay or straight?" Lucy said.

"Straight," said Jane.

"Ned," Lucy told her. "He might be in the storeroom. One of them is. The other went to get lunch, but I didn't see which of them it was. May I ask what you're planning on doing with him?"

"I'll tell you later," Jane said. "Oh, and if Jessica Abernathy or Posey Frost comes in, tell her you don't know where I am."

"That should be easy," said Lucy. "Because I *don't* know where you are. And why is Posey Frost here?"

"I'll explain that too," Jane promised. "I also want to speak to you about a certain young rabbi."

Lucy blushed. "Good," she said. "Because I want to speak to *you* about a certain young rabbi."

Jane started to head for the storeroom, but came back. "We are both talking about Ben Cohen, right?" she said.

Lucy nodded.

"I just wanted to make sure," said Jane. "It's getting a bit difficult to keep track of everyone."

She walked back to the storeroom and opened the door.

One of the Hawthorne boys was standing beside an open carton of books, a copy of the latest Posey Frost novel in his hand. *How perfect,* Jane thought darkly as she forced herself to smile. "Hello," she said. She had no idea to which twin she was speaking.

"Hi," the young man replied. "We haven't seen much of you around here lately. What brings you in?"

Jane thought frantically for a way to identify the twin without having to actually ask. "Things have been crazy," she said. "Is your brother here as well?"

"Ted? He's out getting lunch. But he should be back in a few minutes if you want to talk to him."

Jane breathed a sigh of relief. She was speaking to Ned.

"That's all right," Jane said. "I was hoping to have a chat with you. Actually, *Byron* and I were hoping to have a chat with you. About a certain young lady whose acquaintance you made?"

Ned set the book down and dusted off his hands. "I thought as much," he said. He looked down. "I don't know what happened. I just got carried away."

Jane put her hand on his shoulder. "It happens to the best of us," she assured him. "But we do need to speak with you. Byron is waiting in the car out back. Come with me."

She went to the door and ushered Ned into the hallway, motioning for him to go out the back. "I'm going to borrow Ned for a little while," she called to Lucy.

"Just don't bring him back dented," Lucy yelled back.

Jane hurried Ned outside, where Byron waited in the idling car. Jane indicated that Ned should get in the front, and she slid into the backseat behind him.

"Well, well, well," Byron said as Ned clipped the seat belt in place. "If it isn't the prodigal son."

"Don't start," Jane said. "I'm sure he feels bad enough as it is."

"I do," Ned agreed. "I really do. I didn't mean to—"

"Don't apologize to me," said Byron. "Apologize to Jane. She's the one who had to turn the girl thanks to your sloppy technique. What were you thinking, draining her to the point of death? Of all the amateurish—"

"Wait a minute," Ned said, swiveling around to look at Jane. "You turned her?"

Jane nodded. "And I'm not terribly pleased about it, young man."

Ned slumped in his seat. "That's not good. Well, I mean it's good that she's not dead."

"But she is," Byron reminded him. "Undead. Thanks to you."

"No," Ned said, shaking his head. "Not thanks to me."

"Don't blame Jane for this!" Byron said. "She was just cleaning up your mess."

"It wasn't my mess!" Ned shouted. "It was my brother's!"

"Ted?" said Jane. "But you're the vampire."

"No, I'm not," said Ned.

Byron looked at Jane. "Do you have any idea what he's talking about?"

Jane leaned back in the seat. "I think what he's telling us is that he's Ted," she said softly. "Is that right?"

"Yes," said Ted. "I just pretended to be Ned to give him time to get away."

"Get away?" said Byron. "Get away where?"

Ted shrugged. "I don't know," he said. "He was totally freaked out by what happened. He thought you'd be mad at him." He looked at them both, and his eyes were wet with tears. "He really didn't mean to do it. And he was scared. He thought she was dead."

"How long has he been gone?" Jane asked him.

Ted looked at his watch. "About half an hour," he told her.

"He couldn't have gotten very far," said Byron. "We have to find him."

A thump from the rear of the car made Jane jump. "What about her?" she asked.

"Her?" Ted said. "You mean she's in the—"

"Yes," Byron said. "She is. And we can't keep her there much longer. So here's what we're going to do. Jane, we'll take you and Chloe back to the set. You'll have to keep an eye on her and make sure she doesn't attack anyone. Ned and I will go looking for Ted."

"You mean Ned," Ted said.

Byron glared at him. "We'll go looking for your brother," he said.

"Why do I have to watch Chloe?" Jane asked.

"Because you turned her," said Byron.

"But you made me!" Jane objected.

Byron held up a hand. "Let me finish. Because you turned her, you have a certain bond with her that I do not. She'll listen to you." He paused. "Possibly. I mean, she should."

"Wonderful," said Jane. "Just lovely."

"Besides," Byron continued, "you already have a rapport with the film people."

Jane sniffed. "Don't even try to flatter me," she said.

Byron smiled at her in the rearview mirror. Jane narrowed her eyes and stared at his reflection as he started the car. He looked away and Jane tried to relax. She was going to have to calm herself down if she was to have any chance of controlling Chloe on the set of the movie.

This was easier said than done. In addition to worrying about her vampire charge, she couldn't stop thinking about her lunch with Jessica Abernathy and Posey Frost. Nor could she forget what she'd seen in Walter's house. Beverly Shrop and Miriam knew about her and Byron. But how? And what were they planning to do? *Nothing good,* Jane thought as they exited the shopping center parking lot and Byron turned the car toward the film site.

Suddenly she remembered something very important. "I forgot to tell you," Jane said to Byron. "Guess who Jessica Abernathy's sorority sister is."

"Someone I know?" Byron asked.

Jane nodded. "An old friend of ours," she said. "Violet Grey."

"How is that possible?" Byron said. "Violet must be—"

"One hundred and fifty-six," said Jane. "Thirty-eight when she was turned."

"That seems a bit old to pass herself off as a schoolgirl," Byron remarked.

"Yes, it does," Jane agreed. "I'm sure she disguised herself. She's a wretched novelist, but she always did have a hand with the powders and paints. I wouldn't be surprised if she'd done herself up as a goth and run about in lots of black eyeliner and pancake makeup. No one would know *who* was under there."

"Violet Grey," Ted said. "Isn't that the name Charlo—"

"Yes," Jane and Byron said in unison.

"We don't say her name unless we have to," Byron told the young man. "Like Old Nick."

"Or Voldemort," added Jane.

"But yes, that is the personage of whom Jane is speaking," Byron said stiffly.

"And what has she done?" Ned asked.

"Just caused a spot of bother," said Jane. "Again." She looked out the window. "I really do wish we'd killed her when we had the chance," she mused.

"There's the bloodthirsty Jane I've been waiting to see," Byron said happily.

"Shut up," Jane said. "But it's true. Things would be easier if we'd been more . . . comprehensive in our last attack."

"We have bigger things to worry about right now," Byron reminded her as he turned the car onto a side street and pulled over. "Stay here," he ordered Ned as he and Jane opened their doors and got out.

Jane met him at the trunk, which he opened with a double click of the key fob. The lid rose slowly, revealing Chloe inside. She was lying on her side, her hands tied behind her, and there was a piece of duct tape across her mouth. Byron reached down and pulled the tape away in one quick movement.

"Santa's ball hair!" Chloe yelled. "That hurt!"

"I'm sorry," said Byron as he reached behind the girl and untied her hands. "It was for your own good."

Chloe scrambled out of the trunk as Byron offered her his hand. When she was standing on solid ground she looked at Jane. "I know you. You're the writer lady."

"I'm pleased you remember," said Jane, eyeing the girl with distaste. She hadn't noticed before how vulgar Chloe's outfit was. It revealed entirely too much midriff.

"Is she a vampire too?" Chloe asked, speaking to Byron.

Byron nodded as he closed the trunk. "She's also fully capable of understanding what you're saying, so feel free to speak directly to her."

Chloe was peering through the car window. "Hey!" she said. "That's the dude who bit me!" She scrabbled at the door handle, trying to get inside, but Byron locked the doors with a click of the fob. Inside the car, Ted was leaning away from the window, watching Chloe with an expression of terror on his face.

"I want to bite him!" Chloe shouted, banging on the glass with her fists. "Open the door!"

Jane looked at Byron. "I see this is going to be loads of fun," she said.

Byron took Chloe by the wrist and pulled her away from the car. "That's not the boy," he told her. "It's his brother."

"That's good enough for me," Chloe snapped. "If they're twins, I'm sure they'll taste the same."

Byron put his hand on her chin and turned her head so that she was looking into his eyes. "Listen to me," he said in a low, seductive voice. "It's very important that you remain calm. I'm going to go find Ned. You're going to go with Jane and do what you've been hired to do. Do you understand?"

Chloe nodded slowly as the glamor took effect.

"Good," Byron said, releasing her. He turned to Jane. "If she misbehaves, stake her."

A look of horror passed over Chloe's face as Jane nodded. "You wouldn't really do that, would you?" the girl asked.

"In a heartbeat," said Jane, trying to sound as if she meant it.

Byron got into the car and drove away, leaving Jane alone with her charge. "All right," she said. "The plan is very simple. We're going to go back to your trailer. Everyone thinks you've been in there resting after a fainting spell. You're going to let them go right on thinking that. You'll do whatever it is you're supposed to do today, and then tonight we'll discuss what comes next."

"So, did I become a vampire because that guy bit me?" Chloe asked as they walked.

"Not entirely," said Jane.

"Then how did it happen?" the girl said.

"It's complicated," Jane replied. "We'll talk more about it later."

"And I really *am* a vampire, right?" said Chloe. "I mean, this isn't some kind of joke is it? Because if I'm being punked, I'm going to be really pissed off."

"You're not being punked," Jane assured her. "Whatever that is. This is very serious. Although I must tell you, you're taking it rather well."

Chloe shrugged. "I played a vampire on *High Stakes* once," she said. "You know, that show about vampires who run a casino in Vegas. I'm used to it. Besides, now I never have to worry about turning forty and not getting parts. I'll always be young and pretty. Sounds like a win-win to me."

"Be that as it may," said Jane, "there are a lot of things you're going to have to learn."

They were approaching the film site. It was crawling with people, and Jane was hopeful that they might actually get to Chloe's trailer without being seen. Then, to her horror, she saw approaching them the trio of Julia Baxter, Jessica Abernathy, and Shirley.

"There you are," Julia said to Chloe. She looked at Jane. "Is she feeling better?"

"I'm fine," Chloe told the director. "I just fainted or whatever."

"Come with me," said Julia, taking the girl by the hand. "We need to get you into hair and makeup. And I want to talk to you about your scene. I think you . . ."

Her voice trailed off, and Jane found herself faced with Shirley and Jessica. "I'm sorry I had to leave our lunch so precipitously," she said. "There was a bit of an emergency."

"So we heard," said Jessica. "Listen, I spoke with Kelly and Julia, and everything is set. Shirley will work on any changes Julia wants in the script, and you're free to write that novel I've been waiting for."

"Well, you seem to have it all worked out," Jane said sharply. Now that Jessica had laid all her cards on the table, Jane no longer felt compelled to adhere as strictly to rules of polite conversation as she normally would. Besides, she intended to call Kelly as soon as she could and straighten things out.

Jessica smiled. "I guess I have," she said. "Isn't it wonderful when everything works out for the best?" A chirping sound filled the air, and Jessica reached into her handbag. "Excuse me," she said as she removed a cellphone. "I need to take this."

The editor walked off, leaving Jane and Shirley alone. As soon as Jessica was out of earshot Shirley said, "I'm really sorry. I had no idea that Jessica did all of this behind your back. I never would have agreed if I'd known."

"Oh, it's all right," said Jane. "I really didn't want to work on the script anyway. And she's right that I need to get this book written. Maybe it really is all for the best."

"Don't count on it," Shirley said.

Jane looked at her, surprised. "What do you mean?" she asked.

Shirley snorted. "Jessica edited my first book," she said. "I didn't even have an agent then. I sent the manuscript in blind. Anyway, Jessica bought it. I was so excited. I thought this was going to be my big break."

"Wasn't it?" asked Jane. "That book did very well."

"It did," Shirley agreed. "And do you know how much I was paid for it?"

Jane didn't want to ask. She assumed the amount was obscene.

"Five hundred dollars," Shirley said.

Jane gasped. "But surely the royalties made up for that," she said.

Shirley shook her head. "It was a work-for-hire contract. No royalties. Jessica told me it's what all publishers did with first-time authors. What did I know? Until then I'd only ever published in my garden club's newsletter."

Jane was appalled. "What did you do when you found out she'd lied to you?"

Shirley shrugged. "I didn't find out until the book was on the bestseller list and another writer friend asked what I was going to do with all the money coming in. By then the damage was done. But I got myself an agent *and* a new editor."

"If you don't mind me asking, why are you still friends with her?" said Jane.

"Oh, we're not friends," Shirley said. "I trust her about as much as I trust a rabid dog. The only reason she hooked me up with this project is because I know a few things she doesn't want her husband to know about."

"You're blackmailing her?" Jane said, thrilled by the prospect.

Shirley laughed. "I prefer to think of it as making her pay for her sins," she said. "Our deal is that at least once a year she finds me easy work for big money. Working on scripts. Ghosting celebrity bios. Whatever. In return I don't send her husband a certain set of photographs I had a private detective take of her and someone who isn't her husband in room 1287 of the London Hilton."

Jane shook her head.

"I know," said Shirley. "I'm supposed to channel my anger into my work. Can I help it if I prefer good old-fashioned extortion?"

Jane laughed. "It isn't that," she said. "I just can't believe someone as horrible as she is has a husband."

This time Shirley laughed along with her. When they were through Jane said, "How come you're telling me this? Aren't you afraid of *your* secret getting out?"

"I can read people," Shirley said. "You're one of the good ones. You won't say anything. Besides, I feel bad taking this job from you. I figure it's a trade. I take your job, and you have information that could ruin my life. Seems fair to me."

"As I said, it's not really important to me," said Jane. "I just don't like being bullied, especially by someone who resembles a praying mantis in heels."

"I can always get you a set of those pictures," Shirley said, grinning.

"I might just take you up on that someday," said Jane, watching as Chloe emerged from a trailer and stormed toward the set. "Right now, though, I have to do some babysitting."

Chapter 18

KEEPING AN EYE ON CHLOE PROVED TO BE MORE DIFFICULT A TASK than Jane had anticipated. She had assumed that the actress would be before the cameras for most of the day, making it relatively easy to know where she was and what she was doing. However, she had failed to take into account the enormous amount of time between shots when the actors were doing absolutely nothing. Five minutes of acting were followed by half an hour of fussing with hair and makeup, worrying about the angle of the sun, trying to locate wayward assistants (everyone had an assistant, even the assistants), and trying to coordinate the half dozen pedestrians, bicyclists, and dog walkers who were required to move in and out of the frame while the actors spoke their lines.

In short, it was all very tedious, and Jane quickly became bored. This was a disappointment to her, as she'd expected the making of a film to be endlessly thrilling. She said as much to Chloe during one of the breaks, while the two of them sat in Chloe's trailer and Chloe chain-smoked a pack of Marlboro Lights.

"I know, right?" Chloe said as she lit a new cigarette from the butt of the one she'd just finished. "I thought the same thing about making records. But you know what you do? You stand in this glass box and sing the same line two thousand times. You don't even sing a whole song at once. You know my song 'Primitive,' right?"

Jane nodded, although she had no idea what the girl was talking about.

"I recorded that in, like, four different places," said Chloe. "Mostly on the tour bus between gigs on my last tour. And the parts that Monkee Bidness raps? He did those over the phone from *jail*." She inhaled, then blew the smoke out in one long blast. "This is pretty much the same."

"Then how do you stay in character?" Jane asked her.

Chloe looked perplexed. "What do you mean?"

"Your character," said Jane. "Barbara Wexley."

"Is that her name?" Chloe said. "It just says Chloe in the script. How did you know what she's called?"

"I wrote the novel," Jane told her, trying to mask her shock at the girl's ignorance. "The one the movie is based on," she added when Chloe seemed not to understand her meaning.

"It's based on a book?" said Chloe. "No wonder my agent wanted me to be in it. It will make me look smarter."

Smarter than what? Jane wondered. She decided to abandon the topic of Chloe's ability to remain in character despite constant distraction. Unfortunately, the only other topic in which they both had any interest was a more painful one.

"You probably have all kinds of questions about what it means to be—like we are," Jane said.

Chloe lit another cigarette, her fourth in half an hour. "Not really," she said. "I mean, what is there to know? You bite people and drink their blood. How hard can it be?"

"Well, that's a good question," said Jane, relieved to have found an opening. "It's easy to think of feeding as simply—"

The sudden appearance of Byron in the trailer startled her, and she stopped talking.

"Now *that* is cool!" Chloe exclaimed. "How do you do that? Show me."

"Later," said Byron. "Right now we have more pressing matters to attend to." He looked at Jane. "We've found Ned," he told her.

"Where?" Jane asked.

"At the train station," Byron explained. "He was heading to Montreal."

"Ned," said Chloe. "He's the one who made me like this."

Byron glanced at Jane. "You didn't tell her yet?"

"I was getting to it," Jane said.

Chloe tapped some hot ashes onto the carpet, where they burned for a moment and fizzled out, leaving a black circle in the pink shag. "Tell me what?" she said.

"It's too complicated to get into right—"

"Ned bit you, but Jane turned you," Byron said. He ignored the furious look from Jane. "But she had to do it to save your life," he added. "So don't blame her. We'll talk about it later."

"She—" said Chloe.

"I—" said Jane.

"*Later,*" said Byron. "Jane, you come with me. Chloe, don't eat anyone. We'll be back for you later."

"Fine," said Chloe. She pouted and kicked at the spot on the carpet. "Whatever."

"Then it's settled," Byron said. He looked at Jane. "Best go invisible so no one sees you running away," he said.

Jane sighed, closed her eyes, and concentrated. To her great satisfaction, she disappeared almost immediately.

"You have to teach me how to do that!" Chloe called out as Jane and Byron left the trailer.

When they were several blocks away Byron materialized behind a hedge. Jane followed suit.

"You're getting very good at that," Byron remarked as he walked toward his car, which was parked at the curb.

"Aren't I?" Jane agreed. "I'll be turning into a bat in no time."

"A what?" said Byron as he opened the door.

"A bat," Jane repeated. "You promised to show me how, remember?"

"Of course," said Byron, starting the car. "It slipped my mind."

He pulled away from the curb and started driving. "Ned is at my house," he explained. "With Ted, of course. They're still dressed alike, and I'll be damned if I can tell one from the other even now."

"We should tag one of them," said Jane. "Through the ear. Like they do with cows."

"We could brand them, I suppose," Byron said thoughtfully. "We used to do that with sheep, remember?"

"I do," said Jane. After a moment she sighed. "It all seems so long ago," she said.

"It *was* long ago," Byron replied.

Jane looked out the window at the passing houses. "Do you ever get tired of it?" she asked.

"Of what?" said Byron.

"Living," Jane said.

Byron stopped at the corner, looked for oncoming traffic, and turned left. "No," he said. "I never tire of it."

"I don't believe you," Jane said. "But let's assume for the moment that you are not lying to make me feel better—which you are. Don't you ever think about that last day?"

"You're a confounding young woman," Byron said. "What last day?"

"*The* last day," said Jane. "Of existence. Of everything."

"We're immortal," Byron said. "There doesn't have to be a last day."

"I don't mean *our* last day," Jane said. "I mean, I do, but I'm speaking about the last day of the world. It has to end sometime. At some point the sun will die and everything will go black and freeze, or whatever happens when suns die. I don't know. But it's sure to be grim and very final."

"Oh, that," said Byron as he turned onto his street. "I don't worry about that."

"How can you not?" Jane asked. "If we indeed live forever, we're going to be here when it all comes to its dreary end."

"By then we'll have figured out how to live on the moon, or Saturn, or somewhere else," Byron said.

He reached his house and drove up the driveway, coming to a stop and turning the car off. "Look," he said. "I know you're going through this existential crisis about Walter, and that's to be expected, but—"

"This is *not* about Walter," Jane exclaimed.

"Yes it is," said Byron kindly. "You just haven't figured that out yet. But you will. Right now, however, we need to go deal with our wayward child. Would you like to be the nice parent or the mean parent?"

Jane stared at him. She wanted to argue with him some more about what he'd said about Walter. To her annoyance, however, she realized that he was right. "I'll be the mean parent," she said. "He won't be expecting that."

"Frankly, neither was I," said Byron as they got out of the car. "I must say it's rather arousing."

"Shut up," Jane snapped.

Byron smiled seductively at her as he opened the front door and waved his hand. "After you, *mistress*," he purred.

Ted and Ned were in the living room, seated next to each other on the J. and J. W. Meeks sofa Byron had recently purchased from an antiques store in New York. He'd had it reupholstered in garnet velvet, and it reminded Jane of a sofa that had been in the villa at Lake Geneva the summer she'd met Byron. She vaguely remembered him making love to her on that sofa, and for a moment she became flustered.

She calmed herself, stood in front of the boys, and looked down at them with what she hoped was an expression of disappointment and anger.

"Just where did you think you were going?" she asked. Unable as yet to determine which brother was which, she addressed the space between them.

The brother on the left lifted his head and looked at her. "I was afraid you would be angry," he said. "I wasn't thinking."

Jane narrowed her eyes. "Fangs," she barked. "Show me."

The young man opened his mouth. A second later a pair of fangs clicked into place. Jane nodded. "Ned," she said. She looked at the other brother. "You can go," she said sharply.

Ted looked up. "But—"

"Go!" Jane repeated. "Back to the store. Lucy will be wondering where you are."

Ted's eyes darted to Byron, who stood in the doorway.

"Don't look at him," said Jane. "Just do as I say."

Ted stood, gave his brother a worried look, and walked out of the room. Jane waited until she heard the front door open and close before she continued.

"Do you have any idea how much inconvenience you've caused?" she asked Ned. "Not to mention what you did to Chloe. You do realize she's one of the biggest pop stars in the world, don't you?"

"I didn't know that at the time," Ned told her. "I just thought she was pretty."

Jane made a noise of disgust. "You thought she was *pretty*," she said, the sneer in her voice only partially manufactured. "Perhaps in the future you should do your thinking with this," she said, rapping Ned on the head with her closed fist, "and not with . . . little Ned," she concluded, glancing meaningfully at the young man's crotch.

Out of the corner of her eye she saw Byron trying very hard not to laugh. This caused *her* to want to begin laughing, and she was forced to turn her back to Ned and bite her lip while she regained her composure. Clearing her throat, she said, "I have half a mind to stake you."

"No!" Ned said, clearly startled.

Jane winked at Byron and turned back to face the now frightened young man. "And why not?" she asked. "You've broken one of the vampire commandments. The punishment for that is staking."

Ned looked at Byron. "But he never told me about any command—"

"And that's his failing," Jane snapped. "But my concern is with you." She clasped her hands and tapped the tips of her index fingers together. "I'm afraid we have no choice."

Ned began to weep. It broke Jane's heart to see him cry, and she had to try very hard not to sit beside him and comfort him. It occurred to her that perhaps she had not fully considered the difficulty of playing the bad guy.

"Wait a moment," Byron said. He moved to the couch and took the place to Ned's right, putting his arm around the young man's shoulders. "He's right," he said, looking up at Jane. "It's my fault for not instructing him properly."

"He still should have known," Jane argued. "It's only common sense."

"Please," Ned said, sniffling. "There must be some way I can make up for what I've done. I'll do anything. Just tell me what to do."

Jane and Byron exchanged glances. It was time for Byron to take over, and Jane wondered what he'd come up with.

"There *might* be an alternative," Byron said cautiously.

Ned looked up. "What?" he asked. "What is it?"

Byron appeared to think. He shook his head. "I don't know," he said. "Perhaps not."

Ned looked as if he might burst into tears again as he said, "Whatever it is, I'll do it."

Byron looked at Jane. "There is the option of penance," he said. "If the guilty party commits an act of selfless devotion to our people, he might be forgiven. Is that not correct?"

Jane had no idea whether it was or was not. As far as she knew, they were making the entire thing up out of whole cloth. "I suppose so," she said.

"Then perhaps he could assist us in the matter of Beverly Shrop," said Byron.

"How so?" Jane asked, wanting very much to hear the answer herself.

Byron addressed Ned. "We've recently discovered that Beverly Shrop is one of our kind."

Ned blinked. "She's a vampire?" he said.

Byron nodded. "Yes. But in name only. I'm afraid she's aligned herself with a human vampire hunter." He looked at Ned, appearing concerned. "I don't know if I can ask this of you," he said.

"You can," Ned assured him. "What is it?"

Byron took a deep breath. "If we had someone who was close to Beverly, someone in whom she might confide, we might be able to find out exactly what she and her human master have planned."

Jane realized what Byron was asking before Ned did. The idea sickened her, but she said nothing. It was Byron's game to play out now.

"Why would she tell me anything?" asked Ned. "She doesn't even know who I am."

Byron stroked the young man's arm. "That's exactly the point, my boy," he said. "She already knows who—and what—I am. I could never gain her trust. But you are a complete mystery to her. Fresh blood, as it were."

Ned swallowed hard. "What makes you think she would be interested in me?" he asked.

Byron laughed lightly. "You're a very attractive young man," he said, stroking Ned's neck. "As you know, I myself was overcome by your considerable assets."

"You thought I was my brother," said Ned.

"Yes, well, there was a great deal of wine involved," Byron

replied testily. "Anyway, that's not the point. The point is that Beverly Shrop is sure to find you desirable."

Ned, understanding dawning on him, wrinkled his nose in disgust. "You want me to sleep with her?" he said.

"Crudely put," said Byron. "But yes."

Ned shuddered. "But she must be at least fifty," he said. His eyes darted to Jane. "No offense," he added.

Jane started to speak but was cut off by a look from Byron. *Fifty!* she thought. *He thinks I'm fifty!*

"I realize that the idea of romancing Miss Shrop may be distasteful," Byron told Ned. "But it would help us—all of us—immensely. Besides, the alternative is not entirely pleasant."

Again Ned looked at Jane. She saw fear in his eyes, and in order to keep herself from telling him that this was all a ruse she reminded herself that he thought her too old to be attractive.

"Byron is right," she said firmly. "It's either penance or staking. The law is *very* clear on the matter."

Ned swallowed hard. "All right, then," he said. "I'll do it. I'll be Beverly Shrop's cougar bait."

Byron smiled at Jane. "See?" he said. "I knew we could work something out." He ran his fingers through Ned's hair. "Grrrrowwwllll," he purred.

Chapter 19

WHEN JANE WALKED INTO FLYLEAF BOOKS ON TUESDAY MORNING she found Lucy in a peculiar mood. The manager was going through the mail and humming a tuneless but cheerful little song as she tossed the various envelopes into two piles. She seemed slightly more dressed up than usual, having traded her habitual summer combination of jeans and a T-shirt for a short-sleeved white silk shirt and a flowy skirt made out of deep purple batik fabric patterned with orange and gold birds. Her dark curly hair hung loose about her shoulders, and even from forty feet away Jane's keen nose detected the scent of violets rising from her skin.

"What's going on?" Jane asked, setting the cup of takeout coffee in her hand on the counter.

"Hmm?" Lucy said. "Nothing. Why?"

"You're wearing real clothes," said Jane. "And you smell nice."

"Are you saying that I usually stink?" Lucy asked.

"Something's up," Jane insisted. "Out with it."

Lucy smiled. "Ben and I have a lunch date," she said. She then made another sound that turned into a cough.

"Did you just giggle?" said Jane. "And then try to cover it up?"

Lucy coughed again, but her attempt was halfhearted at best. "I did not giggle," she said. "I do *not* giggle."

"How many times have you seen him?" Jane asked.

Lucy shrugged. "Twice, I guess," she answered. "Why?"

"Twice?" said Jane. "In the past year you haven't gone out twice with anyone. You've gone out twice with Ben in five days. Three and a half, really, since you met him Friday night and it's not even nine o'clock yet."

"To be fair, one of those times was a picnic with Sarah," Lucy said. "That's not really a *date* date."

"What did you do on the *date* date, then?" asked Jane.

"We *were* going to go out to dinner," Lucy said. "But we ended up ordering in Chinese and watching a movie."

"Interesting," said Jane. She was enjoying teasing her friend. She didn't often get to do it, so now she wanted to make the most of it. "And what was the movie?"

"I don't remember," Lucy said.

"Liar," said Jane. "What was it?"

Lucy sighed. "I don't want to tell you," she said.

"Why not?" said Jane.

"Because," Lucy replied, "I know what you're going to say."

"I don't see how that's possible," Jane told her, trying not to smile. "How can I have an opinion when I don't even know what the movie is?"

Lucy took the largest pile of mail and dropped it into the recycling bin beneath the front desk. "Fine. We watched *Tarantula*. You know, the one with John Agar and Mara Corday."

"Yes. And Leo G. Carroll," Jane said. "There's a line about him and the movie in the song 'Science Fiction/Double Feature.'"

"From *The Rocky Horror Picture Show*," said Lucy. "I know. When I was in college I used to play Magenta in an audience participation show every Friday night at the local dollar movie theater."

"*I* played Magenta in an actual stage version," Jane countered. "Well, a touring company, anyway. In England."

"You?" said Lucy, her mouth agape. "You played *Magenta*? In *The Rocky Horror Picture Show*?"

"It was just *The Rocky Horror Show* then," Jane said. "But yes, I did. Why are you so surprised?"

"Oh, I don't know," said Lucy. "Maybe because I've never heard you sing. Maybe because you've never mentioned it. Maybe because the idea of Jane Austen playing Magenta in *The Rocky Horror Picture Show* is so freaking awesome I could die."

Jane rolled her eyes. "I told you, it was *The Rocky Horror Show.* And it was for a very short time. I might as well have been an understudy."

"How did you even get involved in it?" asked Lucy.

"Well, you know the show," said Jane. "It's really all about monsters of one kind or another. There were several vampires in it. Real ones, I mean, not characters. One of the creators was—is—a vampire as well. Lovely fellow."

"I'm still not sure I believe you," Lucy said. "It's too weird."

"Please. It was the seventies," said Jane. "We did all kinds of peculiar things."

"What name did you use?" Lucy asked. "Jane Fairfax?"

"Heavens, no," said Jane. "I really don't remember what I called myself."

"Now you're lying," Lucy said.

"I am not!" said Jane.

"Are too," Lucy argued. "Out with it. You made me tell you something I didn't want to. Now it's your turn."

Jane sighed. "Oh, all right," she said. "Meadow Brightstar. I was Meadow Brightstar."

Lucy paused only a moment before laughter poured from her mouth. "Meadow Brightstar!" she shrieked.

"I told you, it was the seventies!" said Jane as Lucy laughed even harder. She waited for the young woman to calm down. This took a good minute and a half, during which Jane tried very hard to remain dignified in the face of Lucy's mirth.

Finally Lucy stopped laughing and took a deep breath.

"Meadow Brightstar," she said hoarsely. "I am *never* going to forget that."

"Oh, good," Jane said. "Now, enough about my illustrious theater career. Let's get back to you and Ben. A giant spider movie is an interesting choice for someone who doesn't care for the creatures."

"It gets worse," said Lucy.

"Worse?" Jane asked.

"We might have watched some of *Deadly Mantis*," Lucy said. "And possibly *Them!*"

"*Three* giant-insect movies," said Jane. "It really must be love."

"They were running a B-movie marathon!" Lucy said defensively. "And you know I *love* those campy monster movies from the fifties."

"Oh, yes," said Jane. "You talk about them *all* the time."

Lucy made a face. "I do," she insisted. "Anyway, Meadow, it's your fault for introducing us in the first place."

"My fault?" Jane exclaimed. "Are you saying you'd like me to get rid of him for you?"

Lucy pouted. "Okay," she said. "I don't like movies about giant bugs. But Ben does, and it wasn't like that's all we were doing."

"Oh?" said Jane, raising an eyebrow.

"We were *talking*," Lucy said. "He is a rabbi, you know."

"What, rabbis don't like to kiss pretty girls?" Jane said, feigning—badly—a Yiddish accent.

"Ha ha," said Lucy. "For your information, he kisses quite well. He also fed me walnut prawns using chopsticks and didn't drop a single one. That's talent."

"Prawns?" Jane said. "Prawns aren't kosher."

Lucy waved a hand at her. "Please," she said. "Everyone knows it doesn't count if it's in Chinese food."

"Since when?" asked Jane.

"Since forever," Lucy said. "Ask anyone."

"I might have to," said Jane. "So you had a good time. And now lunch today. This sounds serious."

Lucy shook her head from side to side but said nothing.

"Is that a yes or a no?" Jane asked.

"It's a 'we'll see,'" said Lucy.

"That means yes," Jane teased.

"It means we'll see," Lucy repeated.

"Are Ted and Ned in?" Jane asked.

"They are," said Lucy. "I put them to work in the storeroom packing up all the books that have to go back to the distributor. It was the nastiest job I could think of."

"They really don't like to get dirty," Jane said. "Good thinking."

"I also turned the air conditioner off," Lucy continued. "I told them it was broken. That should make it even more pleasant. By noon it will be ninety-five degrees in there."

"I heartily approve," said Jane. "And now I am going back to the set to make sure Chloe doesn't undo us completely. I just stopped in to see how things are going."

"Before you go you might want to call Kelly back," Lucy said. "He called about ten minutes before you got here. He said he tried you at home first, but you must have just left."

Jane groaned. She really didn't want to speak to her editor-turned-agent, but she knew she had to, if only to settle the situation with Jessica.

Kelly answered on the second ring. "I was just going to lunch," he said when he heard Jane's voice. "But that Reuben sandwich can wait until I've had a chat with my favorite client. How's everything?"

"Somewhere between dreadful and unbearable," Jane answered. "Jessica Abernathy is here. She's trying to pry the manuscript out of me, and I have no doubt she would insert a probe into my brain if she thought she could siphon the words out that way."

"Wouldn't that be fantastic?" said Kelly. "Imagine if you could just *think* a story and have it appear on your computer screen."

"A novel idea," Jane said. "Oh, and she apparently decided that I was too busy to do any work on the film script and very thoughtfully suggested her friend Posey Frost for the job."

"Yes," Kelly said. His voice had an odd tone, as if he were suddenly occupied with doing something that required all his attention.

"Yes what?" asked Jane.

"Yes," Kelly said again. "I know about Jessica. And Posey. I meant to tell you."

"You *knew*?" said Jane. "So Jessica wasn't making that up? Why didn't you say something?"

"I said I meant to," Kelly reminded her. "I just didn't exactly get around to it."

"You knew she was coming here to ambush me and you didn't think I might want to know about it?" she said, the anger in her voice making it tight.

Kelly sighed. "Jane, it's complicated," he said. "You *are* very late with the manuscript, and we don't have a lot of options at this point. Jessica thought that if she could speak with you face-to-face it might light a fire under you."

"That's not the point!" said Jane. "The *point* is that none of you told me what was going on. Can you imagine how I felt seeing that woman on my doorstep? And the way she spoke to me at lunch, I—"

"Jane, it's going to be all right," Kelly said. "You just need to calm down."

"I will not calm down!" Jane said loudly. "And if you even *think* about uttering the word *hysterical* I will not hesitate to get on the next train to New York and show you exactly how not calm I am!"

"I'm sorry," said Kelly. "You're right. I should have told you what was going on. But Jessica is there now and she's more than willing to work with you on hammering out a plot for the new book."

"I don't want her help," Jane snapped. "I want her to go away. As soon as possible. Preferably yesterday."

"I wish I could make that happen," said Kelly. "But I can't. So please, just try to work with her. You don't want to antagonize your publisher."

"What about my publisher antagonizing me?" Jane asked. "Why can't we just get another publisher? Surely someone else would want me."

"Someone probably would," said Kelly. "But switching publishers never looks good. I'd rather stick with Browder."

Jane tapped her fingers angrily on the desk while she tried to compose herself. "In other words, I have to play nicely with Jessica Abernathy," she said.

She considered telling Kelly about Jessica's connection to Violet Grey. But that would complicate things too much, and besides, she was no longer sure she entirely trusted Kelly. She had yet to tell him that she was a vampire, and although a week earlier she would have entertained doing so with no reservations about his ability to keep her secret, now she had doubts.

"That's pretty much where things stand," Kelly said in answer to her question.

Jane considered this. Did she really care if she published another novel? She'd waited almost two hundred years to see *Constance* published. She could do it again.

No, she told herself. *You couldn't.*

This was true. Having once again tasted the joy of seeing her words in print, she was not willing to give that up. She would write the novel for Jessica Abernathy, and it would be a good novel. Better than anything she'd yet written. But she wasn't going to be happy about it, and she wasn't going to let Kelly off the hook quite yet.

"I'll think about it," she said stiffly. "We'll talk later."

She hung up.

The happiness she'd felt from sharing Lucy's excitement about her new relationship had completely disappeared. Now all she could think about was how she was, in essence, Jessica Abernathy's employee. Added to the fact that she had to spend the rest of the day keeping an eye on Chloe, this put her in a decidedly unpleasant mood. *Maybe I'll bite somebody,* she thought darkly.

She got up and opened the office door. A woman was browsing the fiction shelves. Deciding it might cheer her up to help someone find a good book, Jane approached the customer.

"Are you looking for anything in particular?" she asked.

The woman turned around, and Jane was horrified to discover that it was Miriam Ellenberg. Miriam presented Jane with a tight smile. "Do you have *Jane Eyre*?" she asked. "It's by Charlotte Brontë."

"So it is," said Jane. "I believe we do have a copy or two."

"It's such a good book," Miriam remarked as Jane led her to the appropriate section. "I don't know why, but I woke up this morning with a desire to read it again."

"Probably because of the festival," Jane said. "It starts on Friday. You likely saw posters for it all over town."

"That's probably it," said Miriam as Jane found the novel and handed it to her.

Of course she's a Brontëite, Jane thought as she watched Walter's mother examine the book as if she were checking it for defects. She wondered if Miriam had come by herself and if she was there for any other reason.

This question was answered a moment later when Walter entered the store. He was holding two cups of coffee from the bakery a few doors down. When he saw Jane standing beside his mother a decidedly uncomfortable look crossed his face.

"Good morning, Jane," he said stiffly.

"It is, isn't it?" said Jane.

"Did you find the book, Mother?" Walter asked Miriam.

Miriam nodded. "Yes. But I think perhaps I don't want to read it after all." She handed the book back to Jane. "I'll just look around."

Walter watched his mother wander over to the gardening books. "How are you?" he asked Jane.

"I'm well," Jane told him. "And you? Your mother seems to be enjoying her visit."

"At least one of us is," said Walter. He looked at Jane. "I know my mother has a lot to do with what's happened between us," he said. "I should never have lied to her about you, and I should never have asked you to think about converting. I'm sorry."

Jane didn't know what to say. How could she tell Walter that the reason she couldn't be with him was because his mother knew she was a vampire? He would think she was insane.

"There's nothing to be sorry for," she said. "Sometimes Mother knows best."

Walter reached out and took her hand. Jane found herself glancing toward Miriam to see if they were being watched. Walter's mother, however, seemed engrossed in a book about the successful growing of daylilies.

"Jane, it doesn't matter to me what she thinks," Walter said. "So if that's the only reason you don't think you can be with me, don't let it come between us."

Jane squeezed his hand. "Walter, she's your mother," she said.

"Do you love me?" Walter asked, surprising her.

Jane looked into his eyes but said nothing.

"Because I love you," Walter continued. "You know that. And I think you love me. So if my mother is the only thing keeping us from being together, then just say so. Because I can handle my mother."

I'm not so sure you can, Jane thought as she struggled for words.

"It's a simple question, Jane," said Walter. "Do you love me?"

Jane glanced at Miriam. The woman had put the book down and now was staring at Jane and Walter. Jane saw a look of pure hatred on her face. What Miriam knew about her could be disastrous for all of them.

Then she looked at Walter. His blue eyes were pools of still water, but there was worry reflected in them, as if a storm were gathering. Jane longed to hold him and tell him that everything was going to be all right. But it wasn't. It couldn't ever be.

She opened her mouth to tell him this but heard herself say, "You know I do."

Walter embraced her. "Then everything will be all right," he whispered in her ear. "You'll see."

Jane looked over his shoulder. Miriam met her gaze. She shook her head once, then turned and walked out of the shop.

Jane closed her eyes and let Walter hold her.

Chapter 20

JANE AND BYRON KNELT BEHIND THE PEONY BUSHES AT THE SOUTH end of Walter's yard. Very old and very large, the bushes sported huge pink and white flowers, and their dark green leaves provided excellent screening from the house. The only drawback was the bees, which buzzed sleepily around the flowers like tiny astronauts exploring new worlds. Jane eyed them warily as she peered through the bushes.

"Tell me again why we can't just go invisible," she said. When Byron had suggested the mission to her earlier that day she'd assumed they would make use of their ability to disappear. He, however, had insisted on maintaining corporeality.

"It's difficult to use two abilities at once," he said. "For instance, invisibility *and* glamoring. You end up making both weaker. You *can* do it, but it takes practice."

"But you've had a great deal of practice," Jane reminded him.

"Not with this particular ability," said Byron. "I've done it, but not often."

Their conversation was cut short by the opening of the back door. Miriam appeared on the porch, and a moment later Lilith descended the short flight of stairs into the back garden. She ran using her peculiar three-legged hop into the grass, where she began sniffing around.

"This is a terrible idea," Jane whispered. "Miriam is watching. There's no way we'll be able to get the dog."

"Just be quiet," said Byron. "And have the bag ready."

Jane was holding a pet carrier of the kind used to take cats or small dogs on airplanes. Entrance was through a rectangular opening on the top, and mesh panels on all four sides let in air. The bag was unzipped and waiting.

Lilith had moved farther away from the porch. Miriam watched her as she explored the garden. "Go pee, sweetie," she called out to the Chihuahua.

Lilith ignored her, smelling a clump of lavender and moving on. She spied a butterfly and barked at it, sending it fluttering away. Lilith chased it as it came toward the peonies.

"Just a little more," Byron said softly.

"Lilith!" Miriam called. "Not too far!"

"Shut up, old woman," Byron hissed.

Lilith was only a few feet away now. The butterfly had flown off, but the little dog had found something new to investigate. *She's a nosy thing,* Jane thought. *No wonder Miriam uses her as a spy.*

Miriam's voice rang out again. "I'm going to get my hat," she shouted. "You stay right here."

"Now's our chance," said Byron. "Ready?"

Jane nodded. As the back door shut Byron reached through the bushes and grabbed Lilith. The dog gave a sharp yip and tried to bite his hand, but Byron held tightly as he pulled her through the leaves and dropped her into the open bag. Jane zipped it shut as Lilith snapped at her fingers.

"Go!" Byron said.

They dashed out of the garden and made their way around the side of the house. Byron's car was parked on the street parallel to Walter's, and they had to cut through a neighboring yard to reach it.

Jane jumped into the front seat just as Miriam's voice rang out. "Lilith! Lilith!" she cried. "Come here!"

In the bag Lilith growled. Byron started the car, drowning her out, and drove off with a whoop of triumph. "We got her!" he said.

"But what are we going to *do* with her?" asked Jane.

"I told you, we're going to interrogate her," Byron replied.

"I thought you were being metaphorical," Jane said. "You're serious?"

"Of course," said Byron. "I told you, we can communicate with animals. What did you think I was doing back there?"

"Sitting behind a bush," Jane said.

"I was using my ability to call the dog," Byron said. "Honestly, do you *ever* listen to me? When I said I was going to use an ability, which one did you think I meant?"

"It's just that I didn't *hear* you," Jane explained.

"That's because it's all done in here," said Byron, tapping his head. "You don't actually speak to them. Well, you can, but why bother when you can do it psychically?"

"So what has Lilith told you?" Jane asked.

"Nothing yet," said Byron. "I used a very gentle call to get her to come to us. I haven't actually spoken with her yet."

"Miriam is going to be frantic," Jane said. "I feel bad for Walter. She'll probably make him drive all over town looking for the dog."

"That's not our problem," Byron said. "We just need to find out what she knows."

Because they suspected that Miriam and Beverly might be watching their houses, and because they didn't want to cast suspicion on Lucy or the twins by involving them in the dognapping, Jane and Byron had rented a room at a motel outside of town. They went there now, parking the car behind the main building and walking quickly to room 119. Lilith had stopped growling and was now resting quietly in the carrier.

Once inside, Jane set the carrier on the room's lone queen-size bed as Byron drew the curtains closed. He then turned on the overhead light, casting a yellow glow over the walls, which were painted a sickly coral color. It also did no favors for the faded brown carpet, although for some reason it improved the painting affixed to the wall over the bed—a poorly done scene of what Jane imagined was supposed to be a Mexican village market.

"Let her out," Byron told Jane, with a wave at the pet carrier.

Jane glanced at the carrier. "Are you sure?"

Byron nodded.

Jane approached the bed and reached for the zipper on the top of the carrier. Lilith remained quiet. Cautiously, Jane unzipped one side, then an end, and then the remaining side. As soon as the carrier was open Lilith sprang out with a loud growl, landing on the hideous pink-and-brown-striped bedspread. Her three legs acting as a tripod, she glared at Byron and Jane, her teeth bared and her small ears sticking up. Jane backed away, but Byron calmly sat in one of the room's two tattered armchairs.

"Now then," he said. "Let's give this a try. Jane, you should be able to listen in."

"Me?" said Jane. "I can't communicate with animals."

"I believe you can," Byron replied. "Tom and Jasper tell me they sometimes get flashes of it from you."

"Tom and Jasper?" said Jane, shocked. "My cat and my dog talk to you about me?"

"Don't worry," Byron said. "They haven't said anything unpleasant. To the contrary, they're both fond of you. Although Tom would like you to know that he doesn't appreciate being called Mr. Fuzzybum. Just so you know."

Jane wanted to find out what else they'd said about her, but Byron was focused on Lilith, so instead she asked, "What do I do?"

"It's similar to when you go invisible," said Byron. "Empty your mind and focus on Lilith. Let her thoughts enter your mind."

"That's a little vague," Jane said, taking a seat in the other chair and keeping her eyes on Lilith, who was looking from Jane to Byron as if deciding which would be easiest to take down.

"It's one of those things that can't really be explained," said Byron. "It either happens or it doesn't. It helps if you make eye contact with the animal."

Jane tried. She looked into Lilith's eyes and tried to empty her mind. At first all she heard was the little dog's growl. But after a minute or two she thought she understood some words. She concentrated harder and the words came again.

"Oh my," Jane said. "That wasn't very nice."

"So you heard that," said Byron. "She has a filthy mouth for such a cute dog. Were you able to hear what I asked her?"

Jane shook her head.

"Try again," Byron said.

Jane took a deep breath and once again focused on Lilith's eyes. For a few seconds she heard what sounded like static. Then Byron's voice cut through.

"Who is Miriam Ellenberg?" he asked.

"You know who she is," said a high, thin voice that could only be Lilith's.

"*What* is Miriam Ellenberg?" asked Byron.

"Why should I tell you anything?" Lilith replied.

"Because if you don't I'm going to put you back in that carrier and toss it into the river," Byron told the little dog.

Jane was horrified. *He wouldn't do that*, she thought.

"Good to know," said Lilith. "Thank you, Jane."

"You're wel—" Jane began.

"Jane!" Byron's voice was sharp. "A little discretion, if you please!"

"Sorry," Jane said aloud.

"Don't speak!" said Byron. "Just *think*. Only don't think about anything you don't want overheard."

Immediately Jane began thinking about exactly those things.

"Ted and Ned?" Lilith said.

"Stop thinking!" Byron commanded. "Or focus on something to mask your thoughts. A poem or song, anything to occupy your mind."

"She really isn't very good at this, is she?" Lilith remarked.

Jane thought quickly, searching her mind for something to distract her from thinking about things she shouldn't. She suddenly could remember not a single nursery rhyme or song, and although she searched and searched for a poem with which to occupy herself, the only lines she could recall came from Chaucer's *Canterbury Tales,* which she'd learned as a child. *It will have to do,* she told herself, and began to recite them in her head.

> *Whan that Aprill, with his shoures soote*
> *The droghte of March hath perced to the roote*
> *And bathed every veyne in swich licour,*
> *Of which vertu engendred is the flour*

She found to her dismay that she could remember no more. She said the lines again, hoping that would jar her memory, but it did not. Worse, it made her think of her siblings, with whom she had learned the verses and performed them for their parents, eliciting much laughter with their attempts at Middle English.

Don't think about them, she thought even as she failed in this. Her own name—her real name—was threatening to reveal itself, and this she could not allow. If Lilith discovered her identity, then surely Miriam would, and no good could come of that.

Name the monarchs. The suggestion came to her as if Cassie herself had spoken the words. It was a challenge their father had set for them, listing all the rulers of England in chronological order. Jane and Cassie had often used the game as a way to make themselves fall asleep. Now Jane used it to keep her true thoughts hidden from Lilith.

Egbert, she began, surprised at how quickly it came to her.

Ethelwulf. Aethelbald. Ethelbert. Ethelred. Her memory faltered here, but after a few moments she recalled the next ruler. *Alfred the Great. Edward the Elder. Athelstan. Edmund. Eadred. Eadwig. Edgar. Edward the Martyr. Another Ethelred, this one the Unready. Edmund Ironside. Canute.*

"Jane!"

Byron's voice made her start, and she looked over at him.

"What are you doing?" he asked.

"Not thinking," said Jane.

"You're also not listening," Byron said. "You were just supposed to distract yourself long enough to focus on what we're doing."

"Oh," Jane said. "Sorry. Um, what are we doing?"

"Asking questions," said Byron.

"Right," Jane said. She straightened herself in her chair and once more looked at Lilith. The little dog was now lying down, her one front leg stretched out in front of her. She was no longer growling. "What are we talking about?"

"You were trying not to think about being Jane Austen," Lilith said. "So much for that."

"Damn it!" Jane said, hitting the arm of her chair with a fist.

"Nothing to be done about it now," said Byron. "Anyway, Lilith has given me some very interesting information."

"Such as?" Jane asked. She was very annoyed at having given herself away, and only half cared about what Byron was saying.

"As I suspected, Miriam is a hunter," he said.

"She was recruited in 1962 by a college professor," said Lilith. "She was studying ancient history and showed particular interest in the Sumerian legends of the undead. Gradually her mentor introduced her to the truth about vampires, and eventually she trained with six others, including Lee Harvey Oswald."

"Oswald?" Jane said. "The man who assassinated John F. Kennedy?"

"Yes," said Lilith.

"Are you saying Kennedy was a vampire?"

"And people thought his being Catholic was a problem," Byron remarked.

"Oswald thought he was," Lilith said. "Miriam didn't. Anyway, that's not important."

"So how did you get involved with her?" Jane asked.

"The story she told you is true," said Lilith. "She found me in Jerusalem. Actually, she rescued me from a vampire who had decided I would make a nice dinner. That's where my leg went."

Jane felt instant sympathy for the little dog and reached out to pet her. Lilith snarled and jumped back. "Don't touch me, fang face!" she said.

"I'm not going to hurt you," Jane said.

"Right," said Lilith. "You just like to stuff little dogs in boxes."

"We had to talk to you," Byron said. "Would you have come if we'd asked?"

Lilith eyed him suspiciously. "That depends," she said. "What do you have?"

"What do you mean, what do I have?" Byron asked.

"Just because I don't like your kind doesn't mean I can't be bought," said Lilith. "I'm a mercenary. I go where the money is."

"What about your allegiance to the Ellenberg woman?" said Byron. "You'd betray her?"

"I've already repaid her a dozen times," Lilith said. "I've helped her find and stake vamps all over the country. I don't owe her anything."

"Then why stay with her?" Jane asked.

"The food's good," said Lilith. "And I like to travel."

Byron chuckled. "I like this one," he said to Jane. To Lilith he said, "What's your price?"

Lilith blinked and licked her paw. "Like I said, what have you got?"

Byron smiled. "How about bacon?" he said.

Lilith looked up. "I'm listening," she said.

"I imagine Miriam never gives you bacon," said Byron. "You know, what with keeping kosher and all. Am I right?"

"You're not wrong," Lilith told him.

Byron nodded. "Then how about this. For every piece of solid information you give us about what Miriam and her defanged stooge are up to, we'll give you a quarter pound of premium hickory-smoked bacon."

Lilith licked her chops, and Jane sensed her thoughts humming busily. *She's thinking about it,* Jane told herself.

"Half a pound," Lilith said. "And you cook it for me."

"Naturally," said Byron. "Then we have a deal?"

"I'm still her dog," Lilith said. "Well, as much as I'm anyone's. So don't think I'm on your side. You're buying information, that's it."

"That's all we want," said Byron.

"Then we have a deal," Lilith told him.

Byron grinned. "Excellent," he said.

Lilith stood up and shook herself. "Now get me out of here," she said. "Miriam's probably freaking out."

Jane got up and went to the carrier.

"Uh-uh," Lilith said. "This time you carry me."

"May I pick you up?" Jane asked.

Lilith nodded. Jane scooped the dog up and held her to her chest. Lilith turned her head and looked up. "Jane Austen," she said as Jane walked to the door. "If Miriam knew this, she'd stake you on the spot. She hates your books."

"What about you?" Jane asked. "Do you like them?"

Lilith cocked her head. "Don't be ridiculous," she said. "Who ever heard of a dog that could read?"

Chapter 21

"KNOCK KNOCK."

Ben Cohen looked up from his desk to see Jane standing in the doorway of his office. He smiled at her and waved her in.

"I'm sorry to bother you," Jane apologized as she took a seat across from him. "Do you have some time to talk?"

Ben nodded. "I'll make time," he said as he shut the book he'd been perusing. "Have you come to talk more about conversion? I sort of got the impression that was off the table."

"It is," Jane said. "For now, anyway. I want to talk about relationships."

Ben smiled. "Okay," he said. "Any one in particular?"

"Let's say it's a hypothetical one," said Jane.

Ben nodded. "We can do that," he said.

Jane folded her hands in her lap and stared at them, trying to decide how to begin. Although both she and Ben knew that they were about to talk about her and Walter's relationship, Jane wasn't ready to use their names. In part this was because she was embarrassed, but more than that, it allowed her to pretend they *weren't* talking about her and Walter. That made it easier for her to ask the questions she needed to ask, as she could pretend they were discussing other people, or characters in a book.

"Let's say that you love someone," she began. "And that some-one loves you back."

"You think this person loves you back, or you know for sure?" asked Ben.

"You're quite certain about it," Jane said. "He—this person—has told you so."

"Got it," said Ben. "Go on."

"You want to be with this person," Jane continued. "In fact, you know that being together will make you very happy." She paused a moment. "But you also know that being together will ul-timately cause this person a great deal of misery."

"How can you know something like that?" asked Ben.

"You just do," said Jane. "Let's say there's something about yourself that the other person doesn't know, and that if he—if the other person found out, it would make that person very unhappy."

Ben leaned back in his chair. "What kind of thing might this be?" he asked.

Jane, feeling very uncomfortable, cleared her throat. "Does it matter?" she asked.

"Yes," said Ben. "For instance, let's say this thing is something you—and I'm using *you* hypothetically here—have done. Com-mitted a crime and spent time in jail, for example. You're afraid that if your partner finds out about this, he—and again I'm being hypothetical—will be horrified and think badly of you. That's one kind of problem. But your problem might be something bigger, something more—ongoing, for lack of a better word."

"Ongoing," Jane repeated. "Ongoing how?"

"That you have a child you never mentioned," said Ben. "Or that you're addicted to something or have a gambling problem. Anything that isn't limited by time."

"I still don't see how it matters," Jane said.

"Events in the past—isolated things we've done that might be upsetting to a partner—are generally easier to accept," Ben ex-plained. "Especially if they occurred before the relationship began. But an issue that's ongoing, that is in some way still occurring, that's often more difficult to handle. We can't compartmentalize it and say, 'Okay, this happened in the past but it's over now and my partner isn't the same person who did that thing.' Instead, we're now looking at this partner as someone we never really knew at all."

"Wouldn't that happen in either case?" said Jane.

"Possibly, but often no," Ben replied. "We're far more likely to forgive things in our partners that happened in the past."

"Time heals all wounds," said Jane.

"Or in this case, time makes it possible to accept nasty surprises. So which situation are we dealing with here?"

"Ongoing," Jane told him. "Well, a little of both, actually. But mostly ongoing."

"And this thing—whatever it is—is something the partner won't be able to handle?"

Jane thought about this. Could Walter handle finding out she was a vampire? She suspected he could, or at least he would think he could. And maybe for a time things would be fine. But what would happen when the perceived age difference between them became obvious? Then how would he feel about being with her?

Jane suddenly realized that she'd been asking the wrong question. Yes, Walter was the one who would have to accept something about her he could never have imagined. But she would be the one left alone when he died, as he inevitably would. In some ways he would live out his life as he always would have, except that his wife would never age. But it was Jane who would be left with the loss of him, Jane who had to watch everyone she loved leave her over and over again.

There was, however, another option.

"You know the story of Beauty and the Beast, don't you?" she asked Ben.

"Of course," he said. "It's one of Sarah's favorites."

"What does she like about it?" asked Jane.

"She likes that Beauty sees that the Beast is really a good man," he said.

Jane nodded. "Exactly. Now let me ask you this—how would she feel if instead of the Beast becoming a prince because Beauty loves him, Beauty became a beast? They would still live happily ever after, but Beauty would be someone that others were afraid of."

"I don't think she'd like that very much," said Ben. "The whole idea is that love sees what others can't, the real us beneath the dirt and grime."

"Sure," Jane said. "But if the two beasts love each other, isn't that all that matters? Can't beasts have happily ever after without becoming princes or princesses?"

"I guess Shrek and Fiona kind of have that," said Ben.

"Who?" Jane asked.

"Sorry," said Ben, laughing. "You probably don't get dragged to a lot of animated movies. Shrek is an ogre who falls in love with a beautiful princess. Long story short, she's under a curse that turns her into an ogre at night. Only true love's kiss can break the spell. Eventually Shrek kisses her and the spell is broken. But instead of returning to her human form Fiona remains an ogre. She's horrified, but Shrek tells her she's beautiful and she realizes that his love for her is all she's ever really wanted."

"But everyone else still thinks she's hideous, right?" said Jane.

Ben shrugged. "Some of them," he said. "But not everyone."

Jane sighed. "That's the problem right there," she said. "Even if the person you love accepts the real you, you haven't changed who you are. Just ask King Kong. Fay Wray came to love him, but he still fell off the Empire State Building."

"Jane, whatever it is you're worried about, I'm sure you and Walter can get through it," Ben said.

Jane smiled. "So much for being hypothetical," she said.

"I haven't known you long," Ben told her. "But I think I can safely say that there's nothing about you that the right man couldn't accept."

"How can you say that?" Jane said. "For all you know I might have murdered a family of five by mixing ant paste into their tea."

"Did you?" asked Ben.

Jane shook her head. "No," she said. "I lured them one by one into the woods and bashed their heads in with a rock."

Ben laughed. "Look, whatever it is you think Walter won't be able to accept, the only way you're going to find out is if you tell him what it is. May I ask, have you told *anyone*?"

Jane thought about Lucy. "Yes," she said.

"And does he or she still accept you?"

Jane nodded. "But Walter is different."

"Different how?" asked Ben.

"I'm in love with him," Jane said. "That changes everything. If I lose him . . ." Her words trailed off, for she could think of no way to adequately explain how she felt.

When Ben spoke, his voice was gentle. "So rather than have him reject you, you're not giving him the chance," he said.

It was some time before Jane answered. "I suppose I am," she admitted.

"Then you're a fool," Ben said.

Jane, surprised, looked at him.

"Well, you are," said Ben. "Don't expect me to pretend you're right, because you aren't. You're not giving Walter a chance. And why? Because you're scared he won't love the real you."

"I don't see anything so unusual about that," Jane argued. Her feelings were slightly hurt by Ben's brusqueness, even if deep down she knew he was right.

"Oh, it's not unusual," said Ben. "But that doesn't make it any less stupid. Now get out of my office."

"What?" said Jane. "Why?"

Ben stood up. "Because you're wasting my time," he said. He came around to the other side of his desk, took Jane's hands, and pulled her to her feet. "And you're wasting *your* time," he said. "You're a wonderful woman. But you're being a fool."

"Are you this direct with everyone who comes to you for advice?" Jane asked.

"Only the ones I like," said Ben. "Now go. I have work to do."

Jane walked toward the door, but Ben called her name. "Take this," he said, walking over and handing her something.

"What is it?" Jane asked.

"A DVD of *Shrek*," Ben told her. "It's one of Sarah's favorites, so I always keep a copy here in the office in case I need to entertain her."

"I don't think—" Jane said.

"Just watch it," said Ben. "And don't come back until you do."

Jane read the description of the movie on the back of the DVD as she walked to her car. She had no intention whatsoever of watching an animated movie about an ogre and a talking donkey, even if it *was* based on a William Steig book (she adored his picture book *Dominic*). She put the DVD in her purse and forgot about it.

Having not entirely had the conversation with Ben Cohen that she'd wished to have, Jane now did something she had never done before. Driving to the area of Brakeston closest to Meade College, she parked her car, removed from the backseat a bag containing her laptop, and walked to the nearest coffeehouse. There she ordered a latte, took a seat at a table near the front window, and began to work on her novel.

She had often seen people—mostly students from the college —busily engrossed in doing something (she assumed writing) on their laptop computers in coffeehouses all over town. Although the idea of working on one's craft in public had never seemed to her to be quite polite, she wondered if perhaps a change of scenery might not give her a new perspective on her book.

After ten minutes she decided that it apparently did not. Despite staring doggedly at the screen of her laptop, she had not written a word. She glanced to her left and saw a young man with papers and books spread across his table tapping manically at his keyboard. Pretending to stretch, she leaned in his direction to get a look at what he was doing.

The screen was filled with what appeared to be a picture of a factory. A series of pink shapes moved up and down, as well as from side to side, as something round and blue bounced between them. The man appeared to be guiding the blue ball by tapping the keys of his computer.

The blue ball dropped into a basket at the bottom of the screen and a series of numbers flashed rapidly on the lower left-hand side. The man, noticing that Jane was looking at his screen, said, "It's a total waste of time, but I'm addicted to it."

"What is it?" Jane inquired.

"It's called Sushi Cat," said the man. "See all of the little pieces of sushi?"

Jane moved her chair closer and peered at the screen. "Why, so they are," she said. "How clever."

"And here's the cat," the man said, pressing a key. The blue ball appeared at the top of the screen and Jane saw that it was in fact a cartoon cat.

"You drop the cat from anywhere up here," said the man, demonstrating. "It falls between the gears or the balls or whatever and it eats the pieces of sushi. If you can get him to eat enough pieces, you go to the next level."

Jane watched as the cat ate piece after piece of sushi, growing fatter with every bite. She saw absolutely no point in the game, but she found herself fascinated. "Can I try it?" she asked the young man after he'd successfully finished a level.

"You can play it on your laptop," he answered. "Just do a search for Sushi Cat and you'll find it. It's a free game."

"Thank you," Jane said, leaving him to his game. She opened

the browser on her computer, found that she could connect to the Internet through the shop's free Wi-Fi, and soon located the Sushi Cat website.

An hour later, having made it to level nine, she paused to get another latte and a scone. She promised herself that once she cleared level ten she would begin writing.

The completion of level thirteen saw her coffee cup empty and the scone reduced to crumbs, but not a word had been written. Jane glanced at the clock and discovered that she'd been sitting in the shop for more than two hours and had accomplished nothing. *If you can call a score of 654,890 on Sushi Cat nothing*, she argued.

Annoyed with herself, she closed the game and opened her word-processing program. Locating the file for her novel, she clicked on it and prepared to read what she'd written so far.

> The koi pond was filled with the detritus of fall. Staring into it, Lydia searched in vain for the fish she had watched swim there in the summer. She had fed them from her hand, their whiskered lips breaking the water as they competed for her attentions. Now she prayed for the briefest flash of orange or gold, the merest flip of a tail to indicate that something still lived in the brown water.

"Koi?" she said under her breath. "When did I write about koi? And why?"

She had no memory of putting those words to paper, as it were. But there they were. She read more, but it was equally hideous. She thought hard and vaguely remembered a bottle of merlot. Possibly two. Had there also been some typing involved?

"Apparently so," she answered herself.

It was all dreadful, every last word. Lydia (and she had not the foggiest idea who Lydia was or why she was looking anxiously into a koi pond) was dull and a bit of a whiner. There seemed to be no plot whatsoever, nor really any incentive to keep reading at all. Hoping to stumble across something she could use—some bit of prose that might be salvaged and used to build something better—Jane skimmed over several paragraphs about a pair of woolen mittens. When she arrived at some dialogue between Lydia and a child holding a balloon, she highlighted the entire document and deleted it.

She closed the computer, shut her eyes, and wished she hadn't eaten the scone. It was disagreeing with her. Also, she had a headache, and now the music from Sushi Cat was playing in her head.

She got up and left, tossing her coffee cup in the trash and angrily pushing the door open. The afternoon sun was hot and the light hurt her eyes. Finally, to make things even worse, she walked two blocks in the wrong direction looking for her car before remembering that she was driving a loaner from the garage where her car was being repaired.

She considered going to the bookstore and having a chat with Lucy, but decided to go home instead. Lucy would almost certainly still be giddy over her new relationship with Ben Cohen, and although Jane was sincerely happy for her, she didn't want to be exposed to that much joy. She just wanted to go home, open a bottle of wine, and not think about anything.

It wasn't until her phone rang and she recognized Byron's number on the caller ID that she remembered she was supposed to be watching Chloe. She'd promised to relieve Byron at four. It was now half past. For a moment she considered just not answering. *You could always tell him you got busy writing and lost track of time,* she thought.

"Like he'd ever believe that," she said as she answered the call. "I'll be there in ten," she told Byron, and turned the car around.

Chapter 22

"How nice of you to come," said Byron as Jane entered Chloe's trailer. "I hope we aren't inconveniencing you."

"Just a little," Jane sniped.

Chloe was seated in one of the chairs, a script open on her lap. Her eyes were closed and she was silently mouthing some words. She was dressed in a white poodle skirt and a pink angora sweater. Jane couldn't bear to look at her.

"What is she doing?" she asked Byron.

"Learning her lines," Byron explained. "She's shooting a scene with Tucker Mack this afternoon. It's the scene where Jonathan seduces Barbara after taking her for a ride in his new Chevy Bel Air convertible. Wait until you see the car they got. It's a beauty. Red and white. I had one exactly like it in 1955." A dreamy look appeared on his face. "I took Scotty Mulligan to see *Rebel Without a Cause* at the drive-in in that car. He was captain of the football team."

"How romantic," Jane teased. "Did you go to the malt shop afterward?"

"Of course not," said Byron. "We went necking." He clicked his fangs into place and gave Jane a lecherous leer. "I think I still have his class ring somewhere."

"Wait a minute," Jane said, ignoring him. "There's no scene in

Constance where Jonathan seduces Barbara, let alone in a convertible."

"There is now," said Byron, getting ready to leave. "What's-her-name wrote it not an hour ago."

"Who?" Jane asked.

"The Frost woman," said Byron. "And I must say, she's quite good. You could learn a thing or two from her."

"Out!" Jane ordered.

Byron, laughing, went invisible and slipped out the door, leaving Jane alone with Chloe. The girl had said not a single word during Jane and Byron's exchange and seemed almost to be in a trance as she continued to mouth her lines. Now, as Jane stared at her, her eyes opened.

"Hey," she said. "When did you get here?"

"Ages ago," said Jane, now in a foul mood. "Thank you for noticing."

"Run lines with me," Chloe said, thrusting her script at Jane.

"Excuse me?" said Jane.

"Run lines," Chloe repeated. "You read Tucker's lines and I'll say mine. It's how we practice."

Jane took the script from the girl and plopped down in the trailer's other chair. She looked at the script and found Tucker's first line.

"'I hope you had a nice time,'" she read.

"Don't use your voice," Chloe said. "I can't do a romantic scene with a *woman*. Try to sound like a man."

Jane began to object, but Chloe said, "Please. It will really help."

"Fine," Jane huffed. She cleared her throat and began again, this time making her voice lower and gruffer. "'I hope you had a nice time,'" she said.

"That's better," Chloe said. "Now me. 'I had a swell time, Jonathan. Thank you for asking me. To tell the truth, I wasn't sure you liked me.'"

"Swell?" said Jane in her own voice. "Who says *swell*?"

"Just read the lines," Chloe said. "I didn't write them, so don't get mad at me."

Jane gritted her teeth. "'Why would you think that?'" she read.

Chloe shrugged. "'I don't know,'" she said in a breathy voice. "'I guess because you're always talking to Connie, and you gave her your letterman sweater.'"

"Please tell me she didn't rename Constance Connie," Jane said, putting a hand to her forehead. "Please tell me that."

"You really suck at this," Chloe replied, snatching the script from Jane's hand. "Forget it. I'll do it myself."

"I'm sorry," said Jane. "I can do it. It's just that this is all very upsetting."

"I don't know why," Chloe said. "They're making a *movie* out of your book. You should be happy about it."

"You wouldn't understand," said Jane. "You've never written a book."

"No," Chloe agreed. "But I know if I did I'd be pretty excited if someone liked it enough to make a movie out of it."

Jane sighed. "I suppose you're right," she said. "Still, it's not really my book anymore. It's someone else's story now."

"Oh, boo-hoo," said Chloe, picking up a pack of cigarettes and tapping one into her hand. She began to light it, then suddenly stubbed it out. "Shit. I can't smoke."

"Why not?" Jane asked.

"Tucker has a thing about cigarettes," Chloe explained. "If you're going to kiss him, you can't taste like cigarettes."

"That sounds like a reasonable request," said Jane.

Chloe snorted. "Yeah, except that *he* always tastes like garlic." She looked at Jane with a worried expression. "Do I have to worry about that?" she asked. "You know, the whole garlic thing?"

Jane shook her head. "Probably not," she said. "That's pretty much a myth, although some vampires do have an allergic reaction to it. But you should be fine."

"How will I know if I'm allergic?" Chloe said.

"Well, you'll probably break out in hives," Jane explained.

"Hives?" said Chloe. "Like beehives?"

Jane wondered if the girl was joking, realized she wasn't, and said, "Not like beehives, no. Like welts." Chloe looked at her blankly, so Jane added, "Small red spots that itch."

"Right," Chloe said. "I get those when I'm around cats."

"So you're allergic to cats?" said Jane. "Then you know."

"Oh, I'm not allergic," Chloe said. "I just get all itchy and sneeze and stuff."

Jane decided against further discussion of the subject and said simply, "I'm sure you'll be fine."

A knock at the door interrupted them. "Come in," Chloe shouted.

A young woman holding a clipboard and looking very anxious poked her head in and said, "They're ready for you on set, Chloe."

Chloe stood up. "You coming?" she asked Jane.

"I don't know," said Jane. "I might be in the way."

"Oh, come on," Chloe prodded. "It'll be fun."

Jane hesitated a moment, then stood up. "Maybe it will," she said.

The two of them left the trailer and walked over to where a camera had been set up near a convertible parked in front of the house that in the movie belonged to the Wexley family. In reality it belonged to Agatha Martin, the town librarian. In a stroke of good fortune, Agatha had maintained the house exactly as it had looked in 1955, when she'd been a sixteen-year-old sophomore at Brakeston High and lived there with her family. As a result, the set decorator had only to remove the satellite dish from Agatha's roof and add a few more garden gnomes to those already occupying the petunia beds.

Julia Baxter was peering at a monitor when Jane and Chloe

approached. Seeing them, she straightened up. "All right, people!" she called out. "Let's make a movie!"

All around them crew members scrambled to do their various jobs. Jane watched in amazement as what had moments ago seemed like total chaos turned into an operation of military precision with Julia Baxter as the commander.

"I should have eaten something," Chloe said to Jane as lights were adjusted and someone polished the convertible's hood. "My stomach is growling."

Jane stiffened. "Your stomach is growling?" she asked.

Chloe nodded. "I should have had a muffin or some toast or something."

"No," said Jane. "That wouldn't help."

What Chloe needed was blood. It hadn't occurred to Jane that the girl might be hungry. She'd assumed Byron had taken care of that. But perhaps Chloe hadn't realized what was happening to her. It was difficult the first few times it happened to differentiate the need for blood from normal human hunger.

Before Jane could do anything, Tucker Mack appeared. Like Chloe, he was dressed like a 1950s student, wearing jeans, a striped polo shirt, and a varsity jacket with PEARSON HIGH SCHOOL written on the back in white letters. His dark hair was slicked back.

"Pearson High School," Jane said, distracted by the jacket. "There's no Pearson High School in *Constance*. There's no high school at all."

"I had to write it in," said a voice.

Jane turned to her right and saw Shirley standing there. She was holding a script on which were numerous cross-outs and arrows and words scribbled in the margins.

"Pearson is the name of one of the producers," Shirley continued. "He wanted to be in the movie somehow, and this was an easy way to do it. Just be glad Elena Wawrzyniak-Kobayashi settled for an extra half a percent of the gross. We'd never have gotten that on a jacket."

"Chloe, get in the car," Jane heard Julia Baxter say.

"Wait a moment," Jane said, grabbing the girl's wrist. "You need to eat something," she whispered in Chloe's ear. "And I don't mean a muffin. You need blood."

"Chloe!" Julia called.

Chloe pulled away from Jane. "There's no time," she said. "Besides, I'll be fine. This won't take long."

Jane watched, tension rising in her belly, as Chloe got into the convertible. Tucker Mack was already seated behind the steering wheel, one arm on the edge of the door and the other stretched along the back of the seat.

"All right," Julia said. "Chloe, I want you to lean into him as he says his lines. But look a little bit afraid, as if you don't know what he's going to do."

Julia put a pair of headphones over her ears and took a seat behind the camera. A boom was lowered over the car so that the microphone was only a few feet above the heads of the actors.

"And action!" Julia called out.

"'I hope you had a nice time,'" Tucker said.

"'I had a swell time, Jonathan,'" Chloe said. "'Thank you for asking me. To tell the truth, I wasn't sure you liked me.'"

Despite her worries about Chloe's hunger, Jane found herself entranced by what was happening. The lines that only minutes ago had been just words on paper were now coming to life. It still wasn't the story Jane had written, but it was exciting nevertheless.

"'Of course I like you, Barbara,'" Tucker was saying. "'I like you just fine. Connie doesn't matter to me.'"

Chloe ducked her head. "'You're just saying that,'" she said.

Tucker put his arm around her. "'That's not so,'" he said. "'Honest I'm not. Would I do this if I didn't really like you?'"

He pulled Chloe to him and kissed her. Chloe's hand went to his neck as their lips met. Tucker put his other arm on her waist. Then, all of a sudden, Chloe pulled away.

"Shit!" she said, no longer sounding like demure little Barbara. She looked at her face in the convertible's mirror. "You've been eating garlic," she said to Tucker.

"Yeah," he answered. "But I used mouthwash."

"That's not the problem," Chloe said, getting out of the car. She ran over to Jane. "Are these hives?" she asked, thrusting her face into Jane's. "They itch like hell."

Jane looked closely at the girl's face. Where Tucker had kissed her lips and cheek there were now red blotches. Chloe reached up and scratched at them. Jane pulled her hand away. "That will just make it worse," she said.

Julia Baxter walked over to them. "What's the problem?" she asked, sounding annoyed.

"She has allergies," said Jane. "To garlic, apparently."

"Fantastic," the director said. "Makeup!" she yelled.

A man came running carrying a small case.

"Cover the spots," Julia told him, pointing to Chloe.

"No," Jane said. When Julia and the man looked at her she added, "You can't just cover them up. They'll still itch."

"Then she'll have to not scratch them," Julia said. "Not until we've got the scene shot. Then she can scratch all she wants."

Chloe, who at that very moment was scratching at her cheek, stopped when Julia glared at her. "It's not that bad," she said.

"Ansel, fix her face," said Julia.

The man opened the case and removed a tube of foundation. "This should do it," he said as he dabbed some on each of Chloe's hives and smoothed it out. "Just don't touch it," he told her as he dusted powder over the makeup.

"Chloe, I really don't think this is a good idea," said Jane.

"I'll be *fine*," Chloe hissed, trying not to move her mouth as Ansel applied a fresh coat of lipstick.

"Jane, why don't you stand over there," Julia suggested. Her voice was friendly but firm, and Jane decided now was not the time to argue. Maybe Chloe could get through the scene without further incident. Then they could take care of both her hives and her hunger.

"Is everything okay?" Posey asked when Jane came over to her.

"Fine," Jane said. "Everything is going well."

"I want to tell you again how sorry I am that I have to make changes to your book," Shirley said. "If it's any consolation, when the first Vivienne Minx book was made into a movie they decided that instead of being a black girl from Alabama whose ancestors were slaves who used their monster-hunting skills to fight the Klan she should be a white girl from California who got her skills from a magic amulet she found while scuba diving in the Bahamas."

"You're joking," said Jane.

"I'm not," Shirley said. "The good news is that the books weren't hugely popular then and the movie only made it to cable. When we did the first real Vivienne Minx movie I had enough clout that I could insist they stick to the book. Well, more or less."

"How did you explain the first movie?" Jane asked.

"Easy," said Shirley. "We said it was all a bad dream Vivienne had after being bitten by a werewolf."

"Do you think Julia would let you work a werewolf into this script?" Jane said.

Shirley laughed. "Don't tempt me," she said.

"Quiet on the set!" someone yelled as Jane stifled a giggle.

Once more the scene began. This time Tucker and Chloe were only a few seconds into the kiss before Chloe began beating at him with her hands. As soon as he let go she leapt from the car and ran toward her trailer, her hands clawing at her face as she shrieked in pain.

"Get her back here!" the director barked.

An assistant started toward the trailer, but Jane intervened. "I'll get her," she said. As she walked away she heard Tucker Mack say loudly, "It was only hummus, for Christ's sake!"

Jane found Chloe scrubbing her face with a washcloth. "Don't," she said. "It will just make it worse. We need to put some calamine lotion on it."

"It burns," Chloe whined as Jane took the washcloth away. "I thought you said it wouldn't."

"I said it *probably* wouldn't," said Jane. "Apparently you are allergic."

"Great," Chloe said. "How am I supposed to get through the scene?"

Jane thought for a moment. "Maybe if you feed," she said. "You might be particularly sensitive to the garlic because you're hungry."

Chloe scratched her chin. "And how am I supposed to do that?" she said. "I can't just go off looking for someone to bite."

"No, I suppose you can't," Jane agreed.

Chloe brightened. "I could bite Tucker," she said. "When he's kissing me. I mean, his neck will be *right there.*"

"That's a splendid idea," said Jane. "And it will all be caught on film, so the entire world can see it."

"Oh," Chloe said. "Right. I forgot about that."

"It's all right," said Jane kindly. "Being hungry makes you a little stupid." She batted Chloe's hand away from her cheek as the girl went to scratch it again.

"What are we going to do?" Chloe moaned. "Julia's going to have a fit if I don't get back out there soon."

As Jane searched for a solution there was a knock on the door. A moment later a young man's face appeared. Jane recognized him as one of the several assistants who always seemed to be trailing after the various producers. "Chloe, she wants to know how long you're going to be," the young man said. "We're losing the light, and we can't afford to get behind."

"Tell her she can go—" Chloe began.

"Actually, I'll go speak to her," Jane interrupted. She looked at the boy. "What's your name?"

"Cedric."

"Well, Cedric, would you be a dear and help Chloe apply some lotion?"

Chloe looked at Jane with a confused expression. Jane leaned down. "He's already half in love with you," she whispered. "I can tell. He'll be very susceptible. But just drink a *little,* do you understand?"

She turned to Cedric. "I believe there's a bottle of calamine lotion in the bathroom," she said. She stared into his eyes and cast a glamor. Cedric's eyes glazed over and he nodded. "I can do that," he said.

Jane looked at Chloe. "Five minutes," she said. "And *not too much.*"

She left the trailer, shutting the door behind her. She hoped Chloe would do as she was told. If not, it would be a disaster, or at least a very big mess. She was taking an enormous risk leaving the girl alone for her first feeding, but it was the only way.

"Where is she?" Julia Baxter asked as Jane came up to her.

"She'll be out in a few minutes," said Jane. "She just needs to put some calamine lotion on."

The director shook her head. "I hate working with pop stars," she said. "If it isn't allergies, it's cocaine addiction or being in a cult or some other bullshit."

"She's trying very hard," Jane said, suddenly feeling very protective of Chloe. "It's not her fault she's allergic."

Julia snorted. "It's never their fault," she said. "It's not *their* fault they can't remember their lines. It's not *their* fault they got drunk and fell down. It's not *their* fault the sex tape got leaked the week before the premiere and Disney totally freaked out. It's never their fault."

Jane tuned Julia out as she continued to rave about the irresponsibility of pop stars, how no one respected directors anymore, and how she ought to have signed on to the independent film about the Brazilian street orphan who was found to be the reincarnation of the Dalai Lama.

"I bet Kathryn Bigelow doesn't have to put up with this crap!" she raged. "I'm giving that girl two minutes to get out here or I'm quit—"

"Here I am," said Chloe.

Jane looked up to see the girl standing there smiling. The hives were gone and her skin was flawless. There was a glow about her that hadn't been there five minutes before. Jane recognized it at once, and she looked at Chloe with raised eyebrows.

Chloe nodded slightly. Then she looked at Julia and said, "I'm sorry about before."

"Then you're ready to shoot now?" asked the director.

Chloe beamed. "Of course," she said. "I just needed a little snack."

Chapter 23

IF THE HEART-SHAPED GATES FESTOONED WITH HUNDREDS OF RED and pink roses weren't enough to let anyone entering the fairgrounds know that love was the theme of the carnival, the half dozen men dressed like cupids walking around handing out candy hearts would have provided an additional clue. One—an attractive, well-muscled redhead wearing a short white tunic and little else—approached Jane and held out a basket. Jane shook her head firmly and walked away.

Lucy, however, took a handful of hearts. She handed one each to Byron, Ben, and Sarah. "What do they say?" she asked.

Ben peered at his. "'Kiss Me,'" he read.

"Don't mind if I do," said Lucy, giving him a peck on the cheek.

"Mine says, 'You're Cute!'" said Sarah. "I already know that. I should get another one."

Lucy looked at the candies in her hand. "This one is perfect for you," she told the little girl as she handed her another heart.

"'Girl Power,'" Sarah read. "Only it's spelled G-R-R-L. I like that." She popped the candy into her mouth, then growled. "Grrrl power," she said.

"And what's written on your hard little heart?" Jane asked Byron, smiling tightly.

"Mine is slightly less thrilling," Byron said. "It says 'Love Bug.' I have absolutely no idea what that means."

"It means you're infested," said Jane.

"You're just determined to have a horrible time, aren't you?" Lucy said to Jane. She hooked her arm through Jane's and walked beside her. "Come on. It isn't that bad."

"It's worse," Jane countered.

Lucy laughed. "Cheer up, or I won't tell you what my heart said."

"Let me guess," said Jane. "It said 'Sour Puss.'"

"That would be for you," Lucy teased. "Guess again."

"I don't want to guess," said Jane. "I want to go home."

"Quit being a big baby," Lucy said. "Revel in the hideousness of Beverly Shrop's festival of romance."

"It's more like a nightmare," Jane groused.

"Fine, I'll tell you," said Lucy. "It said 'Marry Me.'"

Jane raised an eyebrow. "No wonder you ate it so quickly," she said.

"Oh, I didn't eat that one," said Lucy. "I saved it. The one I ate said 'Tell Jane to take the stick out of her butt and have a good time with her friends.'"

"Cheeky candy," Jane said, feigning offense. Then she laughed. "And why are you saving the other one?"

Lucy leaned in. "Maybe I'll give it to Ben later."

"You wouldn't!" said Jane.

Lucy shrugged. "You never know," she replied. "I'm feeling impulsive."

"What are you two whispering about?" Ben called out.

"Yeah," Sarah agreed. "Whispering is *rude.*"

"I'm just telling Jane that she needs a funnel cake," said Lucy.

Jane groaned. "You live to see me suffer, don't you?" she said.

The five of them continued to stroll through the festival. Jane had to admit—albeit very grudgingly—that Beverly Shrop had managed to put together a fairly impressive event. Although many of the vendors and attractions were typical of any small carnival, they had been altered slightly to highlight the theme of romance. A ring toss game was played with giant fake diamond rings. Pink cotton candy was puffed into the shape of hearts. Strolling clowns made balloon flowers and handed them to happy passersby.

Even the prizes for winning the games were apropos of the romance motif. Those who were able to hit a target, select the winning rubber ducky from a pool, or correctly guess under which coconut shell the red ball was hidden received copies of popular romance novels instead of stuffed bears or tacky plastic toys. Beverly had thoughtfully provided each booth with stacks of pink canvas book bags embroidered with her website's name and logo. Everywhere they went Jane and her friends were among a sea of advertisements for ShropTalk.com.

Jane very much wanted to talk to Byron about Beverly, specifically about the progress Ned was making with romancing her. She knew that he had asked Beverly out for dinner the night before last, but she'd had no report on his results. She wondered now if it had been worth trying. Given Ned's past behavior, Jane feared he might inadvertently give them away.

Not that she and Miriam don't already know Byron and I are vampires, she reminded herself. *But they don't know that we know that they know that we're vampires. That's something. And hopefully they don't know about Chloe.*

Although Lilith had seen Jane bite Chloe, it seemed she had not realized that Jane was turning the girl and not just feeding on her. Further discussions with the little dog had turned up no evidence that Miriam knew anything about any other vampires being in Brakeston (and they had been careful not to let Lilith know that there were any, lest she tell her mistress). Jane found this both interesting and befuddling, as they still didn't know how Miriam had found out about Byron. Lilith didn't know either, or was lying when she said she didn't, but Jane was fairly confident the dog was telling the truth. Bacon had a way of bringing out the truth in her.

She was trying very hard not to imagine Ned on a date with Beverly when they turned a corner and found themselves blocked by a group of women. They were all looking in the direction of a large tank of water. Perched above the tank on a small seat connected to a metal arm was Ned. He was dressed in the costume of a Regency gentleman, and above him was a sign reading DUNK DARCY.

Beverly Shrop herself was standing on a raised platform beside the tank. She too was done up in a costume suitable for a woman of Jane's time, although Jane thought the dress slightly too young for a woman of Beverly's age.

"Who will try to dunk our Mr. Darcy?" Beverly cried out, her amplified voice trembling with excitement as it trickled from a tinny speaker. "Five dollars gets you three chances to send him into the drink. As you can see, he is still dry. Won't you be the first to get him wet?"

"Well he's gone and got himself into it, hasn't he?" Byron remarked. "Good boy, our Ted."

"Ned," said Jane. "I think."

"Come now," Beverly called. "Surely there's one among you who has always wanted to give Mr. Fitzwilliam Darcy a good dunking. How about you, madam?"

Beverly pointed to a middle-aged woman dressed in too-tight red pedal pushers and a T-shirt reading TEAM EDWARD. The woman giggled and covered her mouth with one hand, the other being occupied with holding a bulging pink ShropTalk.com tote. The woman's friend, equally middle-aged and wearing what appeared to be a tribute to Scarlett O'Hara, nudged her friend forward. "Go on, Ellie," she said.

Ellie handed her bag to her friend and made her way through the crowd of onlookers. Beverly stepped down from the platform and handed the woman three softballs.

"Take your time," she said. "And make sure you hit it hard."

Ellie threw the first ball, which sailed very close to Ned's head, making him duck.

"No, dear," Beverly said, laughing gaily. "Don't throw the ball at Darcy. Throw it at the big red heart to the left of him. *That's* the target."

Ellie, embarrassed, covered her face and turned to the crowd, which erupted in applause and urged her on. "Go for it, Ellie!" someone cried. "You can do it."

The second ball flew wide, missing the heart target by a good four feet. By the time Ellie took her third throw she was so anxious that the ball didn't even make it across the tank, falling into the water with a soft plop as the crowd groaned its disappointment. Ned looked down at it bobbing beneath him and seemed relieved.

A second woman, much younger and more athletic than Ellie, took her turn. All three of her pitches came close to the target, missing by only a few inches each time. Ned, apparently having decided that he was invincible, began calling out to the audience.

"Can't any of you throw?" he yelled, grinning madly. "Come on! Show me what you've got!"

Beverly scanned the crowd, and her eyes stopped at Byron. "You, sir!" she called out. "Come up here."

Byron hesitated, but Jane whispered to him, "Don't give her any reason to suspect we're on to her." Nodding his agreement, he walked through the crowd.

"Ladies and gentlemen," Beverly said, "I am very, very pleased and honored to welcome Mr. Tavish Osborn."

At the mention of the name a collective gasp went up from the crowd. Byron, turning, waved at them all. "Hello!" he said cheerfully.

"As you all surely know, Mr. Osborn is the author behind the Penelope Wentz novels," said Beverly. "He will also be joining us for tomorrow morning's panels, where he will be talking about the real Jane Austen."

Byron looked in Jane's direction, caught her eye, and winked. Jane frowned. She'd forgotten about his talk. Now that she remembered, she was annoyed anew. *I'll have to have a chat with him about that,* she thought.

Beverly handed Byron three softballs. "Let's see what a man can do," she said. Jane thought she heard a note of mockery in the woman's voice, but Beverly's face was all smiles.

Byron hefted one of the balls, aimed it at the target, and began to throw it. At the last second he cupped the ball in his hand and brought it back. "You know what I think I need?" he said loudly. "I think I need a good-luck charm."

"A good-luck charm?" said Beverly, clearly taken aback. "Such as?"

"A kiss from a pretty lady," Byron answered.

Beverly blushed. "Well, I suppose I—"

"Sarah, will you come help me out?" Byron interrupted.

Beverly balked. "Sarah?" she said. "Who is Sarah?"

Lucy, holding Sarah's hand, called for the crowd to let them through. She led the little girl to the front of the tank, where Byron bent down and said, "How about a kiss for me?"

Sarah kissed him on the cheek and Byron pretended to swoon. Sarah and the crowd laughed, but Beverly scowled at the little girl for a moment before the fake smile returned to her face. Jane, who had been watching her, was pleased to see that Byron's stunt was annoying her.

Byron took aim once again and threw the ball. It narrowly missed the target, eliciting oohs from the crowd, who were now hungry to see poor Ned get a dunking. Byron took up the second ball and once again knelt for Sarah to give him a kiss.

"He certainly has a way with the ladies, doesn't he?" Ben said to Jane.

"By—I mean Tavish?" Jane said. "Yes, I suppose he does. And then some."

She wondered what Ben would say if he knew his daughter

had just kissed Lord Byron. *For that matter, what would he say if he knew he was standing next to Jane Austen?* she thought. She felt sympathy for the rabbi. Having fallen for Lucy, he was getting far more than he'd bargained for. *Unless we never tell him,* Jane told herself.

Suddenly she was overcome with a deep sadness. She was thrilled that Lucy had found someone she could love. But it meant that eventually Jane would have to give up their friendship. Unless Ben knew about her, he would start wondering why Jane never aged. Lucy would always be hiding something from him, and Jane knew from experience how difficult that was.

This was exactly the situation she'd wanted to avoid. Telling Lucy about herself had been a great relief. But part of her had always worried that it would lead to heartache. Now it seemed destined to do just that. Expecting Lucy to keep such an important secret from the people she loved most was too great a thing to ask. And the more people who knew, the riskier it was for all of them.

I've already put them in danger, Jane realized. *Just by letting them be my friends.*

Another groan from the crowd snapped Jane out of her thoughts. Byron had missed again. With one ball left he once more bent down for Sarah's kiss. This time, though, she said something in his ear. He nodded and, grinning, stood up.

"Sarah has decided that the third and final throw should go to someone else," he said. He paused a moment. "Miss Jane Fairfax, would you please join us?"

Jane heard her name repeated by several people in the crowd. She also saw Beverly Shrop search the sea of faces, a bitter expression on her face. Jane had been tempted to slink away, but seeing Beverly's reaction, the sadness in her turned to anger. *Who does she think she is?* she thought.

"Excuse me," she said firmly, making her way toward Byron and Sarah.

"Well, this is a pleasant surprise," Beverly announced. "Our very own Jane Fairfax, author of *Constance*, has joined us. Jane, say hello to your fans."

"Hello," Jane muttered as Beverly thrust the microphone in her face. "Cheers. Thanks for coming."

She felt like an idiot. But there was no time to sulk. Byron was handing her the softball, and Sarah was tugging at her hand. Jane bent down to see what the girl wanted.

"I saved this for you," Sarah whispered, tucking something into Jane's hand. It was small and sticky, and when Jane looked she saw that a pink candy heart was stuck to her palm. Written across it in red letters was YOU WIN.

She looked at Sarah. "Thank you," she said. "This is exactly what I needed."

She tucked the heart in her pocket and took the softball from Byron. "Stand back and let a woman show you how it's done," she said.

She stood and looked at Ned seated on the platform. But she didn't see Ned. She saw Fitzwilliam Darcy. To many he was Jane's greatest creation, the ideal man to whom no living man could measure up. To Jane, however, he was something else. Not a curse, exactly, but a hindrance. She sometimes felt that ever since creating Darcy she, along with her characters, had been overshadowed by him. He was the one to whom all the others were compared, and more often than not they were found wanting. And as she had yet to create a character equal to Darcy, she too sometimes felt bested by him.

These feelings combined with the sadness that still clung to her, and she felt herself growing very angry. She was angry that Walter's mother had interfered in their lives, that Miriam was planning the destruction of Byron and herself, that Beverly was taunting her with the ridiculous festival, and that Jessica Abernathy regarded her with distaste. She was angry with Kelly for abandoning her, with Ned for his lack of self-control, and with

Julia Baxter for butchering her novel. Most of all, she was angry with herself for allowing it all to happen and for not standing up for herself sooner.

She thought of all of these things as she took aim at the heart-shaped target floating next to Ned's shoulder. She hadn't thrown a ball in years, and it felt odd in her hand, too big and unwieldy. She pushed these thoughts from her mind as she pulled her arm back and flung the ball.

It hit the target smack in the center. For a moment Ned's surprised face stared back at her. Then he dropped into the tank with a colossal splash. As he flailed around trying to get his footing, Sarah's arms went around Jane's waist and she said, "I knew you could do it! The heart helped you!"

"Yes, it did," Jane agreed as the thunderous applause of the crowd filled her ears. Then Beverly Shrop was beside them.

"It looks like we have a winner!" she crowed, glancing sideways at Jane. "And here's your prize." She thrust a giant stuffed teddy bear into Jane's arms. It was made of red plush and had a pair of white wings sewn to the back. In one paw was a bow and arrow. It was hideous.

"Now if you'll all follow me I'll take you to the outdoor theater for a pantomime production of 'Dick Whittington and His Cat.'"

"Outdoor theater," Lucy sneered. "She means the ring where the 4-H kids show their lambs."

"Still, 'Dick Whittington and His Cat' is quite good," said Jane.

"Oh, it is," Byron agreed. "I played Sarah the cook in that one at the Surrey Theatre." To Ben, who was listening with a puzzled expression on his face, he said, "You know, I was quite a respected panto dame at one time. My Widow Twankey was the talk of Drury Lane."

Jane began to laugh, not even caring that Byron's slip would require some explanation and coverup later. Then she saw that they were being watched. A dozen yards away, Walter and his mother stood observing them. Miriam's face was set in a stony frown, while Walter's eyes were fixed on Jane as he ignored the strawberry ice cream that was dripping from the untouched cone and down his hand.

Lucy followed Jane's gaze. "Hi, Walter!" she called out. "Hi, Ms. Ellenberg!"

Walter waved, but Miriam turned and walked away. A moment later Walter followed her, giving Jane one last glance as he went after his mother.

"What a mama's boy," Lucy said.

"He isn't really," Jane said. "It's just that he . . . it's complicated," she said inadequately.

"He needs to tell her to mind her own business," said Lucy.

Jane ignored the remark, turning to Sarah. "I believe this belongs to you," she said, handing the girl the bear.

"Me?" Sarah said. "But I didn't throw the ball."

"Ah, but if you hadn't given me a good-luck charm, I never would have hit the target," said Jane.

Sarah accepted the bear, putting her arms around it and squeezing. "Thank you!" she said.

"You're very welcome," said Jane. She looked at Byron. "Now let's go home. I've had enough romance for one day."

As they walked back to the parking lot and their cars, Jane looked at the people having fun around her. Some she was sure were there because any fair was an opportunity for fun. Others, though, were there because they were in love with romance, with the idea of love. These were the ones she envied. How wonderful it would be to be so innocent again, to believe that love really would conquer all. It was sentimental and foolish to think such a thing. She knew that. All the same, she wished she could be one of those people.

"I'm surprised to see *you* here."

Jane almost ran into Jessica Abernathy, who stood in front of her holding a corn dog on a stick. She surveyed the group as if checking them for weapons, then said, "I thought you would be home working on your novel."

Byron came to Jane's defense. "We thought it would do Jane some good to get out of the house for a few hours," he said. "You know, to unlock her brain."

"I had no idea her brain had locked up," Jessica remarked. "That would certainly explain some things."

"I'm going home right now," said Jane. "To work."

Jessica smiled. "Excellent," she said. "I'll expect to see some chapters tomorrow."

"Have a lovely time at the fair," Byron said to Jessica.

The editor put the tip of the corn dog between her lips and bit it off. "Oh, I intend to," she said as she began to chew.

"How I hate that woman!" Jane exclaimed as they walked away.

"Daddy says hating people is wrong," said Sarah. "Isn't it, Daddy?"

Ben looked at Jane. "Well . . ."

"Your father is absolutely right," Jane said quickly. "I shouldn't say I hate her."

"But you do," said Sarah. "I can tell." She walked in silence for a few moments, then added, "I don't like that woman either. She looks mean."

"She's not mean," Byron said. "She's evil."

"Like the Wicked Witch in *The Wizard of Oz*?" Sarah asked.

"Worse," said Byron as Jane motioned for him to shut up.

Sarah looked up at Jane. "Maybe somebody will drop a house on her," she said brightly.

Jane glared at Byron, who grinned, patted Sarah on the head, and said, "We can only hope."

Chapter 24

JANE GLANCED SLEEPILY AT THE MAILBOX ICON ON HER COMPUTER screen. Seeing that she had three messages, she clicked on the box to see what had arrived during the night. *Maybe one of them will be something thrilling,* she thought as she yawned. She touched the tip of her right fang with her tongue and vaguely wondered if it might be wearing down. Tom, seated on the desk, twitched his tail over the keyboard and meowed.

"Don't start with me," Jane told the cat. "Now that I know how to listen in, I know all the horrible things you and Jasper say about me when you think I'm not listening."

This was not true. Try as she might, she hadn't been able to pick up anything from either of them. But she suspected them— at least Tom—of harboring traitorous thoughts. Jasper, being a dog and a good-natured one, was less likely to be critical of her, she imagined. Still, she wanted them to think she might be on to them.

Tom blinked his big golden eyes, licked a paw, and turned his back on Jane to lie down in a puddle of sunlight that came in through the window. Whether he'd understood or her not, Jane didn't know. *Maddening beast,* she thought in the direction of Tom's back.

She looked at the three messages awaiting her. The first was a note from one Mr. Raymond Obatangu, the son of an unfortunately deceased official of the Nigerian government, asking her assistance in transferring $3.8 million from his father's accounts into an American bank. She deleted this and went to the second email, which was a bill from the electric company. Finally she opened the third message and read it.

Jane:

Meet me this morning at 8:30 at Sunnyside Up.
Bring chapters.

Jessica

Jane groaned. "When she said she wanted chapters *tomorrow* I thought she meant *whenever*," she told Tom, whose lack of reaction suggested he didn't care about her problems. Jane looked at the clock and groaned again. It was 7:45. And she wasn't dressed.

She considered not going and then telling Jessica she'd received the email too late to make the meeting. But she was already in hot water with her editor, and she had to at least try to make the relationship work.

"Of course I have no chapters to show her," Jane informed Jasper as she pulled open her dresser drawers in search of clothes. "So she's going to be annoyed with me anyway."

She pulled a black turtleneck over her head. "Why is she still here, anyway?" she asked the spaniel, who was now lying on his back with his front paws flopped over and his ears splayed on the carpet. "Does she really think breathing down my neck is going to get me to write any faster?"

She slipped her foot into one leg of a pair of blue jeans, repeating the process on the other side. "As far as she's concerned,

I can't write," she told Jasper as she pulled the jeans up and zipped them closed. "Which of course is all thanks to your former mistress," she added, pointing a finger at the dog.

Jasper rolled onto his side and looked at her with his big brown eyes. "Don't give me that look," Jane told him. "I only rescued you from her because Lucy made me."

The nub that was Jasper's tail wiggled furiously. Jane knelt beside the dog and ruffled his ears. "I can't even imagine what it was like for you living with Our Gloomy Friend," she said as Jasper licked her hand. "You poor thing."

Five minutes later she had brushed her hair, found her shoes, and located the car keys. Fifteen minutes after *that* she was pulling into a parking spot outside Sunnyside Up. Being a Saturday, the popular breakfast place was already busy. Jane went in and searched the tables of customers for Jessica. She wasn't there.

Jane looked at her watch. It was 8:31. She could easily imagine Jessica leaving precisely one second after 8:30, just so she could tell Jane she'd waited for her but given up when Jane was late. It would be just one more strike against Jane.

She decided to wait outside. The inside of the restaurant smelled like bacon and old coffee, and it was upsetting her stomach. Jane suspected she might need to feed soon. Often when her body needed blood she found herself more sensitive than usual to odors. Now, for instance, she could easily make out the scent of half-cooked yolk as someone broke open a lightly fried egg. It mingled with the smells of syrup and hash browns, making her feel queasy.

It was better outside, although there she had to contend with two elderly men who, forbidden to smoke inside, had brought their coffee outdoors and were now seated on a bench puffing defiantly on their cigarettes. The smell filled Jane's nostrils and made her gag.

"You know, you're not supposed to smoke here either," she said testily.

One of the old men waved her away. "I've been smoking since before you were born, missy," he said. "Hasn't hurt me any."

Jane fixed him with a stare. "That's a matter of opinion," she said. "And just so you know, I've been dealing with nasty old men since before your great-great-great-great-grandfathers were born. Now put those out before I get *cranky.*"

The men looked at her for a moment, then stubbed out their cigarettes and hurried back into the restaurant, where no doubt their wives were enjoying being able to have a conversation without their husbands interrupting with talk of sports and lawn mowers. Jane felt only the slightest bit of remorse for having scolded the old fellows, but she didn't miss their cigarettes at all. Nor did she feel so much guilt that she was prevented from taking a seat on the bench they'd vacated.

She had been sitting there for approximately fifteen minutes (which she thought was the shortest amount of time good manners required she wait for Jessica) and was about to return home when Sherman Applebaum appeared. As always, he was dressed impeccably, this morning in a brown suit of summer-weight wool complete with waistcoat, a crisp white shirt, a silk tie in a subtle pattern of tiny orange and gold flowers against a pink background, and a smart brown herringbone ivy cap.

"Don't you look dapper this morning," Jane said.

"Ah," Sherman said, sounding genuinely delighted to see her. "There you are." He took a seat next to her on the bench. "It's going to be a lovely day," he said.

"It certainly looks that way," said Jane. "And where are you on your way to or from? Church?"

Sherman looked at her with one eyebrow raised. "My dear, you know me better than that," he said. "God and I have an understanding. I don't bother him and he doesn't bother me. I dare say that might change one of these days, but I don't intend to be the one who blinks first."

Jane laughed. "If anyone can win that contest, it's you," she said.

"Indeed," said Sherman. "Also, I should point out that this is Saturday. Let's not get ahead of ourselves."

"Of course it is," Jane said. "I've been so busy, what with the film and the new book, I don't know if I'm coming or going. Which reminds me, I owe you an apology. I haven't spoken to Julia Baxter about that interview yet. I just haven't had a chance."

"No worries about *that,*" said Sherman. "At the moment I'm more interested in the young woman they found floating lifeless in the dunk tank at the festival."

"What?" Jane said. "Who?"

"One Jessica Abernathy," said Sherman. "I believe you've made her acquaintance."

Jane felt her jaw drop. "Jessica Abernathy?" she said. "She's dead?"

"Very much so," said Sherman. "Although one has to wonder how she could have drowned in water no deeper than her shoulders. It seems to me she might have saved herself a great deal of difficulty by simply standing up. Of course, someone might have *held her down.* I wouldn't know."

Jane was still processing Sherman's news and wasn't paying attention to his chatter. "You're absolutely sure it's Jessica Abernathy?" she said.

Sherman nodded. "Officer Pete Bear told me himself not twenty minutes ago. He's the one who fished her out."

"And you're absolutely sure she's dead?" said Jane.

"Well, I'm not a physician," Sherman replied. "But Officer Bear was kind enough to let me have a peek at her, and she certainly looked dead to me. Quite blue around the face. Not at all pleasant to look at. Also, and I hope you'll forgive me for mentioning this, given your attachment to Walter, but I distinctly remember that Evelyn Fletcher looked very much the same when she was pulled from the lake."

At the mention of Walter's deceased wife Jane felt a pang of sadness. Evelyn had drowned during a Fourth of July picnic a little more than fifteen years earlier. Jane of course had never met her, having lived in Brakeston for only a decade, but when Walter spoke about her (which he did very rarely) it was with such affection that Jane was sure she would have liked her very much. It was an odd thing to feel for a woman some might consider a rival for Walter's love, but Jane had never thought of Evelyn in that way. She was simply a part of Walter's history.

"It was rude of me to bring up the past," said Sherman. "I hope you'll forgive me."

"Oh," Jane said, realizing that to Sherman she must appear to be in a daze. "It's not that. It's just that, well, I'm actually waiting for Jessica. We were supposed to have breakfast and talk about my book. She's my—was my—editor."

"So I understand," said Sherman. "Do you have any idea who might want to do her harm?"

"Only anyone who's met her," Jane said before she could stop herself. She blushed. "That was a terrible thing to say."

"It was," Sherman agreed. "Which is why you must say even more. She sounds like an absolute terror."

Jane glanced at Sherman, who she could tell was working very hard not to smile. "One shouldn't speak ill of the dead," she told him with mock reproach.

"Who better to speak ill of?" he replied. "They're not around to hear you!"

Jane bit her lip. Part of her was thrilled to hear that Jessica was no longer going to be a problem. But she also had to wonder who might have killed her, and why.

"I hesitate to say so," she told Sherman. "But the only person I can think of who would want her dead is I."

"How thrilling," Sherman said. "It isn't often I get to sit beside a murderess. It will make a wonderful chapter for my memoirs." He patted Jane's knee. "Unfortunately, I don't believe you have it in you."

You have no idea, Jane thought, although she appreciated the sentiment. "I wonder how long it will take for the news to spread," she said.

"That is also an intriguing subject," Sherman answered. "It seems the police are going to hold off on making an announcement until Monday."

"Monday?" Jane said. "Why?"

"They don't want to interrupt the delightful festival that has taken over our fair town," said Sherman. "It's bringing some much-needed capital to our coffers, and they fear news of a possible murder might spark needless concern among the more sensitive among us."

"But what if the murderer strikes again?" said Jane. "They should let people know what's going on."

Sherman nodded. "I agree with you on that point," he said. "Do you recall in the movie *Jaws* when the town council voted to overrule the sheriff's wishes and keep news of the shark's presence a secret so as not to spoil the lucrative summer tourist trade?"

"I'm afraid I haven't seen the movie," said Jane, surprised that Sherman had.

"The council's decision was a grave error," Sherman continued. "A great many more people died because of it. Of course it was necessary for the plot, and this is real life, but the principle is the same." He sighed happily. "I do so love a good monster movie," he said.

Jane looked at Sherman and wondered what other surprises were in him. "Do you think whoever killed Jessica might do it again?" she asked.

"It's always a possibility," said Sherman. "But let us hope not."

Something puzzled Jane. "If the police want to keep this quiet for now, why are you telling me?"

"First, because of your connection to the Abernathy woman. Second, because you are a writer."

Jane didn't understand. "What has that got to do with it?"

"You're used to considering multiple possibilities for a plot," Sherman replied. "Perhaps something you think of will aid in the investigation."

Another question occurred to Jane. "Who found the body?"

"Beverly Shrop," Sherman said. "At least she's the one who telephoned the police last night, so I assume she was the first to see the body."

"Last night?" said Jane.

"Just before midnight," Sherman said. "As I understand it, Miss Shrop was leaving the fairgrounds following the closing of the festival and walked by the dunk tank, where she saw the body."

"And how did you find out about it?" Jane asked him.

Sherman's eyes twinkled. "I am a newspaper editor," he said. "It's my business to know everything that happens."

"In other words, you have a friend in the police department," said Jane.

"I have many friends," Sherman said. "It's possible that some of them work in the police department. As I said, it's my business to know what's going on."

"And yet you're going to keep this a secret until they make an official announcement on Monday," said Jane. "Interesting."

Sherman chuckled. "Isn't it though," he said, standing up. "And now, my dear, I have a date with a bowl of oatmeal and a poached egg. I bid you a good day." He walked toward the door of the restaurant. "Of course, if you think of anything that might be of interest regarding this story I would be most appreciative if you would think of me."

"Of course," Jane said. "You'll be the first to know."

Sherman disappeared into Sunnyside Up, leaving Jane to ponder what she'd learned. Again she was left with just one question: Who had killed Jessica Abernathy?

She supposed it could be a coincidence and that the murderer had chosen Jessica for reasons having nothing to do with who she was. In fact, that made the most sense. *She was, as they say, in the wrong place at the wrong time,* Jane thought. Although it seemed more accurate to say that she was in the *wrong* place at the *right* time or the *right* place at the *wrong* time, depending on your perspective. At any rate, she had been there at the same time as the murderer, which ultimately was the only thing that mattered.

There was nothing to be done about it at the moment, though, so she drove home. After making herself a cup of coffee, she went into her office. Jessica's email was still open on the screen. Jane looked at it, wondering if it was the last email the editor had sent.

She was about to delete it when something caught her eye. The email had been sent at just after midnight that morning. "But Sherman said Beverly Shrop called the police just *before* midnight," Jane informed Tom, who was still asleep in the sunspot on her desk. "How could Jessica have sent this message if she was already dead?"

Chapter 25

"YOU MISSED MY PANEL THIS MORNING," BYRON SAID AS HE handed Jane a cup of punch. "In which I revealed to an enrapt audience the real Jane Austen."

Jane sipped the punch, which was overly sweet and tasted of ginger ale and cranberry juice. "On the contrary," she told Byron. "I didn't miss it one bit."

Byron laughed. "Everything I said was most complimentary," he assured her. "I told them that despite whatever criticism has come your way by virtue of your being a *popular* author, your ability to capture the caprices of the human animal are unmatched."

Jane bent her head slightly in his direction. "I thank you," she said. "That was very kind."

"Of course, I also told them you were a frustrated virgin and possibly a lesbian," Byron added.

Before Jane could reprimand Byron they were interrupted by the arrival of Lucy and Ben.

"How did your panel go?" Lucy asked Byron.

"Did no one come to hear me?" said Byron in reply. "I'm deeply wounded. But as it happens, Jane and I were just discussing that very subject. If I do say so my—"

Jane cut him off. "They've done a wonderful job with the decorations, don't you think?" she said. "It hardly looks like an Elks Lodge, does it?"

The building in which they were standing was a simple wooden structure built in the 1930s to house the local Order of Elks. To be exact, it was the home of Lodge 1372. The lodge currently had seventeen members, almost all of them over the age of seventy. Two of them—Grady O'Byrne and Felix Malden—happened to be the gentlemen with whom Jane had quarreled that very morning.

In addition to the Elks' regular Wednesday meetings (at which they mostly smoked cigars, drank whiskey, and told dirty jokes) the lodge was used for monthly spaghetti suppers sponsored by the fire department, Saturday night bingo organized by the local Red Hat Society, and any other community event that had no other permanent home. It had a kitchen, a single bathroom (there were no lady Elks when the lodge was built and so they had not anticipated the need for a women's restroom), and a storage area for chairs and whatever else needed storing. Other than that, the lodge was one enormous room, which made it ideal for events involving large numbers of people.

Tonight it had been turned into a re-creation of a Regency drawing room, or at least as reasonable a facsimile as could be manufactured using flowers, card tables, and half a dozen large sofas and twice that many chairs arranged around three sides of the room. On the fourth side was a small raised bandstand on which stood a piano.

Several dozen people moved about the room, sitting on the sofas, talking in excited voices, and enjoying the various edibles arranged on the tables. With very few exceptions they were all dressed in period costumes. This included Lucy, Ben, and Byron. Jane, however, wore a simple red silk dress, sleeveless and hemmed above the knees.

"Where's your costume?" Lucy asked.

She was teasing. She knew full well that Jane had never

intended to wear one to the dance. In fact, Jane had never intended to even come to the dance. It was only because Lucy had asked her that she was there. And why Lucy was so eager to attend still baffled her.

"I feel quite underdressed," Jane remarked, looking around at the outfits being sported by other attendees. She examined Lucy and Ben's costumes. "Those are rather good," she remarked. "Where did you get them?"

"We lucked out," Lucy answered. "Last year the college theater department put on *The School for Scandal.* I have a friend who worked on it, and she managed to snag these from the wardrobe closet for us."

"Ah, yes," said Jane. "Walter and I saw that. I believe your dress was worn by Lady Teazle in act two." She patted the lapel of Ben's jacket. "And this belongs to the dastardly Sir Benjamin Backbite," she informed him. "Fortunately for you, the clothes do not make the man."

"I don't know," Ben said, winking at Jane. "This getup does make me feel a little rakish." He nodded at Byron. "You look pretty sharp yourself. Where did you find that suit?"

Byron, whose attention had been elsewhere, said, "In my closet. Why?"

"Well," Jane said, "I imagine *I* will be the scandal this evening, being the one out of costume."

"Just like Bette Davis's character in *Jezebel,*" Byron remarked. "Julie Marsden. She wore a red dress to the Olympus Ball. Everyone was horrified. She only redeemed herself by volunteering to care for victims of the yellow fever epidemic, which of course likely meant her own death."

"I'll have to live with my tarnished reputation, then," said Jane. "I was never very good with epidemics."

A low whistle from Byron made them all turn their heads in the direction of his gaze. Entering the room was a girl in a beautiful pale blue silk ball gown. Her face was ghostly white, and on her head was an enormous white wig. Behind her were two young men dressed identically in the uniforms of French footmen.

"Is that Chloe?" Jane asked.

"I believe so," said Lucy. "With Ted and Ned."

"Why is she dressed like Marie Antoinette?" said Ben.

"Well, it's roughly the right period," Byron told him. "Just the wrong country."

The trio approached the group. When she arrived before them Chloe gave an awkward curtsey. Ted and Ned, looking mortified, bowed from the waist.

"What do you think?" Chloe asked. "I had the wardrobe people whip it up."

"Whip it up?" said Jane. "That must have taken them days."

"Don't the two of you look adorable," Byron said to the twins, who eyed him balefully.

"I know," said Chloe. "Couldn't you just eat them up?"

"Don't you dare," Jane whispered in the girl's ear.

Chloe ignored her. "I only get one of them anyway," she said. "Ned already has a date."

"Do you?" said Byron. "And who might that be?"

"Beverly Shrop," said the twin on the right, thereby identifying himself as Ned. His voice was flat, almost lifeless, and Jane would have felt sorry for him if he hadn't brought his predicament upon himself.

"Speak of the devil," Byron said as Beverly appeared. He appraised her costume and added, "Why, that looks as if it might have come from the closet of Jane Austen herself!"

More likely from my mother's closet, Jane thought as she shot Byron a withering look.

"Thank you," Beverly said sweetly as she patted Byron's arm. Jane wondered how he could stand having her touch him, especially as they knew what her and Miriam's plans for them were. *Or at least the outcome of their plans*, Jane thought darkly.

"Jane, I'm disappointed that you didn't make it to the panel today," Beverly said. "I think you would have found it most enter-taining."

"So I hear," said Jane.

"Tomorrow's should be equally fascinating," Byron said. He turned to Ben and Lucy. "Three romance editors are going to talk about what they look for in a manuscript," he told them. "One of them is Jane's editor, Jessica Aber—"

"I'm afraid Jessica won't be able to join us," Beverly inter-jected.

Jane held her breath, waiting to see how Beverly would han-dle the moment. For her own reasons she herself had said nothing to anyone about Jessica's death. As far as she knew, fewer than half a dozen people were aware of what had happened at the fair-grounds.

"Oh?" Byron said. "Why not?"

Beverly looked around. "She was called back to New York," she said. "A family emergency."

Byron frowned. "What a pity," he said. "Jane, did you know about this?"

"No," Jane said. "This is the first I've heard of it." She looked at Beverly. "That certainly is a disappointment."

"Yes," Beverly said. "Well, these things happen. Now if you'll excuse me, I need to see about the music for this evening."

Jane watched Beverly leave. *I'd love to be inside her head,* she thought. *Only for a moment, of course.* She imagined being trapped in Beverly Shrop's head forever and shivered.

"Hello, Jane."

Jane thought she heard Walter's voice. Then she turned around and discovered that in fact she had. He was standing be-hind her, dressed in a handsome pair of tan breeches, a cream-colored waistcoat, and a jacket of royal blue velvet that was cut away in front and ended in tails at the back. His cravat was tied in a small bow at his throat, and his hair was tousled, as if he'd just come in from riding. He was breathtakingly handsome, and Jane found herself staring into his blue eyes and unable to look away. *It's as if he's glamoring me!* she thought.

"Walter!" Byron said jovially, putting his arm around Walter's shoulders. "It's a pleasure to see you."

"And you," said Walter.

"Where is your *delightful* mother?" Byron asked.

Walter looked around. "Over there," he said, pointing toward a spot as far away from where Jane and her friends stood as it was possible to get. Miriam had her back to them as she looked over the various plates of cookies and pies laid out on the table before her. Then, apparently finding none of them to her liking, she turned and fixed Jane with a steely stare.

"Such a handsome woman," said Byron. "I see that, like Jane, she's opted not to dress for the occasion."

"No," Walter replied. "Mother isn't really one for costumes." Looking at Jane, he added, "I hope it's all right that we came."

"Of course it's all right," said Jane. "I'm very pleased to see you, Walter."

Walter smiled shyly. "I should go keep her company," he said, nodding slightly in the direction of his mother. "Perhaps we can talk later."

Jane nodded. "I look forward to it," she said.

As Walter walked away Byron came close to Jane. "Have you asked yourself why it is you keep falling for unavailable men?" he asked.

"First of all, there have only been *two* men," Jane said. "And you don't count, as I was a silly girl who didn't know any better. As for Walter, he pursued *me*. So I hardly see how I can be blamed for that."

"I suppose you're right," said Byron. "Still—"

"Still nothing," Jane snapped. "And that's the last we'll speak of that subject."

Byron opened his mouth to reply, but suddenly the air was

filled with a crackling sound that came from speakers on either side of the bandstand. All heads turned to see what was happening. Beverly Shrop, a microphone in her hand, stood on the stage.

"Hello!" she said. "And welcome to what I know will be a magical evening. I'm sure you're all anxious to begin, so please join me in welcoming our musicians for this evening, the wonderful Haymeadow Trio, as well as English country dance expert Katherine Threadgood."

As the audience clapped, four people—two men and two women—mounted the steps to the bandstand. One of the women held a flute in her hands, one of the men had a violin, and the second man seated himself at the piano. The second woman took the microphone from Beverly.

"As Beverly told you, my name is Katherine Threadgood," she said. "I don't know that I'm an *expert* on English country dancing, but I'm certainly a great fan. Tonight we want to give you a taste of what a typical night of dancing might have been like in the time of Jane Austen."

"Oh, joy," Jane groused.

"Cheer up," said Byron. "It's going to be fun. Perhaps they'll have us do Buttered Pease, or maybe All in a Garden Green."

Jane groaned. "I couldn't remember the steps to those when they were all the rage," she said. "How am I supposed to remember them now?"

"To get us started, we're going to do a simple circle dance," Katherine Threadgood announced. "If you would please pair up into couples and form circles with even numbers of couples but no more than twelve couples to a circle, I'll walk you through the steps."

As couples began forming, Katherine added, "Don't be shy. I promise you this is very simple."

Jane moved to take a seat on one of the couches, but Byron took her hand. Before she could object she found herself standing in a circle in the middle of the dance floor. Also in her circle were Ben and Lucy, Chloe and Ted, Beverly and Ned, and several couples she had never seen before. To her surprise they were joined a moment later by Sherman Applebaum and Posey Frost.

"All right," Katherine called out. "Now within each circle form two circles, men on the outside and women on the inside, facing one another."

Jane took her place between two women she didn't know and waited for the music to begin. She detested circle dances. They involved touching numerous hands, all of them sweaty, and inevitably someone broke the pattern and it all ended badly. *I'll just do this one,* she promised herself. *Then I'll go home.*

"Excuse us."

Two men to Byron's left parted, and Jane saw Walter and Miriam enter the circle. Miriam looked annoyed, but Walter had a gleeful expression on his face as he took his place. Jane could tell that he'd forced his mother to participate, and she imagined he was getting no small amount of satisfaction from subjecting her to the indignity. *Good for you, Walter,* she thought. She smiled at him, but he was not looking in her direction.

"This should be interesting," Byron said to her, grinning.

"One more thing before we begin," said Katherine. "I need you to count off in pairs. It doesn't matter where you begin, so one couple in each group volunteer to be couple number one."

"We'll be couple number one!" Beverly said excitedly.

"Once you've decided who the first couple is, count off starting with the man to the left of the man in the first couple," Katherine continued.

Beverly looked at Sherman and Posey. "That makes you number two," she said.

They continued to count off. Jane and Byron were couple number six.

"Don't forget your number," Katherine announced. "It will be important later."

"Do you think you can be trusted to remember?" Byron teased Jane.

"I've written it on my hand just in case," Jane joked back.

"Here's how this dance works," Katherine said. "For the first four bars you link left arms with your partner and swing around two times. This will put you back where you started, facing each other. Stay in place and clap for a count of eight. Then each lady links arms with the gentleman to her right and they swing around two times. You do this until each woman has danced with each man. When you're back with your original partner stay in place and clap hands. I'll call out further directions when we get there. Now when the music starts, I'll count you off and tell you when to begin."

The three musicians began playing a lively tune Jane recognized as "Jack's Maggot." She had danced it often as a young woman, and it was a favorite. It was not entirely appropriate for the kind of dancing they were now doing, but that did not diminish her joy at hearing it again.

"Here we go!" Katherine called out. "One, two, three, four, and swing!"

Jane locked left elbows with Byron and the two circled each other. "This brings back some memories," Byron remarked.

"It does indeed," said Jane.

"Now clap for eight!" Katherine reminded them.

Jane dutifully clapped for the count and then moved to her right to dance with a gentleman she did not know. He smiled but said nothing as they turned twice around.

Her next partner was Ben. On their first swing he said, "Have you decided what to do about Walter?"

"No," Jane replied. "But I have fifteen bars to think about it."

"Good luck," said Ben as they finished their second swing and parted to stand facing each other and clapping.

"Well," Jane said to Ned as she took his arm for the next measure. "How do you like being Beverly's boy toy?"

"I'm Ted," the young man replied. "Ned couldn't take it anymore. Besides, he wanted to dance with Chloe."

"Sneaky," said Jane. "Let's just hope Beverly doesn't try to take a bite out of you."

Ted paled as he let go of Jane, and as she stepped back she felt obligated to say, "I'm just teasing."

This seemed to do little to make things better, as Ted appeared rattled and mistakenly clapped on the up beat. But there was no time to apologize again before Jane found herself with Sherman.

"Just the woman I wanted to see," said Sherman. He pulled her close in to his body and whispered, "They found a note in the pocket of Jessica Abernathy's jacket, asking her to meet at the fairgrounds."

"Do they know who sent it?" asked Jane.

"Someone called Violet Grey," said Sherman as he released Jane's arm.

Jane stifled a gasp, almost forgetting to clap. Violet Grey? Did that mean Charlotte was in town? Had she killed Jessica—her sorority sister—to send a message to Jane?

"Isn't Chloe's costume *fabulous*?" her next partner asked as they began their swing.

"Don't bother," Jane said. "I know you're Ned. You have some nerve, leaving your brother with that jackal."

"I'm sorry," Ned told her. "I just couldn't stand it anymore. She keeps trying to hold my hand."

"You're lucky that's all she's trying to hold," said Jane. "But you won't have to do it for much longer, so don't worry. We won't let her savage you."

During the two bars of clapping she looked to her right. Walter was dancing with a woman Jane didn't know. But he kept stealing glances at Jane. Moments later they were arm in arm.

"I thought you'd never get here," Walter told her.

"I'm sure your mother is thrilled about it," said Jane.

"Can we not talk about her?" Walter said. "At least for the next count of four."

When he let go of Jane it was reluctantly. As their arms parted his fingers grabbed hers. Just for a second he held them tightly. Then Jane stepped back and the connection was broken. She looked into Walter's eyes as they clapped. *I can't keep doing this,* Jane thought.

Her final partner was a stranger, a short, jolly man who swung her with such vigor that she was almost swept off her feet. She was relieved when their turn was over and she was once again dancing with Byron.

"Did anything interesting happen?" he asked as he and Jane did their final swing.

"Our Gloomy Friend may be in town," Jane informed him. "I think that qualifies."

There was no more time for discussion as they parted and clapped down the final bars. But the music kept playing as Katherine's voice came over the speaker. "Gentlemen, stay in place and continue clapping," she instructed them. "Ladies, your job is a little trickier. Remember your numbers?"

A chorus of laughter and yeses filled the room.

"I hope so," said Katherine.

Jane wished she could sneak out of the circle. But it was too late. Not only was the circle of men keeping her inside, there was simply no way to do it without causing a commotion. Also, it would leave the circle with an odd number of couples, which would make the dance impossible.

"Ladies, turn and face inside the circle."

Jane turned her back to Byron. Across the circle from her was Posey, moving back and forth as she kept time with her feet.

"When I say go, I want the odd-numbered ladies to walk forward and meet in the middle of the circle," said Katherine. "You'll join hands and circle to your right for a count of eight. If you do it right, you should end up back where you started. Walk backward to your starting position. Then we'll repeat those steps with the even-numbered ladies. On the next bar, we'll begin!" said Katherine. "And two, three, four, go!"

Jane watched as Beverly, Chloe, and the two unknown women walked forward and joined hands. As they circled she counted down the bars until she would have to move forward and take Miriam's hand. She comforted herself with the knowledge that Lucy would be on her other side.

The women on either side of Jane returned to their places. At the beginning of the next bar Katherine called out, "Even-numbered ladies!" and Jane willed herself to move. When she reached the center she gladly reached for Lucy on her left. She hesitated a moment and then extended her hand to Miriam on her right.

Miriam's hand was cool and dry. But seconds after Jane grasped it she felt a wave of emotion wash over her, a sickening wall of fear and rage. Instinctively she dropped the woman's hand and stepped away as if she'd been stung. Miriam stared at her, her eyes blazing.

"I'm sorry," Jane said, letting go of Lucy's hand. "I have to go."

Turning, she ran toward Byron, pushed him aside, and ran as quickly as she could toward the door.

Chapter 26

"YOU COULD HAVE MENTIONED THAT JESSICA WAS DEAD," BYRON said. He sounded hurt.

"I'm not apologizing for that," said Jane. "I didn't know Our Gloomy Friend might have had something to do with it, not until Sherman told me at the dance. And anyway, I only found out this morning. I was still basking in the joyous news."

They were in Jane's living room. Jane was stretched out on the couch, an afghan covering her, and Byron was seated in one of the armchairs. He still wore his dancing clothes, but Jane had swapped her dress for a pair of pajamas made from lightweight pink flannel printed with images of small gray mice. They each had a glass of merlot, and the almost empty bottle sat on the coffee table.

"Does Sherman know who Violet Grey is?" asked Byron.

"I doubt it," Jane answered. "I think he was just pleased to have more information about Jessica's murder."

"Being in possession of that information is very dangerous for him," said Byron. "If Our Gloomy Friend really is responsible, she's going to go after anyone who knows anything about her."

"Including us," Jane said.

"Especially us," said Byron. He sighed and glanced at his

watch. "It's almost two," he said. "Do you want to go over the rules of softball so you're ready for tomorrow's game?"

Jane groaned. She'd forgotten all about the big Janeites versus Brontëites ballgame. Having never played softball, she had only a vague idea of what was involved. Byron had volunteered to help her figure it out, and Jane had brought home a book on the subject from the store. She handed it to Byron. "Read," she said.

Byron opened the book. "'Softball is commonly mistaken for an easier version of baseball,'" he read. "'In fact, it is just as interesting and just as complex a game. The fundamental difference between the sports is the size of the ball used and the style of pitching, which in baseball is overhand and in softball is underhand.'"

"I'm already bored," said Jane. "Can you condense it all for me?"

Byron skimmed the page and turned to the next one. After flipping through perhaps a dozen or so he shut the book and sighed. "You stand on a plate, someone tosses a ball at you, and you try to hit it with a stick," he said. "If you succeed in hitting it and no one catches it, you run. If you run far enough, you score a point for your team."

"That sounds rather easy, really," Jane said. "Surely there must be other rules?"

"Well, yes," said Byron. "Quite a lot of them, actually. Do you really want to hear them all?"

"I don't think I do," Jane said. "I imagine if there's anything I need to know they'll explain it to me."

"Pity they aren't playing cricket," said Byron. "That would be much easier. These American games make absolutely no sense."

"Why do you think Miriam hasn't made her move yet?" Jane asked.

"I honestly don't know," said Byron. "And Lilith hasn't brought us any additional information. I'm beginning to think the little bitch is a liar."

"Ned hasn't been any more useful," Jane said. "According to him, all Beverly talks about is how wonderful *you* are."

"I'm not surprised," said Byron. "Just between us, I think she had rather a crush on me."

"She's planning on *murdering* you," Jane reminded him.

Byron waved a hand, dismissing the idea. "The two are hardly mutually exclusive," he said. "There have been plenty of lovers I would gladly have murdered."

"I'm sure there are one or two you actually have," said Jane. She hesitated before asking her next question. "You've never told me: Why *did* you turn Char—Our Gloomy Friend?"

Byron sighed deeply. "I'm surprised it's taken you this long to ask," he said.

Jane poured more wine into his glass. "It surprises me as well, and I really don't know why I haven't asked before. I suppose I didn't really like to think of you with her."

"Your jealousy is flattering," said Byron, lifting his glass to her. "If I didn't know you were in love with someone else, I might just try to seduce you again."

Jane laughed. "And give up on Ted?" she asked.

"I fear that's a lost cause," Byron said. "Anyway, about Our Gloomy Friend. What do you know about her death?"

"Very little," said Jane. "If I recall correctly, she died of typhus."

Byron nodded. "That's correct," he said. "She contracted it from one of the family's servants, an old woman called Tabitha Ackroyd. Did you also know that Our Gloomy Friend was pregnant at the time of her death?"

"No," Jane said. "How awful."

"It was," said Byron. "But if it weren't for the child, I might never have turned her."

Jane sipped her wine. "How do you mean?"

"It was mine," said Byron.

Jane gasped audibly. "It wasn't!" she said.

"It was," Byron said. "I wouldn't marry her, and so she married her father's curate. Arthur, his name was. A peculiar-looking fellow. He rather resembled Stephen King." He paused for a moment. "Now that I think of it, I wonder . . . No, it couldn't be. Could it?"

"Our Gloomy Friend," Jane reminded him.

"Our Gloomy Friend," said Byron. "Yes. Well, as I said, she was pregnant with my child."

"And you refused to marry her," Jane said. "Which was very gentlemanly of you, I must say."

"I was young," said Byron.

"You were sixty-seven," Jane countered. "Did she know who you really were?"

"Not until later," said Byron. "Anyway, she contracted typhus and was near death. Although I wouldn't marry her, I did want the child. I had very little to do with my other children, you know."

"Yes," said Jane. "You weren't exactly father of the year."

"I wanted to try," Byron said. "To be honest, I didn't love Our Gloomy Friend. I never had. But the child was different."

"So to save the baby you killed the mother," Jane said. "Does it work that way?"

"As far as I knew, no one had ever tried it," Byron answered. "She was going to die anyway, and the child with her, so there was nothing to lose."

"For you," said Jane. "Did you give her any say in the matter?"

Byron shook his head. "She was delirious with fever when I turned her. She thought it was all a nightmare."

"And the child?"

"Stillborn," said Byron. "I don't know if the typhus killed it or if I did, but as I said, it hardly matters."

Jane set her wineglass down. "Despite everything, I can't help but feel sorry for Charlotte," she said, momentarily forgetting her own rule against using her enemy's real name. "First you get her pregnant and refuse to marry her, then you turn her into a vampire. And after all of that you don't stay with her."

"I couldn't," Byron said defensively. "She was half mad. All she did was scream at me and demand that I bring her victims to feed from. She wouldn't hunt for herself. I endured it for half a year and then I left before I lost what was left of my humanity."

"But you saw her again," said Jane. "In New Orleans."

"Our paths crossed from time to time," Byron said. "She seemed to have accepted her new life. In fact, she seemed quite happy with how things turned out."

"Except that she had her mummified siblings in her house and had dinner with them every night," Jane reminded him.

"There is that," Byron agreed.

"Have you given up trying to convince Ted to let you turn him?" Jane asked.

Byron was quiet for a long moment. "It has to be his idea," he said. "It was a terrible mistake turning Ned. Even if I did think he was his brother, that doesn't excuse what I did. And trying to get Ted to become like us won't change any of that. I don't think even Ned is trying to sway him."

Jane thought about Ted growing old as his twin stayed young. She had gone through that with Cassie, although Cassie had never known that Jane still lived. Jane had watched her from afar.

"Why didn't you ever give her the choice?" Byron asked.

"How did you do that?" asked Jane. "Can you read my thoughts?"

"Thankfully, no," Byron said. "But I know how you felt about your sister, and given the similarity in circumstances, I thought it likely you might be thinking of her."

"I am," said Jane. "I don't know if Ned and Ted are as close as Cassie and I were, but I have to imagine they are. If that's the case, then I know why Ned isn't asking Ted if he'll consider being turned."

"And why is that?" Byron inquired.

"Because," said Jane, "he's afraid Ted will say yes."

Byron looked at the floor. When he looked up his eyes were filled with sadness. "Is it really so bad?" he asked quietly.

"It's not about whether it's good or bad," said Jane. "It's about knowing the other person will choose eternal life because she wants to be with you, not because she wants it for herself."

"I never gave Our Gloomy Friend a choice," said Byron. "I never gave you a choice, or Ted."

"Ned," Jane said. "It was Ned."

"The point is I never *asked* any of you what you wanted. I turned you because *I* wanted to."

Jane patted the seat beside her on the couch. "Come here," she told Byron.

He did as she said, and when he was next to her Jane spread the afghan over both of them. "You're very good at turning people's lives upside down, aren't you?" she said.

"It seems that way," Byron said.

"It's not an attractive trait," Jane informed him. "And it hasn't served you well."

"It hasn't, has it?" said Byron.

"And now we're both sitting here wondering when we might be killed by either your ex-lover or a vampire hunter," Jane continued. "Some people might say that's all your fault."

Byron groaned and leaned his head back, looking up at the ceiling. "I'm sure this isn't going to help my situation," he said. "But I feel the need to point out that you're the one who tried to kill Our Gloomy Friend."

"I wish people would stop bringing that up," Jane said. "It hardly compares."

"I really do think she hates you more," said Byron. "Do you suppose it's because she's jealous of your success, or is it because I favor you over her?"

"You've learned a great deal from our conversation, haven't you?" Jane said.

Byron took her hand and held it. "I'm merely trying to put off considering what it all means," he told her. "I thought it might help if I put some of the blame on you."

"Well tried," Jane said. "But not this time. This could be the last evening we spend together. Do you really want me to remember you like this?"

"Me?" said Byron. "Why do you assume that I'm the one they'll be successful in killing? I might remind you that your skills are far less developed than mine."

"Through no fault of my own," Jane argued. "You never told me I could do any of these things."

"Because you ran away," said Byron. "Had you stayed around, I might have. I mean I *would* have. At least I would have considered it."

"Mmm," Jane said, drinking more wine. "Your dedication is awe-inspiring. You can see why I was so anxious to remain by your side."

Byron tried very hard not to laugh but was unable to maintain his composure. "I really am a shit, aren't I?" he said when he could speak again.

"You are," Jane said. "But I do love you."

Byron looked at her. "I love you too," he said.

He continued to look at her, so Jane added, "This doesn't mean we're going to kiss."

"I know," said Byron. "I wasn't thinking that. I was just thinking how lucky Walter is to have you."

"I don't want to talk about Walter," Jane said.

"Now who's evading the subject?" Byron said.

"I'm not evading the subject because it never *was* the subject," Jane argued. "We were talking about what a frightful shit you are."

"Which I acknowledged," said Byron. "Now it's your turn to acknowledge that you love Walter."

"Of course I love Walter," Jane said. "That doesn't change the fact that our relationship is impossible."

"Let me ask you this," said Byron. "Would you marry Walter if you knew he had cancer?"

Jane didn't even have to think about her answer. "Yes," she said. "That wouldn't make any difference to me."

"Then why should the fact that you're going to outlive him because you're a vampire?" Byron asked. "In either event he's going to die before you do."

"You know it's not that simple," said Jane. "Death from cancer is natural. It's terrible, but it's natural. Living forever because you've been turned into a monster isn't."

"We aren't monsters," Byron said.

"They don't know that," said Jane. "All they know is what they see in the movies."

"There's also that television show," Byron said. "The one with the girl with the odd name. Spooky? Cookie?"

"Sookie," said Jane. "Her name is Sookie. And there were books before there was a television show."

"Really?" Byron said. "I didn't know. Anyway, it's very popular, and we're portrayed very sympathetically."

"That's beside the point," Jane snapped. "Walter isn't some giggly little goth girl who thinks it would be neat to have a vampire boyfriend."

"Lucy doesn't think we're monsters," said Byron.

Jane sighed. "I know all of this," she said. "But I just can't."

Byron cocked his head. "You don't have to tell him, you know."

Jane snorted. "I think he'd notice eventually," she said. "If his mother doesn't tell him first."

"Forget her for a moment," Byron said. "She can always be dealt with. Has it occurred to you that Walter might *like* having a young, beautiful wife for the rest of his life?"

"He's not shallow," Jane scoffed.

"You don't have to be shallow to appreciate a young, beautiful face," said Byron.

"You know what we should do?" Jane said. "We should make a pact. If neither of us has found someone by the time we're, I don't know, four hundred years old, we should get married."

"That's nearly two hundred years from now," said Byron.

"Exactly," Jane said. "Which gives us plenty of time to worry about it."

"You're just postponing the inevitable," Byron told her. "You're not going to meet a nice vampire man and fall in love. You've met the love of your life. He's right here, right now—and he's human."

He put his arms around Jane and pulled her closer, so that her head was against his chest. She closed her eyes as he stroked her hair. "I didn't give you, or Our Gloomy Friend, or Ted—"

"Ned."

"Ned a chance to say yes or no," Byron said softly. "But it's time you gave Walter his chance."

Jane said nothing. But in her head she spoke the words she couldn't say out loud: *What if he says no?*

Chapter 27

"CROQUET?"

Jane looked at the playing field. Instead of bases and a pitcher's mound there were six perfectly laid out croquet pitches outlined in white chalk. At each one a man dressed all in white was inspecting the six wickets and the striped peg.

"I thought you said croquet was too difficult to arrange," Jane said to Beverly, who was watching the proceedings with a keen eye. Like the referees, she too was dressed all in white, although she wore a full-length dress instead of trousers.

"Did I?" Beverly said. "I don't know why I would have said that. At any rate, we're playing croquet."

Jane looked down at the T-shirt, shorts, and tennis shoes she was wearing. A softball glove—bought just that morning at P.J.'s House of Sports—was tucked under her arm, and her hair was pulled back into an unflattering ponytail and hidden by a baseball cap (purchased along with the glove) emblazoned with the name and logo of a team she had never heard of but which the salesman helping her had assured her was very popular.

"You asked me to be a team captain not two weeks ago," Jane reminded her. "Remember, it was going to be the Janeites versus the Brontëites?"

"Oh, it still is," said Beverly. "And you're still captain of the

Janeites. But we're playing croquet. You *do* know how to play, don't you?"

"Yes," Jane said. "But I look ridiculous."

Beverly looked Jane up and down. "I'm sure no one will notice," she said.

They'll notice, Jane thought. *And you did this on purpose to make me look like a fool.*

"This is so exciting," said Beverly. "There will be six matches played concurrently, with four players per match. Whichever team wins the most matches will be the victor."

"And if each team wins three matches?" Jane asked.

"Then we'll have a playoff game, of course," said Beverly.

"That's sensible," Jane said. "Who is the captain of the Brontëites?"

"Why, I am," Beverly replied. "Oh, and did I tell you that we have mascots?"

"Mascots?" said Jane.

Beverly nodded. "Every sports team needs a mascot," she said. "The fans love it. It generates excitement."

"I suppose," Jane said doubtfully. "What are they?"

Beverly craned her neck. "There they are now," she said, pointing behind Jane.

Jane turned to see two creatures walking toward them. One of them was pink and tubular, with a large flared head. The other seemed to be some kind of bird. It was black with an orange beak.

Jane indicated the pink mascot. "Is that a—"

"It's a squid," said Beverly. "See the tentacles?"

"It looks like a—"

"It's a *squid*," Beverly said.

Jane decided not to press the issue. "And is the other one a crow?" she asked.

Beverly sighed and rolled her eyes. "It's a moorhen," she said. "It's the mascot for the Brontëites. I think it's very appropriate."

"You were able to find a moorhen costume?" said Jane.

"I had it made," Beverly explained.

"And why a squid for the Janeites?" Jane asked. She found it a peculiar choice, and wondered why Beverly thought it appropriate to represent her work.

"It symbolizes the—"

"Good morning, ladies." Byron's greeting interrupted Beverly's explanation. He then looked at the two approaching mascots. "Is that a—"

"It's a squid!" Jane and Beverly said in unison. Jane glared at Beverly, who pretended not to notice.

"And a moorhen," said Byron. "I imagine that's for the Brontë fans."

Jane turned on him. "Why would you assume that?" she asked. "What is it about a squid that says Austen?"

Byron shrugged. "It's just that—"

"Time to begin!" Beverly shouted. "Players, please gather round."

The twenty-four croquet players assembled around Beverly. All of them, Jane noticed, were dressed in pristine white. Only she was dressed for softball. *I look like a tourist,* she thought. *All I need is a fanny pack.* She realized she was still holding the softball glove, and she tried to hide it behind her back.

"We'll be playing by International Association laws," Beverly informed them. "If you don't know all of them, don't worry. Our referees are here to help. I will be captaining the Brontëites and Jane Fairfax, one of our illustrious local authors, will captain the Janeites. Let us now break up into our respective teams and discuss strategy. Brontëites, follow me."

Beverly moved off, taking half of the players with her. Jane couldn't help but notice that the Brontëites as a whole were a dour-looking team. Almost none of them smiled, and they seemed uncomfortable in the warm, sunny weather. Several of them kept looking up at the sky, as if praying for dark clouds and rain.

Jane turned her attention to her own group. In contrast to

Beverly's team, the Janeites were a far cheerier bunch. Equally comprised of men and women, they chatted gaily and seemed eager to begin. This lifted Jane's spirits considerably. She was also very pleased to see that Sherman Applebaum—dressed in a white suit—was among her players.

"Good morning," she said. "We have a lovely day for playing today, so I hope you're all excited."

All around her heads nodded vigorously.

"Brilliant," Jane said. "Now, before I pair you up, how many of you have croquet experience?"

She expected eleven hands (not counting her own) to be raised. After a suitable amount of time had passed, however, only three were seen. Two of them belonged to a pair of elderly men whose white hair and mustaches matched their clothing. The third was that of a girl who appeared to be no older than thirteen.

"I see," said Jane, her hopes sinking quickly. "Well then, the three of you will be captains of your individual teams. You may choose your playing partners. The rest of you can pair up as you like."

There was a minute or two of looking around, finger-pointing, and raised eyebrows as the players assembled themselves into duos. At the end of this time one player remained unpaired. Sherman smiled at Jane. "I believe this puts us together," he said, coming to stand beside her.

Jane gave him a smile of gratitude. If she had to suffer through the next two hours, she preferred to do it with a friend.

"Very good," she said. "Now each team will go to a pitch and we can begin." She pointed at the first team. "You'll play on one." She went through the remaining teams in succession, sending each to its respective pitch. "And that leaves us with the sixth pitch," she said to Sherman as her layers dispersed.

"I must confess that I told a small untruth," said Sherman as he and Jane walked across the field. "I *have* played a bit of croquet in my time."

"How much of a bit?" asked Jane.

"Grand Champion of St. Basil's Preparatory School for Boys, 1959," said Sherman. "Although I haven't played much since. I know I might have been of service assisting those who have not had as much experience, but frankly, I am a poor teacher." He looked at Jane. "Also, I hate to lose."

"You are a treacherous old goat," Jane said, adopting a scolding tone.

"Positively diabolical," Sherman agreed as they reached their pitch. "By the way, we haven't discussed the note found in Jessica Abernathy's pocket."

"I'd almost forgotten," said Jane. "Is there any more to it?"

Sherman shook his head. "No more than I told you last night," he said. "Apparently this Violet Grey person was to meet Miss Abernathy. That's all I know. I was hoping you might have some thoughts on the matter."

Jane considered whether or not she should tell Sherman that she did indeed know Violet Grey, and that Violet was one of Jessica's sorority sisters. She could not, of course, reveal Violet's true identity, but she felt she owed Sherman something.

"There's a Violet Grey who writes a blog about romance literature," she said. "I don't know if it's the same one, but given Jessica's position, it wouldn't surprise me that the two knew each other."

"Is this the same Violet Grey who wrote some unflattering things about your novel?" Sherman asked.

"Yes," said Jane, slightly horrified that Sherman had read Violet's crushing review of *Constance*, in which she'd stopped just short of accusing Jane of plagiarism.

"I wonder if we ought to mention this to Officer Bear," said Sherman. "Not now, of course, but when the festivities are over."

"You're probably right," Jane said. "It might be helpful."

"Right now, however, I believe it's time for us to kick some serious ass," Sherman said.

The two of them met their opponents, neither of whom they knew, at the edge of the pitch. After introductions the referee performed the coin toss, which Sherman and Jane won after calling tails. They elected to go second.

Unfortunately for their opponents, neither of whom appeared to have any experience, the match was a massacre. Starting at the A baulk line, one of the opposing players placed the black ball into play by hitting it out of bounds. The referee placed it back on the yard line, and Jane then struck the red ball so that it too went out of bounds. She then watched as the second opponent inexplicably placed the blue ball on the B baulk line and attempted to roquet his partner's ball. The distance between them was too great, however, and he succeeded only in rolling past the south boundary, resulting in his ball being placed on the yard line a short distance from the black ball.

After that it was all over. To the amazement of Jane and the consternation of their opponents, Sherman passed through all the wickets on his first turn. Unnerved by this display of prowess, the other team made blunder after blunder, and after only three turns Jane too had traversed the course forward and back and knocked her ball against the peg. The game over, she and Sherman shook hands with the other team and with the referee then went to watch the other matches.

The remaining games took far longer to complete, but one by one they ended until the score stood at three matches for the Janeites and two for the Brontëites. The final match pitted Jane's youngest player and her partner against Miriam Ellenberg and Walter. Seeing them there, Jane wondered how she could have missed them earlier. Had Beverly hidden them from her, or had Jane simply been too preoccupied to notice them? Ultimately it didn't matter, but Jane was still unnerved by the situation. She was particularly distressed to see Walter playing for the Brontëites, although she knew this was due to Miriam's literary preferences and not his.

The game was nearing its end, and it was a close one. Each team had two balls out of play, and only Miriam's and the girl's remained on the pitch. The girl had played her red ball through the penultimate wicket, and Miriam was on the 4-back. It was her shot.

Her first hit delivered a roquet to the yellow ball, which she then deftly hit back toward the number two wicket while sending her own ball back toward its starting point. Her next stroke took her ball through the penultimate wicket. That entitled her to an additional stroke, which she used to hit her ball toward the rover.

With her chances running out, the girl attempted to roquet Miriam's ball. Her nerves got the better of her, however, and her shot rolled past Miriam's ball by inches. Miriam seized the opportunity to roquet the red ball and then croquet it toward the southwest corner while positioning herself to pass through the final wicket. She did this on her next shot, and with her final tap her ball struck the peg.

As the dejected girl was comforted by her partner and teammates, Walter hugged his mother in celebration. Only then did Jane realize what the win meant—she and Sherman would have to play Miriam and Walter for the championship.

The final event was played on a pitch neither team had used. The Janeites took up position on the north end of the pitch, while the Brontëites claimed the south end as their territory. The mascot for each team moved among the fans, urging them to clap and call out for their players. The excitement was very much not in keeping with the croquet tradition of silence and decorum, and the noise only added to Jane's anxiety.

The coin toss was a blur. Jane heard Miriam call heads and saw the coin in the referee's palm, tails up. He looked at Sherman and Jane, and Jane called first shot. Miriam gave her barely a glance as she turned away, and Jane felt an echo of the sickening emotion that had washed over her when she'd grasped Miriam's hand at the dance. But then Walter held out his hand to Jane and said, "Good luck."

Jane played the black ball. As her cheering section was situated on the north end, she began on the B baulk line. Not knowing what strategy Walter and Miriam might employ, she hit her ball past the third and sixth wickets so that it came to rest near the peg. Sherman nodded his approval but said nothing.

Walter played next, sending the blue ball through the first wicket and earning a chorus of cheers from the Brontëites. The moorhen jumped up and down, flapping its wings. In response the Janeites' squid waggled its tentacles provocatively as the team booed.

This is all ridiculous, Jane thought as she watched Walter send his ball through the second wicket and earn more cheers from his teammates. He used his extra stroke to move the ball in the direction of the third wicket.

This was his undoing. Sherman, playing as Jane had from the B baulk line, sent his ball into Walter's. He then cleverly croqueted Walter's ball toward the fourth wicket, where it came to stop almost exactly at the fourth corner. Sherman's ball, in the meanwhile, went toward the number one corner and collided with Jane's ball near the peg. His turn thus continued, Sherman croqueted both Jane's ball and his own toward the first wicket and used his additional stroke to move his ball into position to the right of that wicket.

It was a clever move, well done, and the Janeites applauded madly. As they screamed their approval Miriam took up position on the A baulk line and hit her ball into Jane's. On the croquet she looked at Jane and continued staring at her as she hit Jane's ball back toward the number two corner and subsequently sent her own ball back toward the baulk line.

The game proceeded in this way for some time, with neither side gaining an advantage and each player gradually passing through wicket after wicket. Every time one of them played a beautiful shot it was responded to with an equally clever one, so the balls moved across the pitch like marbles and the players were constantly changing directions.

As play crept toward the two-hour mark the tension rose higher and higher, until the match more resembled a prizefight than a lawn game. Every well-placed croquet earned applause from the supporting team, and the two mascots were kept busy working the crowd into a frenzy.

Finally Walter and Sherman had pegged out and the match, as Jane had known it inevitably would, came down to her and Miriam. Jane's wrists ached from holding the mallet and the back of her neck was sunburned. Miriam, by comparison, looked as fresh as she had on her first stroke. She moved around the pitch calmly and methodically, like a cat stalking a mouse that was becoming more and more desperate for escape.

Oh no you don't, Jane thought. *You're not going to make me look foolish.*

Jane's ball had passed through the 3-back and was lying halfway between it and the next wicket. Miriam's was through the 4-back and lined up to reach the penultimate wicket on her next stroke. It was Jane's turn to hit. She could either take a simple hit through the 4-back, hope Miriam faltered on her turn, and then try to roquet Miriam's ball, or she could attempt a much more difficult move and try to roquet Miriam's ball on this turn and hope it gained her an advantage.

She looked at Miriam, who gazed implacably at the peg as if daring it to elude her grasp. This was the deciding moment. Jane could feel it. If she played it safe and waited for Miriam to make a mistake, she could win. Or she could go on the offensive and take the win from her by force. If successful, this would humiliate Miriam utterly. If it failed, however, Miriam would be victorious in more than one arena.

It's time to show her who the stronger woman is, Jane told herself. *If she wants a fight, that's what she's going to get.*

Standing beside her ball, she acted as if she was going to take the easier road. At the last moment, however, she turned her mallet and sent her ball rolling to the left of the wicket. She saw a look of surprise on Miriam's face as they both watched the ball's progress. For a moment it looked as if Jane might miss the mark, but then her ball tapped ever so gently against Miriam's.

Trembling with excitement, Jane positioned her ball behind Miriam's and hit it from the side. Miriam's ball rocketed toward the baulk line on her team's end of the field, while Jane's rolled toward the east side and came to rest only inches in front of the 4-back wicket. The Janeites went wild.

Now it was Miriam's turn. There was no way she could roquet Jane's ball, as the penultimate wicket was between them. However, she hit it neatly into the space between the 1-back and the 4-back, placing it in position near Jane's ball.

Again Jane had a choice—roquet Miriam once more or pass through the 4-back and dare her to attempt her own roquet. She chose the latter option, using a quick, neat strike to pass through the wicket. She was now directly in line with Miriam's ball, and it was Miriam's turn to decide on a strategy.

When Miriam opted to hit her ball through the penultimate wicket Jane knew she was afraid. She was now simply trying to get to the peg before Jane. Sensing this, Jane felt a surge of excitement.

Because of the angle she could not pass through the penultimate wicket behind Miriam. It would take two shots. She knew that Miriam expected her to attempt a roquet. But she didn't. Instead she merely tapped her own ball and lined it up to go through the next wicket.

Miriam, sensing that Jane was toying with her, hit her next ball to the left of the peg, going toward the final wicket. She hit it too hard, however. Jane could hear the collective gasp from the crowd as the ball stopped just shy of the 3-back wicket.

Jane saw her chance. If she could roquet Miriam's ball now, she had a good chance of passing her in the race to the peg. But it was a tricky shot, with the peg in the way. Still, if she could bounce her ball off the peg at just the right angle, her ball might hit Miriam's. It was a ridiculously stupid shot to attempt, and Miriam would never expect it. Which is precisely why Jane chose to attempt it.

She approached her ball and stopped. Closing her eyes, she took several deep breaths. She felt her wrist muscles tense as she brought the mallet back. Then she struck the ball and prayed.

The ball rolled toward the peg, struck it, and changed course slightly. At first it appeared to be wide, but then Jane saw that it was heading for Miriam's ball. She watched, her heart pounding, as it slowed down. *Go, go, go,* she willed the ball.

When the soft click of contact sounded you could hear a pin drop. Both teams knew what might come next, and no one made a sound as Jane walked to the two balls. Nor did they make a sound as she placed her ball against Miriam's, struck it, and sent the blue ball back to the southwest corner. This lined her own ball up perfectly with the final wicket. A moment later it sailed through and connected with the peg.

Jane found herself caught up in a tangle of spongy tentacles as the Janeites' mascot lifted her up and swung her around. Her teammates encircled them, yelling madly, and there was much backslapping and general carrying on. Finally the celebration quieted and Beverly appeared with a trophy, which she handed to Jane.

"Congratulations," Beverly said. "It was a fine match, and either of our finalists could have won it."

Jane looked at Miriam, who stood on Beverly's other side, her mouth set in a rictus of a smile. *Anyone* could *have*, she thought. *But only I did.*

Beverly handed Jane the trophy. "Austen wins this time," she said. "But Brontë will have her revenge next year."

Again the Janeites cheered, while the Brontëites looked glumly at one another and shook their heads.

"I hope you'll all join us for the picnic lunch," Beverly called out. "Baskets can be picked up at the refreshment tent at the far end of the field."

Byron approached Jane, who was sharing her victory moment with Sherman. "Shall we lunch?" he asked them.

"By all means," Sherman said. "In fact, I've been looking forward to talking to you."

"Really?" said Byron. "I can't imagine why. I'm dreadfully boring." He looked at Jane. "Are you coming?"

"In a moment," Jane said. "I want to change out of these shorts. I have some jeans in the car."

"Well, give us the trophy," said Byron, taking it from her. "We can celebrate by drinking champagne out of it. It will make the Brontëites furious."

Jane left the two men talking and walked back to where she'd parked her car. It was some distance from the playing field, and she had to walk through the corridor of now-shuttered game booths. It wasn't until she was halfway down the row that she realized she was being followed.

She turned just in time to see the moorhen running at her. It held a croquet peg in one hand and a mallet in the other. Jane only had time to raise her hands in defense before the bird was upon her.

"Die!" the moorhen screamed as the two of them fell to the ground. Jane ended up on the bottom, the weight of the mascot knocking the breath from her. She stared in horror as the bird raised the peg and prepared to bring it down on her.

Jane twisted to the side, throwing the moorhen off balance. The bulky costume slipped sideways, and the bird dropped the mallet. It righted itself however, and once more the pointed end of the stake hovered over Jane's chest.

Her fingers found the handle of the mallet and closed on it. With great effort she swung her arm up. The mallet connected with the moorhen's head. It slid sideways, the long beak grazing Jane's cheek. Then it fell off.

A sweaty, dirt-streaked face stared down at Jane with murder in its eyes.

"Charlotte?" Jane said.

"Yes," Charlotte hissed. "And this time you won't get away." Her hands went around Jane's throat, the wings attached to her arms flapping wildly as she began to shake Jane up and down, her head hitting the hard-packed dirt beneath her.

Jane again brought the mallet up, but this time it only glanced off Charlotte's shoulder.

"You killed Jessica," Charlotte said as Jane struggled to breathe.

Jane tried to deny this, but she couldn't speak. Why was Charlotte accusing *her* of killing Jessica? It didn't make any sense. At the moment, however, she was more concerned with getting Charlotte off her.

Wrapping her legs around Charlotte was difficult due to the shape of her costume, but Jane managed to get a purchase on the tail. Twisting to the side, she threw Charlotte off and scrambled away from her. Charlotte lay on her back, her bird feet kicking in the air as she shrieked.

"You killed her!" she wailed. "You killed her!"

"I did no such thing," Jane said. "And you know it."

Charlotte's arms flailed as she managed to right herself. As she pushed herself up Jane grabbed the dropped croquet peg. She held it out in front of her, the pointed end toward Charlotte. "I didn't kill Jessica," she said. "You did."

"Lies!" Charlotte said.

"No," said Jane. "They found the note."

"What note?" said Charlotte. "I don't know anything about a note."

Jane didn't know what to say. Charlotte seemed to believe that Jane had killed Jessica, and if she knew anything about a note, she was certainly hiding it well. *She thinks she's telling the truth,* she realized.

"Jane?"

Jane looked over Charlotte's shoulder and saw Byron running toward them. Charlotte too turned and saw him. Her head snapped back to Jane. "This isn't over," she said as she turned and ran. Before Byron could reach them she was gone. Only the head of her costume remained on the ground.

"What was that about?" Byron asked.

"Our Gloomy Friend is back," said Jane. "And I don't think she killed Jessica."

Byron looked confused. "Then who did?" he asked.

"That," said Jane, giving the moorhen head a good kick, "is the million-dollar question."

Chapter 28

BYRON WAS LATE. THIS WAS NOT AN UNUSUAL OCCURRENCE, AND SO Jane wasn't yet worried, but she'd also had a peculiar feeling all afternoon that something was wrong. She'd attributed this to the fact that Charlotte was indeed in Brakeston, but now she wasn't sure. The dread surrounding her seemed larger somehow, more all-encompassing.

As if there's going to be a storm of some kind, she thought. *A very large storm.*

They didn't really have a plan, which was part of the problem. Byron was going to come over and they were going to see if they could track Charlotte down and find out what exactly was going on. Byron had even gently hinted at the idea of a truce while they figured out who had killed Jessica Abernathy and why that person apparently was trying to lay the blame on Violet Grey. Jane thought this to be a terrible idea and had said so in no uncertain terms. That's when Byron had told her to go home and calm down. And *that* was when Jane had said some regrettable things.

It was all very confusing, and that made her cross. She preferred it when there were defined issues to be dealt with. At the moment things were all jumbled together, and knowing where to start was near to impossible. She hoped Byron had thought of something.

A scratching at the front door caught her attention. At first she thought she had imagined it but a moment later she heard it again, a frantic *skritch-skritch-skritch*. Wondering what it could be, Jane went and opened the door.

Lilith ran inside. She was panting, and immediately sat down on the carpet and leaned against the sofa, her one front leg propping her up.

Jane looked at the clearly exhausted and frightened dog. "What's the matter?" she asked. "Is someone chasing you?"

Lilith shook her head. Then she barked. Jane stared at her and she barked again.

"Oh," said Jane. "Right. You want me to read your thoughts. I can't. You'll have to wait for Byron. He's the one who can do that."

Lilith barked again, several yips in quick succession. Jane, leery of the dog's teeth, backed away. Lilith continued to bark.

"I don't know how," Jane told her. "Really, I don't."

Lilith yipped frantically.

"All right," said Jane. "I'll try." She closed her eyes and tried to focus her mind on the sounds Lilith was making. At first she could make no sense of the barking. Then, in the midst of it, she thought she heard a single word: *captured*. She opened her eyes. "Byron has captured Charlotte?" she asked.

Lilith barked some more, which Jane took to mean she had guessed incorrectly. Again she closed her eyes. This time the Chihuahua's barks changed tone and Jane distinctly heard her say *Walter*.

"Byron has captured Walter?" Jane said. "That doesn't make any sense. Why would he do that?"

"No, you moron. Byron has been captured and is being held in Carlyle House." The voice was crystal clear, and Jane knew she was hearing Lilith speak.

"I did it!" she said. Then the words sunk in. "Byron has been captured!"

"That's what I've been trying to tell you," Lilith said. "Miriam and Beverly have taken him to Carlyle House."

"All right," said Jane. "We need to rescue him. Let's go."

Lilith yipped. "And how are you going to do that?" she asked.

"I don't know," Jane answered, scooping the little dog up and carrying her. "We'll figure that out when we get there."

She drove quickly. Lilith, trying to sit still on the front seat, was toppled first one way and then the other. Each time she slipped she swore.

"Where did you learn such colorful language?" Jane asked her after one particularly foul outburst.

"You pick things up living on the streets," said Lilith.

"Can Miriam understand what you're saying?"

"No," Lilith answered. "Only your kind can. And before you ask, no, I don't know why. And I don't care."

When they neared the house Jane parked the car a block away. She and Lilith walked the rest of the way, and Jane went around to the side of the house where she could look through the windows with less chance of being seen.

They were in the living room. Byron, tied to a chair, was in the center of the room. Beverly stood behind him, her hands on his shoulder, and Miriam was in front of him. She held something in her hand.

"What is that?" Jane asked.

"What's what?" said Lilith. "I can't see from down here."

Jane picked the dog up and held her to the window.

"Fang extractor," Lilith said. "She's going to defang him."

Jane gasped. She set the Chihuahua down. "Why?"

Lilith snorted. "Are you stupid?" she said. "Why do you think?"

Jane looked through the window again. Byron was shaking his head from side to side as Miriam tried to get the extractor into his mouth. For the first time Jane noticed a small pool of blood on the floor by Byron's feet. Something white lay in the red puddle. It looked like a fang.

"That's it," Jane told Lilith. "I'm going in."

Lilith trotted behind Jane as she went to the back door of the house. Lifting the mat, Jane took out a key and fitted it into the lock.

"Not the best place to hide a key," Lilith remarked as Jane opened the door.

"Hush," said Jane as they went into a small mudroom off the kitchen.

"Just what are we going to do?" asked Lilith.

"I don't know," Jane admitted. "I should probably think of something."

A loud howl came from inside the house. It was followed by a thump, as though something—or someone—had fallen over.

"Or we can just make it up as we go along," said Jane, running into the kitchen and down the hall.

Miriam whipped around when she heard Jane's footsteps. Jane looked at the bloody extractor in her hand, then at Byron lying on the floor. He was still tied to the chair, and was trying to inch himself away from Miriam.

"She broke one of my fangs!" he yelled.

"What is *she* doing here?" another voice asked.

Jane looked to her right and saw two more chairs set against the wall. Tied to one of them was one of the twins. Tied to the other was Charlotte.

"What is *she* doing here?" Jane said.

"All of you shut up!" Miriam bellowed. She pointed the extractor at Jane. "Tie her up," she ordered Beverly.

Beverly came at Jane so quickly that Jane had no time to respond. She felt herself being pushed to the floor. Then her wrists were pulled together and rope was wrapped around them. She was now lying on the floor facing Byron.

"That was very well done," Byron said.

Jane ignored him, turning her head as well as she could to see what Miriam and Beverly were going to do next. Miriam was looking at all of the captives and smiling. "I think that's all of them," she said to Beverly. "I hadn't anticipated taking care of this one so soon," she added, nodding at Jane. "But we might as well stake them all at once."

She came over to where Jane and Byron lay on the floor and bent down. "Are there any more of your kind polluting this town?" she asked, shaking the extractor in Jane's face.

"I'm not telling you anything," Jane said.

Miriam laughed. "I bet you'll talk once I start pulling those fangs of yours," she said. "I'll be particularly happy to pull yours. You deserve it after trying to take my son."

"For your information, *he* asked me out," Jane said.

"Only because you glamored him," said Miriam. "He would never fall in love with a creature like you. He might think he loves you, but once you're dead and the spell is broken he'll come to his senses."

"And just what are you going to tell him about where I've gone?" Jane asked. "Or where any of us have gone?"

"That's easy," Miriam replied. "You and Mr. Fancypants here ran off together. The young man decided to move on. Young people do that. As for this other one, I don't even know who she is."

"I'm Charlotte Brontë, you dolt!" Charlotte screeched.

Miriam laughed. "She's Charlotte Brontë," she said, clearly not believing what she was hearing. "And I suppose *you're* Jane Austen and Mr. Fancypants is Oscar Wilde."

"Here now!" said Byron. "I most certainly am not. Do I look like a tired old washerwoman to you?"

"I've had enough out of you," said Miriam. "Beverly, bring me the stakes."

Jane couldn't see what was happening, but she heard Beverly walk to another part of the room. Half a minute later she came back.

"Excellent," said Miriam. "We'll start with the boy."

Again Jane heard movement. Then she heard the trussed-up

twin say, "Wait a minute. I'm not even a vampire! That's my brother."

"Ted?" Jane called out. "What are you doing here?"

"Ned paid me to take his place tonight," said Ted. "He said he couldn't stand one more date with Beverly."

Beverly hissed. "He said he cared for me," she whimpered.

"It doesn't matter," said Miriam. "We'll use this one as bait to get the vamp after we finish the others off. Let's do Miss Brontë instead."

"You can't kill me," Charlotte shouted. "I'm Charlotte Brontë."

"Well, I do love your books," said Miriam, clearly still not believing Charlotte. "Even so, I'm afraid your time is up."

"Jane!" Charlotte yelled. "Tell her who I am."

"She's Violet Grey," Jane yelled back.

"She's lying," said Charlotte. "Do you know who she is? She's Jane—"

She was cut off by the sound of Miriam's body hitting the floor. The woman had fallen several feet in front of Jane and Byron, and Jane could see the gash where she had been struck in the head. A thin line of blood trickled from the wound.

"I've been wanting to do that for a long time," Beverly said.

A moment later Jane felt herself pulled to a seated position and pushed against the wall. Byron was likewise arranged. The two of them were facing Ted and Charlotte, who were still tied to their chairs. Charlotte glared at Jane but said nothing.

Beverly walked over to Miriam's body and pushed her with her foot. Miriam didn't respond. Beverly then turned to the others. "I suppose you all want an explanation," she said.

"Just untie us," Charlotte said, straining against the ropes holding her still.

Beverly laughed, but there was no humor in her voice. "Untie you?" she said. "Why would I want to do that?"

"That's enough, Doris," Charlotte said. "Do as I say."

"Doris?" said Jane. "Who's Doris?"

"I am," Beverly said.

"Doris!" Charlotte said. "Untie me. Now."

"I don't understand," Jane said. "What's going on here?"

Beverly—now Doris—sighed. "I suppose I do owe you an explanation," she said.

"She's my servant," said Charlotte. "And if she knows what's good for her, she'll untie me at once."

Doris ignored her. "It's true," she said to Jane. "I am her servant. At least I was." She turned back to Charlotte. "But that's all over with. I no longer take orders from you."

"What are you talking about?" Byron said.

"And *you*," said Doris, wheeling around to look at him. "None of us would be here if it weren't for you."

Byron looked at her, squinting. "I don't remember turning you," he said.

"You didn't," said Doris. "You turned her." She nodded at Charlotte, then took a deep breath. "And she turned me as revenge against my mother, then made me serve her."

"Your mother killed me!" Charlotte yelled. "She gave me typhus!"

"Your mother was Tabitha Ackroyd?" Byron asked.

Doris nodded. "After you turned Charlotte she came after me, turning me because she blamed my mother for her death."

"I took her child because she took mine!" said Charlotte.

"I was no child," Beverly snapped. "And my mother no more caused your death than I did." She stepped toward Charlotte. "But now I will have my revenge."

"You wouldn't dare kill me," said Charlotte.

Doris laughed. "I don't intend to kill you," she said. "I'm going to have you arrested and jailed for the murder of Jessica Abernathy."

"You're the one who killed her," Jane whispered.

Doris nodded. "Yes," she said. "And I put the note from Violet in her pocket."

"They'll never believe you," Charlotte said. "Jessica was my sorority sister."

"Please," Doris said. "You only befriended her because you hoped she would publish your novels once she established herself. Then when she became Jane's editor you saw an opportunity to get your revenge on your enemy." She clapped her hands together. "No, I think you'll be going to prison for murder. Or maybe you'd like to tell them that you're Charlotte Brontë, as well as a vampire. What do you think they would do to you then?"

"I'll kill you," Charlotte growled.

"What do you think it would be like being a vampire in prison?" Doris asked, addressing Jane and Byron. "Not much fun, I wouldn't think. And what would a life sentence be when you're immortal? How long do you think it would be before other prisoners started turning up drained of blood? And how soon would it be before someone noticed that the prisoner in cell block C looked exactly the same as she did when she entered her cell sixty-eight years before? I suspect the scientists would be *very* interested in such a specimen."

"It doesn't sound very nice," said Byron. He looked at Charlotte. "I hope you have a good lawyer."

"I'm still confused," Jane said. "You killed Jessica to frame Violet. That makes sense. But what about Miriam? Why were you working with her?"

"That was Charlotte's idea," Doris said. "You see, after your last run-in Charlotte decided to look into your boyfriend's family to see what kind of mischief she might make. Imagine her surprise when she discovered that his own mother was one of the world's most feared vampire hunters."

"I don't know how you couldn't have known," Charlotte said to Jane. "You're really very stupid."

"Says the vampire who just got framed by her own servant," said Jane.

"I'm not her servant!" Doris said. "Stop calling me that. Both of you." She waited until both Jane and Charlotte were quiet, then continued. "Charlotte arranged for Miriam to catch me," she said. "I then begged her to let me live and made a bargain with her. I would help her find other vampires."

"But you had to agree to be defanged," said Byron. "Now I see."

"At first we thought we would tell Miriam that her son's girlfriend was a vampire," Doris said. "Then Charlotte decided it would be more amusing if she found out by accident, so I told Miriam I knew of a vampire living here."

"That would be me," said Byron. "Correct?"

"Yes," said Doris. "As it happened, it was very convenient for all of us. By having Miriam kill you, Charlotte would have her revenge on you for turning her. It would also put Miriam in contact with Jane."

"A little something for everyone," Jane said. "It's very nice, but there seem to be an awful lot of coincidences in this story."

"Please," said Doris. "As if the two of you don't have books filled with convenient coincidences. You can't have an entertaining story without them."

"My novels are not entertainment," Charlotte said. "They are literature."

"They're tripe," said Doris. "The only people who like them are miserable little girls who have never been kissed and likely never will be and the occasional boy who finds a copy of *Jane Eyre* in his sister's bedroom and thinks there might be dirty bits in it."

Jane giggled.

"Yours are only slightly better," Doris told her. "Supposedly independent women trotting about the countryside after impossible men."

"But they *are* better," Jane said. She looked at Charlotte and winked.

"Not that this isn't a brilliant plan," said Byron. "And it is. But it seems like a lot of fuss to go through just for a spot of revenge."

"Not at all," Doris said. "I really do love romance literature, and the festival was great fun. When this is all over with I plan to go right on as Beverly Shrop. Seeing Charlotte jailed and the two of you staked is just an added bonus."

"But why me?" asked Jane. "I've done nothing to you."

"Perhaps not," Doris said. "But you've treated me rudely. Admit it—you thought I was just some silly woman trying to make money off your work, didn't you?"

"Well, yes," Jane admitted.

"You wouldn't give me the time of day," Doris continued. "And yet I brought busloads of fans to see you. It's very ungrateful of you. Besides, having you dead will explain why Miriam is dead. I'm sorry about that. Well, a little sorry."

"Is Miriam dead?" asked Jane. "I thought she was just knocked out."

"She is," Doris said. "But she'll be dead soon enough. Then I can lay claim to having destroyed one of the greatest vampire hunters of all time."

"About that," said Jane. "How exactly did Miriam come to be a hunter?"

As Doris started to answer, Ted sprang from his chair. Only then did Jane notice that while they had been talking Lilith had snuck in and chewed through the ropes tying his hands. Now she ran at Doris's ankles, growling and biting them as Doris danced from foot to foot in an attempt at kicking her. Ted grabbed her from behind and pinned her arms to her sides.

"Now what?" he shouted.

"Knock her out!" Jane yelled.

"Break her neck!" said Charlotte.

"Lock her in the closet!" Byron suggested.

Ted opted to follow Byron's advice. With Lilith still clawing at

Doris's ankles, Ted dragged her to the hall closet, opened the door, and pushed her inside. He then placed the chair from which he'd escaped against the doorknob, making it impossible for Doris to open it. She pounded on it from the other side, cursing him and the dog.

"Now untie us," Jane said when Ted returned. "And keep away from Charlotte."

Ted worked on the ropes. "Is she really Charlotte Brontë?" he asked Jane as he undid the knots.

"She is," said Jane, rubbing her wrists where the rope had scraped them raw.

"And are you really . . ."

Jane nodded. "I am," she said.

Ted looked at Byron. "I suppose you're not just an English professor, are you?"

"I'll give you a clue—"

"Oh, for heaven's sake. He's Lord Byron," Charlotte said.

"Did I say you could out me, Charlotte?" said Byron. "I don't recall going around telling everyone who *you* are."

"Don't talk to me like that," Charlotte shot back. "Not after what you did to me and our child."

"I *tried* to save—"

"Enough!" Jane barked. "We have to figure out what we're going to do." She looked at Miriam's still figure. "No one is killing Walter's mother," she said. "Even if it *would* make things easier for some of us." Turning to Charlotte, she said, "And although the idea of you spending eternity in jail is indeed amusing, you didn't kill Jessica and I see no reason why you should pay for that crime."

"I should say not," said Charlotte.

"Right, then," Jane said. "Let's make a deal. We'll let you go. In return, you must promise to bother us no more. Also, you will take Doris with you. You created her; you deal with her. Are those acceptable terms?"

Charlotte chewed on her lip. Jane could see she was struggling with her answer. Finally she nodded. "Yes," she said. "They're acceptable."

"Untie her," Jane told Byron.

"What are you going to do with Doris?" Byron asked Charlotte as he loosened her bonds.

"I have a few ideas," Charlotte said darkly. "I don't think she'll be pleased about any of them."

She stood up. Facing Jane, she said, "I won't thank you, as you've done nothing I couldn't have done myself had I tried. However, I will say you've comported yourself admirably."

Jane nodded. "And I won't say you're an evil genius, but I will say you make a very fine moorhen."

"Bite me," Charlotte said, swirling around and storming out. They heard the closet door open, then squeals of protest as Charlotte dragged a gibbering Doris down the hall. There was a slam as the front door opened and closed.

"Now what to do with Mother Ellenberg," said Byron.

Jane looked down at Walter's mother. Her chest rose and fell steadily, and the blood on her forehead had dried. "Leave her to me," Jane said. "I think I know just what to do with her."

Chapter 29

"WHERE AM I?"

Jane turned down the volume on the television. "You're in my guest room," she told Miriam. "We're watching *Shrek*."

Miriam looked around. She put her hand to her forehead and winced. "What have you done to me?"

"It's not what I've done, it's what your friend Beverly did. Although her name isn't really Beverly and she murdered Jessica Abernathy. But I have a feeling Our Gloomy Friend has taken care of her."

"Who's Our Gloomy Friend?" asked Miriam.

"It doesn't matter," Jane told her. "What matters is that I saved your life."

Miriam snorted. "Unlikely," she said. "Your kind thinks of no one but themselves."

"And what might my kind be?" Jane asked her.

"Vampires," said Miriam. She spat the word out as if it were a piece of spoiled fruit. "Bloodsuckers."

"And just how many of us have you actually known?"

"Enough to know what vile creatures you are," said Miriam.

"At least you didn't try to tell me that some of your best friends are vampires and that you only kill the bad ones," said

Jane. "That's a point in your favor. If you're going to be racist, you might as well go all the way."

"I'm not racist!" Miriam said.

"Oh?" said Jane. "You want to kill me just because I'm a vampire. What would you call that?"

"Being sensible," Miriam said.

"You know, I could have just left you on the floor in Walter's living room," said Jane. "Doris wanted to kill you. So did Charlotte. But we told them no."

"Doris?" said Miriam. "Who's Doris?"

"I'm sorry," Jane said. "That's Beverly's real name. Anyway, the point is, you're not dead, and that's because of me. So the way I see it, you owe me."

"Owe you?" said Miriam. "I don't owe you anything."

"I think you do," Jane said. "So here's what's going to happen. I'm not going to tell Walter that you tried to kill me, and you're not going to tell Walter that I'm a vampire."

"And why should I do that?"

"Because I love your son and he loves me," Jane said. "It's as simple as that."

"My son couldn't love a vampire," said Miriam.

"Well, he does," Jane told her. "And you're just going to have to accept it. Times are changing, Miriam. This isn't the eighteenth century. And I'm not going anywhere."

Miriam said nothing. She just lay back against the pillows and looked at the television set. Jane had paused the movie just as Shrek was getting ready to kiss Fiona, whose true form had been revealed to be that of an ogre.

"This is a good part," Miriam said. "Turn it on."

Jane hit the play button and the film resumed. She and Miriam watched for the next ten minutes without speaking. Then the credits came on and Jane turned the DVD player off.

"Maybe you're not so bad," said Miriam. "But I have a condition."

"What condition?" Jane asked, afraid of what was coming next.

"You have to give me a grandbaby," said Miriam.

"A grandbaby?" Jane said.

"I don't care if it's a boy or a girl," Miriam said. "As long as it's healthy. Can you have babies?"

Jane scratched her head. "I really don't know," she said. "I've never tried."

"No baby, no deal," said Miriam. "As far as I'm concerned, until there's a baby you're fair game. But give me a grandchild and we'll see what we can do. We have to put a time limit on it, though. I'm not getting any younger. Let's say a year."

"A year," Jane repeated.

"A year," said Miriam, nodding. "If within a year you get pregnant and it looks like things are going fine, I won't say anything to Walter. If not . . . ." She made a motion as if driving a stake through Jane's heart.

"A baby," Jane said, as if sampling the word to see how it tasted.

"And it has to be Jewish," said Miriam. "So you're going to have to convert."

"Well, I was taking the class anyway," Jane said.

"I can't believe I'm having this conversation," Miriam said, ignoring her. "I'm telling a vampire that I won't kill her if she marries my son and gives me a grandchild. Next I'll be buying a ham for Passover."

"Why should I trust you?" Jane asked her.

"Why should you trust me?" said Miriam. "The vampire is asking me why she should trust me? What's wrong with this picture?"

"I'm sorry," Jane said. "I think it's a reasonable question given the circumstances."

"Don't talk back to your mother-in-law," Miriam said. "Show some respect for your elders."

"Technically, I'm the oldest one around here," said Jane.

"Again with the talking back," Miriam said. She pointed her finger at Jane. "Don't make me stake you, because you know I will," she said.

"All right," Jane said, holding up her hands. "I give. I give. We have a deal."

"All right, then," said Miriam. "Now get me something to eat. I'm starving. I don't imagine you can make a Reuben, can you?"

"It's three in the morning," Jane told her. "And Walter is probably very worried about you."

Miriam waved her hand. "Please. Walter thinks I go to bed at nine o'clock. How do you think I got out of the house? As long as I'm back before eight he'll never know I was gone."

Jane smiled to herself as she stood up. "I'll go make that sandwich," she said. "Yell if you need anything."

"A gin and tonic would do wonders for this headache," Miriam called as Jane went downstairs. "If it's not too much trouble."

"Not at all," Jane called back.

In the kitchen Byron was standing by the sink, the broken part of his fang in his hand. "Do you think I can get it fixed?" he asked, holding the broken bit to the jagged stump in his mouth.

"Maybe if we can find a good vampire dentist," Jane said. "Or you could file it down."

"And be lopsided?" said Byron.

"Why not?" Jane said. "It will match your limp."

"Not funny," said Byron, putting the piece of fang in his pocket.

"I'm just teasing," Jane said as she opened the refrigerator and scouted around for the ingredients for Miriam's sandwich.

"How's the killer?" Byron asked her.

"Awake," said Jane. "And she's made me a most interesting proposition."

As she made Miriam's sandwich she told Byron what the two of them had agreed to. "So, *can* I get pregnant?" she asked as she slathered mustard on the corned beef.

"I really don't know," admitted Byron. "I suppose we'll find out."

"What if the baby is a vampire?" Jane said. "Apart from the teething issue, what would it be like? We stop aging when we're turned, so would it always be a newborn? Would it grow to a certain age and then stop?"

"A vampire embryo," said Byron. "What a hideous thought."

"Don't tell me you didn't think about all of this when you turned Charlotte," Jane said. "You must have."

"I didn't think about much, really," admitted Byron. "I assumed it would all work itself out somehow. And you know what?"

Jane turned to him. "What?" she said.

Byron smiled. "It will."

"I'll remind you of that when the baby turns into a bat and flies away," Jane said. "Which reminds me. You promised to show me how to do that. I think I've proved myself worthy of knowing the secret now, don't you?"

"I do," said Byron. "Unfortunately, it's not possible."

"What do you mean?" Jane asked. "You mean you won't tell me? After everything we've been through?"

"I would tell you if I could," said Byron. "I mean that we can't turn into bats. I lied."

"Lied?" Jane said. "Why?"

Byron shrugged. "You needed incentive," he said. "I thought if I told you that you could turn into a bat you would be more interested in your studies."

Jane shook her head. "You insufferable man," she said. She thrust the plate with the sandwich on it at Byron. "Just for that you get to take this up to her."

Byron held up his hands, refusing to take the plate. "I'm not going near her," he said. "She scares me."

"She's going to scare you even more when I tell her that you're going to be her grandbaby's godfather. Now go make nice."

Byron took the plate, gave Jane a wounded look, and stomped out. He was halfway up the stairs before Jane remembered the gin and tonic. Rather than call him back, she decided to make it herself.

She was adding a twist of lemon when someone knocked on the door. Wondering who could be calling at such a late hour, she peered through the peephole, afraid that she might find the police or Charlotte standing there.

"Walter?" she said when she saw him standing on the porch. "What on earth?" She opened the door.

"I know it's late," Walter said. "But I saw your lights on and I know you stay up late sometimes and—"

"Come in," Jane told him.

Only when Walter was inside did she remember that his mother was upstairs in her guest room.

"I want to talk to you about my mother," Walter said.

"What about her?" Jane asked, keeping her eye on the stairs in case Byron made an appearance. She hoped Miriam would keep quiet long enough for her to get rid of Walter.

"She'd kill me if she knew I was here," Walter said. "I had to wait for her to fall asleep before I snuck out of the house." He chuckled. "I swear, she makes me feel like I'm fifteen years old."

"Well, you'll always be her little boy," said Jane.

Walter nodded. "You're right," he said. "I will. But I don't have to *act* like her little boy."

"What do you mean?" Jane asked.

Walter reached into the pocket of his jacket and took out a box. Getting down on one knee, he said, "I know we've been back and forth and up and down and all around this issue. I've been afraid of my mother and you've been afraid of, well, whatever it is you're afraid of. But Jane, the only thing that matters is that I love you and you love me. Nothing else is important. Just love." He took a deep breath. "So, Jane Fairfax, I'm asking you one last time. Will you marry me?"

Jane heard a noise. Glancing up the stairs, she saw Byron and Miriam huddled together at the top. Byron had one hand over Miriam's mouth and the other over his own. They were both staring wide-eyed at the scene below.

"Jane?"

Walter's voice brought Jane's attention back to the moment. She looked into his eyes and saw the air shimmering around him.

"Yes, Walter Fletcher," she said. "Yes, I'll marry you."

Chapter 30

"IT'S CERTAINLY BEEN AN EVENTFUL COUPLE OF WEEKS."

Jane accepted the glass of wine Lucy was holding out to her. They were standing on Jane's deck, looking out at a yard teeming with people. It was early evening, the air was warm, and Jane was reminded of the summers in the English countryside.

"This is how it all started," said Lucy, leaning against the railing of the deck. "With a barbecue."

"Well, it started a bit before that," Jane began. Then she saw the smile on Lucy's face. "You mean you and Ben," she said.

"Are you surprised that he and I got together?" asked Lucy.

Jane thought about telling Lucy how she'd seen the sparks flying between her and Ben that night. But she decided not to. That particular talent was one it was probably best to keep secret. *You never know when it will come in handy,* she told herself.

"Delightfully surprised," she said in answer to Lucy's question. "I think you make a lovely couple."

Lucy sighed happily. "As do you and Walter," she said. "Show me the ring again."

Jane held out her left hand. On the ring finger was a small but flawless diamond in a beautiful antique setting. Lucy held Jane's hand, admiring the ring for a moment. "And you say it belonged to Walter's great-grandmother?" she said.

Jane nodded. "Calpernia Higgenbotham," she said. "Apparently her husband, Hector, saved his earnings from his job as a newspaper copy boy for a whole year to buy it for her. Calpernia's family came from money, and her father objected to Hector because he wasn't wealthy. But he was so impressed by Hector's perseverance that he gave his blessing to their engagement. He also bought the newspaper at which Hector worked and made him an editor, so everything worked out splendidly."

Lucy looked at Jane and a mischievous twinkle filled her eyes. "Miriam must be beside herself," she said.

Jane looked around for Walter's mother. Miriam was seated in a chair beneath one of the old elm trees. Lilith was on her lap and Miriam was having an animated discussion with Sherman Applebaum, whose hands moved about gracefully as he spoke.

"I thought she was going to have a stroke when she saw me wearing it," Jane said, causing both her and Lucy to laugh happily.

"What's so funny?"

Walter and Ben emerged from the house, each with a beer in one hand. Walter stood beside Jane, while Ben put his arm around Lucy. She leaned her head on his shoulder.

"Everything is funny," Jane said. "Just look around."

"It is a pretty odd group we've got here," Walter admitted.

Jane nodded. "Perhaps," she said. "But we have so much to celebrate—our engagement, the end of the film shoot, good friends."

"Jessica's murder," Walter added.

"I don't know if that's something to celebrate, exactly," Jane said.

"You *did* get Kelly back because of it," Lucy reminded Jane.

Apart from becoming engaged to Walter, this was indeed the best thing to happen to Jane since the beginning of the summer. As it turned out, Kelly was not as happy being an agent as he had been being an editor. Upon Jessica's untimely retirement he had been offered his old job back and had taken it.

Jane feigned shock. "You are all positively ghoulish," she said. "As if I could possibly take any enjoyment from the misfortunes of others."

"We're sorry," Lucy said softly. A second later she added, "But Jessica really *was* kind of a bitch."

Jane pressed her lips together, fighting a smile. It was wicked of her, she knew, but she couldn't help feeling some small measure of relief that someone as awful as Jessica Abernathy was no longer in the world. *She had no literary taste,* she thought. *Besides, it's not as if she's going to hear us and have her feelings hurt.*

Her thoughts were interrupted as a camera was thrust into her face.

"Ant!" Shelby said. "Enough already!"

"I just want to get some footage of the wrap party," he said. He turned to Jane. "How was the experience of seeing your book turned into a movie?" he asked.

"I didn't actually see much of it at all," Jane said. "They really didn't need me for anything."

"Are you excited about seeing how it turns out?"

"I'm aquiver with joyous anticipation," Jane said.

Ant lowered the camera and turned it off. He sighed. "You're still boring," he said, shaking his head. "Never mind. I'll go talk to some of the actors."

"Sorry about that," said Shelby as her brother walked away.

"I've told you a dozen times, there's no need to apologize for him," Jane told the girl. "He's not your responsibility."

"I know," Shelby said. "It's just a habit."

"Maybe it's a habit you need to break," said Lucy. "Do you even like doing this kind of work?" she went on.

Shelby shook her head. "No," she said. "It's really boring. If Ant didn't need me, I wouldn't do it at all."

"Then stop," Lucy said.

"And do what?" said Shelby. "This is all I've done since I got out of school."

Lucy glanced over at Jane and a silent word passed between them. Jane nodded.

"Come work for us," Lucy said. "At Flyleaf. You know, until you decide what it is you really want to do."

Shelby looked at Jane. "Really?" she said.

"She's the manager," said Jane. "What she says goes."

"I don't know," Shelby said.

"Why?" asked Jane. "Because it's so much fun taking care of Simple Simon over there? You need to take care of *you*. And believe me, when an opportunity for happiness comes along, you take it." She patted Walter's hand, and he wrapped his fingers around hers.

Shelby shrugged. "Okay," she said. "I'll do it." She laughed. "This is totally crazy. Ant's going to freak." She looked at Lucy again. "You're *really* sure?"

"Ask one more time and you're fired," Lucy said. "Now go tell your brother he's going to have to find someone else to hold his stick."

"His boom," said Ben quickly. "She meant hold his boom."

Shelby ran off in the direction of her brother, who was annoying several of the cast of *Constance* by trying to film them while they were eating. A moment later Byron appeared.

"Hello," he said gaily. "Did you all miss me?"

"Were you gone?" Jane asked.

Byron kissed her on the cheek. Then he looked at Walter. "I suppose I'd better kiss you as well," he said, and did. "I don't want you to think I'm after your woman."

"I'm not his woman," said Jane. "Honestly, how primitive."

Walter pulled her close. "But you are," he said. "You're my woman, and no one's going to take you away from me, no matter how good-looking he is or how nice his accent is."

"You think I'm good-looking?" Byron said, lifting an eyebrow.

"Fine," said Jane. "I'm your woman."

Walter kissed her neck. "And you love it," he said.

"This reminds me," Byron said. "Are Ted and Ned about?"

"Ned is over there," said Lucy, nodding in the direction of the picnic tables. "He's talking to Chloe. Actually, I think they're more making out than talking."

Everyone looked at the two young people, who were kissing each other and laughing, oblivious to the fact that they had an audience.

"That's a paparazzo's dream," Ben remarked.

"What do you mean?" asked Jane.

"Are you kidding?" said the rabbi. "The gossip magazines would kill for a photo of Chloe kissing a guy. Ned there would be the envy of people all over the world. Everybody would want to know who he is."

Jane, Byron, and Lucy exchanged glances. How Chloe was going to manage being a vampire and a pop star/actress was something they had yet to discuss with her. But she at least had experience with Hollywood and its ways. Ned didn't. Jane couldn't imagine what might happen if he suddenly found himself the center of attention. Questions would be asked. People would want to know everything about him. It could be a disaster.

"We'll have to have a little chat with Mr. Hawthorne," Byron whispered to Jane. "Soon."

Jane decided not to worry about it. *I'm too happy,* she thought. Whatever happened with Chloe and Ned could be dealt with when it happened.

So when are you going to tell Walter about yourself? The question came to her unbidden, as if someone else had asked it. Jane tried to ignore it, but it came back like a persistent fly. *When are you going to tell him?*

"I don't know!" she said.

"Don't know what?" asked Walter.

Jane realized that she had spoken aloud and that everyone was looking at her, waiting for an answer. "I'm sorry," she said. "I thought someone asked where Sarah was."

Walter looked at her. "No," he said. "Anyway, we know where she is. She's over there playing with Jasper."

"Of course she is," Jane said. "Would anyone like another drink?" She looked at Lucy and furrowed her brow.

"I would," said Lucy, draining her wineglass in one long gulp.

"We'll be right back," said Jane as she and Lucy went into the house.

"What was that?" Lucy asked when they were safely in the kitchen.

Jane put her hand to her forehead. "I was thinking about Walter," she explained. "How am I going to tell him?"

"Tell him?" said Lucy. "Oh," she added a moment later. "You mean about..." She thrust her upper incisors out and made sucking sounds.

"Charming," Jane said.

"Sorry," said Lucy. "We watched *Dracula* with Sarah last night."

"She wasn't scared?" Jane asked.

Lucy shook her head. "She thinks monsters are neat," she said. "I thought she was going to cry when Dracula was killed at the end."

"What an interesting child," said Jane. "I look forward to knowing more about her."

"So do I," Lucy said. "Now what about Walter? What are you going to do?" When Jane didn't answer right away she added, "You're not going to break up with him again, are you?"

"No," said Jane. "At least I don't think I am."

"Jane!" Lucy said sternly.

"All right, I'm not," said Jane.

"Promise," ordered Lucy.

"I promise," Jane said.

"Cross your heart and hope to die?" Lucy asked.

Jane made a face. "Not much chance of that, is there?"

Lucy ignored her. "Now listen to me. You are going to stay engaged to Walter. You are going to *marry* Walter. I am going to be your maid of honor, and if I have to, I'm going to drag you down the aisle by your feet."

"You're going to be my maid of honor?" Jane said.

"Oh," Lucy said. "Did I say that? I didn't mean to—"

"But you would be?" said Jane. "If it comes to that?"

"Are you asking me to?" Lucy said.

Jane nodded. Lucy nodded. They both burst into tears and hugged each other. "There's so much to do," Lucy said between happy sobs. "We need to make a list. Have you thought about flowers?"

Jane laughed. "I think we have time," she said as she wiped her eyes. "We haven't even set a date. Anyway, there's still the tiny matter of my having to tell him I'm a . . ." She imitated Lucy's earlier imitation of a vampire.

"More important, what kind of dress do you want?" said Lucy.

Jane hesitated. "I don't know," she said. "Maybe something with an Empire waist?"

Lucy wrinkled her nose. "We'll look at magazines," she said. "And don't worry about Walter right now. We'll figure something out."

"Maybe I should tell Ben," Jane suggested. "Then *he* can tell Walter. I imagine he's very good at that sort of thing, being a rabbi."

Lucy's face brightened. "Ben can marry you!" she exclaimed.

"I think he'd probably rather marry you," said Jane.

"I mean you and Walter," Lucy said. "Ben can perform your ceremony."

Jane leaned against the counter. "This is all coming together rather quickly," she said. "This morning it was all very vague in a we'll-get-married-one-of-these-years way. Now we're talking about flowers and dresses and rabbis."

"You are going to be such a bridezilla," said Lucy.

"A what?" Jane asked.

"A nightmare," said Lucy. "Now snap out of it. Today is supposed to be a celebration. You can fret later."

"That's very easy for *you* to say," Jane reminded her. "Let's see how composed you are when Ben asks for your hand."

Lucy picked up a bottle of wine and refilled their glasses. "It's going to be *fine*," she told Jane as she handed her a glass. "Trust me. We'll get you through this."

Jane took the glass. Lucy lifted hers and tapped it against Jane's. "Have I ever let you down?" she asked.

"No," Jane said. "You haven't."

"And I won't this time," said Lucy. "Now let's get back to the boys before Byron has glamored them both into taking their shirts off."

Jane took a sip of wine. "Actually, I wouldn't mind so much if he did," she said.

"Why, you sly old cougar," said Lucy.

Back on the deck they found Walter, Ben, and Byron talking to Miriam. Seeing her there, Jane bristled slightly. Although she and Walter's mother had declared a truce of sorts, her presence still made Jane uncomfortable. She would be relieved when Miriam was safely on a plane back to Florida.

"Jane," Walter said, "my mother just gave us some wonderful news." From the tone of his voice, Jane sensed that the opposite was true.

"I've decided to move to Brakeston," Miriam announced. She fixed Jane with a steely stare. "I'm tired of the heat in Florida."

Jane forced a smile. "That's wonderful," she said. She embraced Miriam, feeling the woman tense beneath her touch.

"Remember, a grandchild or I stake you," Miriam whispered.

"Walter and I will get to work on that immediately," Jane whispered back, "Mother." She emphasized the final word and gave Miriam a peck on the cheek.

"Well," she said, letting go of Miriam and lifting her glass. "Let's have a toast, shall we?"

The others, even a reluctant Miriam, raised their glasses.

"As an old friend once said to me, 'Forever is composed of nows,'" Jane said. "Here's to the many nows to come."

They all drank. Afterward their various conversations resumed. Jane separated herself from the group and stood at the edge of the deck, thinking about her future and what it might hold. A minute later Walter walked over to her.

"That quote," he said. "It's from an Emily Dickinson poem, isn't it?"

"Yes," Jane nodded. "I'd forgotten that."

"You said it came from an old friend," Walter continued.

Jane thought back to the lovely fall day that she and Emily had enjoyed together in Amherst. "I suppose that's how I think of her," she told Walter. "Isn't that what our favorite writers become to us, old friends?"

Walter smiled. "I suppose they do," he said. "Does that mean you and I are old friends?"

Jane took his hand. "We will be," she said. "We will be."

Acknowledgments

Writing a sequel to a book has been, for me, an undertaking fraught with peril. Often I have forgotten what characters look like, what they did in the previous book, and sometimes even what their names are. This admission frequently horrifies people, but it's true. I am not a good literary parent.

Therefore it is an enormous relief to me that there are people to keep me from doing irreparable damage to my hapless creations. Chief among them are my editor, Caitlin Alexander, and my agent, Mitchell Waters. I cause them no end of worry, and they are very kind about not yelling any more than is absolutely necessary. I also owe a debt of gratitude to the copyeditors and proofreaders who caught my errors and made sure everything came out all right in the end.

Finally, I am enormously grateful to every single person who read and enjoyed *Jane Bites Back* and wrote to say so. Thank you.

Read on for an excerpt from *Jane Vows Vengeance*

by Michael Thomas Ford
Published by Ballantine Books

❦

Chapter 1

"WHAT ABOUT THIS ONE?"

Jane glanced at the magazine Lucy was holding up, opened to a picture of a bride standing in a field of daisies. She wore a sheath-style dress of ivory silk and a birdcage veil to which was affixed a huge pale pink gardenia. Not far behind her stood a Holstein cow, gazing at the camera with a disinterested look.

Jane grimaced. "I don't think I have the upper arms for that," she said.

"Of course you do," said Lucy. "Well, with a little work you could."

Jane ignored her. "Why would a bride go tromping around in a field of cows?" she said irritably. "If there's any train at *all* on that dress she's going to drag it right through a pile of—"

"It's *one* cow," Lucy said wearily. "And it's a photo shoot for a fashion magazine, not an article in *National Geographic.* Get a grip."

"I'm sorry." Jane sighed, closing the magazine she was paging through and tossing it onto the pile covering the top of the kitchen table. "It's just that they're all starting to blur together. Cap sleeves. Bateau necklines. Basque waists. Mermaid this and sweetheart that and princess whatever. It's maddening."

Lucy picked up another magazine. *"Victorian Bride,"* she read, looking at the cover. She glanced at Jane. "Really?"

Jane chewed the nail on her left index finger. "I grabbed everything they had," she said. "I think I have wedding sickness."

Eight months had passed since she'd accepted Walter's marriage proposal. Shortly before the Christmas holidays she'd moved into Walter's house. It was now February, and although Walter was not pressuring Jane to pick a date for their wedding, a different deadline hung over Jane's head like the ominous dark clouds of an approaching thunderstorm.

Jane had so far avoided telling her fiancé that she was a vampire. Her undead condition was, however, known to Walter's mother. Miriam Fletcher had turned out to be even more of a challenge than mothers-in-law generally are. Miriam was a vampire hunter, and not surprisingly she disapproved of her son's girlfriend. Initially she had vowed to dispatch Jane at the earliest convenience; however, after Jane had rescued Miriam from almost certain death at the hands of a deranged vampire–turned–book reviewer, a truce had been declared. With one condition: Jane had a year in which to produce a grandchild. Should she fail, all bets were off and Miriam and she would once again be mortal enemies.

In addition to not having planned a wedding, Jane had not become pregnant. She wasn't even sure she *could* conceive. To make matters worse, Miriam had decided to move from Florida to upstate New York so that she could keep an eye on her daughter-in-law-to-be. Thankfully, Walter had not suggested that his mother move into the house with them. However, he *had* suggested that Miriam buy Jane's former home. As neither Jane nor Miriam—despite both thinking very hard—had been able to come up with a good reason why this course of action should not be taken, a deal had been struck, and the week after Jane had moved herself, her pets, and her possessions into Walter's house, a trio of anxious young men had unloaded Miriam's belongings from a truck under Miriam's scrutinous supervision.

The matter of Jane's barren state was becoming a greater problem with each passing week. With only four months left in which to become pregnant, she felt Miriam becoming increasingly impatient. To her credit, Miriam had never once reminded Jane of the looming deadline, and she and Jane were cordial enough to each other that Walter had often remarked on how pleased he was that they were getting on so well. Still, Jane knew that she was being watched.

She was not surprised, then, when Miriam made an appearance in the kitchen just moments later. She was dressed in a variation of the peculiar ensemble she'd adopted following the first snowfall of the winter. Unused to cold, let alone snow, she had opted for warmth over fashion, exchanging the lightweight pantsuits that had served her well in Florida's tropical climate for sturdy corduroy trousers and heavy wool sweaters in Irish fisherman and Norwegian ski patterns. At the moment she was wearing moss-green pants and a cream-colored Aran sweater with a rolled neck. Below the knees her pants were tucked into a pair of brown Wellingtons, and on her head was a black-and-red buffalo-plaid hunter's cap with earflaps and a shearling lining.

"It's cold enough to freeze a bear's ass," she said as she pulled the cap off and sat down. "I need some coffee."

In addition to her new wardrobe, Miriam had also acquired a collection of sayings generally used only by residents of the New England states. No matter how many times Walter told her that New York—despite its name—was not considered part of New England, Miriam persisted in behaving as if it were, occasionally even taking on an accent that was more Maine lobsterman than Jewish mother.

Jane got up and poured Miriam a cup of coffee, then refilled Lucy's mug. She herself was drinking hot chocolate. Although her vampire metabolism didn't require that she eat, she still enjoyed the activity, particularly if it involved sweets.

"Still looking at dresses, I see," Miriam remarked, nodding at the magazines.

"Yes," said Jane. "Still looking." This was not a conversation she wanted to have, yet she knew it was unavoidable.

"I really don't see what the problem is." Miriam sniffed. "Choosing a dress shouldn't be any more difficult than choosing a paint color. Just pick the one that's going to hide the problem areas the best. Take you, for example. You've got a wide—"

"I believe I've narrowed it down," Jane said. "The dress choices," she clarified as Miriam started to reply.

Miriam peered at her through the steam from her mug. "And have you set a date?" she asked. "Summer's right around the corner, you know."

Was Miriam referring to the approaching anniversary of their agreement or just remarking on the fact that a summer wedding would be lovely? Jane chose to believe it was the latter, although Miriam's tone could go either way.

"Why don't you and Walter just elope?" Lucy suggested.

Miriam and Jane both turned their heads to look at her.

"What?" said Lucy. "It would save a lot of fuss and bother."

"I thought you were excited about being my maid of honor," Jane said.

"I am. I'm just saying, if this is making you so crazy, just get married at the courthouse and go to Tahiti for two weeks or something."

"That *would* be nice," Jane mused. "We could lie on the beach and have fruit drinks."

"Nonsense," said Miriam. "You're going to be married right here so that I—so that all of your friends can join in the celebration."

Jane looked at Lucy, who rolled her eyes and puffed out her cheeks. "It was just a suggestion," she muttered.

"Walter's *first* wedding was simply perfect," Miriam informed them. "Evelyn was absolutely stunning."

And now she's dead, Jane thought, immediately mortified that such a thing would pop into her head. But it was true. Besides, it was becoming far too common an occurrence for Miriam to compare Jane to Walter's deceased wife. The week before, when Jane had tried her hand at cooking a brisket because Miriam had mentioned how much she enjoyed one, Miriam's response was to tell her how Evelyn's brisket had been so much moister and how she had served small roasted potatoes with it instead of mashed.

"Miriam, what kind of dress do *you* think Jane should wear?" Lucy asked.

Miriam waved a hand at her. "Oh, you know I don't care. I'm sure whatever she wants is fine."

Jane felt her fangs click into place. She closed her eyes and concentrated on forcing them to retract. *You can't bite her,* she reminded herself.

Miriam looked at Jane. "Do you have a headache, Jane?" she asked. "You look tense."

"I'm fine," Jane snapped. She opened her eyes. "I'm fine," she repeated, giving Miriam a tight smile.

The front door opened and closed. "Jane?" Walter called out. "Where are you?"

"In here," Jane called back. "With Lucy and your *mother.*"

Walter came into the kitchen, brushing snow from his hair. "I have great news," he said as he bent to kiss first his mother and then Jane.

"You got the Thorne-Waxe House job!" Jane said. Walter had recently been asked to submit a proposal for restoring a run-down Victorian house that had been cut up into four apartments. The new owners wanted to bring it back to its original glory.

"Oh, yes, I did," said Walter. "But that's not the big news."

The three women looked at him. "Well?" Jane said after a long pause.

"I've solved our wedding problem," Walter said, beaming. "Well, not so much the wedding problem, but the honeymoon problem."

"What do you mean the honeymoon problem?" Miriam asked.

"Jane and I have been trying to decide where to go on our honeymoon."

"What honeymoon?" said Miriam. "You haven't even set a date for the wedding!"

"We'll figure that out," Walter said. "The important thing is, I know where we're going afterward."

"Tahiti?" said Lucy. She'd been pushing that suggestion for months.

"Europe," said Walter.

"Europe is a big place," Jane reminded him. "Can you narrow it down a bit?"

"That's the best part," said Walter. "We don't have to narrow it down. I've been invited on a tour of historic houses with the International Association of Historic Preservationists. They're spending two weeks looking at homes in Ireland, France, Germany, Switzerland, Italy, and England. Maybe Scotland and Spain too. Oh, and Holland or somewhere. I can't remember the exact details. Doesn't it sound fun?"

"How many other people will be going on our honeymoon with us?" Jane inquired.

"I don't know, two dozen or so, I guess. But we don't have to do *everything* with the group. There's a lot of free time built into the itinerary. And it's not really our honeymoon. We can add another week on at the end for just the two of us. Anywhere you want to go." He looked at the three women, who sat there saying nothing. "Well?"

"When is this trip?" Jane asked.

"March," said Walter.

"March!" Jane, Lucy, and Miriam shrieked in unison.

"March what?" asked Lucy.

"We leave on the ninth," Walter answered.

"The ninth!" the three women chorused.

"Walter, that's—" Jane counted on her fingers.

"Seventeen days from now," said Miriam. "We can't possibly plan a wedding in that short a time."

"Why not?" Walter asked. "You're my only family, and Jane has none."

"Hey!" Lucy exclaimed.

"You know what I mean," said Walter. "No parents or cousins or other people who would need to make travel plans. Everyone we want to invite already lives here in Brakeston. All we have to do is get married."

Lucy looked at Jane. "It sounds so simple when he puts it like that."

"It does rather, doesn't it?" Jane smiled.

"See?" said Walter. "It's all settled."

Jane looked at Miriam. Her mouth was set in a grim line, and she scowled at Jane with undisguised dislike. *She's been hoping all along that the wedding would never happen,* Jane realized. *She* wants *me to run out of time. Well, we'll just see about that.*

"I think it's a splendid idea," she said. "Don't you, Miriam?"

Miriam narrowed her eyes. "Just peachy," she said through gritted teeth.

Walter put one arm around Jane's shoulders and the other around his mother's. "I knew you would be thrilled," he said. "Hey, I just thought of something. Once Jane and I are married, you'll both be Mrs. Fletcher."

Miriam let out a little yelp, which she covered by pretending to cough.

"You should take care of that, Mom," Walter said. "You don't want it to turn into something worse."

"I don't think it's possible for it to get worse," said Miriam, reaching for her coffee.

"Well, maybe you should go home and rest," Walter told her. "We want you in fighting shape for the big day. Right, Jane?"

"By all means," Jane said, flashing her teeth at Miriam. "I know I will be."

About the Author

MICHAEL THOMAS FORD is the author of numerous books, including the novels *Jane Bites Back, Z, The Road Home, What We Remember, Suicide Notes, Changing Tides, Full Circle, Looking for It,* and *Last Summer.* Visit him at www.michaelthomasford.com.